Dea

By

Ray Lawrence

Front Cover illustration by

Georgia Crewe

To FRADA,
Best Wishes
Ray Lawrence

To My darling wife, Kath, who always
stands by me

****

Also, by Ray Lawrence

Books of Comic Verse -

"It Could Be Verse"

"This is Much Verse"

"Nonsensical Rhymes for Nonsensical Times"

****

Evidence of Evil – A Jacqueline Caine Mystery

Available from Amazon Kindle.co.uk

in electronic (e) form or Paperback.

Death Track

CHAPTER ONE

At 3.30 pm on Friday 7th December 2013 the London
-Ipswich express roared out of the railway tunnel just north
of Fen Molesey, Essex. Fifteen seconds later it left the rails
and crashed.

Six people were found dead in the wreckage. Five of
them had perished from their injuries; the sixth, a nurse by
the name of Marion Winters, had been garrotted.

CHAPTER TWO

The CID officers' shoes squelched in the mud as they made their way up from the metalled track. With a nod of recognition to the police constable watching over the body, Detective Sergeant Mark Dolby of Fen Molesey CID bent over and drew back the polythene covering. The dead woman's eyes were closed, her lips, a scarlet rip against the paleness of her face, were drawn back to reveal her tongue. Her arms were bent upwards, her hands clutching at the collar of her light blue tunic. She had been fighting for breath when she died. With a glance across at his colleague, DS Dolby eased away the plastic sheet, letting it drop to the wet grass at the foot of the corpse.

"A nurse," commented Detective Chief Inspector Jacqueline Caine, noting the uniform style and colour of the woman's skirt, her black stockings and heavy, sensible shoes. She looked across at the constable. "Do we have any ID, Bailey?"

"I believe her handbag's still in the carriage, Ma'am." PC Bailey glanced over at the shattered train carriage that lay on its side across the tracks, just a few meters away. "We were told not to touch anything until you and DS Dolby arrived."

Dr Peter Williams, the Police Surgeon, approached from one of the other coaches. He stopped in front of the three officers and rubbed his tired grey eyes, wiping a hand across his brow before partly unzipping the front of the orange coveralls he wore over his dark suit. "Ah! It's the lady and gent from the CID. I didn't recognise you in all that gear." He was referring to the bright yellow protective jackets they wore over their suits. Dolby's was quite a good fit on his tall, lean frame. Caine's, however, was far too large for her and hung loose about her trim figure, as unflattering as the bright blue hard hat perched at an odd angle on her head.

She acknowledged the Doctor's arrival with a nod. "Hello, Peter. Any idea what may have caused this?"

"If you're referring to the crash - no, that's anybody's guess." The Doctor grimaced, pulled off his hard hat and scratched his thinning hair. "But if you mean what happened to *her*," he gestured towards the woman's body, "Well, that seems to have been brought about by a piece of double stranded rope - well, *cord* would be a better word. It was placed about her neck and pulled - very tightly - by someone with a great deal of strength." He dropped his leather bag onto the mangled grass and squatted on his haunches behind the head of the corpse. "Of course, I've only been able to carry out a cursory examination, but if you take a look under here..." he lifted the dead woman's chin gently upwards with his gloved hand "...you'll see the marks left by the cord."

The two police officers leaned forward. "She was garrotted, then," said Dolby.

"Not strictly speaking," said Williams. "If I wanted to be pedantic I'd say you need wire to make a proper

7

garrotte. This seems to have been done using string or cord, two strands. But the effect was the same. It did the same job." He removed his fingers from the woman's chin and her head flopped back down again. He knelt on his knees beside her. "I'd say the killer came up behind her, tossed the cord about her neck like this," he used his hands to demonstrate, "wound it around a couple of times to get purchase and then pulled the two ends towards and across each other, like so, throttling her."

"You say **seems** to have been done with cord," said Dolby. "You're not certain then?"

"Not absolutely, until we've carried out tests. But the marks are consistent with string. They certainly weren't caused by wire - that would have cut right into the flesh, probably sliced through her neck like so much ripe cheese." The doctor yawned and rubbed his tired eyes. "And unfortunately, the killer didn't have the courtesy to leave his weapon behind. At least the people who found the body didn't see it."

"Was she sexually assaulted?"

"At first sight, no. There's nothing to indicate that. The motive, whatever it was, doesn't seem to have been of a sexual nature. We'll know more after the autopsy."

"Right, Peter. Thanks. You'll let us have your report as soon as possible?" Williams nodded. Caine looked away, her eyes ranging slowly across the scene. The place was buzzing with emergency crews working frantically in the shattered ruins of the overturned coaches, attempting to free the trapped victims of the rail crash. They worked quietly, murmuring encouragement to each other, their voices low, but above this controlled flow of human intercourse the air was thick with the shriek and whine of heavy cutting and lifting machinery. She looked upwards to the dim outline of the grass-covered slope that lay beyond the glare of the lights, up to the cold winter sky where a mountain of dark cloud scudded against a star-studded background. Less than two hours earlier - at about the time of the train crash - the sky had been split by thunderous flashes of sheet lightning amidst a deluge of tempestuous rain. She wondered whether the accident had

9

been caused, in some way, by the extreme weather. She dismissed the thought as pointless, none of her concern – it certainly had not caused the death of the young woman lying on the grass in front of her. Caine sighed and turned her gaze directly on the doctor. "And she was alive before that? She wasn't killed in the crash?"

Williams shrugged. "You'll have to wait for the path report to be absolutely certain, Jackie, but she was definitely badly injured in the crash. She may even have been unconscious when her assailant came upon her. That would have made it easier for him to do what he did, of course, but I really couldn't say definitely what actually killed her - not at this stage." He paused, shook his head. "Either way he wound a rope around her neck and yanked it tight - that was not an act of mercy by anyone's definition!" He shook his head again, dolefully. "I've seen a lot of things in my time, but I still find it hard to believe anyone would do a thing like this - you'd think the crash itself would have caused enough mayhem, but *this*!" He threw up his hands in a gesture of helplessness. Caine, barely six months in the Fen Molesey area, had only recently met the doctor, but Dolby had known Williams for years, had met him at many a murder scene. His attitude had always been detached and clinical, even facetious. Now the Detective Sergeant was surprised to see raw anger in the doctor's eyes and hear his voice shake with emotion.

"Where was she found?" asked Caine.

"She was in that carriage over there," Williams indicated what was left of the nearest coach. "A couple of fire officers got to her first. They realised she was dead, but they naturally thought she was a normal accident victim. It wasn't until they laid her down out here that one of them noticed the marks around her neck. That was when the alarm bells started ringing."

"Excuse me, Doctor, but I think it was the paramedic who first noticed something was wrong," this, apologetically, from PC Bailey,. "I spoke to her when I arrived. As you say, she - the paramedic - didn't notice the marks on the dead woman's neck until after they'd carried her out of the carriage. She said she'd been sort of *preoccupied* with the other woman."

"What other woman?"

"The one in the carriage, Ma'am. The one that wasn't dead," Bailey looked embarrassed, as though he was speaking out of turn. "According to her there were *three* ladies in the carriage when she and the fire officers got to it. One was dead, they could see that straight off, then there was this lady, the nurse, who was also dead, of course, but there was another woman in there as well - she had some injuries, but she was still alive and conscious - in shock, of course, as you can imagine."

"So, *she* probably couldn't have strangled our victim," observed Caine, "*but* she may have seen the killer." The Detective Chief Inspector smiled for the first time since hearing news of the rail crash, a reserved, thoughtful smile. "Did she say anything about that to the paramedic?"

Bailey rubbed the back of his neck, trying to ease away the stiffness steadily creeping into his tall, beefy frame after his long vigil standing over the dead woman. "I don't think so, Ma'am. Apparently, she didn't say much that made any sense - she was hurt and in pain, of course! The young lady, the paramedic..." he consulted his notebook, "her name's Hammond, by the way, Sandra Hammond - well, she did say the woman seemed to be trying to tell her something, but it didn't make any sense."

"Something about the killer?" Dr Williams interposed.

"I don't know - as I say Miss Hammond said she wasn't making any sense. But she thought it was something about being afraid."

"You mean afraid of the killer?" Dolby made the supposition. "Well, you can understand her being scared of *him*!"

"I don't know, Sergeant." Bailey blushed with confusion. "As I say I only got the story second hand. And there was a lot to do at that time, just after the accident. Perhaps you should ask the paramedic what the woman actually said."

Caine nodded thoughtfully. "Yes, we will, Bailey. And nothing was touched after the body was brought out here?"

The question was addressed to both the medical man and the police constable. The doctor answered, raising his hands helplessly. "I really don't know, Inspector. You'll have to ask the people that found her. I received a call to help with the general emergency, so I happened to be in the vicinity when they hollered for a doctor. Pure coincidence I can assure you! I came over and examined her, but I couldn't say what happened before that."

"Any ideas, Bailey?"

The constable shook his head. "No, Ma'am, sorry."

"So, neither of you would know if there was **anyone else** in the same carriage - apart from the two other women that we know about - one dead and the other one injured?"

The doctor answered again. "No. But I gather the train was pretty empty, not more than thirty passengers all told in the five carriages. Which was a bloody Godsend, of course, or there'd be a whole lot more than five people

lying about dead…killed by the actual accident, anyway –
especially as there was a bit of a fire to start with, just after
the crash. It didn't spread very far, thank God and
nobody's quite sure how it got started or, for that matter,
who put it out!" He shook his head again and scowled.
"Hopefully, there won't be any more fatalities! But who
the hell would *do* this? Running around throttling injured
women after an accident! And a nurse into the bargain! A
few years ago, of course, I would have said he has to be a
psycho, some sort of raving lunatic, but nowadays these
idiots attack nurses and medical staff as a matter of course,
the bloody barbarians!"

"It was probably a passenger," mused Caine. "There
could have been someone else in the carriage with the three
women."

"It's more likely than not," agreed Dolby.
"Fortunately, one of them survived, so she should be able
to give us a detailed description."

"Unless, of course, he came from one of the other
carriages *after* the accident, and she was unconscious,"

said Caine. She shot a quick glance at Dolby. "I suppose, Mark, that somebody who's co-ordinating this little lot is keeping a proper record of the passengers who were on the train?"

Dolby nodded. "Yes, apparently it's normal routine."

"There's a young lady up by the recovery area checking them all in as they load them into the ambulances," Williams confirmed. "They put tags on them, even the dead."

"I hope there aren't any more so-called *accident victims* who turn out to be murder victims," said Dolby darkly. "I suppose someone has checked?"

"No worries on that score - as soon as we realised what was going on here, we double checked all the others." The doctor looked down at the body. "This poor lady seems to have been the only one to receive the attentions of our murderous mystery man - assuming, of course, it was a man."

"So, if all the passengers are accounted for," said Dolby thoughtfully, "The name of the killer must be on the list."

"Not necessarily," said the doctor. "It may not be that easy. There's no reason why the mad beggar couldn't have just walked away from the scene of the crime." He gestured towards the steep incline beside the track. "Up there and across the fields. That'd be no problem for a fit person and because it's so wet and muddy you'd have a fat chance finding his footprints after the emergency wallahs have clomped their way up and down dozens of times!"

"A fit person, yes," Caine agreed. "But how fit would he be after being involved in an accident like this?"

The doctor shrugged. "There's nothing to say he wouldn't be perfectly fit. It happens like that sometimes. Some people are fatally injured in a disaster, while others walk out of it totally unhurt. There's no sense to it but believe me it happens!" He picked up his bag. "Now, there's not much more I can do here, so if you don't mind I'll see if I can be more useful elsewhere. By all accounts

17

there are a lot of unhappy rail travellers with bruises and broken bones in amongst that lot." He nodded towards the shattered remains of the other coaches and then set off in the direction of the tunnel, picking his way carefully through the scattered wreckage.

"The Doc's right," said Dolby, grimacing. "The sadistic bastard could've just walked away up the hill. He'd have been well away before the emergency services arrived."

Cain nodded slowly. "Yes, but in that case there's a chance someone may have seen him leaving the train, or maybe a motorist saw him when he got to the road. We'll have to issue an appeal for information." She paused thoughtfully. "*And* we'd better organise a search from here to the nearest road, just in case he dropped something incriminating on the way."

"Like what?" queried Dolby, dubiously. "The murder weapon? It'll be very difficult to find anything significant in the dark, especially after that rainstorm. Besides - what area do we search? He could have gone just about anywhere, in any direction."

"Logically speaking he would have headed for the nearest road. He may even have had a car waiting for him." Caine frowned. "The rail tunnel's about a third of a mile from the A12 - he may have headed there or maybe he was aiming for some minor road that's not so busy, but has houses on it."

"Well, there's the Rivenhall Road, I suppose - Hoo Hall to the north west and Rivenhall End going the other way towards Braxted. They're not what you'd call well populated areas, but there are people there and someone may have seen something." Dolby was unenthusiastic. "But even if he did make his getaway like that, Jackie, we haven't got a clue which route he took."

"We'll start with the most obvious," suggested Caine.

"Okay, but we'll still need an awful lot of our people to cover all the possible escape routes. The Super isn't going to like that - our manpower's stretched by this train accident as it is, not to mention the virus everyone's been going down with. And you know how cost conscious our Great Leader is. He'll need some convincing I can tell you, especially as we're not even certain the killer walked away from the scene. He might just as easily be one of the passengers."

"Nevertheless, we should carry out a search as quickly as possible," said Caine. "The longer we postpone it the less chance we'll have of finding anything useful."

"If there *is* anything useful to find." Dolby sighed. "Yeah, well, I suppose you're right - it wouldn't help much if the only clue gets eaten by a cow before we get to it!" He zipped up his heavy day glow jacket as a blast of cold wind rippled through the narrow valley formed by the railway cutting. "Looks like we're in for a cold one tonight, it must already be pretty close to zero!" He shivered. "But you're right, Jackie, we do need that search. Come to think of it, if this murder was premeditated the killer may have had a car parked somewhere near. We should get our people to knock on house doors and see if anyone saw any strange cars."

"But if it **was** premeditated why do it here?" PC Bailey chipped in. "It doesn't make sense to me. Don't forget, it was broad daylight when he done it!"

Caine smiled grimly, pulling the tie strings of her too-large jacket more tightly about her. "But it **wasn't** broad daylight in the tunnel," she pointed out. She took her mobile phone from her pocket. "The murder **may** have taken place **before** the crash! As I recall it that tunnel's not particularly long - and the driver doesn't normally bother to switch the lights on. It takes less than a minute for the trains to pass through, but that might be long enough to garrotte someone."

"But in that case how was the killer planning to get off the train afterwards?" insisted Dolby. "He couldn't have known the train was going to crash. If he did get off it was just a stroke of luck. He couldn't have got off otherwise!"

"It's not impossible, not if he's fit," suggested PC Bailey, enjoying the discussion, "he could have come in from the next-door carriage, done the dirty deed and then jumped off the moving train."

Dolby shook his head. "That's a bit bloody unlikely, if you'll excuse my French!"

"That's the big problem," said Caine - we don't know *how* it was done and we can't afford to take the chance of missing anything." She punched her PIN number into the phone. "I'll get on to the Super and organise a few more bods to assist in the search." She pursed her lips, taking a last look at the dead woman. "You can cover her up again, gentlemen." She checked her watch. "The SOCO team shouldn't be long now, Mark. When we've finished here we'll go and take a look at the carriage she was in when the accident happened." She paused again, turned back to Bailey, who was helping the Detective Sergeant spread the polythene sheet over the woman's body. "I think we'd like a word with the people who found her, Bailey. Ms Hammond, the paramedic, in particular. Could you organise that?"

The constable flipped open his notebook. "Yeah, the fire officers are Officers Blake and Hunt, from the Chelmsford 2 Brigade. I'll see if I can get hold of them. And Ms Hammond."

In the violence of the train crash the carriage occupied by the murder victim had turned on its side, one of its walls splintering, bringing part of the roof away with it. Caine and Dolby could see through the resultant hole into the interior where some of the seating had been torn from its holdings and lay in a chaotic heap by the windows and doors, the wall that had contained them now having become the carriage floor. Various items, Caine presumed the personal belongings of the passengers, lay strewn about this newly orientated surface, intermingled with still glistening blood stains, broken glass and pieces of splintered plastic and torn seat fabric.

Dolby pulled his hard hat tight down on to his head and leaned into the carriage through the gaping hole in what had once been the roof. "We ought to have a look at that stuff on the floor, Jackie. The killer may have left something behind." He took a pair of thin plastic gloves from his pocket and pulled them over his hands.

Caine nodded "Okay, Mark, after you. But we'd better be careful, it doesn't look that safe!"

The thin metal of the carriage's side wall, now the floor, was badly weakened and trembled under Dolby's weight, bowing downwards as he placed his foot on it and pulled himself inside. Caine followed him in, treading carefully, thankful she was wearing sensible footwear. Dolby skirted the edge of a door, the glass of which had smashed, and bent down to examine a pair of spectacles lying on what was now the floor. The frames were made of blue, slightly iridescent plastic and the glass of one of the lenses was bloodstained and crazed as if hit by a heavy object. He held them up in his gloved hands.

"Lady's," said Caine. "Presumably, they belonged to one of the passengers."

She moved across the carriage, her eyes catching the gleam of a metal stud beneath the edge of an overturned seat. She knelt down and teased out a black leather purse.

24

Beside the seat was a partially crumpled paperback book that, she assumed from the lurid title, was some sort of romantic novel, easy reading for a train journey that had ended in disaster.

"There's a carrier bag here," Dolby picked it up and peered inside, "there's a couple of drums of health food capsules still in it, but it looks like the rest of the stuff has spilled out - they're all over the place, a packet of lady's tights, some deodorant - oh - and there are some pages from today's papers - The Daily Mail and The Sun - over here." He stooped to examine them more closely. "Plus, a couple of women's magazines. Oh, and a half eaten packet of Extra Strong Mints." He paused, making his way further into the carriage, moving carefully, aware there was a long split in the plastic bulwark of what once had been one of the sides of the carriage, and that it was splitting further beneath him as it took his weight. He reasoned that the coach was resting on the rails and even if the surface did give way he did not have far to fall. "There's a couple of ladies' handbags tucked over here in the corner, near what's left of the seats. Let's see if there's any ID." He picked up the first bag and undid the clasp, flipping the black leather top over, unzipping each compartment and examining the contents. "Credit cards in the name of a Dorothy Hartnell - Mrs." He took his notebook from his pocket and made a note of the name. "And a building society book - that should give us her address." He repeated the operation with the second bag, noting the owner's details from a bankbook before moving on.

Caine had reached the end of the carriage. "There's a children's book here. Were there any children on the train?" She read out the title, "'*Grimy Tales'* ..." Her humourless laugh echoed hollowly about the carriage. "Funny things they give children to read these days!" She started on her way back. "Hello, here's another handbag - that makes up the third woman." She stopped to open the bag and note down its owner's name and address.

Dolby had retraced his steps to the opening. "Right, so we've got three names for the three women in the carriage - what we don't know is which one was killed in

26

the accident, which one was murdered and which one was the lucky survivor."

"We'll have to wait for formal identification, unless by any chance there are photographs somewhere in the bags. No doubt the families will be ringing in - news of the accident must have gone out over the radio by now." Caine picked her way carefully across the shattered train carriage. "I wonder what the one who survived actually saw of the killing - she must have seen *something*."

"Hopefully, something significant." Dolby reached the hole in the roof through which he had clambered and turned back to look once more into the carriage. "We'll obviously have to go through this stuff when the SOCOs have finished, but on the balance of what we've just seen the killer hasn't left much for us to go on!" He stepped down and, shielding his eyes from the glare of the banks of floodlights set up to illuminate the scene, squinted up the embankment, following the slow downward progress of a tall man laden with expensive camera equipment. "I think that's Tony Ash on his way down."

Caine looked up the hill out of the shattered carriage and nodded to the approaching officer. He waved in recognition. "We'd better leave him to his photography." She turned and made her way back to PC Bailey who was still standing vigil over the body. He was speaking on his radio and nodded to her before finishing his conversation.

"I've just got those interviews organised for you Ma'am - Fire officers Blake and Hunt will be waiting for you up at the RCV in about five minutes. That's up the top of the embankment, in the field just above the mouth of the tunnel. And Miss Hammond, the Paramedic who first examined the body, she'll be along as well." He looked around, surveying the scene of the wreckage and the frenetic activity of the yellow-coated rescue workers. "It seems they've almost done with getting the passengers out, Ma'am."

Sandra Hammond was sitting on the rear bumper of the Rescue Co-ordination Vehicle when they arrived. She had taken off her hard hat and laid it beside her on the muddy, boot crushed grass and she was using one hand to

28

wipe grime off her face with a moist tissue, the other to push her thick auburn hair back, away from her forehead. Her yellow and white waterproof tunic was partly unzipped revealing the line of her bosom beneath her white blouse. She looked up as the two police officers approached and nodded when Dolby called out her name. She made no attempt to stand up.

"Fire Officer Blake said we'd find you here, Ms Hammond," said Caine. She hoped the young paramedic would have more helpful information than the two fire officers who had found the murdered nurse's body. They had talked to her and Dolby for nearly fifteen minutes without saying anything of any consequence, partly she guessed, to take their minds off the gruelling and grisly rescue work that had occupied them for most of the last two hours. Caine nodded sympathetically to the young woman. "I'm sorry to trouble you with questions at this time, you must be exhausted."

It was relatively quiet here beside the big antennae festooned van, but they could hear the buzz of activity from inside, where messages were being transmitted and received with calm efficiency by the emergency services co-ordination staff. The rescue effort had been turned down a few notches at the welcome news that the driver and all the passengers were now out of the wrecked train and most of the activity was now taking place at the bottom of the steep embankment, at the side of the track. The long and complicated task of examining the wreckage to determine the cause of the accident had begun.

The young paramedic nodded, managing a smile. "Yeah, exhausted would be a good word, although I prefer to use the word knackered!" She waved a hand as a colleague carrying two mugs of tea came slowly towards her out of the spot-lit area, treading carefully over the mangled grass. "Over here, George!" She took one of the cups from him and sipped at it thirstily. "Thanks! I needed that. I'll be with you as soon as I've finished helping the police with their inquiries - you can manage without me, can't you?" The yellow-coated man smiled his agreement, nodded to Caine and Dolby and then set off across the mud in the direction of a group of emergency vehicles. She gestured in his direction, "my crew mate, George."

"We're investigating the death of one of the passengers," said Caine. "We believe she's a nurse, at least she seems to be wearing a nurse's uniform. We understand you were there when she was moved out of the carriage." She had squatted down to speak to the young woman and now she stood up again, flexed the muscles in her legs to relieve the strain. Dolby, who had squatted beside her, shifted position uncomfortably before rising.

Sandra Hammond scowled. "If you mean that poor woman who's been murdered - yes, I was there." She pushed herself up from the bumper of the van. "Two of the fire men actually found her, but they thought she'd died in the accident. Same as the other dead lady in that coach."

"There were three women altogether?"

"Yes. Well, that's all we found. Two were dead - the other one was injured. She was still alive, but in shock, as you can imagine. We managed to do something for her." She took a long draught of the hot steaming tea and nodded

31

her appreciation. "Best stuff in the world, tea – gets right down inside!" She returned to Dolby's question. "There were three passengers in that carriage when I got there. I'd split off from George by then. Well, there were a lot of us around and I wasn't needed where he was, so I went along to the next carriage. The woman in the nurse's uniform, she was laying on the floor all scrunched up and I knew as soon as I saw her there wasn't any hope." She sighed. "Well, you see a lot of it in my job, I'm afraid and you get to know the signs."

"When was it you realised there was something wrong?"

The young woman looked puzzled for a moment. "Oh - right - you mean with the one who'd been murdered? The nurse? Not until after she'd been carried out of the carriage. Naturally, after my first look, as soon as I realised she was no longer with us I turned my attention to the lady who was still alive. It was only after I'd seen to her and got her away that I went over to take a second look at the nurse - just wanted to make sure I suppose - and I noticed those marks on her neck. It shook me, I can tell you, seeing them there - well, there was only one thing that could've caused them, they were so deep. Made me feel quite faint for a second - and I've seen some things in my time. I'm not exactly squeamish." She mopped her forehead. "It was then I hollered for you lot."

"Tell us about the other lady - the one who survived. Did she say anything to you?"

Sandra sipped her tea thoughtfully before answering. "She seemed to be in a great deal of pain from whatever happened to her in the accident. We won't know until she's had all the tests and X-rays, but I shouldn't be surprised if she's broken a few bones, not to mention any internal injuries she might have. Anyway, she wasn't making much sense."

"She *was* trying to say something then?"

"Oh yes, but I couldn't catch much of it. She was wheezing a lot – it could have been the shock or maybe she'd broken her ribs. Her voice was strange and I think she was a bit delirious."

33

"But did she say anything about the killer - the person who killed the nurse?" asked Dolby with a note of impatience.

"You mean she may have seen who did it? I hadn't thought of that." The wind picked up again, whistling across the fields from the east. The young paramedic shivered involuntarily and took a quick gulp of her tea. "No, she didn't say anything about the - er – the murderer. Nothing. Not directly. She just sounded like she was afraid. She kept saying 'it's you, it's you!' and asking for someone to help her; and then she said 'Leave him alone! Leave him alone!' And then something about 'there's hell fire in his hair!' 'Hell fire' – I'm sure that's what she said, but I couldn't really get it. I think she must have been delirious. She was rambling. I could understand that she wanted me to help her - she was obviously in pain, the poor dear - but the rest of it, well, it didn't make any sense!"

"And she didn't say who this 'him' was?" asked Caine, puzzled.

"No. I suppose she could have meant 'her'. As I say, she wasn't making any sense. She was delirious - must've been. I wouldn't attach any importance to it."

"And that was all she said?"

Miss Hammond nodded. "Yes. A bit more of the same, but none of it made any sense to me. She was out of her head, the poor dear. Then I gave her a shot of morphine for the pain and she went off."

"But she was afraid." said Dolby. It wasn't so much a question as a statement.

"Are you surprised?" The young paramedic drained the tea from her mug. "She'd just been injured in a train crash and then she had to lie there and watch a woman done to death by a homicidal maniac! She must have thought she'd be next on his list, mustn't she! If I were you lot I'd give her protection - around the clock surveillance - if she saw the murderer he's going to be coming after her sooner or later, isn't he!"

CHAPTER THREE

"Why *wasn't* she murdered?" asked Caine.

Dolby looked up from the contents of the murdered woman's handbag. It was just after 7.00 pm and they were in Caine's office back at Fen Molesey Central Police Station. Their inquiries had quickly established the identity of the murder victim. A qualified Nurse, her name was Marion Winters and she had lived in Heckford, a small village just south of Colchester. The local police had been asked to call on the premises and break the news of her death to her next of kin. Meanwhile, the contents of the train carriage in which she had been murdered had been brought back for examination. The various items, previously photographed, catalogued and dusted for fingerprints, were now spread out across Caine's desk.

The Detective Sergeant interrupted his perusal of an address book taken from the victim's handbag. "Why wasn't she what?"

"Why wasn't she next on the murderer's list? I'm just thinking, Mark, about what that paramedic said about the other woman passenger - the one who survived both the accident and the killer." Caine perched her spectacles on her nose and consulted her notepad, "Mrs Hartnell, Mrs Dorothy Hartnell - there she was lying in agony watching the other woman, Nurse Marion Winters - being done to death in a pretty horrible way. She must have been afraid she'd be next. So, the question is - why *wasn't* she?"

"Maybe she would have been, but the killer ran out of time."

Caine shook her head. "No, Mark, he had all the time in the world. It was nearly seventeen minutes before the emergency services got to the scene of the accident - it was in the middle of nowhere. How long does it take to garrotte someone?"

Dolby shrugged. "I don't know, I've never tried, thank God! But I imagine no more than a couple of minutes. It would probably be quicker, though, if the victim happened to be badly injured in a train crash a few minutes beforehand and couldn't put up any resistance." He thought for a moment. "But we're making the assumption that the killer was there on the spot as soon as the train crashed, i.e. that he was a passenger. But what if he wasn't even on the train? What if he was walking in the fields by the railway track, heard it crash and ran down the hill to do the dirty deed?"

"That's not very likely is it?" Caine insisted. "It's not a likely MO for a killer. And the place where the accident happened is pretty remote. There aren't even any public footpaths close by that he might have been hiking on."

"And the field search has turned up nothing so far," admitted Dolby, "apart from a few footprints in the mud, hundreds of yards away from the railway track. They could have been put there by anyone."

"They may still be useful," said Caine. "If we can find a suspect to match them - a little bit of corroborative evidence. But anyway, Mark, if the killer was out there in the fields on a cross country trek - in the extremely unlikely possibility that he *was* there - why pick on Marion Winters when he had so many other passengers to choose from?" She shook her head, "No, it's an interesting idea, Mark, but until I know otherwise, I'll stick to the theory that the killer was actually travelling on the train."

Dolby resumed his appraisal of the address book, finally closing it and putting it into the paper bag containing the other 'exhibits'. "Funny. She's a Mrs, but there's no mention of her husband's address in here."

"What's funny about that? Do you write your wife's address in your address book?"

He laughed. "No, of course not. That was a bit stupid of me - I guess I'm getting a little addle-headed looking through all this stuff!" He examined a set of door keys he had taken from the handbag before he went on slowly. "Jackie, the murdered woman's name - *Marion Winters* -

does that name ring a bell with you? It's been nagging at me ever since I heard it."

"Yes, now you mention it, it is vaguely familiar," said Caine. She opened one of her desk drawers and groped around for the bottle of ink she knew was in there. "I keep thinking I've heard it somewhere before, but I can't think where. Get Wendy to run a check on it will you, Mark? There may be something significant in Nurse Winters' background, something relevant to the case." She found the ink and unscrewed the lower section of her fountain pen, squeezing the bladder in readiness to immerse the nib in the reservoir. "But it still worries me that Mrs Hartnell wasn't attacked."

"I shouldn't think it worries her, though. She must be pretty pleased about it if you ask me," said Dolby, flippantly. He was scrutinising the entries in Marion Winters' building society passbook and looked up for a moment from the closely printed figures. "Maybe the murderer prefers younger women."

"Or brunettes to women with mousy, lacklustre hair. Or even nurses." Caine doodled on her blotting pad with her fountain pen. "Or maybe he was out to get Marion Winters specifically. Perhaps he'd been following her."

"You mean he followed her on to the train and, when the accident happened, he took the opportunity to polish her off? I suppose it's possible." Dolby closed the passbook and dropped it back onto the desk. "Nothing interesting in there... But look, if he was stalking her - why? What was his motive?"

"Discouraged admirer? Some sort of professional animosity? I don't know," said Caine. "He would obviously have to have a reason to kill her, but it *would* explain why he targeted Marion Winters and ignored Dorothy Hartnell." She paused thoughtfully. "Although for my money, if he knew she'd seen him killing Marion Winters he'd have disposed of her too, if only to conceal his own identity. Mrs Hartnell was badly injured - she couldn't have put up much of a fight. And as for screaming for help there's no way she would have been heard -

everybody else on the train was probably screaming their head off at the same time!"

"Maybe he was wearing a stocking or something over his head to hide his face or perhaps Mrs Hartnell didn't actually *see* him at all," suggested Dolby. "We don't know that she did. For all we know she may have been out for the count and came to *after* the murder, just before they found her. Also, those things she said to the paramedic didn't make any sense, so perhaps she *was* out of her mind." Dolby pushed his chair back from Caine's desk and stood up, turning to look out the window. The heavier traffic of the afternoon had subsided and he watched a lone bus, emblazoned with the turquoise and cream colours of the Arriva transport company, manoeuvre its way around the one way street system, halting at a bus stop to let passengers off.

"It does mean, though," he continued reflectively, "that if she didn't see the killer at work any hope we have of our key witness giving us a useful description could have flown straight out the window. That would leave us with nothing at all to go on."

"Patience, Mark, patience," cautioned Caine. "We've got a long way to go before we can say we've got **nothing** to go on, though I must admit there does seem to be precious little at this very moment." She was doodling aimlessly and the nib of her fountain pen described two sweeping loops over the surface of her notepad. "There's something else that bothers me about this murder, Mark. Why garrotte her?"

Dolby turned and sat down again. "How do you mean?"

"Just *that*, Mark. Why garrotte her? Or being a little more pedantic, like Doc Williams, why use a double loop of rope or cord to strangle her with? Why not just pick up a handy piece of metal or something left over from the crash and bash her over the head with it?"

"I don't know. Maybe he had the rope to hand and thought he'd use it?"

"I don't think so, Mark. How many people walk about with a length of string in their pocket just in case they come across a likely candidate for strangulation?" Caine wrote the word '*premeditation*?' on her notepad. "But, he **did** have it to hand didn't he, and that makes it look like he planned it."

Dolby was silent, thinking. "But if it **was** premeditated," he said after a pause, "then our man has no imagination - even when he was given a golden opportunity to cover-up the murder he didn't deviate one iota from his original plan, which was to strangle her with rope or string or whatever you want to call it. As you say, he could have just beaten her brains out with a heavy object - then nobody would have even suspected she'd been murdered."

"Premeditated or not, it looks like he's an obsessive," said Caine, grimacing. "For some reason he **had** to strangle her with his piece of cord. Nothing else would satisfy him." She shivered. "I hate obsessive killers - until you discover what motivates their obsession, they're totally unpredictable. And they do, often, kill again!"

Dolby nodded slowly. "And what if the train hadn't crashed? Would he have killed her anyway *and* the other people in the carriage?"

Caine shrugged. "An interesting question. If he didn't kill the others he'd risk them identifying him, of course. But maybe it wouldn't have happened at all if there'd been no crash - maybe he just saw his opportunity when it happened. Either way we're dealing with someone with a peculiar mind set."

There was a subdued knock at the door and DC Wendy Doyle looked in hesitantly. "Sorry, Ma'am, but it was open!" She came into the room carrying a thin sheaf of papers. "I've got the list of passengers for you. The Transport Police have just e-mailed it over to us."

"Thanks, Wendy," Caine took the papers from her and ran her eyes quickly through the three sheets. The names and addresses and other relevant facts concerning the unfortunate passengers of the ill-fated 3.30 pm

Liverpool Street to Ipswich train were given in detail. "Is this all of them?"

Wendy nodded. "So, they tell me. Everyone who was on the train at the time of the accident is there, including the driver. They checked them all in as they left for the hospital."

"Do you know how many are being kept in for treatment?"

"No, but I can find out."

"Good - we've got some people up there haven't we?" DC Doyle nodded. "Make sure they tell everybody on the list who leaves the hospital they're to be available for questioning. And tell our people to double check these addresses and phone numbers. We don't want *anyone* slipping through the net. Our murderer is almost certainly amongst them."

"Right. Jean Baker and Tommy Scott are over at the hospital. I'll give them a bell when I get back downstairs." Doyle hung back. "There was something else, Ma'am."

Caine motioned her to a seat. "The murder victim - Marion Winters - she's on record."

"Is she, indeed?" said Dolby. "I told you that name rang a bell, Jackie! Bit of a mind reader, our Wendy, isn't she!" The young police officer looked confused. "The name seemed familiar to us too, Wendy. We were about to ask you to run a check on it, but there you are - you've anticipated us."

"I - er - I knew I'd heard the name before, so I ran a quick check on the online," Doyle explained.

"So, what did you find out?"

"Well, Marion Winters doesn't - I mean *didn't* actually have a police record, not for a conviction. She was tried and acquitted about seven years ago - something to do with a hospital in North Yorkshire. She was a nursing sister there and she was accused of being involved, with three other medical staff, in some cases of criminal negligence."

"Yes, I remember that," said Dolby. "It was all over the newspapers at the time. Wasn't it The Ridings General

Hospital? Several children died and the DPP brought charges of criminal negligence."

DC Doyle nodded. "Nurse Marion Winters was one of the principal defendants, but the jury found her 'not guilty'."

"Yes, I think I recall it now," said Caine, taking off her reading glasses and rubbing her eyes. "One of her fellow defendants was also acquitted, but the other two - both of them doctors I think - were sent down and there was a huge shake-up at the hospital itself, a lot of sackings and resignations. It was a very high-profile case at the time and I believe there was almost a public inquiry." She frowned. "The media, of course, were full of it - just as they will be with this murder case. They're going to love it!" She turned to the young police officer. "Thanks, Wendy, that information might just be helpful."

Dolby got up from his chair again and paced the floor. "It does open up a possible can of worms, though doesn't it? Do you suppose any of the families of those children, the ones who died through the hospital's

48

negligence - do you suppose any of them disagreed with the 'not guilty' verdict in favour of Marion Winters and decided to administer their own brand of rough justice?"

"You mean one of the family members may have taken revenge by murdering her? An eye for an eye?" Caine frowned and picked up her pen. "It seems unlikely after all these years, Mark, but it's possible. Anything is possible in this modern world of ours. They could have been stalking her, waiting for the opportune moment - which, of course, would have been immediately after the crash." She turned to the young policewoman. "Wendy, get on to the Yorkshire Force and ask them to check their records and see if any of the other defendants in the case have been attacked. They might also like to email us a copy of their case file."

"I've already been on to them, Ma'am," said Doyle. "They were a bit difficult at first, said seven years was an awfully long time ago and they'd probably ditched the files by now, but I said to try anyway. I've also been on to a couple of Yorkshire newspapers and asked them to email copies of the relevant issues dealing with the case. They said they would."

"You're not telling me they actually agreed to co-operate," said Dolby with a whistle of admiration. "I know we're sort of north of Watford here, but whenever I've had to ask them a favour they've called us a lot of pesky southerners."

Doyle smiled. "I've an aunt lives in Scarborough, Sergeant, and I spent quite a few of my school holidays there when I was a kid. My Yorkshire accent is more than passable."

Dolby grinned. "Oh yes, I've heard some of your jokes - Yorkshiremen figure quite a lot in them. So how did you make use of this undoubted talent for mimicking dialects?"

"I was a bit economical with the truth I suppose. I pretended to be a homesick Yorkshire lass down here on secondment, so they said they'd send the stuff down sharpish, just to cheer me up. It should be here by tomorrow."

"Well done, Wendy," said Caine, "but you've got yourself a little job when that lot comes in. Read up all the articles and see what you can learn about the children's families' attitudes towards the acquittals. Let us know if you find anything we can hang our helmets on. You know, if any of them threatened to take the law into their own hands after the trial, that sort of thing."

"Yes, Ma'am, I'll do my best to get on to it as soon as the stuff comes in, but I do have that other kiddies' case I'm working on? You know – Donna Baker's hit and runs."

Caine nodded. "Yes, I'd forgotten that. How is Donna?"

"Not bad, but this virus really is sweeping right through the station, Ma'am. We're all doing two peoples' work."

"Yes, don't we know it," said Dolby. "Life in Fen Molesey Central's almost normal isn't it!"

"Of course, this notion about family revenge doesn't quite fit in with the 'obsessive' theory and the killer's need to use a rope rather than a blunt instrument," observed Dolby after Wendy Doyle had left.

"It might or it might not," said Caine. "We need to know a lot more about how those kids at The Ridings General died before we can draw any conclusions. There might be something that ties in with strangulation by rope or cord, although I admit it does seem rather a long shot. I suppose the whole theory's a long shot anyhow, after seven years."

"Well, let's see what the Yorkshire Police report says," suggested Dolby. He gestured towards the list on Caine's desk. "In the meantime, how are we going to handle the list of suspect passengers? Presumably, we can ignore all those who were badly hurt - assuming Marion Winters was killed after the crash they're hardly likely to have throttled her if they themselves were injured. We ought to concentrate on those who were mobile enough after the accident to get about easily, the walking wounded if you like."

Caine flipped quickly through the list again. "This does mention their condition and list their injuries, which is helpful. We'll need a team of, say, three to interview the able-bodied ones tomorrow - and Sunday if it runs to it - and try to find out exactly what they were up to after the accident." The telephone rang and she picked up the receiver. "It's Colchester nick for you, Mark." While Dolby took the call, she read more thoroughly through the list, highlighting those passengers whose condition was given as 'fair' or 'uninjured'. Dolby, his face settling into an expression of gloom, replaced the telephone receiver. "So, what did our friends up at Colchester have for us?"

The Detective Sergeant sighed wearily. "It seems there's nobody at Marion Winters' address at the moment. According to the neighbours it's not her house anyway, apparently, she acts as nursemaid cum companion to a very elderly lady by the name of Mrs Millicent Mears. It's Mrs Mears' house."

"And she's not there either?"

"No. The neighbours say she was taken off to hospital in an ambulance yesterday morning. Nurse Winters went with her. They don't know which hospital yet, but Marion Winters was on the Liverpool Street train, obviously going back home to Heckford, so it must be somewhere south of here, between here and London or even in London itself. Anyway, Colchester hasn't been able to trace Marion Winters' next of kin. I suppose it'll be down to me to locate them and break the news that she's dead... A job I could very well do without, thank you very much!"

"We don't even know if she has any next of kin," observed Caine. "There was nothing much in her bag was there?"

"No. But nearly everybody's got *someone*. And she is referred to as 'Mrs' Winters on some of the documents in her bag, so she must at least have a husband."

"Or have had one." Caine doodled the words 'background' and 'relatives' on her notepad. "Anyway, if we're going to get closer to this case we'll have to look

54

into her personal history. It would be useful to get into this Mrs Mears' house and have a look at Marion Winters' personal effects. We'll have to be careful there, though. Strictly speaking, I suppose, we should get the old lady's permission before going into the premises."

"Yes, a chat with her wouldn't come amiss. She must know something about our victim. Perhaps she'll give us a few leads - friends and acquaintances etc. We'll have to find out which hospital she was taken to."

"Maybe the local welfare people could help there. I'll ask Wendy to get on the blower first thing tomorrow morning and find out. And it might be an idea to have a word with the neighbours - they may be able to give us some background. They may even have seen someone stalking Marion Winters."

"Yes, but maybe it would be better to do that when we can get into the house - it'll save two trips up to Heckford." Dolby yawned and looked at his watch. "It's been a long day, Jackie. Okay if I get off now?"

Caine nodded. "Yeah, I'll be off myself in a minute. I'll just get this list copied and organise two or three people to interview the walking wounded and 'unhurts' tomorrow." She dropped the list on to her desk and highlighted one of the names. "I'll also ring the hospital in the morning and try to arrange a talk with our friend Mrs Hartnell - the other woman who was in the carriage. I'll try and make it for 10.00 o'clock, always assuming she's fit to be questioned. I'll contact you when I've made the arrangements and we can meet and go on to the hospital. Unless, of course, they've let Mrs Hartnell out before then."

"I doubt it. They'll probably be carrying out tests on her for the next few days."

Caine nodded. "True. Anyway, if she has by any chance been discharged, we'll interview her at home. Maybe we can also get to see old Mrs Mears tomorrow, assuming we can establish which hospital they've taken her to. I'll be in touch."

"Right. I'll wait to hear from you." Dolby indicated the items taken from the scene of the crime. "Shall I put this lot away or do you want to go through them again?"

"I might do. In any case I'll take care of them, you'd better get home to Lorna and the kids."

Dolby paused at the door. "You ought to call it a day yourself, Jackie - after all it is Friday evening. Go out and have a meal. You don't eat properly you know. See you in the morning."

"Cut it out, Mark, you make more fuss than my mother!" She watched with mixed feelings as the Detective Sergeant closed the door behind him. Sometimes she envied Dolby his stable family life, the fact that when he arrived home his meal would be waiting for him. It had not been like that for her for a long time, in fact not since she left her parents' home to fend for herself. Even when her late husband, Jonathan, was alive, during the very early years of their marriage, before he was gunned down during his undercover work against drug traffickers, they had both had their own jobs to do and they had worked late and unsocial hours, sometimes not seeing each other for days. They had met, infrequently, for an evening meal in a restaurant, but she had never arrived home early enough in the evening to cook more than a tasteless snack; and then when Alison, their daughter, came along, very shortly after Jonathan's death, she had coped as a single mother, picking the child up from the childminder at erratic hours and taking her home to a hastily prepared, unimaginative meal in their dingy little flat in Walthamstow. Even now, living in her newly acquired house in Birch Medley, she rarely cooked a meal for herself.

The thought of food brought on pangs of hunger and she realised she had not eaten since breakfast. Her notes on the train murder case were still to be written up and she wondered if she should go down to the canteen now or tackle the report. Chief Superintendent Hansen had recently laid down the law on report writing - in a ruthless cutting back of superfluous office staff (which included making all but one of the typists in the typing pool redundant) he had ruled that, without exception, all his officers must enter their reports directly onto the networked computers - one workstation from which endured a lonely and neglected existence on a pedestal desk in a corner of Caine's room. It was lonely and neglected because Caine hated using it. When she started work all those years ago she had made a point of not learning to use a keyboard in the firm belief that if she did she would be expected to act as unofficial secretary for the many males who worked in her office. They seemed to think, in those days, that typing was all female employees were worthy of and capable of doing (apart, of course, from making tea). Instead, she had pursued her career as an active CID officer, soon making her mark and carving out a successful future for herself. But here in the second decade of the twenty first century the technological revolution had come full circle and battalions of typists were no longer employed by the police force. Now she would have been the first to admit that a keyboard speed of 60 to 80 words a minute would have been extremely helpful. She decided to eat before writing the report.

Caine gathered up the scene of crime paraphernalia and locked it in one of the metal cabinets that stood against the wall of her office, placing the key in her handbag. The lift that served this end of the building disgorged, in the basement, into a maze of narrow and cheerless corridors leading to a number of temporary prison cells and interview rooms. The canteen, although also housed in the basement, was at the other end of the building and Caine preferred to reach it by taking the lift to the ground floor and traversing the wider, less gloomy public corridors. She would then pass the front desk and descend to the basement via the main stairwell.

Sergeant Bernard Crouch beckoned to her as she passed the desk. "Sorry to trouble you, Inspector, but Sergeant Dolby didn't sign for that bag of exhibits. Would you like to do that now?" He was referring to the objects found on the ruined train carriage at the murder scene.

"Didn't he?" Caine stopped at the desk and read quickly through the list of articles Crouch had pushed across at her. She took the ballpoint pen he held out and scrawled her signature across the bottom of the sheet. "That's not like Mark, he must have been distracted. Sorry." Crouch should not have let Dolby have the bag of exhibits in the first place without a signature, of course, but she did not want to upset him. He was one of the old-style coppers, crusty on the outside, but as soft as wet putty on the inside. He had a heart of gold and was looking forward to his retirement within a couple of years. Crouch was also an extremely useful source of local information, a guy for a relatively new girl to have on her side. She smiled disarmingly and handed the pen back to him.

The front door swung open to admit two police constables who, with their hands clamped firmly to the elbows of a couple of tall, teenage boys, guided them into the hallway and up to the desk. The lads, obviously reluctant to enter the police station, wore black designer jeans and grimy Reebok trainers. One of them sported an expensive black leather jacket, the other a Tommy Hilfiger sweatshirt beneath a light blue Hugo Boss windcheater. The taller of the two, his fair hair worn long and with an arrogant set to his jaw, leered at Caine across the room, turning strangely cold blue eyes on her, the tip of his tongue moving lasciviously across his lips. Involuntarily, and quite illogically, she felt a thrill of unease and dropped her gaze. She pushed the signed form back across the desk to Sergeant Crouch and then turned to continue her progress across the vestibule and into the far corridor. Behind her she heard scuffling sounds as one of the boys shouted at the officers. "You've got no frigging right to bring us in, you frigging pigs! My father'll have something to say about this!" The reply, if there was one, was lost to her as she closed the door to the stairwell and made her way down to the canteen, the cooking aromas arousing her hunger to an even higher state.

She chose cottage pie, chips and peas, knowing it would play havoc with her diet, but too tired and hungry to care. It was heated up quickly and it smelt divine. Apart from two other officers seated at a table on the other side of the room she was the only diner in the canteen and it was quiet save for the occasional clanking of pots and pans from the kitchen. She ate slowly, turning over in her mind the events of the day, searching for meaning and order, something that would point her in the right direction, towards the train crash killer. Finally, wearied by the endless succession of seemingly unconnected and meaningless incidents which paraded themselves before her mind's eye, she pushed her plate away and went to the counter to fetch another cup of coffee, determined to finish her meal and then get off home to a hot bath. The report could wait.

"Ah! I'll have one of those please, Jacqueline. Black, two sugars." Chief Superintendent Edward Hansen was striding across the floor towards her. She groaned under her breath. He chose a table in the centre of the room and indicated she should join him with the two coffees. "I was looking for you, Jacqueline, there's something I'd like you to do for me – strictly in the line of work, of course. And you can bring me up to speed on this train fiasco." Showing an almost naïve faith in the strength of the Police Authority standard issue furniture the Chief Superintendent lowered his tall beefy frame into a light plastic chair and puffed heavily for some moments as though he had just run up two flights of stairs to the canteen rather than come down three in the lift.

"It has been an eventful day, sir, but there's not much to tell, yet." She placed the coffees on the table and sat down opposite him.

Hansen shrugged. "Well, I had to come back to the office for a few minutes anyway, so I thought I'd just stop by and see whether you're on the right track, pun intended." He smiled at his own attempt at levity. "Bernie Crouch pointed me down here." He was wrestling to undo the button of his dinner jacket, which was stretched taut across the vast expanse of his burgeoning belly. He had evidently not seen the inside of the station gym for some considerable time and was obviously on his way to yet another black-tie function, involving vast quantities of free food and dignified small talk. Caine wondered idly if it was a civic affair, a jolly with the local lawyer's association or something to do with the Freemasons. His destination was, of course, inconsequential; wherever he was bound he would not be prevented from first lecturing her on the importance of a quick and successful conclusion to the current murder case and the consequent benefits to her (for which read 'his') personal career advancement.

"Well?"

"Yes, thank you sir, but as I said, there's very little to report at the moment."

He picked up his cup and sipped at the coffee. "This stuff doesn't improve, does it?" He complained. He cleared his throat. "But there must be *some* developments, Jacqueline. What about that search of the area around the scene of the rail crash? I hope you're not going to tell me that all those extra officers we sent out came up with nothing!"

"Nothing yet, sir, apart from some footprints in the mud, which may or may not be significant - we're not certain the killer actually left the scene afterwards anyway. He could be one of the other passengers. I told you I just wanted to make sure we didn't miss anything."

"Well, let's hope you haven't, Detective Inspector, let's hope you haven't." He glowered into his coffee for a few moments before continuing. "The press are getting hot under the collar on this one, you know. Not only do we have a horrendous train disaster on our patch, but a particularly nasty murder has been committed."

"I know that, sir!"

"Of course, you know that! But there's a lot of mileage in it so far as the press is concerned - it's *not* just a *local* issue, we've got half the world's media breathing down our bloody necks. They're loving it, of course - there's something particularly titillating about railway crime, it doesn't matter if it's a rape or a murder or the wife of a cabinet minister being caught cheating on her fares, the so-called ladies and gentlemen of the press just love it! They want to know what's going on, Jacqueline!" He sighed and Caine almost felt sorry for him. "There must be *something* we can tell them that'll convince them we're on the right track." This time the pun was unintentional.

"But the murder only took place a few hours ago, sir," protested Caine. "We've hardly had time to establish who the murdered woman is let alone draw any conclusions on who killed her."

"Who was she then?"

"A woman called Marion Winters. *Nurse* Marion Winters."

"She was a nurse?" He looked aghast. "It would have to be a bloody nurse wouldn't it! The papers'll have a field day writing a lot of maudlin clap trap about angelic Florence Nightingales being done to death in wrecked railway carriages." He slammed his cup down heavily, spilling his coffee into the saucer. "And, of course, they'll be demanding an arrest, double quick."

"Yes, but we should at least arrest the right person, don't you think sir! And that takes time!"

"Of course, we want to arrest the right bloody person, but nobody wants a particularly nasty, homicidal maniac running around our streets either, do they! That's why I need to be able to tell the news hounds we've got something concrete - and soon." His manner softened. "Look, Jacqueline, it's no reflection on you, I don't really expect you to have the name of the murderer - not just yet anyway. It is early days, I'll admit that, but what have you got that they *can* get their teeth into? Are there any hot leads?"

She shrugged. "We have a couple of ideas - you can't call them leads, not yet anyway, our inquiries have hardly got off the ground."

"What *are* they then?"

She told him of Marion Winters' connection with The Ridings General Hospital case. His eyes narrowed and she could almost see his brain ticking. The man - believe it or not - and she found it hard to believe - had once achieved a double First at Cambridge, but during his climb upwards through the ranks he seemed to have devoted his once considerable brain power to the pursuit of political manoeuvring rather than to criminal detection; consequently, he sought quick, politically correct rather than accurate, solutions. "You mean one of the kids' relatives did it? That would be a turn up for the newspapers, wouldn't it?"

"Yes sir, front page stuff, but I doubt it's the answer we're looking for. It was too long ago. If they were planning on taking their revenge, they'd have done something about it long since." She looked up at the large wall clock. It was well past eight o'clock - she revised her assessment of Hansen's plans - he must already have had his dinner somewhere - he never ate later than seven thirty - and be on his way to another function. "I really don't think there's anything else I can give you on the case for the time being, sir. Of course, I'll keep you informed."

"Well, see you get the sod before he does another one. We seem to be getting a new breed of viciousness nowadays, some of these buggars'll cut their grandmother's throat for half a crown!"

"Or even twenty-two and a half pence, sir." The burly shape of Sergeant Bernard Crouch had come into the room while The Chief Superintendent was speaking. He made his way to the serving counter and helped himself to a cup of tea from the urn. "Whoever said youth was wasted on the young wasn't wrong, sir." He said loudly, "I've just had two youngsters in for speeding and I can tell you they gave me a hard time of it. Should know better, kids like that, but do they? Do they heck! I was tempted to throw them both in the cells overnight, just to teach them a lesson. Arrogant little sods!" He took a toasted tea cake from one of the glass display shelves, placed it on his tray beside his tea and carried it over to their table. "Mind if I join you, sir, Ma'am? - It's not exactly buzzing in here tonight!"

"Gave them a piece of your mind did you, Bernard?" asked the Chief Superintendent, waving his hand to indicate he had no objection to the Sergeant joining them. There was a familiar, relaxed relationship between the two; no doubt engendered over the many years they had spent working in the same police station. Hansen finished his coffee and eyed Crouch's teacake covetously. "We don't teach these young drivers enough about the stupidity of speeding, not considering the number of people killed on the roads every year!" He looked across at Jacqueline Caine. "Far more deaths on the roads than in rail accidents, you know and most of them seem to be caused by these young idiots in their souped-up sports cars!"

Caine remembered the two teenagers she had seen at the front desk on her way down to the canteen. "Those boys did seem a bit - er - forward, Bernard!"

"Their language was a bit ripe, if that's what you mean, Ma'am!" said Crouch. "You'd think a school like that would turn out a better product considering what it costs their parents! I call it scandalous myself."

The Chief Superintendent scowled. "Upton Grange again, I suppose?" He turned towards Jacqueline Caine, his hands wandering up his shirt front to adjust his bow tie. If he had not been her boss she might have assumed he was nervous. "As a matter of fact, that's the other thing I meant to discuss with you, Detective Chief Inspector."

"Oh? Someone up there been breaking the law, have they, sir?"

He smiled weakly. "No, nothing like that. At least I don't think so. Maybe you could find out when you make the inquiries."

"What inquiries? What does Upton Grange School have to do with any of my inquiries?"

Hansen looked distinctly embarrassed. "Well, it may not be anything big you understand, Jacqueline. But you're the best person I have to look into it."

"To look into what? You're not making yourself very clear, sir!"

"Fact is, Jackie that Toby Wilson, the Principal of the School, has been on to me. Seems they're having a bit of a problem with the neighbour. I – er – thought you could look into it on my behalf."

"That I could *what*?" Caine stared at him disbelievingly. "Superintendent Hansen, I'm with the CID – I don't *do* spats between neighbours."

Hansen looked longingly at Sergeant Crouch's teacake as if stuffing it into his mouth would help reduce his obviously mounting embarrassment. "It's not just an ordinary neighbour's dispute. At least I don't think so." He became more intense and leaned across the table to speak confidentially. "Toby – that is, Mr Wilson – thinks his neighbour is indulging in black magic rituals."

"Black Magic rituals?" Caine repeated, unsure she had heard him correctly.

"You know the sort of thing. Bonfires at night, dancing around in the nude." Hansen coughed apologetically. "Deviant sexual practices. There's been bonfires at night and naked carryings on in the woods near the school."

Crouch, who had been chewing on his remaining fragment of teacake, grinned widely. "Wouldn't fancy it myself, not in this weather." He shivered theatrically.

"What sort of deviant sexual practices, sir?" Caine asked innocently.

"How should I know?" said the Superintendent irritably. "Naked things, orgies, despoiling of virgins, I suppose." He took a pristine white handkerchief from his trouser pocket and wiped his brow. "But the point is Toby

Wilson's worried his school kids'll see what's going on. Thinks it might give them ideas."

Caine tried to stop herself from smiling. "Well, yes, I can see his point, Super,   but what has all this to do with me?"

"Ah! Well! If there is something going on with the neighbour – his name's Beckett by the way, Marcus Beckett and he runs that big antiques place on the Upton Road, just next door to the School; I've met him a couple of times at Rotary, peculiar character, but he seemed a nice enough chap, if a bit weird – anyway, the point is *if* there is anything going on there it might be illegal."

"Yeah, they often have drugs and illicit materials in those sorts of gatherings," offered Crouch, listening attentively.

"But I still don't see what relevance all that has to me?" said Caine. "Shouldn't we just send in one of the beat boys to find out what's going on?"

"I would, but it's not so easy as all that," said Hansen, again blushing with embarrassment. "I mean it's a delicate sort of thing. We can hardly send in a beat bobby to ask about orgies and strange goings on around bonfires at night. Beckett runs a respectable business and Wilson's school's right next door. It may well be affected if the press were to get hold of the news. We need a more discreet approach."

"And that's me, I suppose?" Caine sighed heavily. "Look, Superintendent. I'm up to my ears in an important murder case and you want me to waste my time chasing after a voodoo witch or Harry Potter style wizard or whatever you'd like to call him. Don't you think, sir, that that might be a complete waste of resources?"

"You don't have to drop everything, Jacqueline. All I'm asking you to do is to drop in on Beckett – when you happen to be in his neck of the woods – and have a discreet word in his ear."

"But why me? I'm a woman, I'm sure you've noticed that sir – wouldn't it be more appropriate for a man to drop in on this complete stranger and talk to him about orgies and virgins and deviant sexual behaviour? That is, if anyone *has* to do it it would make more sense if it was a man."

"Well, as I say, I'm not sure about the details..." Hansen coughed and held up his hand in an effort to placate her. "Jacqueline, you're the most discreet senior officer I've got. I'm asking you to do it because I know you'll do it well. Don't make a song and dance about it. You don't need to mention the sex..." he coughed again. "Just ask Beckett what he's up to, lighting the bonfires in the woods and discreetly get in the fact that he and his acolytes – I think that's the correct word, isn't it? – have been seen *doing things* - you don't need to go into the actual *'what'* of it." He stood up. "Try and see Beckett soon, but I don't expect you to spend a lot of time on it." He made his way across to the door. "Have to get back to the Town Hall, I fear, Chief Inspector, join in with the festivities, though I must confess I've forgotten what this particular shindig is all about. Then I'm away for the weekend so we'll catch up with each other on Monday. I hope you'll have some good news for me by then." He nodded to the Sergeant. "Bye, for now Chief Inspector, Sergeant Crouch"

"The wonders of being a DCI in the Fen Molesey force," said Caine as the door closed on her superior officer. "There's no end to the interesting jobs you get to do here, is there, Bernie?"

The Sergeant grinned and downed the last of the teacake. "Looks like that bloke Beckett's up to something even more interesting!"

"Yes, well, I suppose dancing around a bonfire in the middle of the night might strike some people as suspicious," said Caine. "Personally, I think he must be a complete lunatic to be doing it in this weather. But I suppose there is a chance the kids at the school might see something, not that those two lads you've just booked need any further corrupting." She absently tapped her spoon against her teacup. "Correct me if I'm wrong, but I was under the impression that Upton Grange was one of the best schools in the area, if not *the* best?"

"Used to be, Ma'am," Crouch agreed lifting his cup towards his mouth, but pausing to speak before sipping. "But it's gone rapidly down hill over the last few years. Since that Toby Wilson took over as Head I understand. They do say he has very advanced ideas."

"You mean he runs the place on a free for all basis - no rules?"

"It seems that way. Don't get me wrong; of course, I'm not an expert on education or anything like that. All I know is all the discipline's gone and Wilson lets them do exactly what they like. If you ask me, they're turning into a bunch of little savages." He frowned between sips of tea. "Beats me why he's suddenly so worried about a bit of black magic amongst the neighbours, I should have thought that's just the kind of free-thinking Wilson was in favour of!" He sniggered; he was an avid reader of cheap thriller paperbacks, many of them devoted to horror and the occult. "Anyway, I don't believe it. People running naked around bonfires and having sex amongst the dandelions? Surely not in quiet little Upton Eccles!"

"What do you know about this man, this Marcus Beckett?"

"I know his antiques place," said Crouch. "He has a few acres of woods and then there's a stretch of woodland and a bit of a meadow between his land and the school's. And I've met him once, at his shop. He knows his antiques and he's a smart businessman. He is a bit strange I suppose, *intense,* if you see what I mean, doesn't have much time for small talk. I suppose, at a *stretch*, you could take him for Chief Wizard of Fen Molesey and devoted acolyte of Beelzebub."

Caine smiled, thinking that an interview with Marcus Beckett might after all be an interesting diversion. "I suppose I ought to bone up on Satanic law before I see him, if there is such a thing that is; just in case."

Crouch nodded and chewed on a piece of teacake. "Well, it takes all sorts, Ma'am. Maybe Beckett is the reason the kids at the school are turning into a load of savages. Perhaps Satan's escaped from his place and is busy buying up their souls, precious few of those kids

79

seems to have one!" He laughed. "As a matter of fact, he is a bit weird, that bloke, Beckett. As I say, I met him once when I went into his antiques emporium or whatever he calls it with the wife a year or so back, she was interested in getting a bit of antique furniture, you know, something a bit out of the ordinary for the house - didn't find anything as it happens, well nothing we liked that we could actually afford if you take my point - anyway he is a bit of a strange looking person. Funny eyes my wife says, like he's trying to hypnotise you. And he always wears black clothes. Almost like an undertaker."

Caine nodded thoughtfully. "Sounds a bit sinister to me, but, Bernie, tell me, was it my imagination or was The Super really cut up about the school going downhill?"

"Well, it's his old school isn't it - he's a distinguished Old Boy. I suppose he has a natural affection for the place. I couldn't say too much while he was here, of course, being as how he always used to say how good it was in the old days, but between you and me Ma'am it really has deteriorated; fallen apart might be a better way of describing it. Used to be we'd never hear anything about those kids, but now we get regular complaints from the townspeople about their misbehaviour. And worse." He toyed with a used sugar sachet, twisting the paper in his fingers. "Rich kids most of them. Seventeen and eighteen years old they are and they drive around in their flashy cars like they own the roads. Some of them even have small boats moored in the marina down in Maldon. Spoilt isn't in it!" He lifted the cup of tea to his mouth and Caine thought he was going to interrupt his flow of words, but his arm went down again, the tea with it and he continued. "***And*** they try going into pubs and drinking underage and generally making nuisances of themselves in the town centre - a lot of them are into shoplifting. Last year we even had a case of attempted rape by one of the senior boys - went for one of the lasses out at Upton Eccles village he did. Of course, we couldn't actually ***prove*** he did what she said he did, but by the look of him I didn't have much doubt. Anyway, it didn't get to court. That bloke Wilson nearly dirtied his pants in his haste to hush it all up. For the good of the School, he said it was." Crouch stopped and consumed half the cup of tea in one noisy draught.

"Drugs as well, I suppose?"

"Actually, no - nothing to speak of, so far. But there's plenty of places in town where you'll find kids indulging in that sort of filth - that night club off Church Square, for instance - what's it called? ***Rock A Go Go*** or something equally crass - but Upton Grange isn't one of the regular places for drugs. There have been some rumours, of course, but we've never had the opportunity of raiding the place. Some of the kids have been found in possession, outside the school, but they'll never let on where they get the stuff from. We never get any concrete evidence." He paused to gulp down some more tea. "But why are you so interested? Your daughter's well past school age, isn't she?"

Caine laughed. "Oh, yes - she's well into her twenties, not that she's any less of a worry. I just thought it would be interesting to find out a little more about the school that produced our revered Superintendent. And, of course, I shall have to visit the place in the course of my

inquiries into this black magic story."

CHAPTER FOUR

Detective Sergeant Mark Dolby finished shining his shoes and closed the polish tin, pushing it back into the fabric bag his wife, Lorna, had made out of some abandoned curtain fabric during one of her "tidy-home" periods. He looked around, found she had disappeared into the hall and called out to her. "Do you want me to put the shoe cleaning stuff away, love, or do you think someone else might want to use it?"

Lorna came back into the kitchen carrying the laundry basket and dropped it down beside the washing machine before replying. "If by *someone else* you mean one of the kids, Mark, you must be joking. I don't suppose any of them would even know what it was. I don't think they realise that shoes actually have to be polished. They think they either automatically repel dirt or clean themselves."

"Yeah!" he agreed, "silly of me." He recalled their last visit to the shops when they had tried to find a suit for his son Simon who, at eleven, was already into the designer-creased look. "It's the same with ironing clothes - that's also a totally redundant concept, something you simply do not do in the twenty first century." He opened the broom cupboard and deposited the fabric shoe-polishing bundle on the top shelf before sitting down by the kitchen table and reaching for his shoes. He slipped his feet into them and then glanced up at the clock. "I'll have to be off in a minute. I'm due to pick up the boss at just after eleven."

Lorna emptied out the laundry basket and started sorting the lights from the coloureds. "Did you say you were going up to the hospital?"

Dolby bent over to tie his shoelaces. "Yes. Hopefully this Mrs Hartnell, the woman who was in the same train carriage as the murder victim, will be fit enough for us to

85

interview. With any luck she'll be able to give us a description of the killer."

"I shouldn't think so," said Lorna in her matter-of-fact way. "*Surely* if she'd seen anything useful the murderer would have done her in as well!"

"We were wondering about that, but I suppose you're right," Dolby agreed reluctantly. He watched silently as his wife sorted the light-coloured clothes from the dark with, to his mind, amazing speed, wondering at the fact that she could carry out this chore with such ease whereas he always found it impossible to prevent a vividly dark coloured sock or other hued 'small' from getting into the lights. He had often marvelled over this apparently minor difference between men and women - were females that much more talented in this respect? Was there a washing machine gene hidden in female DNA or was it that women were just multi-talented? He pulled his mind back to the matter in hand, reflecting that if this Mrs Hartnell had no useful information to offer Jackie Caine and himself then they had precious little else to go on. Why *had* the killer let the woman go? He went into the hall, stopping to look in the mirror to adjust his tie before taking his jacket from the newel post where he had hung it earlier, on his way down to breakfast. He brushed the lapels, dislodging a few particles of dust.

"Who's the smart one then?" Lorna came into the hall and stood before him, her blue eyes sparkling. "You know if I didn't know you I'd be getting worried."

"What about?"

"How picky you've been about your dress since your new boss joined the F M fuzz. You didn't wear a suit every day when you were working with Bill Walker, did you? You were quite happy to go out with *him* in sports jacket and baggy trousers. Now it has to be a smart suit and a *very* snazzy tie!" She was pouting and the humorous glint in her eye told her husband she was joshing, but there was also a warning signal implicit in that look.

Dolby blushed in spite of himself. Working closely with an attractive woman could be complicated. The thought of any romantic involvement with Jackie Caine

87

had never really crossed his mind - he wondered briefly why not. "That's not true! I'm no different now - I've always been a natty dresser."

"Nutty, more like! Anyway, it *is* true - you men are so transparent. Not that I'm not pleased, - I'm proud of the way you look!" she kissed him lightly on the cheek and bounced away down the hall towards the kitchen.

Dolby smiled and followed her, pleased at the compliment. "Did you get the picking up the kids' timetable sorted out for this evening?" She was standing at the sink tying a freshly laundered apron about her ample, but still curvaceous hips, running the hot water. He came up behind her and kissed her affectionately behind the ear.

"Mmm! That's nice! Pity you only do that when you're about to rush off to see *her*!" She giggled girlishly, heard one of the children coming noisily down the stairs and answered his question. "Yes. There's no problem. Donna's going to the dance with Sara and Emma and her parents will pick them both up at 8.30 and bring them back again by 11.30. The other two are staying in. They know where we'll be if anything crops up."

"Good. Well organised. But do please warn Donna to be careful what she drinks - you know what the kids get up to nowadays at dances - raves they call them don't they? There's been a big increase in drug usage in F M recently. It worries me."

"You and me both, darling - but you can tell Donna yourself, she's pretty sensible and you'll be seeing her before she goes out." She turned anxiously, brushing back her dark auburn hair with her hand before slipping on a pair of rubber gloves. "You will be back in good time for this evening, won't you?"

"No problem there, dear. I've told Jackie I must be away no later than six. Tom said he'd booked the restaurant for seven thirty, didn't he?" They were going out to dinner with friends. Lorna confirmed the time of the meal and he checked his watch again, kissed her on the cheek and made for the door. "I'm not quite sure what we'll be doing after the visit to the hospital - there are a lot

89

of avenues we've got to pursue - can't call them 'leads' yet, but there's lots to follow up, so I'm not quite sure when I'll be back – but hopefully it will be in time to get changed and spruced up for the meal."

It was just after eleven o'clock when Dolby picked DCI Caine up in the police station car park in the centre of Fen Molesey.

"The hospital says we should be able to see Mrs Hartnell," she told him as she opened the car door and swung herself in, reaching behind her for the seat belt and snapping it into place. She laid her capacious handbag on the lap of her grey business suit and pulled the door closed. "Any further thoughts on our mysterious killer?"

Dolby shook his head. "I spoke to Eddie Briggs earlier - there are no useful fingerprints in the train carriage. Most people wear gloves in this sort of weather so there aren't many anyway," he manoeuvred his way across the car park and positioned the car to turn right out of the gates. "Most of those he did find were smudged beyond recognition and the ones he could identify belong to the people we know were there."

She sighed. "Par for the course, I suppose. This is not going to be easy, Mark." She glanced out of the window as they drove slowly past Hengerts department store and up to the traffic lights prior to turning left towards the Chelmsford road. "And there's no sign of the murder weapon either. It looks like the killer took it with him."

"Well, he would do, Jackie, if it really was just a piece of string!"

The traffic lights turned red as they approached, and Dolby slowed the car to walking pace. As they came to a halt a few feet from the pedestrian crossing a light blue convertible, its top down, drew up beside them with a screech of brakes. Its audio system was blaring pop music and as the vehicle stopped the driver turned the volume even higher so that the resonating beat of the bass almost hurt the ears of the two detectives stopped alongside. Caine turned to look across at the car, which she now saw was a late model BMW convertible and was surprised to see the two teenage boys she had glimpsed at the station desk the previous evening. They grinned back at her. The fairer of the two again ran his tongue across his lips in a way he seemed to think lascivious. As the lights changed and the BMW shot forward with its tyres racing, he waved and blew her a kiss.

Dolby glanced at her curiously. "Noisy bloody beggars. Do you know them?"

"No," she replied. "But I saw them last night at the station - they were being booked for speeding believe it or not."

Dolby manoeuvred the car around the mini-roundabout and onto the Chelmsford Road, picking up speed. "Doesn't look like they've learnt their lesson. And what about that music if you can call it that!"

"It was too loud to hear it properly, whatever it was," said Caine. "I don't know how they can stand it that loud."

"Beats me - but my kids are no better. Simon's only thirteen and Michaela's just turned eleven and they play

92

their music like that most of the time. And as for Donna -
she's fifteen and hers has to be even louder!" He shook his
head sadly. "They'll all be deaf before they're thirty if they
carry on like that! It worries me."

"What do you know of Upton Grange School?" Caine
asked as they reached the dual carriageway and picked up
speed.

"Not much. Why?"

She told him of Hansen's request the previous
evening. "Apparently the Headmaster's worried his kids
might be influenced by Beckett's activities."

"From what I've heard a bit of black magic won't
make any difference. They're already a lot of little devils.
It beats me why their parents send them there anymore."

"Maybe they don't realise. According to Bernie
Crouch the school's only recently gone down the tubes."

Dolby swung the car out to overtake a long vehicle.
"You're going to look into this occult story then?"

Caine nodded. "Yes. Well, Hansen expects me to
now, but I don't intend to waste any time on it. In the first

93

place I don't know if there's anything in it and even if there is, I don't think it's exactly illegal."

"It's not," agreed Dolby. "So long as he's not conducting orgies in public places or ravaging young virgins against their will. I wonder where he gets his supply."

Caine laughed. "Anyway, I'll worry about Beckett when I find myself in his area. So far as I'm concerned his moonlight activities are a long way down my priorities list."

A few minutes later they walked in through the automatic doors of the Chelmsford District Hospital's Accident and Emergency Department and made their way to the reception desk. The frenzied activity of the previous day, when a barely sufficient staff had suddenly to cope with the onrush of more than two dozen injured passengers from the ill-fated train, had subsided and an orderly calm now prevailed. The young lady behind the desk smiled up at Caine, said "Good Morning, Madam, I'm Sally. How may I help you?" in the syrupy tones of a recent participant in a "***How To Greet Guests in Reception Areas***" seminar and then leaned forward to study their Warrant Cards. "Oh yes, Chief Inspector, Sergeant, Dr Hamilton is expecting you. Mrs Hartnell is in…" she checked a notepad on the surface of her desk, "Bartholomew Ward. Doctor Hamilton said he would meet you there when you arrived."

Caine and Dolby found the ward after walking what seemed like half a mile along white painted, busy corridors, the noise of their shoes clattering on the black and white floor tiles. As they pushed through the swing doors and entered the corridor leading to Bartholomew ward, a tall, white-coated man in his mid forties came out of the office and walked towards them holding out his hand. His face was haggard and his eyes bloodshot and he looked almost exhausted. A badge on his lapel announced him as Dr David Hamilton.

"Good morning, you must be DCI Caine," he shook her hand and turned towards her companion, "and DS Dolby - David Hamilton." Stifling a yawn, he led them along the short corridor and stopped in the doorway of a

95

small office. Behind him a nurse sat with her head bowed over a desk, writing. "I must tell you, Inspector that now is not a convenient time for you to call. Many of the patients who were involved in the accident yesterday still require attention and most of us have been up all night trying to cope."

"I fully appreciate that, Doctor," said Caine, "and I can assure you we would not be here if it wasn't absolutely necessary. However, as you no doubt know, a murder was committed on that train yesterday and it's important we interview Mrs Hartnell as soon as possible. We believe she was travelling in the same carriage as the murder victim."

Hamilton nodded. "Well, as I told you on the telephone, Inspector, Mrs Hartnell's injuries were not as bad as we thought. They're mainly superficial, badly bruised ribs and heavy contusions in a number of places. Physically she's..." he paused and shrugged, "I suppose I can say she's better than one would have expected, considering what she's been through. Mentally, however...well, I'm not so sure! She's suffering from shock – we've put her on tranquilisers for the time being, but I'm not sure it'll help much."

"You're saying she won't be able to tell us anything?" asked Dolby.

"I'm saying, Sergeant, that while she is certainly conscious most of the time, at the same time she appears to be delirious. She claims she can *see* strange things and she *says* strange things. I'm by no means an expert, but if you were to ask my opinion, I'd say she's been so traumatised by her experience she's lost touch with reality."

"How do you mean she seems to see 'strange things' what sort of 'strange things?'"

Hamilton hesitated. "Actually - people! People that aren't there! Her husband says she's psychic and that she's seeing the spirits of the dead," he raised his eyebrows expressively. "I don't know what your beliefs are, but personally, I prefer to think she's having hallucinations brought on either by her experience or by the drugs we gave her when she came in."

"We can see her though?" asked Caine. "I hope we haven't come all this way for nothing."

"Oh, you can see her," Hamilton replied frostily. "But whether you'll get anything useful from her I can't say. And I can only let you have five minutes with her - less than that if she shows signs of distress. Is that understood? You can see her as much as you like once she's been discharged, but until then she's my patient and my responsibility. Oh and - er - I shall want Staff Nurse Rierdon to be in attendance throughout." He turned back into the office and called out. "Staff Nurse - if you wouldn't mind."

The nurse brushed away a lock of reddish hair that had escaped from beneath her cap and looked up. She smiled and then yawned, shaking away her tiredness. "I'll be with you in a moment, Doctor," She said in a thick Irish brogue, writing quickly before dropping her ball point pen on the desk and standing up. "What is it you'll be wanting?"

"Inspector Caine here and Sergeant Dolby are going to interview Mrs Hartnell - they seem to think she might be able to help them with their inquiries into the train murder. I'd like you to keep an eye on her, make sure they don't overtax her strength."

"To be sure, Doctor, I'll do that - is it okay for me to come along in a couple of minutes? There are one or two things here I need to attend to first."

Hamilton eyed her for a moment, stroking his chin as if weighing up the justification for her request. "Yes - all right, Nurse, but please, don't forget, we don't want poor Mrs Hartnell to be overtaxed by too many questions. You know the situation I take it?"

She shook her head. "I was in A and E when the accident victims came in yesterday evening, Doctor, naturally, we all of us came in, but I don't know about Mrs Hartnell specifically. I've just come on to the ward."

"Then I suggest you read the notes," he said brusquely. She blushed and a flash of anger burned in her eyes. "I'm taking Inspector Caine and Sergeant Dolby to see her now; I can't hang around here all morning." He relented. "But I'll drop by on my way back and brief you."

They started off along the corridor towards the ward. "Mrs Hartnell is in a private room at the far end, Inspector," Hamilton explained. "She's not a private patient, you understand, but we thought we'd better isolate her when it became obvious you lot were going to be questioning her – at least there'll be a modicum of privacy."

Caine contented herself with a brief "Thank you, Doctor that should help, privacy *is* important – witnesses are sometimes reluctant to talk and Mrs Hartnell may well be our principal witness."

The doctor shrugged. "So long as you don't interfere with her treatment. Of course, I shall want to check she's okay before letting you see her."

Caine nodded, irritated by his attitude, but not wishing to enter into a discussion. She and Dolby followed Hamilton up the ward. He opened the door to a private room.

"I'll just go in and make sure she's well enough to see you," he said, turning towards Caine and Dolby. He went into the room.

A few seconds went by before Hamilton appeared at the door again and beckoned them in. "She's conscious, Inspector, but I doubt you'll get much out of her - I'm not sure she's fully aware of what's going on."

Mrs Hartnell, Caine judged, was in her early fifties. A buxom woman, small and thickset and propped up in the hospital bed, her head and one arm bandaged, her other arm showing heavy bruising. Her face was pale, set on a wide head. Her eyes, green and startlingly vivid, stared at them from behind a pair of cheap NHS glasses and followed them across the room, from the door to her bedside and then flickered back to settle on the doctor. A few strands of frizzy, prematurely white hair peeped out from the bandage wound tightly about her scalp while the long, bony fingers of her free hand clenched and unclenched on top of the thin sheet that covered her body. Beside her bed stood the metal stand of a drip feed machine, the long transparent plastic tube making a series of arcs in the air before disappearing into her arm. Bright sunlight slanted in through the window, dimming the screens of the various monitoring machines perched on wall-mounted brackets beside the bed. As the doctor spoke she turned her head slightly to look again at the two detectives.

"Here we are, Mrs Hartnell, this is Detective Chief Inspector Caine and Detective Sergeant Dolby to have a few words with you. Nurse will be along in a few minutes to see that you're okay and I shall call back in about an hour, so you've nothing to worry about." He turned to Caine and Dolby. "Five minutes, please…if you have any questions for me afterwards Staff Nurse Rierdon will know where to find me." He closed the door softly behind him.

"Good morning, Mrs Hartnell," said Caine approaching the bed. "The sergeant and I won't keep you long, we realise it must be very hard for you - yesterday's experience can't have been pleasant. But we do need your help in answering a few questions." Caine suddenly

102

realised that the woman was staring not *at* her, but *through* her, her brilliant green eyes fixed on some distant point and when she remained silent Caine wondered if the injured woman had heard anything at all of her words. "Do you think you could answer a few questions, Mrs Hartnell?" She repeated loudly, her tone brusque.

The woman said nothing, her eyes still fixed on that same distant point somewhere beyond the wall of the room. Caine looked despairingly across at Mark Dolby, on the far side of the bed. He threw up his hands in a gesture of helplessness. "I thought the doctor said she was conscious, but she doesn't seem to be aware of us, does she!"

At the sound of Dolby's voice the woman on the bed became agitated, her free arm rising jerkily upwards pulling on the plastic of her drip feed tube, her hand arching, her index finger pointing towards that far distant point that had so far been the object of her attention. Her body twitched and she tried to move her bruised arm, but it was stiff, the motion sluggish. When she spoke, her voice was high pitched and hysterical. Her eyes burned with a fiery zeal. "The flames of hell are burning for you - for you!" Then the fire fell from her eyes and her hand jerked back, covering the top part of her face, her head turning away. "Don't - don't - don't…"

Caine had retreated from the side of the bed wondering if she should alert the medical staff, but as abruptly as she had erupted into activity Mrs Hartnell now ceased her frenzied quivering. Her hand dropped away to her side again and her eyes regained that blank, expressionless look, staring into the distance.

"It's hopeless - she's not hearing us," said Caine. "She's off somewhere in another world."

"Perhaps we'd better wait a day or so," suggested Dolby. "Until she's recovered from the shock of the accident."

Caine nodded. "Yes, you may be right." She looked across at the woman lying in the bed. Her eyes were still trained on that far place. Caine wondered what she thought she was looking at as she moved closer towards her. The plastic tubing of her drip line was twisted, and she gently

104

moved the woman's arm to iron out the kink. Mrs Hartnell started, her mouth opened, and her head snapped around towards the Police Inspector. Caine found herself staring into a pair of eyes bright with accusation. "Sorry," Caine found herself mumbling, thrown momentarily off balance and thinking that maybe she should not have touched the device. Perhaps these things were better left to the nursing staff, who knew what they were doing. "Just trying to help," She added lamely.

At the sound of Caine's voice Mrs Hartnell screeched loudly, lashing out with surprising speed and strength to push her away. The flat of her hand caught the side of the Detective Inspector's head and Caine reeled backwards from the force of the blow. Again, the woman on the bed lashed out, this time with frenzied force, catching Caine a glancing blow and sending her staggering across the room.

"Fires of hell! You Devil! You Devil! You keep away from me!" Mrs Hartnell cried, her voice high and hysterical. "You've done for my poor girl, but you'll not get me!"

Dolby moved quickly, catching Caine about the waist, interrupting her passage across the room and stopping her from crashing into the wall. "Are you okay?"

Flustered, Caine nodded, rubbing the side of her head where Mrs Hartnell's hand had made contact. "I've been worse," she said, trying to smile. "That was sudden, though - where did she get the strength from? And what *is* she on about?"

Mrs Hartnell's high-pitched protests went on, becoming ever more strident as Nurse Rierdon came running into the room. "What's going on?" she asked anxiously, approaching the bed.

"It's okay, Nurse," said Caine. "I tried to straighten out her drip line and she lashed out at me. It was my fault."

"There was no call for it, though," said Dolby. "She'd better be careful she doesn't end up being charged."

Caine shook her head wryly. "I hardly think she's in her right mind, Mark. Best forget the whole thing I think."

The nurse hesitated, retreated from the bed and stood uncertainly by the door eyeing her patient. "Yes - well, I

106

think I'd better get Dr Hamilton in again," she said over the keening howl that now issued from Mrs Hartnell's lips. "And I think you'd better leave - the poor woman is in no fit state…"

The door opened and a small middle-aged man came into the room. His oval head was adorned by a shabby brown flat cap, his plump, chunky body by a grey suit, worn and shiny and two sizes too small for him. Alarm flickered in his eyes as he took in the scene. "Is everything all right?" He asked anxiously.

"And you are?" asked Rierdon. She had moved away from the bed now and the howl from her patient had dropped to a low moan.

"Henry Hartnell," said the man. He had taken off his flat cap and stood before them uncertainly in his unkempt suit. "Mrs Hartnell is my wife. Is she all right? She doesn't *seem* all right" A tall, thick set, muscular young man dressed in worn jeans and a thin sports shirt with a crumpled collar had followed him into the room. His mouth was wide open to reveal a tongue that lolled limply between his lips, his eyes dull and expressionless as they ranged over the scene. He was carrying a dark blue donkey jacket slung over one of his arms. A baseball cap of similar colour was pulled down over his head and a metal ring adorned his left ear. Mr Hartnell gestured towards him. "This is our boy, Reginald. Say hello, Reginald."

The younger man had just long enough to nod to them and say something indecipherable before Staff Nurse Rierdon sprang into action, shepherding them back towards the door. "Well, you can see, Mr Hartnell, that your wife needs a little of our attention, so if you wouldn't mind the both of you waiting outside while I call the doctor..." She hustled them out, turning at the door towards Caine and Dolby. "And I think you'd better leave now, Inspector, Sergeant. I'm sure we'll let you know when you can come back and see Mrs Hartnell, but I'm going to call Dr Hamilton now."

"Of course, but we shall want to see her as soon as possible," said Caine as they passed through the doorway. Ahead of them Mr Hartnell and his son Reginald were retreating silently back up the ward their backs hunched, ignoring the inquiring looks of the other patients. She turned to Dolby, "In the meantime, Mark, it wouldn't do any harm to have a quick word with our witness's husband and son. You never know what might be lurking under that flat cap."

They caught up with the little man and his son in the corridor outside the ward.

"We was just going to get ourselves a cup of tea in the canteen," said Hartnell after Caine had introduced herself and Dolby. "Just until we hear if we can go and see Dorothy. We can talk there if you like. I ain't got nothing to hide and neither has Reginald, have you son?" He winked at the young man who was staring silently at the two police officers, his mouth limply open, as though he could not understand what they were doing there, talking to his father. "Please, don't mind him," Mr Hartnell continued, "he's just a little slow on the uptake is Reginald, but he's a good lad!"

They sat at a corner table, Caine opposite Hartnell, Reginald beside his father and waited while Dolby brought four cups of tea, all of them weak and with far too much milk in them, as this appeared to be the only brew available. Mr Hartnell, short and plump, his belly erupting like a sea of lava over his trouser belt, talked almost continuously, intertwining his fingers nervously and then sipping noisily at his tea. Reginald sat quietly, his baseball cap pulled hard down on his head, his dark eyes watching with no apparent understanding.

"Have you seen your wife since the accident, Mr Hartnell?" asked Caine.

"You mean before this morning? Not to speak of really, she was sedated last night when I came. You know, they'd given her something to settle her down." He leaned forward. "You know she's lucky to be alive - some people were killed in that crash. I don't know why she was on that train anyway and that's a fact!" He leaned forward eagerly, "Here, do you think I could sue the railway company for all the hurt and aggro she's been put to?"

"You mean you didn't know she'd been to London?" asked Dolby, ignoring Hartnell's question and stirring his tea in the vain hope it might become a little stronger.

"I didn't know she'd *been,* and I didn't know she was coming back!" declared Hartnell. "She's her own woman is Dorothy and I don't try to tie her down." He became a little bolder, clearing his throat to ask, "I don't know why you're so interested in my Dorothy, Inspector - what's she got to do with the murder of that woman on the train? Seems very peculiar to me! I hope you're not going to make out she's done something!"

"We believe she was in the same carriage as the murdered woman," explained Caine. "She may have seen something, so we need to question her."

Hartnell shook his head. "Oh, I see, but I don't believe my Dorothy would be mixed up in anything funny."

"She probably isn't, Mr Hartnell, but she may well be able to help us. Unfortunately, we haven't been able to ask her anything yet, not the way she is this morning. Has she said anything to you?"

"What? About any killer? No - I told you she ain't been speakable to since yesterday".

Caine turned towards Reginald. "How about you, did your mother say anything to you?"

Reginald's puzzled, anxious expression and the desperate looks across at his father told Caine she was not getting through.

Hartnell intervened. "She wouldn't say nothing to him, now would she? She thinks he wouldn't understand about that sort of thing – overprotective towards him she is. Besides, he ain't seen her since the accident happened."

"He wasn't with you when you visited last night then?"

"No, he was off somewhere on his own, wasn't you Reginald." The young man nodded. "Well, I let him go off to a job by himself, yesterday. His mother doesn't like it – over-protective she is – but he knows his way around - he ain't completely stupid, he just don't talk much, do you Reginald?"

"What sort of work does he do?" asked Dolby.

"I'm a painter and decorator, see and Reginald helps me out. But he does work on his own account sometimes - he's quite a capable little worker is Reginald, I taught him well - he paints good, and you should see him with his plumb bob lining up for his papering. He's got a good eye has Reginald and he's strong, but I must admit he ain't much in the reading and writing line - retarded they said he was at school. And it's true - he doesn't really understand writing and he's no good at numbers - can't even dial out on the telephone - and his reading's very slow. He likes to look at the pictures. That's why his mother won't let go of him – overprotective she is, overprotective." He paused for a moment to take a gulp of his tea.

"You still let him work alone though," said Caine.

"Well, why not? He's all right; he gets by. It's work and it brings in a bit of money. Gawd knows as we need it!"

"I'm sure he does a very good job," said Caine. "But please tell us more about your wife, Mr Hartnell."

"What do you wanna know?" he finished his tea and turned towards his son. "Here, Reginald, do me a favour and get me another cuppa, there's a good lad!" He dug into his pocket and brought out a handful of coins. He looked around. "Anybody else want more tea? No - all right then, Reginald, just the one for me then. You got that?" The young man nodded, took the offered coins and got up from his seat. "That's it, it's over there." Hartnell nodded in the direction of the counter and Reginald set off for the requested tea. "He ain't a bad lad, he's just a bit slow that's all. We can't all be Einsteins!"

"Your wife, Mr Hartnell," said Caine a little wearily, sympathising with this parent of a slow and retarded son who, in spite of his years, still had to be treated like a child, but at the same time impatient to question the husband of their most promising witness. "The doctor thinks she's suffering from trauma caused by the rail accident and, possibly, from seeing the killer murder the other passenger. Is Mrs Hartnell the nervous sort?"

Hartnell pushed his chair back a few inches and scratched his chin reflectively. "I suppose. A bit." He seemed reluctant to continue.

"The Doctor seems to think she's been seeing things," said Dolby, "having delusions if you like."

"I don't like!" said Hartnell sharply. Reginald came back with the tea and he almost snatched the cup and saucer out of his hand. He drank half the cup before continuing in a loud voice. "They ain't illusions. She really sees things does my Dotty. She's what they call psychic!"

"You mean she says she sees dead people?" asked Dolby. He shot a dubious look across at Caine.

"She sees the spirits of those who've passed over if that's what you mean," said Hartnell defensively. "Not that I expect the likes of you to understand."

"Are you and your wife spiritualists, Mr Hartnell?" asked Caine.

The man finished his tea and pushed his cup and saucer away. "We belong to the Spiritualist Church."

"And do *you* see - 'spirits' - as well?" Try as he might Dolby could not keep the cynicism out of his voice.

Hartnell looked at him fiercely, pushing his chair backwards on the tiled floor before standing up. "No - I don't see them, Mr Policeman, but I know my wife does. She's got second sight, not that I expect you to believe that!" He turned towards his son. "Come on Reginald, we'd better go."

Reginald stood up and hurried off towards the canteen exit behind his father. Neither of them looked back to see the meaningful glances exchanged between the two detectives.

CHAPTER FIVE

"There's no point in chasing after them," said Caine watching Hartnell and his son disappear through the door of the hospital canteen. "He doesn't know what his wife saw in that train carriage any more than we do."

"It may be more a case of what she *imagined* she saw," said Dolby gloomily. "It's depressing that our only witness turns out to be mentally unbalanced!"

"We don't know that she's that bad, Mark."

"Oh, come on, Jackie, you don't believe in all that nonsense do you?"

"I like to keep an open mind. Anyway, whatever she is, I shouldn't think we're going to get anything useful out of her today. We'd better start exploring other avenues."

"Such as?"

"For a start, looking for anyone who may have wanted Nurse Marion Winters dead."

Dolby nodded. "Speaking of which, is there anything down from Yorkshire yet on that hospital case?"

"No - I checked before I left the office. Wendy has strict instructions to get in touch as soon as anything comes in."

"It's a long shot though, isn't it, this Ridings Hospital thing. What we really need is more up to date background on the Winters woman!"

"Yes, that reminds me - give Wendy a buzz and see if she's had any joy in discovering Marion Winters' employer's whereabouts. The old lady might be able to give us a few pointers on Marion; where her husband is, whether she had any regular friends, that sort of thing."

Dolby took his mobile telephone from his pocket and looked at it quizzically, pursing his lips. "I never know if we're supposed to use these things in hospitals. Don't they interfere with the electronic instruments or something?"

"Yes, I saw a '***strictly vorboten***' notice on the way in. We'd better be on the safe side and go out to the car before we ring. Anyhow, we can't do any more here for the time being." Caine stood up "Hopefully Wendy will have some news for us, otherwise, to be frank, Mark, I'm not sure where we're going to turn next for a possible lead."

They walked through the corridors in silence for a few minutes tracing their way back to the front of the hospital and the car park, each deep in thought.

"The trouble is that there *is* no apparent motive for this murder," said Dolby as they passed through the automatic doors and turned off to where they had parked their car. "We've got virtually no suspects." He brought out his mobile phone again and pressed the 'unlock' keys. "Let's see if Wendy's got anything for us."

"How do you mean we have no suspects, Mark? Things aren't nearly as gloomy as all that. We have *over twenty* possible suspects, haven't we? There are the train passengers, for a start they're none of them above suspicion, at least any who came out of the accident relatively unscathed. Then there are the relatives of the kids who died under our victim's care up in Yorkshire. That's another dozen or so possibles. Plus, any of Marion Winters' personal contacts, any of those may have wanted her out of the way. It seems to me we have a whole pile of suspects. We'll just have to do a lot of digging."

Dolby nodded then peered at the small, illuminated panel of his telephone, shaking the instrument irritably. "I'm having trouble locating a signal. Ah! Here we are!" He punched the speed dial for Fen Molesey Central Police Station before commenting cynically, "Yeah, I take your point, Jackie, but that makes about forty suspects and that's almost as bad as having none at all!" The telephone at the other end was answered and he asked to be put through to DC Doyle. "Wendy, it's Mark Dolby - do you have anything for us...? Right...yes, I know Stock fairly well ..."

While he was speaking, he and Caine crossed the hospital service road into the car park, passing a small white van with the words "Hartnell & Son, Painters and

Decorators" painted on its side in large red lettering. Henry Hartnell sat in the driving seat reading a tabloid newspaper, his son beside him moving his finger slowly across the page of a comic picture book. Reginald looked up as the two detectives passed, meeting Caine's eye, but showing no signs of recognition. She felt a tiny pang of conscience at the thought that they would have to question the young man's mother during the course of their inquiries, the poor woman surely had enough to contend with without being involved in a murder inquiry. Little wonder she was psychologically disturbed. Caine wondered how *she* would have coped if Alison, her daughter, had been born educationally subnormal - it must surely have changed her life beyond recognition. Still, it was hardly her fault, she concluded, that Dorothy Hartnell was involved in a murder case; it was the fickle finger of fate - the woman had been in the wrong place at the wrong time and she *was* involved, like it or not.

"In a manner of speaking, we have lift off," said Dolby, breaking the connection on his phone and slipping it back into his pocket. "Mrs Mears is in a nursing home for the aged, just outside Stock. Wendy managed to get that out of the social services department, no doubt after a lot of hassle - they're always pretty tight with the information they give out. Then she spoke to the Matron at the home - apparently the old lady - Mrs Mears - had a stroke yesterday morning. It left her with a bit of a muscle control problem on one side, but she's doing quite well in the circumstances. She can have visitors at any reasonable time." He looked at his watch. "It's just gone twelve - it shouldn't take much more than about half an hour to drive down there…"

"Okay, let's do it," said Caine. "The sooner we speak to Mrs Mears the better - we've got to get some sort of a handle on this case, Mark. I feel like we've been going backwards all morning."

Dolby knew the area well, having lived and worked there all his life and by using several short cuts and minor roads, thereby avoiding the heavy Saturday morning traffic on the A12, he managed to reduce the estimated thirty

122

minutes travelling time to just under twenty-five. The place they were looking for, the Tye Green Nursing Home for the Elderly, was on an unclassified road between Margaretting Tye and Stock. As they turned off the road between two tall brick piers that still exhibited the rusting hinges of a once massive wrought iron gate, they saw that the Home was a converted Manor House, the original building having been constructed in the mid nineteenth century. The notice at the entrance to the drive told them the place was now owned by one of the country's leading medical insurance companies and it was obvious they had recently spent a large amount of money on refurbishing and modernising the old house, which stood in the centre of the grounds, surrounded by green lawns and a number of newer, smaller buildings devoted to a variety of medical disciplines, as well as serving as living quarters for the staff.

They followed the curve of the gravel drive between a line of plane trees and around the back of the old manor house - a large grey stone building, with a number of square windowed and castellated towers and turrets. As they passed the two detectives became the subject of inquisitive stares from aged residents sitting out on the partially enclosed terrace, well-wrapped and enjoying a few brief moments of winter sunshine.

"It's like a country house hotel," commented Dolby as he turned off the main path and followed the signs to the car park.

"That's what it looks like," said Caine, "but wait until you get inside. I always find these places depressing." She released her seat belt as the car came to a halt. "It's a reminder of where we're all headed, sooner or later."

Mark Dolby switched off the engine and applied the hand brake. "Unless, of course, you die young," he said. "I suppose it's a toss up which is worse."

They followed a narrow foot path back to the house and climbed the few steps up to the main entrance door, which was open and led through a carpeted lounge area to a large reception hall. The air smelt of chemical fresheners, which only partially masked the variety of other odours

124

common to establishments caring for the elderly and infirm. The area was well lit, brightly decorated in peach and white and deserted but for the receptionist working behind a desk at a computer console. She wore a peach and white uniform matching the room's colour scheme. She looked up and smiled as they entered, rising to greet them, almost too enthusiastically.

"Good day, and welcome to the Tye Green Nursing Home for the Elderly." She looked beyond them as though searching for further members of their party.

"I'm Detective Chief Inspector Caine and this is Detective Sergeant Dolby, Fen Molesey Police," said Caine showing her warrant card. "And we're all there is."

"Sorry?" It took the receptionist a moment to realise what Caine was getting at. "Oh! I'm Deborah Wyngate." She laughed nervously. "Sorry about that. I was expecting a couple bringing in their elderly mother and I thought you were they, only I couldn't see your - *their* - mother. Sorry!" She consulted a notepad that lay on the desk beside the computer keyboard, picking it up and flicking back through a couple of pages. "Oh yes, Inspector - You're here to see Mrs Mears aren't you? If you'd like to follow me."

Mrs Mears was sitting up in bed in her private room playing patience. Her weak, watery eyes darted back and forth behind heavy tortoiseshell glasses, switching between the cards lying on the tray in front of her and the one she held in her gnarled and shaking hands. Every few seconds the left side of her body twitched uncontrollably, and the fingers of her left hand went into spasm, curling upwards into her palms. Beside her bed a number of visual display units, mounted on the wall and connected to her body by a series of slender cables, monitored her heartbeat and bodily functions. Beyond the machines a plain glass vase filled with fresh summer flowers stood on a small cabinet, adding fragrance to the mustiness of the room. Beside the vase, Mrs Mears' dentures grinned through the sides of a large glass jar that looked very much like a goldfish bowl. She looked up and grimaced as Caine and Dolby entered the room.

"Who are *you*? I shall ring the bell for nurse if I have any more interruptions. How am I supposed to finish a game with all these interruptions?" Her voice was shrill and surprisingly firm. She returned her attention to the cards, triumphantly slapping down the one she held in her right hand, on to one of those lined up before her. "You couldn't stop that one though, could you?" She chortled. She turned over another card and peered at it, her eyes moving myopically back and forth for some moments between it and the others.

"That'll go on the seven of diamonds, I think, Mrs Mears," said Dolby. "And the eight of hearts will go there, on the nine of clubs."

The old lady looked up at him angrily. "I don't need you to tell me that!" she snapped, nevertheless placing the cards as he had suggested. She looked up at him again and seemed suddenly to realise he was a stranger. "What are you doing in here?" she asked irritably. "Go away - you must have the wrong room. I don't know you." She glanced across at Caine. "Nor your wife or friend or whoever she is. Go away! Shoo!" She made as if to wave

them out of the room, at the same time returning her

attention to her game.

"Sorry to trouble you, Mrs Mears - it is Mrs Millicent

Mears isn't it?" said Caine, speaking slowly and clearly.

She held out her warrant card. "We're Police officers.

We'd like to ask you a few questions."

"Oh, do go away," the old lady said irritably. "Can't

you see I'm busy?" She had selected a new card and now

held it in her hand, hovering over the others, making a

point of totally ignoring the two police officers.

"Mrs Mears, *please*," said Caine shooting a

despairing look across at Dolby, who raised his shoulders

in an expression of helplessness. "We need to talk to you

about Marion Winters."

Mrs Mears looked up and a flicker of interest lit up

her eyes. "She's dead. Murdered. I know that. They told

me. You should know that too - it's your duty, that is if you

really are the police!" She scowled at Caine. "So why do

you want to come in here and talk to me about a dead woman?"

"We'd like you to tell us about her, Mrs Mears," said Caine "What sort of a woman was Marion Winters?"

For a long moment the old lady seemed to ignore her, engaging her attention once again with the brightly coloured cards. Then she suddenly cackled. "Stupid! That's what she was - stupid!" Mrs Mears turned towards the Detective Inspector and smiled a ghastly smile that was all red gums. Her gimlet eyes were pinpoints almost lost in the wrinkles pitting her leathery old face. "They say that at my age you get simple - I'm eighty-six you know, so, I may have got simple by some people's lights, but I ain't as stupid as that Winters woman!" She cackled again, her whole body shaking with a sort of twisted mirth. There came to Caine's mind the vision of a hunched up, bent nosed witch from a Disney movie. "Only a stupid woman would work for that sort of money."

"Maybe she wanted to help," suggested Dolby. "She was a qualified nurse, you know."

"Of course, she was a nurse, I know that. But she had a past you see, a ***sinister past***! Not something to be proud of! And when I took her on, I knew all about that past of hers, oh yes! She thought I didn't, but I read the newspapers and watch the current affairs programmes on the television." She cackled again, pleased with herself. "Yes, I knew all about her and those little kiddies up in Yorkshire - it might have been three years before and it might all have died down before she came to me for a job, but I remembered all right, oh yes! She was desperate by then of course. She couldn't get another job, not with her past she couldn't - and I knew it!" She leaned forward, showing her gums in a grotesque smile. "Do you know, I was paying her half the going rate and she was still glad to take the job!"

The old lady was evidently not as senile as she had appeared. She had been exploiting Marion Winters' unfortunate background. "She was found innocent of all charges in that case, Mrs Mears," declared Caine, "She was an innocent woman."

"Innocent schminnocent!" She mocked, her rheumy old eyes glittering wildly. "What did it matter to me? She was a nurse and I was looking for someone to help me get about the house. I offered her next to nothing for the job and she accepted. More fool her, I say." She pulled her eyes back to the card in her hand and then peered closely at those displayed on the tray in front of her.

"You didn't like her?" asked Caine.

"What was there to like? She was a servant! All right, these people call themselves 'companions', and they like to pretend they're your friends, but all they *really* are is skivvies. That's why I made her wear her uniform – to keep her in her place. Besides, there was nothing to like or dislike about her. She did her work and what was required of her and in return I gave her board and lodging and a small income. What more do you want?" The old lady turned over a new card and shook her head with disgust. "Useless! I'll never get this game out if you two won't leave me alone to concentrate!"

"Marion Winters was married, wasn't she, Mrs Mears?" asked Dolby. "Where was her husband?"

The old woman shrugged. "I haven't got a clue," she leaned forward as though to get him into focus, "It's Detective Sergeant something isn't it? I don't have the slightest idea where the husband is, Sergeant. I only met him once, a dirty little man he was too and on no account was he going to come and live-in with his wife and me. He was a womaniser he was I wouldn't have felt safe with him in the house. It was bad enough having her about the place, but the two of them together…!" She almost exploded with scorn at the thought of it. Then she stopped chortling and cocked her head to one side, thinking. "Anyway, they hated each other so far as I could tell. He was on the phone to her only a few days ago and you should have heard them shout at each other. Cor Strewth! She had a bit of a mouth on her that one, nurse or no nurse."

"What were they talking about?" asked Caine.

"How should I know? I only heard her part of the conversation."

"Couldn't you guess at it? It is important."

"Well, it was obvious she was divorcing him, cutting him off without a penny – not that she had much to give away, of course!" The old lady chuckled. "Maybe she wasn't so stupid after all! I don't know any more than that."

"We shall have to contact Mr Winters," said Caine. "Would you have any objection to our looking for his details in Mrs Winters' personal papers?"

The old lady turned to peer suspiciously at her. "In my house you mean. So long as you make good any damage you cause. Can't have damage in my house, you know, my nephew wouldn't like that - he'll be around there even now going through my things I dare say, looking for this and that - anything he can steal. He thinks I'm senile and won't notice, but I'm not that stupid, I *know* what he's up to, the little worm, believe you me!" She placed the card she was holding over the bottom card in one of the rows lined up on her bed tray. "You think her husband killed her don't you."

"At the moment we really don't know *who* killed her," said Caine.

"He'd have good reason. Well, it wasn't a proper marriage was it? Them living apart and all that - and besides he hadn't a clue, that man. Couldn't hold down a job he couldn't, he was always trying to borrow money from her. In the end she got fed up with it and decided to divorce him. So, maybe he killed her to get the insurance money before it was too late!"

"We'll certainly look into it," Caine assured her. "But tell me, is there anyone else you know of who might have gained from her death?"

The old lady cackled loudly again. "He! He! He! Of course, there is! Like I said, my nephew, Alec, my sister's boy, for a start. Well, he's not a boy any longer, I suppose, must be well into his forties now - if not his fifties! I forget how old *I* am, sometimes. Little toe rag, he is and my only living relative! He'd love to get his hands on my money - and my house, that's where most of the money is, of course, tied up in the house. Prime building land that is,

134

right on the edge of the village - and a big garden. We couldn't have children you see, my late husband, and me and the garden was a sort of substitute. We'd be out there all day, summer and winter and what a beautiful show of vegetables Claude, my husband, had each year for the village flower show."

"I think we can see that your nephew would be very interested in inheriting your house," said Caine in an attempt to stem the old lady's flow of words, which were drifting off into irrelevance. "It's obviously a sizeable plot and must be worth a tidy sum…"

"And don't forget there's also sixty acres of farmland," Mrs Mears added. "That's mine too. My Claude, God rest his soul, he knew what he was at - nobody ever got one over on my Claude - he made sure we got that land when we bought the house! He wouldn't stand for any nonsense, wouldn't my Claude!"

Caine, hoping that Mrs Mears was not rambling off again, shot a frustrated look across at Dolby. "But what's all this got to do with your nephew - Alec - being better off with Marion Winters' dead? Why would *he* benefit from the death of Mrs Winters?"

The white-haired old lady gave Caine a crooked smile. "Ah! You see - he thought I was leaving it *all* to Winters, lock stock and barrel! *He* thought *she'd* get the lot when I popped my clogs. So, it would be all the better for him if she was out of the way now, wouldn't it!"

"And *would* she have inherited?" asked Dolby. "*Was* Mrs Winters your major beneficiary?"

Mrs Mears guffawed and slapped her side with her right hand causing the monitoring cables connecting her to the various electronic wizardry beside her bed to dance about wildly. "No, of course not! I wouldn't give away all my family's wealth to a complete stranger, would I? We didn't even get on that well, that Marion Winters and me. But Alec thought we did - and he thought she was going to get the lot instead of him!" She sniggered, enjoying the joke enormously. "He gets really mad about it!"

"But why on earth tell him that in the first place?" Caine shook her head and shrugged. It was obvious the old lady was no longer in her right mind. The series of strokes had taken their toll and she had lost touch with reality. Or had she? Perhaps she disliked her nephew so much she enjoyed putting him through what was obviously, for him, some sort of mental torture.

"*Why*? You want to know *why* I pretended to leave it all to Winters," said the old lady, her voice rising to a screech. "Because my nephew ignored me for years, that's why. Him and that wife of his, that Ada, they never came near me until they heard I had a living-in companion. *Then* they started to worry Winters was getting too comfortable, taking over my affections you might say. So, I played up to it, that's what I did! I made them think she really *was* going to get it all when I pass over!"

"And your nephew believed you, Mrs Mears?" asked Dolby.

"Darned right he believed me!" said Mrs Mears, laughing shrilly. "It had him *really* worried! He's in property in a small way is Alec and he has this Tom Fool idea of knocking down my house and taking back the fields

137

my Claude leased to Bill Brightwell, my neighbour who farms the land. He wants to turn the estate into one of these new-fangled shopping areas, does Alex. He reckons he could get the council to let him build there, well, he knows all the right people, I'll say that for him." She smiled wickedly, selecting a new card from the pack and peering at it closely before continuing. "I know that's what he had in mind because he told me. Wanted me to move out and go into one of those warden assisted places where all the old people live. But that's not for me. Anyway, he's a useless businessman is Alec. He's up to his neck in debt on failed property deals he's already done. He really could do with my money - but I say he should earn it, like my Claude did, not expect to have it handed to him on a plate!"

"So, he would have been quite put out if Marion Winters had inherited the property from you," said Caine. "But what did *she* think? Did *she* believe she was going to inherit your house and land?"

"I never discussed it with her!" said the old lady. "It wasn't any of her business what I was going to do with my own property when I died!"

"But your nephew did believe it?"

Mrs Mears nodded. "Oh yes, we had words about it whenever I saw him - not that that was very often. Teased him like mad I did," she smiled gleefully, showing off her gums. "He went wild and shouted and screamed at me, so I told him if he was going to treat his poor old aunt like that then he didn't deserve to inherit my property. Who did he think he was? I told him there were far more deserving people - so maybe Winters overheard us and got to know about it like that. But if she did, she never mentioned it to me!"

"Did she have any regular friends?" asked Dolby.

"Maybe."

"You'd not seen them?"

"No. I didn't go socialising with her, did I? She was my live-in skivvy - she wasn't my friend!"

"How often did she go out?"

"Once a week, for half a day or so. I kept her too busy for any messing around I can tell you!" The old lady grinned smugly, remembering. "She may have had someone, though, someone she didn't want *me* to know about…"

"How do you mean?" asked Caine.

"She used to put on make-up before she went out, the hussy. A woman doesn't do that unless she's going to see a man."

"She might. Most women like to look their best when they go out," suggested Dolby. "My wife thinks it gives them confidence."

"No, she had a man!" declared Mrs Mears. "I didn't ever see him, but she had a man all right. And it wasn't her husband."

Caine sighed. She was not sure the old lady was telling the truth. She seemed to be enjoying herself in some perverse sort of way, criticising her former companion and running her down in a most unfriendly manner that the Detective Chief Inspector found hard to stomach. Old Mrs

Mears seemed to know nothing about Marion Winters' man friend - or friends - if, indeed she had had one, but she was making the most of being the centre of attraction.

"Turning back to your nephew, Mrs Mears, where was he yesterday?" asked Dolby.

The old lady shrugged. "How should I know? Yesterday I had my third stroke - I woke up this morning to find myself here in the hospital. Some would say I'm lucky to be alive. So, what do I care where Alec was yesterday - or anybody else for that matter?"

"We'd like to eliminate him from our inquiries." said Caine.

"Then you'd better ask *him* where he was, hadn't you? I didn't even know where *I* was yesterday!"

"Do you have his address?" asked Dolby.

"Somewhere near Colchester. Oh, I don't know - never been there have I, never got invited by him and his skinny wife, Ada, did I? So why *should* I know? But you ask here at the hospital - they'll have a record of it. You bet they will - they'd have wanted that would Alec and Ada -

141

in case anything happened to me *they'd* want to be the first to know!"

"And what's your nephew's surname, Mrs Mears."

The old lady thought for a moment. "Lassiter. My younger sister, Dora, married this most unsuitable man named Norman Lassiter when she was much too young to know what she was doing. I told her it would never work out, but she would insist. Of course, I was right. He ran off with a window dresser – or was it a window undresser? Either way she was a real little tart!"

Caine heard only the first part of the old lady's diatribe against her sister. Her mind was busy puzzling over the nephew's name. *Lassiter. Alec Lassiter. A. Lassiter.* Where had she seen that name before, recently? She glanced across at Mark Dolby. He was smiling. Maybe something was beginning to fall into place at last. "And you don't have his address, Mrs Mears?"

The old lady scowled. "No, I told you! They never so much as asked me there for a cup of tea!" Angrily, she ran her hands through the cards neatly lined up before her,

142

scattering them across the tray. "Perhaps I **should** change my will! The trouble is, now that Winters is gone there's nobody I can leave it all to. Not family anyway. Perhaps the cats' home…but I never was one for cats!"

"Are you thinking what I'm thinking?" asked Dolby as they closed the door to Mrs Mears' room a few minutes later and made their way back along the corridor to the reception area.

Caine stopped and propped her large handbag against the sill of a window looking out onto the grounds, flicking the clasp and pulling open one of the side compartments. "Maybe, but what a malicious old woman! She didn't have a good word to say about anybody - and the way she treated poor Mrs Winters…That sort of exploitation shouldn't be allowed." She rummaged in her bag. "I think she was inventing most of what she was saying, though and it wasn't down to senility, don't you believe it. She was just being vicious! She told us two things, though that might be important. Firstly, Marion Winters may have had a friend, possibly male; and secondly about her nephew -

143

but if we're right in what we're obviously both thinking we won't need to get his address from the hospital administrator." She pulled a sheaf of folded papers from her bag and opened them up, running her finger down the typed list. "Pity they didn't put these in alphabetical order, but I suppose they were in a bit of a hurry." She flipped over to the second page. "Yes, here it is - '*A. **Lassiter**.* Suspected fractures - ribs, legs and right arm. Cranial contusions'."

"Oh, that's great!" said Dolby, disappointed, "I was pretty sure I remembered his name being on the list, but I was hoping he'd be down as one of the 'uninjured'. Fit to kill, so to speak!"

"Yes, so was I - but, Mark, the important thing is *he was on that train*!" Caine refolded the papers and pushed them back into her handbag. "It's too much of a coincidence. And don't forget, this list was made up just a few minutes after they got the crash victims off the train - the injuries they mention here might be completely wrong.

144

He may have walked away from the accident comparatively unharmed."

Dolby nodded, pleased at the thought. "Then we'd better get over to the hospital and find out, hadn't we? It's the first real lead we've had."

CHAPTER SIX

Mrs Mears' nephew, Alec Lassiter, had a broken leg, two broken arms and extensive damage to other parts of his anatomy in the form of cuts, abrasions, dislocations and heavy bruising. Always assuming she had been killed after the rail accident there was no conceivable way he could have carried out the murder of Nurse Marion Winters.

Lassiter was heavily dosed with painkillers, his arms encased in plaster of Paris from wrists to shoulders, with his broken leg, similarly bound up in a white plaster cast, suspended from a wired pulley system engineered into the frame of the hospital bed. Slender cables connected to sensors snaked from his arms, chest and abdominal regions to monitoring screens behind the bed. His round, almost bald head, his face and the upper parts of his body were pock marked with large expanses of adhesive plaster, bright pink islands against an ocean of pale skin punctuated with dark, heavy bruising. Nevertheless, when Caine and Dolby entered the ward, Lassiter was awake, propped up in bed and trying, with some difficulty, to read the morning's Daily Mail; the front page of which carried lurid pictures of the local train disaster beneath banner headlines reading "***Mystery Killer Slays Nurse in Rail Accident***."

"Would you mind telling us what you were doing on that train, Mr Lassiter?" asked Caine after they had introduced themselves.

"I hope you're not suggesting that *I* murdered the bloody woman," he said irritably, having some difficulty in getting the words out clearly through his bruised lips. He moved his rigid arms a few millimetres up and down in protest.

"We don't know *who* killed her," said Dolby. "It's clear you couldn't have got very far with these injuries, but that's on the assumption Mrs Winters was killed *after* the crash. We don't know that that's the way it happened, Mr Lassiter, not for sure anyway. So, we'd still like to know *why* you were on that train."

147

"I tell you I didn't go near her!"

"That may well be so, sir," said Dolby patiently, "But it is a bit of a coincidence you and your aunt's companion being on the same train in the late afternoon, you've got to admit that - unless, of course, for some reason, you were travelling together."

Lassiter sucked in his breath and shook his head a number of times. "I think one of my teeth is loose!" He groaned. "You've got a cheek coming in here at a time like this, do you know that?" He went on. "Bloody coppers! I could've been killed, do you realise that? And I'm going to sue that sodding Railway Company for every penny it's got. I'm going to bleed them dry!"

"That's your prerogative, Mr Lassiter," said Caine. "But in the meantime, the sooner you tell us what we want to know the sooner we'll be out of your hair. So, what made you get on that train?"

"It's obvious isn't it!" the man snapped, "I was on my way home."

"Where had you been? You're self employed and your office is in Colchester, so what were you doing boarding a train at Liverpool Street station in the middle of a Friday afternoon?"

"I wasn't at Liverpool Street, was I? I got on at Chelmsford." His voice was thick as he sucked on a loose tooth. "Look, you may as well know, I've got nothing to hide. I'd been to the Nursing Home to see if my aunt was okay. I wanted to make sure them taking her to hospital wasn't some scam dreamed up by that cow Winters, to help her feather her nest."

"Then you were at the Tye Green Nursing Home yesterday afternoon?" Dolby paused from writing in his notebook.

Lassiter responded angrily. "Yes! That's what I just said, didn't I? Nothing wrong in that is there?" Caine could not help noticing that his formerly pale face was now suffused with patches of vivid red. She glanced at the monitor screens on the wall behind him. If she was reading them correctly his blood pressure was soaring. They had

149

better get their questioning over quickly before one of the nursing staff noticed the man's condition and threw them out of the ward.

"Your aunt, Mrs Mears, gave us to understand you very rarely see her. How did you know she had been taken to the Nursing Home?"

Lassiter made an attempt at shrugging but succeeded only in twitching the upper part of his body. "One of my aunt's neighbours rang me, didn't they? Look, I know how aunt Millicent makes out I'm a terrible nephew, only out for what I can get etcetera etcetera but my wife and me, we *do* actually care about her…" Caine nodded her head dubiously. "… "and I've always had this arrangement with her neighbours that they let me know if anything serious happens to her. They rang yesterday morning to say she'd been taken off in an ambulance and that the Winters woman had gone with her, so I decided I'd better go and investigate. Find out what Winters was up to."

"So, you left the Nursing Home together with Mrs Winters and you took the train from Chelmsford back to Colchester?" asked Dolby.

"No, I didn't go anywhere with the bloody Winters woman! I had business to attend to in Chelmsford, so when I'd finished at the Home - when I'd checked my aunt was okay and it was all above board - she had a stroke, the doctors confirmed that - there was nothing else for me to do there, so I took the opportunity of seeing a man in Chelmsford about some ongoing business." He yawned, grimacing with pain as he stretched the muscles of his bruised jaw. "Then I took a taxi to the station and got on the Colchester train. I didn't even know the Winters woman was on the same train! I didn't see her - but if I had I would have avoided her. I can't stand the woman!"

"You didn't get along with Mrs Winters?"

"That's what I just said, didn't I - are you thick or something? If you want the truth, I hated her guts," Lassiter's eyes burned passionately. He really did hate her thought Caine. "Ada, that's my wife, and me we could see

151

right through her. We knew what game *she* was playing, bloody little gold digger. I kept an eye on Winters, don't you worry about that!" He yawned again. "If you ask me she got her just desserts yesterday! I didn't kill her, but I'd shake the hand of the man who did!"

"Would you mind telling us the name and address of the person you went to see on business?" asked Dolby.

"His name's Pemberton. Harry Pemberton," Lassiter told him without hesitation. "Pemberton Estates in the main shopping precinct. You can check with him if you want."

"Just one more question," said Caine, rising from her chair. "Why didn't you drive down to the Nursing Home, Mr Lassiter? You do have a car don't you?"

"My wife had it - she does a part time job in an estate agent's office in town - Colchester - she left for work before I got the news about aunt Milly. So, I took a train down to Chelmsford and a taxi from there to the Nursing Home. Satisfied?"

"For the time being, Mr Lassiter. Which carriage were you on?"

He made another attempt at shrugging. "I don't know what carriage I was on. It's not the sort of thing you notice is it?"

"Before you got on the train at Chelmsford," said Dolby. "What part of the platform were you standing on? Did you walk further along after you came on to the platform?"

"I don't know that this has anything to do with anything, but yes I did - I believe I turned right from the entrance. So, I suppose I must have got on one of the rear carriages."

"The last one?"

"It may have been. I think it was. Why?"

"Just trying to get things sorted out in our minds," said Caine.

He grimaced again and yawned. "Now, if you don't mind, I'm going to sleep. The quacks have pumped me full of bloody pills!"

They were twenty feet away from the car before Dolby noticed the wheel clamp. "I don't believe it! What sort of swine would do this? We're here on police business and we get clamped!"

"We *are* in a no parking zone," said Caine without much sympathy. "And it is an unmarked car."

"You know as well as I do that it's here because there was nowhere else to park," Dolby spluttered reaching the car and giving the clamp a hefty kick, "not without causing an obstruction, anyway. And why do you think I put *that* on the dashboard?" He pointed at the large white card printed in six-inch high letters with the word "POLICE". "They must be blind, the lot of them, not to see that!"

"You know what they say, Mark," said Caine. "…There's none so blind as those that don't want to see. This clamping business is private enterprise now and there's sixty quid or more in it for every car they clamp. No wonder they're blind!"

"But it is a bl…ruddy hospital…" It was sweet, though exasperating, Caine thought, that Dolby, after working with her for some months now and knowing that she was not averse to using the occasional bit of bad language herself, still chose his words carefully when speaking to her. "…What do people do when they're visiting a sick relative and they can't park? Blame *us* I suppose, not these ruddy cowboy clamp operators!" He sighed and looked at his watch. "It's nearly three thirty. It'll probably take a couple of hours to get this little lot sorted out," He unlocked the car doors. "I promised Lorna I'd be home at a reasonable time tonight - I really ***do not*** need this!"

"Get someone from the station to deal with it then," suggested Caine. "Come back to the station in a cab with me."

"No, I can't do that - it's my own car isn't it. Hansen has these stupid rules." Dolby wrenched open the car door. He looked daggers at the clamp again and gave it another, half-hearted kick. "Do you want to sit for a minute and just go through where we're at with this blood - ruddy murder?"

"Yes, okay, we may as well both be depressed, but at least we'll be in the warm. You can turn the heating on." She opened the passenger door and sat down pulling it shut behind her. "I can't say we're at anywhere in particular. The killer isn't exactly making himself obvious, is he?"

Dolby sat beside her and switched on the car's ignition, turning the heating controls to maximum. He drummed his fingers on the steering wheel before answering her question. "He could have done it, you know, Lassiter. He was there on the train at the time."

"What? With both his arms and one leg broken?" said Caine. "I know you're upset because your car's been clamped, Mark, but you don't have to take leave of your senses. Okay, I know I'm making the assumption she was killed *after* the train crash, but to do it before - well, it just doesn't make much sense. Marion Winters was in a carriage with two other people. Surely, one or both of them would have seen something and pulled the communication cord."

"What you're forgetting, though, Jackie, is that he could have done it while they were in the tunnel - it's quite a long stretch and it gets pretty dark in there for a few seconds. Besides, neither of our two witnesses has been able to tell us anything. One of them's dead and the other's gone totally loopy!" Dolby had opened his notebook and was flipping abstractedly through the pages. "Just because Lassiter says he didn't see Marion Winters on the train doesn't mean to say he's telling the truth!"

"I suppose it is possible," admitted Caine. "But it's not much of a case is it? We know Lassiter and the murder victim didn't get on - he hated her - and maybe we could prove that, but we haven't any proof that he actually **killed** her. It's just as likely that one of the other passengers did it - and there are more than thirty of them to choose from. Once you assume she may have been killed **before** the crash you open up the possibility that any of them could have done it."

"Well, he **did** know her and he **was** on the train," Dolby persisted. "If only that Hartnell woman would get sensible and tell us what she actually saw!" He sighed. "I still say Lassiter's the closest link we've found so far. *And* he had both motive *and* the opportunity!"

Caine gave a hollow laugh. "Not much of an opportunity, though was it? Fifteen - maybe thirty seconds - in the dark, to get from his own carriage into hers, which - if he was telling the truth just now - was four or five carriages away. Then he'd have to find her in the dark, top her and get back out of her carriage again. I don't think so, somehow." She closed her eyes for a moment, thinking. "I suppose we'd better confirm what carriage Lassiter was *really* on… see if the other passengers agree with what he told us. Then we'd know if he had the time to get into her carriage."

"One or two of the passengers may even remember seeing him," suggested Dolby. "We'll need to show them a photograph."

"Yes, but we'd better make it clear Lassiter isn't a prime suspect, we don't want a bloody defamation charge on our hands - we've got enough to contend with." She rested her handbag on the glove compartment and drummed her fingers on it for a few seconds. "Look, let's wait for the post mortem before we spend time and effort hawking Lassiter's picture around the other passengers - it might well tell us whether the Winters woman was killed before or after the crash." She paused thoughtfully. "You know, Mark, it would help a lot if we could establish whether or not the killer left the train after the accident. I've been thinking about that and it occurs to me there *is* a way of establishing whether he did or he didn't... It'll take time and a lot of boring plod work, but we might just bring it off."

"What exactly do you have in mind?"

"Video cameras. All train stations have video cameras don't they? Surely it must be possible for us to match the people left on the train after the accident with everyone who boarded or disembarked from it at each station. There were only about thirty people left on board after the crash - at that time of day the numbers wouldn't have gone up or down dramatically from station to station, so I shouldn't think it'd be all that difficult."

Dolby nodded slowly, considering her point. "I see what you mean. I suppose it's possible, but it presupposes being able to match the passengers to the video pictures. Those cameras don't take very clear images, not generally speaking, anyway. And they've all got to have been working properly at the crucial times."

"Yes, I know - it's not foolproof, but it's worth a try. It might just give us a lead. I'll get on to Network Rail as soon as I get back to the office. Get them to let us have the video recordings from the stations the train stopped at - mind you, I don't know who we're going to get to go through the recordings, we're short enough staffed as it is." Caine pushed her door open. "I'd better let you get on with your de-clamping exercise, Mark. I'll be back in the office as soon as I can rustle up a taxi." She stepped out of the car and closed the door. "See you tomorrow morning?"

Dolby nodded. Another weekend ruined. Lorna and his children would be disappointed not to have him around tomorrow, when they were off school and therefore available for family activities, but they had long since come to terms with the fact that when there was an unsolved murder DS Mark Dolby's time was not his own - not even his so-called free time. He watched DCI Caine make her way towards the hospital reception area before getting out of the car, giving the clamp a last frustrated kick, and trudging slowly after her.

Caine's mobile telephone rang just as the taxi swung through the gates of Fen Molesey Central Police Station and drew to a halt beside the steps leading up to the entrance doors. She let it ring for a moment while she paid the driver and then, slipping it out of her handbag, ran quickly up the steps and pushed the swing doors open before answering.

"Oh! You're here!" Sergeant Crouch was standing behind the public counter with his telephone to his ear, looking straight at her. "That's a waste of a phone call if ever there was one!"

Caine heard his voice both from across the office and from the tiny microphone of her mobile and quickly shut off the instrument. "What's up, Bernie? Giving me hassle already?" She strode over to the counter and placed her handbag on the surface while she put her phone away.

A slim man in his early thirties, dressed in a white T-shirt and scuffed jeans rose from one of the guest chairs in the corner and came towards them.

"This gentleman wants to speak to the officer in charge of the rail track murder case, Ma'am. Name of Hickman…" he glanced down at his notepad, "Mr Terence Hickman. Says he has what might be an important clue."

"That's right," said Hickman. "I heard the appeal on the radio this morning."

Caine turned towards him and held out her hand. "Detective Chief Inspector Caine. I don't suppose you'll want to see my warrant card?"

Hickman glanced at Crouch and shook his head. "No problem. You won't keep me long will you? Only I couldn't get into the bill's- *your* - car park and I'm parked

162

on a double yellow. I left my mate in the van, but he can't drive - he's been disqualified on account of him trying to snog a bird and drive at one and the same time - so I need to get back out there quick."

"I can't tell how long I'll keep you until I hear what you have to say, Mr Hickman," said Caine reasonably. She turned to Crouch. "Okay for us to use your back office for a few minutes, Sergeant Crouch?"

Hickman consulted his wristwatch twice during the short time it took them to walk around the counter, go through the inner door and settle themselves into chairs in the back office.

"If I get a ticket I'll tell 'em I was in the nick giving important information to the Police," he suggested as he sat down opposite Caine. "That ought to do the trick - you'll back me up, won't you Inspector."

"I can certainly confirm you were in here with me, Mr Hickman, but I'm not sure it'll carry enough weight to get you off a parking fine," said Caine, wondering how Dolby was getting on with his clamping problem. "They're nothing to do with us anymore, you see. Now, what is it you want to tell me?" Hickman dug into his pocket and produced a packet of cigarettes. Caine nodded in the direction of a 'No Smoking' sign on the wall. "Sorry."

He grimaced and put the cigarettes back in his pocket. She noticed his hands were very large, with big fingers, gnarled at the joints. "I heard the appeal for help on the radio this morning." He was missing his smoke and fidgeting, flexing his fingers, missing something to do with those large hands. "About whether anyone saw anybody near the scene of the train accident yesterday afternoon. I thought I ought to report what we - me and Trevor - saw."

Caine leaned forward, interested and unzipped one of the compartments of her handbag looking for her notebook and pad. "First let's have your address, Mr Hickman."

"If it's really necessary for you to have it," he said, a little reluctantly. "14, Union Road, Fen Molesey."

"Okay, Mr Hickman, tell me what you saw."

He rubbed his chin, marshalling his thoughts. "Me and Trevor, me mate, we'd just come from the school -

164

Upton Grange, over by Upton Eccles - where we'd been taking the top off this big Sycamore tree…"

"You're a tree surgeon?"

Hickman looked blank for a moment. "Well, all sorts really, we cuts down trees and we lops the tops off of 'em. We also do forestry, hedge clipping, general gardening, that sort of thing. Anyway, we had this call a couple of days ago from the school. They wanted the top took off their sycamore - they reckoned it was dangerous after being struck by lightning in that storm we had a few days ago - even worse than yesterday's it was, you might not have noticed it, being as you work in an office building like this…" Caine nodded, remembering the almost Armageddon like thunder and lightning of the Wednesday evening. She and Dolby had stood at her office window struck with awe by the primeval violence of the storm. "I know it's winter and we've got to expect bad weather, but strewth! That storm was something else! It's all this global warming we're getting nowadays I reckon. It's changing the whole of our climate, as you know, what with the

165

floods and storms and heat waves we've been having all over the country, like a tropical hell it'll be." He waved his huge hands about like a prophet of doom, seeming to have forgotten the purpose of his visit and the impending disaster of a parking ticket.

"So, you'd been taking the top off the sycamore tree at the school?" prompted Caine, thinking of all the work that was waiting for her in her office and wishing he would get on and say what he had to say.

"Yeah, right." He ran his hands through his thick black hair that seemed to be heavily plastered with some sort of setting gel to hold it in place. "Anyway, we was coming back after the school job, going on to our next job down in Wickham Bishops and we was on one of them little roads near Inworth, when we sees this bloke walking across the fields away from the railway lines. Going in the direction of Rivenhall End he was."

There was a large-scale road map of Fen Molesey and the outlying areas on the wall behind him and Caine asked him to show her exactly where, on the map, he had seen the man. Hickman spent some moments deciding which road he and his mate, Trevor, had been on before pointing out a definite location.

"And you're sure it was there?" Hickman's finger was indicating a point in the middle of a group of fields, no more than two thirds of a mile from the scene of the rail accident. Caine found a drawing pin on one of the nearby desks and stuck it in the map to mark the place. "What time was this?"

"About a quarter to four."

The time fitted, thought Caine. "How far away was this person?"

Hickman shrugged. "I dunno – forty, maybe fifty yards. The land's pretty flat around there, you can see for miles."

"And what was he like?"

"Like? I don't know what he was like - he was too far away to see any real detail, if you see what I mean. And it was starting to get dark." He frowned and looked at his watch again.

"Well, can you give us any sort of a description at all? Was he tall, short, fat, thin?"

Hickman shrugged again. "Well, he must've been tall, I suppose, cos he looked fairly big, even from that distance. And not really fat or thin - sort of average really. But I couldn't tell you what his face was like or anything. He was walking away from us, you see, so we didn't see his face."

It was just within the bounds of possibility that Hickman's information might prove valuable, thought Caine, but he had so far given her precious little to distinguish the man from ten thousand other men living in the Fen Molesey/Chelmsford area. "Mr Hickman, what makes you think there was any significance at all in this man walking across the fields. He could have been a farm labourer couldn't he?"

"What Miss? Wearing a suit?" Hickman said scornfully, as if she had been in possession of this information all along. "You might get a farm labourer in the middle of a field but he wouldn't be wearing a suit, would he?"

"Oh! So, he was wearing a suit? Your eyesight must be very good, Mr Hickman. I don't think I could tell if a man was wearing a suit from that far off and in the twilight. But as I recall it was pretty cold yesterday – why wasn't he wearing a coat?"

"He was, but it was short, like a car coat and you could see the suit trousers underneath. And my eyes are good, as a matter of fact," he added proudly. "Never had to wear glasses I haven't and I'm top player in the local darts team. Have been for the last five years. You need a good steady eye for that game."

"So, what colour suit was this man wearing, Mr Hickman?"

"Blue - I think - he was a long way off wasn't he. It looked blue to me."

"What about your mate Trevor - what colour did he think it was? You have discussed it with him I take it?"

"Yeah - we had to talk about it to decide whether to come in and see you. He thought it was blue too, though at first he said it was grey. Well, the light wasn't that good was it, it was practically dark by then."

"Okay - we'll ask him for his own statement." Caine made a quick note. "Was there anything else you noticed about this man in the suit? Was he in a hurry?"

"Well, he wasn't running if that's what you mean. But he wasn't hanging about either. The fields must've been pretty muddy after that cloudburst we'd had a couple of hours before and it was probably heavy going. That must have slowed him down."

"Anything else?"

"No - can't think of anything. As I say, he was a long way off and it was nearly dark." Hickman looked at his watch again and stood up. "Can I go now, Inspector, I've got a bit of regular gardening work to do out near Pods Wood, not to mention that ticket I might get if I leave the van any longer!"

"No - you can't go just yet, Mr Hickman, I'd like you to sign a statement. And then I'd like Trevor to come in and make one."

Hickman's face dropped. "Here! What is this? I come in special to help like a good fu- frigging citizen and what do I get? Hasslement that's what! And a fu - frigging ticket as well I dare say, the time you've kept me talking in here. I wanna speak to the Guv'nor!"

"The Guv'nor, as you put it is away for the weekend," said Caine. "For the moment I'm *it*. But I'll tell you what I'll do for you, Mr Hickman - we are grateful to you for coming in with this information, it might well be helpful in solving the case - so I'll find you a place in our car park. Then you and Trevor can both make statements and be on your way. How would that suit?"

A preliminary postmortem report from the pathologist was on Caine's voice mail when she finally made it back to her office and it confirmed that certain injuries on Marion Winters' body indicated that she had definitely died *after* the train accident. Apart from that

171

there was very little Caine did not already know. Marion Winters had been garotted, the method employed being a twin stranded cord wound around her neck and pulled tight. There were traces of some fibres from the cord clinging to her skin - if they could find the cord used in the murder, they could easily match these to them. Samples of the fibres, together with her clothing - which might be found to harbour traces of the murderer's hair, skin, even his after-shave lotion (!) - had been passed to the forensic labs for examination. It was not certain whether the victim had put up a fight, but there were no traces of the killer's skin or blood under her fingernails. The only other point of interest was a faint bullet shaped mark, about 2.5 centimetres long, impressed into the flesh of her back, between the shoulder blades. The pathologist offered no explanation for this mark, except to comment that, whilst bullet shaped, it had not been caused by a bullet, but probably by some other hard, possibly metallic, object. His full report would be on DCI Caine's desk by Monday afternoon and, no doubt, forensics would be in touch at some time.

Caine listened to the report again and made a few notes. Next was the fingerprint report. The inside surfaces of the carriage in which Marion Winters had died were liberally covered with multitudes of prints, the vast majority old and smeared; in spite of the fact that the glass, wood and fabric of the train were supposed to be cleaned every night, most of the prints were probably vestiges of those left over from many days before. Those found on the personal belongings of the murder victim and her fellow passengers, those that were not impossibly smudged, had been matched to them. On the newspapers, magazines and books there were one or two other fingerprints that did not seem to match, but these might be explained, the report suggested, as those of the shop assistants who had sold them. Those on the half-eaten packet of extra strong mints were smudged beyond recognition. After reading it carefully and pondering over one or two aspects of the report Caine pushed the two sheets of closely typed words into her pending tray for later consideration.

Some reports were in from the team Caine had delegated to question the surviving train passengers, but after skimming through them she decided there was nothing there of any significance. Quite understandably, the occupants of the train had been far too busy taking care of themselves and their immediate neighbours to take note of any person or persons who might have been seen leaving the train after the crash.

PC Bailey knocked on her office door.

"Sorry to disturb you, Ma'am," he said as he pushed the door open, "but here are those two statements from the tree people," he entered the room with a wad of papers. "And there's these emails from North Yorkshire. They're marked for Wendy - er - DC Doyle, but Sergeant Crouch said you'd probably know what they were about so to bring them up to you."

She looked up, puzzled. "Tree people? Oh, you mean Hickman and his mate, Trevor. And the stuff from Yorkshire, I'll have a look at that too. Thanks." She took the papers from him. "Oh, and thank Sergeant Crouch for sending it up to me."

After Bailey had gone she picked up the statements from Hickman and Trevor and read through them quickly, wondering if, indeed, the man they had seen had had anything to do with the murder of Nurse Marion Winters. Whoever he was he had been in the general vicinity of the murder scene; the crash had taken place at approximately three thirty - it would take a fit man no more than ten to fifteen minutes to walk the two thirds of a mile from the railway track to the location in which he had been seen, but what would have been his destination? She took a large-scale map of the area out of her drawer and unfolded it, spending the next few minutes considering the question before deciding it was a waste of time speculating where he might have been going when she was not even certain he *had* actually come from the scene of the accident, or was even connected with the murder. Still, anyone who walked across that distance of muddy fields in a suit was suspect and would be bound to get a fair quantity of mud on his trousers. Maybe it would be worthwhile alerting all the dry-cleaning outlets in the area - the man, if he was involved in the murder - might just be stupid enough to take his suit in for cleaning. She made a note to ask Wendy Doyle to look into it. It was also possible that someone else - someone in, say, one of the few houses in the areas around Inworth and Rivenhall End - may have seen a man in a blue suit walking across the fields or through their village at about that time and might have got a better description of him. He might, perhaps, have had a car parked somewhere near the point at which Hickman and Trevor had seen him - in that case somebody might have noticed a strange vehicle parked and made a note of its description. It wasn't likely they'd have the number, of course, but generally speaking she had found country folk more likely to notice such things than towns people, who were too busy trying to cope with their faster pace of life and tried, generally, not to 'get involved'.

Caine refilled her fountain pen and made a few more notes before opening the thick pile of papers brought in by

PC Bailey. On top was a note from a Detective Constable Ted Bottomly of the North Yorkshire Constabulary, addressed to DC Wendy Doyle, referring to their telephone conversation and informing her that copies of the file on the Ridings Hospital Case were attached. In return for his prompt and personal service (the note continued), she should make herself available for a date in two weeks time when Bottomly was due to come down and visit his brother who lived in Slough (which, he thought, was only a stone's throw from Fen Molesey). Caine smiled to herself, wondering both at DC Bottomly's abysmal grasp of greater London geography and at how the sexual harassment rules could have so effectively missed the attention of the North Yorkshire Force. More importantly, however, there was a postscript informing Wendy that Bottomly had looked up the local computer records for information on Marion Winters' fellow defendants in the Ridings case; none of them had suffered revenge attacks connected with the case, but two of them – a doctor and a nurse – had been killed in road accidents; apparently, they had both been run down by

177

hit and run drivers – on separate occasions and in different locations. The Yorkshire Police had noticed the similarities in the two deaths and had treated them as suspicious but had been unable to trace the drivers of the cars that had killed them.

Caine skimmed through the attached pages of the report, not really expecting to find anything else of interest, especially after the years that had elapsed since the Ridings Hospital Case and Nurse Winters' acquittal. She was surprised to find that no fewer than seven of the relatives of the children who had allegedly died as a result of the hospital's negligence had made threats against the medical personnel involved. If Bottomly's note to the effect that no revenge attacks had been carried out was correct – and assuming there was no real connection with the hit and run road deaths - then they had been empty threats; but one of the relative's details caught her eye - Patrick O'Hanlon , father of Timothy, two and a half years old when he died in the hospital, apparently from neglect and incorrect diagnosis and treatment. O'Hanlon had made vociferous

178

and frequent threats against those responsible for his child's treatment at the hospital. He was noted as having a previous record for attempted murder, grievous bodily harm, assault and battery and striking a police officer in the pursuit of his duties. He had been released from prison only a few weeks before the Ridings Case and, according to a note in the margin - presumably put there by a very helpful - and, perhaps, hopeful - DC Bottomly - had found himself back in prison a month or so later for the aforementioned murder attempt. Most interestingly, however, he had been released from this latest period of incarceration, *only three months ago*. Caine underlined O'Hanlon's name and, for good measure, outlined it in red highlighter pen. Had the man sought revenge for his child's death as soon as he could put his plans into action? Marion Winters had left the Ridings area some years before and it would have taken him some time - quite possibly three months - to trace her present whereabouts. Chronologically O'Hanlon fitted beautifully into the profile of Marion Winters' killer. Could she be the first of his intended

179

victims? Were the other defendants in the Ridings case now at risk?

Caine picked up the telephone and dialled the Yorkshire number given on the first page of the report - perhaps DC Ted Bottomly would like to undertake a little investigation as to O'Hanlon's whereabouts at the time of Marion Winters' murder? He might also like to know that his report had ended up not on Wendy Doyle's desk but on her boss's, also a woman, but not one likely to enjoy a date with an immature Yorkshire copper...On the other hand, fantasy images of an attractive god-like Bottomly danced in her head as she waited; when he answered the telephone she might have second thoughts...

Bottomly wasn't in the office. The Police Constable who answered, a smart and efficient young woman Caine thought, took details and said she would pass the message on to him. She might even, if she had time, start the investigation into O'Hanlon's movements herself. Caine hung up feeling moderately more hopeful than a couple of hours before and re-read the various papers in the report.

There was a lot of medical detail concerning the causes of the child deaths, most of which was beyond her meagre technical grasp, but none of it seemed remotely connected to death by strangulation. The question as to why the killer had despatched Marion Winters by means of a twin stranded cord rather than hitting her over the head with a heavy instrument was, so far as she was concerned, still unanswered.

Caine brought herself a cup of instant coffee from the machine along the corridor, returned to her office and turned her attention to the report she had omitted to finish the day before, assembling the relevant papers and switching on her computer workstation. She sat for some minutes staring at the screen, not certain how to proceed from the desktop display and regretting her decision not to get involved with the new technology, before clicking the mouse savagely on the "Start" button and closing the machine down again. She sipped her coffee. It was bitter, too bitter for her taste, but at least it was hot. Her daughter Alison had frequently admonished her for drinking too much coffee, insisting that the caffeine was not good for her and she had recently persuaded her mother to switch to herbal teas - the real ones, not those with merely a fragrance of herbs - which Caine had tried and found palatable, but unexciting. She was insufficiently keen on them to remember to bring an assortment of herbal tea bags into the office. Thinking of Alison reminded Caine that she was coming for one of her infrequent flying visits tomorrow and that there was hardly any food in the pantry for the high tea she had been promised. Caine looked at her watch and was appalled to see that it was well past seven – Fortunately, there was an all-night Tesco just outside the town - it would mean a trip out in her car in the wrong direction before she went home, but that could not be helped. At least she could go at any time, when she was ready. She finished her coffee and sat looking at the blank screen of her computer, finally taking the top off her fountain pen and starting to write the report in longhand.

Soon after she had started on her second page DC Wendy Doyle knocked and peeped around the door.

"Thought you'd still be here, Ma'am. Bit like me, I suppose, not often we get a Saturday evening off nowadays, being as that's the night when all the baddies are out in force in the town centre." She came into the room with her arm around a large cardboard box and dropped a set of keys onto Caine's desk. "Marion Winters' front door keys," she explained. "I've just come from her place, or at least the place she was living in."

Caine pushed her handwritten report away with a sigh of relief. "Sit down, Wendy. You look tired."

The young police officer put the cardboard box down on the edge of Caine's desk, and smiled before sitting down gratefully and stretching out her long legs. She sighed and flexed her toes in her calf length leather boots. "Thanks. I've got to admit it hasn't been an easy day, Ma'am. I'll be glad when Donna's over the virus and I can hand the hit and run cases back to her. They really are upsetting and I'm getting nowhere with them."

"No ID on the car yet then?"

"No, all we know is it was blue, possibly a Vauxhall Corsa, but it could have been anything – they all look the same nowadays. The witnesses are pretty vague. You can't blame them really. It's shattering enough having your kid run over, you can't expect the parents to remember any of the details."

"How many is it so far?"

"Three; and a couple of near misses. All of them kids under three years. Fortunately, there haven't been any deaths yet, but we've had a couple of really nasty injuries."

"Anything linking them together?"

Wendy Doyle shook her head. "Not really. They were all born in Fen Molesey General, they all had the same midwife, and they're all still living in the Fen Molesey area, but apart from that they've nothing at all in common. I'm finding it quite depressing interviewing the parents, I can tell you. I was glad to get on to this other job."

"The train murder?" Caine nodded her understanding. The case was anything but boring. "So – found anything of interest?"

184

Doyle shifted her bottom on the guest chair, adjusting her skirt to enable her to cross her long and shapely legs. She indicated the box. "I've brought everything back with me that was of the slightest interest, but I haven't been able to discover much about our victim's recent background. She seems to have led a very sheltered life since she came down from the north. She didn't mix much and she had no friends to speak of - at least the neighbours didn't seem to think so, they never saw her with anyone and nobody went to the house apart from her employer's friends, a few old biddies who could put up with old Mrs Mears' astringent tongue - I don't think the old lady's well liked amongst her neighbours."

Caine thought she could understand that. "What about Mrs Winters' husband? I suppose it's too much to ask for him to have been seen hanging around during the past few days. We're a bit short on good suspects - we need someone to get our teeth into." She indicated her report. "It'd be nice to be able to put something vaguely positive into that thing!"

185

"I may be able help you there, Chief, although nobody's seen her hubby or anyone else in the least bit suspicious around the place over the last few weeks," Doyle grinned and ran a hand through her hair. "She doesn't seem to have had a stalker either, but there *are* one or two other interesting things."

"Such as?"

"She was in the process of changing her will," Doyle uncrossed her legs and lifted the cardboard box down to rest on her lap, opening the top and extracting a sheaf of papers encased in a transparent envelope. "Her old will's here - dated more than ten years ago, it was made just after she got married and her husband is sole beneficiary. But - and this is the interesting bit - there are a couple of recent letters from Winters to a Solicitor in Colchester - apparently she was in the process of cutting her old man out of the picture completely."

"You mean divorcing him? Old Mrs Mears said she thought that was on the go."

"Well, she hadn't actually done it yet, but that was what she intended. Her solicitor was advising her how to go about it and there was also a draft of a new will being prepared."

Caine reached over for the papers. "Now that *is* interesting. What sort of an estate did she have?"

"Nothing spectacular." Doyle consulted a sheet of notes she had made whilst going though Marion Winters' personal effects. "A bit of cheap jewellery, some cash - only a few hundred - in a building society account and a house she was letting, in Halifax. According to the correspondence with the solicitor it's worth about eighty thousand in today's market."

"Not bad as a lump sum," mused Caine. "You say she was letting the house? Her husband isn't staying there?"

"No, from what I can gather - again, from the Solicitor's correspondence - the house was entirely hers, she'd inherited it from her mother before she was married and she made all the payments on it - everything, including the insurance and the rates or council taxes, plus repairs,

187

that sort of thing. When they had all that trouble with the hospital and she split up from her husband she slung him out and made it clear she didn't want him to get anything. I don't know whether she could enforce that or not under the inheritance rules, but it goes without saying that her old man wasn't all that happy about the whole thing."

"But was he unhappy enough to kill her?"

"Well, he certainly had a motive," said DC Doyle. "And if he was going to do anything about it now was the time - the new will hadn't been formalised yet so, presumably, the house still goes to him. That's the way I read it and presumably he'd do the same." She riffled quickly through the papers and pulled out a single sheet. "I've got his address. He rents a flat in Scarborough."

"Good." Caine pushed the North Yorkshire report across her desk towards the young Detective Constable. "Perhaps you'd like to get lover boy to pay him a visit. See what sort of an alibi he's got for yesterday afternoon."

"Lover boy?" Puzzled, DC Doyle put the box onto Caine's desk and picked up the file. She read the covering note quickly and blushed. "Cheeky sod! Who does this Bottomly guy think he is? I'll soon set him right on a few things, Chief." She turned over a few pages of the report. "Any clues amongst the rest of it, or is he just wasting our time?"

"There are one or two things that might be significant," said Caine. "For instance, two of the other defendants in the hospital negligence case were killed by hit and run drivers only a few months ago. There's nothing to connect the two, not on the face of it anyway. Both cases are still open."

"You think they might be revenge killings by one of the relatives?"

"Maybe. Interestingly enough there's a report on a man called O'Hanlon. His kid died as a result of the trouble at Ridings General and he seems to have made some pretty lurid threats against Winters and the others in the case - that was seven years ago, just after she was acquitted."

"Did he try anything?"

"No - apparently he was slung in the clink again immediately afterwards. But the point is he has form - and lots of it. He's down for violent behaviour, assault, attempted murder, you name it. But most interesting of all, he was released from prison only a short while ago."

"So, he could be in the picture! Knocking off the defendants one by one."

"Yes," Caine agreed, cautiously, "but on the other hand he could be a complete red herring. Yorkshire weren't able to connect him with the two hit and runs. Anyway, I've been in touch with them and they're going to run a check on him, see where he was yesterday."

Doyle smiled and put the file down again. "We might be getting somewhere then. At least we have two strong suspects. Do you think they might know each other, Marion Winters' husband and this O'Hanlon character?"

"It's possible O'Hanlon came across Winters while he was checking on Marion's present whereabouts, in fact it's quite likely, if he really is our man." Caine rolled her fountain pen thoughtfully between her fingers. "But you

190

mean could they have been working together? Quite possibly. Winters could have paid O'Hanlon to do the job. He himself may not be suited to it, very few people are when it comes down to it, not for cold-blooded murder."

"And they'd both gain from having his wife dead," suggested Doyle. "Winters would get the house and O'Hanlon would convince himself he was avenging his son's death, plus he'd get a bit of cash to help him on his way back into civilian life or at least, back into the booze."

Caine picked up her pen and doodled a wavy line across the bottom of her report. "But that does *not* explain why the killer used a twin threaded cord. I'd say hitting her over the head with a plank of wood or a broken metal rail would be more in keeping with O'Hanlon's MO, or of course, a bit of hit and run. But he doesn't sound like your average garrotter, does he?" She sighed. "Anyway, let's establish their whereabouts at the time of the murder and we may find they eliminate themselves from our inquiries." She leaned over and switched on the computer. "You know how these things work don't you Wendy…"

Doyle stole a look at Caine's handwritten report. "Having problems with it then, Ma'am?"

"That's the understatement of the year, Wendy. I don't even know where to start."

Doyle made her way around the desk and stood behind her, eyes fixed on the screen as the windows desktop took shape. "You just use the "start" button." She moved the mouse under her hand and manoeuvred the cursor arrow to the bottom left-hand corner of the screen. "Just click on that and then up here to 'new office document'." She clicked the mouse.

Caine watched as the 'new office document' dialogue box appeared on the screen "That's good - you're very proficient. What happens next?" Doyle moved the cursor arrow upwards to settle over the 'blank document' icon. "You wouldn't like to do the report for me as well, would you, Wendy?"

Doyle laughed and clicked the mouse. "I couldn't write a report as well as you, Ma'am," she said tactfully. "Besides, I'm sure you can master this yourself - it really

192

isn't at all difficult." She remembered they had got this far the last time Caine had tried to dump her report writing on her. That time, just as she was beginning to weaken, they had been interrupted.

As if on cue Caine's telephone rang. It was Sergeant Bill Wallace from the front desk, Bernie Crouch's night duty counterpart.

He sounded agitated. "Sorry to land this one on you, Chief Inspector, but it's a bit of a tricky one and there isn't anyone else around. Super said to get a DCI to handle it."

"Handle what, Bill?"

"A fourteen year old kid has climbed up onto the roof of a four storey block up at Upton Grange School, Ma'am. He's dancing about up there. It looks like he's going to jump!"

CHAPTER SEVEN

The vision of a long-forgotten scene swam before Caine's eyes. A young girl balanced on the guardrail of a balcony on the tenth floor of a high-rise block in Walthamstow. Years ago, just after Caine joined the force and was on the beat with a more experienced officer. In spite of his additional years in the force he had emptied the contents of his stomach into the gutter at the exact moment the girl hit the surface of the concrete pavement. She was no more than a schoolgirl, the daughter of working-class parents, unwanted at home, bullied at school and consumed by drugs. Caine had received counselling, but she had never been able to eradicate the scene from her mind. She had prayed she would never again be called upon to endure a similar experience.

"What am *I* supposed to do about it, Bill?" A note of desperation crept into her voice. "He needs a psychiatrist or a counsellor, not a CID Inspector."

"I don't know about that, Ma'am," Wallace said wearily, "Sounds like the kid's on drugs – probably ecstasy. Amongst other things he thinks he can fly." He sighed. "Anyway, for what it's worth one of our cars is on its way with a psychiatrist and I've sent a couple of uniformed men up to the school. There's a fire rescue team on the way as well." He paused and then spoke more quickly. "The school Head rang the Super - they know each other - and he got straight on to me. Says he wants a senior officer out there on the double... if the kid jumps..." He sighed, "well, Ma'am, it looks like there's drugs involved and even if he doesn't it'll need investigating..."

Caine did not want this job. "I'm still not sure what good me being there is going to do, Bill...And drugs aren't my patch."

"The Super just wants somebody senior up there, Ma'am, a senior officer - delicate matter and all that.

195

Hopefully, it won't come to anything and they'll get the boy down safe and sound, but if not..."

"Right. Okay, Bill, leave it to me, I'll get over there right away." She replaced the receiver and slumped back in her chair.

"What's up?" asked DC Doyle, "Anything I can do to help?"

Caine explained. "It's not going to be pleasant, Wendy, but if you've nothing pressing…well, to tell the truth I'd like the company."

Wendy nodded her understanding. "How terrible. It's always kids. Those drug pushers have a lot to answer for!" Her eyes returned to the computer screen. She clicked the mouse to shut down the system. "We'll go in my car if you like."

"Thanks." Caine stood up, pushing the pile of papers away from her. "You know, Wendy, maybe we need to buck up our ideas here in Fen Molesey. It was only yesterday evening Bernie Crouch assured me there was *no* drugs problem up at Upton Grange School. Practically

196

every other problem, but not drugs." She closed her mind against the pictures of what she now thought of as the Walthamstow Incident and crossed the office to take her coat down from the row of hooks on the wall. "I'm just praying that by the time we get there they'll have the poor kid down safely."

Nicholas Rebus, aged fourteen years, fell to his death from the roof of the four-storey dormitory building just a few minutes before Jacqueline Caine and Wendy Doyle arrived at Upton Grange School. For almost half an hour he had paraded back and forth along the ridge tiles, silhouetted against the moonlit December sky, his arms flung wide, giggling and laughing. Members of the school staff and, finally, a fire brigade officer had made a desperate, but futile, attempt to reach and drag him down from his precarious perch.

"Nobody could get to him - he just jumped off, launched himself like he was a bird," Sergeant Thomas

Poole told Caine and Wendy as they made their way

through the group of silent onlookers, many of them fellow

pupils of the dead boy, their faces pale in the emergency

spotlights bathing the quadrangle with surreal illumination.

"I'd bet my pension the kid was on ecstasy."

They watched as two tight lipped paramedics slid the

black body bag into the back of the ambulance. The crew

of a fire engine, its blue light flashing redundantly, huddled

watching, their faces grim and silent. A young woman,

presumably a member of staff, comforted a tearful middle-

aged lady in a nurse's uniform, whom Caine took to be the

school matron. Other teachers, male and female and pupils

of both sexes stood in numbed, hushed groups. To one side

journalists harassed a well-dressed bespectacled man in his

early fifties, one of them squinting through the eyepiece of

a video camera, the other two thrusting microphones under

his bearded chin.

"I was told only yesterday there was no drug

problem here," Caine told Poole sharply. She looked up at

the mid nineteenth century building, still bathed in

floodlight from the emergency vehicles, her eyes following the profusion of creepers encrusting the first three storeys. A few particularly tenacious tendrils had reached up beyond the third floor, snaking their way towards the fourth storey, and thence to the roof. "So where did he get the stuff from?"

"We don't know the full story yet, Ma'am," Poole said lamely.

The doors of the ambulance closed and one of the paramedics, a man in his early thirties, looking tired and a little desperate, came across to them. "We'll be taking the kid away now, Sergeant. The pathologist'll carry out a proper examination at the hospital." He pushed a lock of lank dark hair up over his forehead, away from his eyes and continued apologetically, "Well, there's nothing more we can do here, is there?" He paused, shook his head, sadly. "I hope you find out where he got the filthy stuff!"

"You can count on it," said Poole grimly.

The ambulance man nodded. He looked across at the fire engine. "Maybe he would've survived if they'd had the proper equipment, but what do you bloody well expect with all these cuts…?" He turned away and walked quickly back to the ambulance. His colleague had started the engine and he climbed in and slammed the door before the vehicle moved slowly away across the quadrangle towards the tall archway marking the exit to the drive.

"What did he mean by 'the proper equipment'?" asked DC Doyle who had not spoken since she and Caine arrived.

"One of those inflatable mattresses they use to break the fall when someone jumps from a high building," explained Poole. "Not that it would have made any difference - the kid was charging up and down that roof like a mad thing. The fire people wouldn't have had a clue where to put their bloody mattress, even if they'd had one."

"I know, Sergeant, that's the way it is sometimes," said Caine. "But that wasn't what killed the boy – not really. Right now, I want to know where the boy got the drugs. Let's see what the school authorities have to say." She glanced towards the huddled groups of teachers and pupils who were beginning to move slowly away from the scene, their silence now replaced by the low hum of muted conversation. "Who's in charge?"

Poole nodded towards the bearded man embroiled with the small group of journalists. "That's Douglas Maynard, the school's Deputy Head. I was speaking to him earlier, before the boy jumped. Between you and me I think he was aware there was a drugs problem well before this happened."

"Well, let's see what he has to say for himself," said Caine.

As she moved towards Maynard he shook his head angrily at the reporters and broke away from them, walking quickly in her direction. She realised he was more youthful than he had at first seemed; the small, stubby beard had an aging effect.

Caine introduced herself, showing her warrant card. "DCI Caine, Fen Molesey police. This is DC Wendy Doyle. I believe you've already met Sergeant Poole."

Behind Maynard's thin-lensed wire-framed spectacles burned a pair of angry brown eyes, but his lips parted in a subdued smile of greeting. "I'm Douglas Maynard, Deputy Head Teacher," His grip was firm, but his hand shook with pent up anger. "There will be a full inquiry into this affair, Detective Inspector, I can assure you of that."

"There will also be a thorough search for drugs, Mr Maynard, starting with the boy's quarters," Caine told him coldly. She turned to Poole. "Get that organised, please Sergeant. Bring in as many men as necessary. I want the place turned over before whoever's behind this destroys the evidence."

"Do you think that's entirely necessary?" asked Maynard, dismayed. "You don't even know that drugs were involved."

"It was drugs all right, sir," said Poole firmly. "I saw that lad before he jumped – I should say 'tried to take off' - like he was a bloody bird," he glanced in Caine's direction.

"Sorry, Ma'am, but it was a classic case if ever I saw one – and I've seen enough!"

Maynard scowled. "But I can assure you Detective Inspector, the school has never had problems with drugs."

"There's always a first time."

"But do we have to have the place crawling with police officers? It's unsettling for the children."

"Yes, you do," replied Caine, "I won't be handling this case, drugs are not my field, but I'm the most senior officer present and I'd be lacking in my duty if I didn't start the investigation immediately. There's a young boy dead. I know you're worried about this getting out – it's not something parents like to hear about, but that's just too bad – you should have thought about that before you let the drug pushers into the school." She shot a quick glance at Poole. "Are you still here, Sergeant?"

Poole nodded. "Right. I'll get right on to it, Ma'am." He turned on his heel and walked quickly back towards his car gesticulating to two uniformed constables who stood to one side talking quietly to the crew of the fire appliance.

Caine turned back to Maynard. "Seeing that it's Saturday evening I assume the boy was a boarder?"

"Yes." He took off his glasses and rubbed his eyes. "I can show you his dormitory."

"Have you taken steps to inform his parents?"

He scowled again. "They're abroad, Inspector. The Middle East, Dubai, I believe, one of the Gulf States. That's one of the reasons he boarded here. Rebus – that is – *was* - his name, Nicholas Rebus - very rarely saw his parents. One of the staff is trying to get in touch with them at the moment." He sighed, his shoulders slumping. "Look, I'm sorry…this should never have happened. We never dreamed…And My God the press are going to crucify us…" he realised he was rambling and abruptly stopped speaking.

"Have you any idea where the boy obtained the stuff, Mr Maynard?"

"You mean drugs? Look, you don't even know if he had any drugs." He caught the look on her face and went on hurriedly. "I really don't know, Inspector" Maynard was

204

shaking his head as though he could not believe what was happening. "But, obviously, if there's anything we can do."

"It's a bit late now, don't you think?" said Caine. "I think we'd like a look at the boy's room." She called across to Sergeant Poole. "We're going up to look at the boy's dormitory, Sergeant. I think you'd better join us; it'll be a good place to start the search. Organise a bit of back-up and then follow us up." She turned back to Maynard. "After you Mr Maynard, if you'd like to lead the way."

"Rebus was in a dormitory on the third floor," Maynard explained as he started to walk across the quadrangle. He led the way through a small side door into the school building and then along a passageway to a steep narrow staircase dingily illuminated by naked light bulbs that hung down from the ceiling on thin brown cable.

"These are the back stairs," he explained unnecessarily. He was speaking to fill the silence and to cover his nervousness. They began to climb the stairs. "I'm sorry there's no lift. We had thought of putting one in using this space, but the fire department insisted we have at least two stairways – the front stairs and these - apparently a lift doesn't count for the purposes of fire regulations." He slackened his pace. "It is rather a long way up, but it's one way of getting the boys to do a bit of exercise." Neither Caine nor Doyle made any comment. When he continued, his voice was low, the words punctuated by small breaks as though he was trying desperately not to go to pieces. They had reached the second floor now and although Maynard looked reasonably fit, he was beginning to breathe heavily with the strain of the climb. "Of course, we'd no idea there was any sort of drug problem here – I'm sure if any member of staff had even an inkling we'd have heard about it"

"How many other boys are housed in Rebus's dormitory?" DC Wendy Doyle, trim and fit, a regular visitor to the gym, showed no signs of flagging as they turned the stairwell to begin the next flight.

Maynard stopped on the landing between the second and third floors to answer her question. "Seven. The senior pupils have their own rooms – well, they share with just one other person, but we find a dormitory arrangement works better for the younger boys. The third-floor dormitory of this wing is for third year boys. Rebus had just started his third year." He shook his head as if he could not believe this was happening to him and then took off his glasses to massage the bridge of his nose. "He'd only recently turned fourteen…a young life totally wasted!"

They continued to follow him as he climbed the next flight, finally coming out on to the third floor. They went through a fire door and into a long corridor stretching the full length of the building. There were three doors spaced at long intervals on either side of the corridor. Maynard explained they were doors to the six dormitories.

"Each dormitory has a separate toilet and shower room area at each end." He opened the nearest door and ushered them through into a long room brightly lit by a series of strip lights. A couple of teen aged boys, lying on their backs on two of the eight beds evenly spaced down the room, sat up quickly as they came in. "This is – *was* – Rebus's dormitory. I believe his bed was the one before the far end – is that right, Collins?" The question was directed at one of the two boys who pushed himself up from the bed and nodded, smoothing his fair hair nervously with one hand. Maynard turned back to the two police officers. "Collins and Armstrong are fellow boarders."

"Is Rebus going to be all right?" Collins asked anxiously.

"I'm afraid not," Maynard gestured towards Caine and Doyle. "These two ladies are police officers. They're going to want to search this room, so I'd like you to – er – go down to the refectory for a few minutes." He turned to Caine. "I really need to organise things a little better you know. What am I supposed to do with all the children while your men are invading the place?"

"I'm sure you'll work something out," said Caine. She was finding Maynard's attitude tiresome but told herself that he was probably venturing into new territory; the realisation that his young charges were involved with Class A drugs had probably hit him hard. "But I think we'd like a few words with Collins and Armstrong here, before they leave."

Hearing his name the second boy, Armstrong, stood up quickly. "Is it true then, Nick's really dead?" he blurted out, his face pale.

Caine nodded. "I'm afraid he is." She indicated their beds. "Just sit down for a second or two before you go."

The two boys sat down heavily.

"Were either of you aware that he was taking drugs?"

"Not Nicky," said Armstrong quickly.

"Someone else then?"

Collins shot a quick glance of dismay across to his companion.

"Some of the seniors," said Armstrong. He looked down and moved his feet nervously.

Caine looked directly at Collins. The boy turned his gaze away, looking towards the blackness outside the window. "Some of the senior boys have had drugs?"

Collins shrugged. "Dunno. Maybe."

Maynard strode across the room to stand beside him. "If you know anything about this, Collins, Armstrong, we need to know."

"I'm sure they'll tell us everything they know," said Caine, "Won't you, boys. You know how important it is."

"Yes, Miss," Collins looked down. "But we don't know anything for definite. It's just rumours."

Maynard frowned angrily. "About whom exactly?"

"Like Collins says, it's just rumours," said Armstrong. "We don't know any names."

Sergeant Poole, who had followed them up the stairs, put his head around the door and looked in. "You want us to start searching now, Ma'am?"

Caine nodded. "Yes. You can start in here. It's the dead lad's dormitory." She turned to the two boys. "You can go now, boys, but we might want to speak to you again." They got up eagerly and made their way to the door, pushing past Poole and two uniformed police officers as they made their way into the room. She turned to the Sergeant. "When you've finished in here you might like to

210

go straight up to the top floor and go through the Senior Boy's quarters. I want that stripped down to the floorboards if necessary."

Poole nodded sagely. "Right you are, Ma'am. Get to it lads, we haven't got all night."

"Let me know as soon as you find anything." Caine turned to the window and looked out. The lights of the small housing estate, known in the area as 'Little Cornwall', could be clearly seen in the distance and, beyond them, buildings marking the outskirts of Fen Molesey. To the South, partly hidden by a thin band of trees, was the outline of a large house, now in darkness.

Maynard had come to stand beside them.

"I assume that's Beckett's house, the antiques dealer," said Caine.

Maynard seemed nonplussed by the question. "Yes. Unfortunately, his place is very close to the school. The woods bordering our land belong to him, apart from a few old sycamore trees." He leaned closer to the glass, shading his eyes with his hand. "Hmm! Unfortunately, we seem to have scored an own goal having that tree pruned yesterday – we can see even more of his house than we could before."

Caine remembered the Superintendent's request that she should pay Beckett a visit. "I believe he's been causing you a bit of trouble recently."

"Yes," Maynard seemed reluctant to talk about it. "I don't know that now's the time to discuss it, but there have been some funny goings on in his woodland."

"How do you mean 'funny'?"

"There are rumours he's involved in some sort of witchcraft."

"You don't mean dancing naked around bonfires, do you?" asked Wendy Doyle flippantly. "I've heard talk myself, but I didn't attach any importance to it."

"Well, something like that. As I say, we've heard rumours. From the children mostly – none of the school staff have actually seen anything like that, well they've seen the bonfires in the woods, but no naked dancing." Again, he seemed reluctant to discuss the matter.

"But a complaint went through to us," said Caine. "It seemed serious. I take it you want us to make a few inquiries?"

Maynard shrugged. "Yes. We would like it looked into, naturally, if there is even the hint of something going on that the boys and girls shouldn't be exposed to; but in the light of what's happened here this evening I wouldn't have thought it should trouble us at the moment."

Caine nodded thoughtfully and turned away from the window. She had attached little importance to Hansen's request, reasoning that rumours of black magic rites were probably wildly exaggerated, but maybe there was something in them. However, as Maynard so rightly said, now was not the time to discuss them.

They left Poole and his search party in the boys' dormitory turning out cupboards and looking in the hundreds of different places that might be used to hide such things as small as packages of drugs and made their way back along the corridor to the stairs. Caine stopped at one of the windows on the stairwell and looked out on the scene in the quadrangle. Someone down there, probably one of the senior members of staff she surmised, had at last begun to organise the huddled groups of teachers and pupils, dispersing them in an orderly fashion towards the various buildings. "Does the school have a drugs policy, Mr Maynard?"

He was waiting, holding the fire door open. "Oh yes, I put it together myself. Not that we ever make any use of it." The two police officers walked past him and started to descend. He let go of the door and followed them.

"You mean the policy has never been enforced?" asked DC Doyle, pausing briefly on the small landing before continuing down the stairs. "You had a policy, but you never bothered to enforce it."

Maynard gave a short, derisive laugh before replying. "Oh, our dear Headmaster was quite willing to agree that an anti-drugs policy is a good thing in principle; a very good thing - but not at Upton Grange. We've had a lot of very bitter arguments about it, I can tell you, but so far as he's concerned, it's pointless here, in this school."

"Why?"

"For the simple reason that, so far as he was concerned, there was - *is* - no drugs problem at Upton. It's what you might call a top school, a school with a long tradition - it's more than a hundred years old and we have an excellent reputation for high standards - we teach a wide range of subjects, from modern languages to advanced mathematics, the sciences, the rudiments of such things as geology, even astronomy, plus technologies such as computer science and basic photography. *And* we have a very high number of our pupils who go on to University, particularly Oxbridge. Mr Wilson really can't stomach the possibility that this school - *his* school - is anything short of perfect. To his mind, therefore, it follows that an active policy against drugs was - *is* - a complete and utter waste of time and effort!"

"The man's a blockhead," said Doyle.

"Where is he by the way?" asked Caine. "Why isn't he here?"

"He's away for a long weekend in Cornwall - an educational seminar. I rang him earlier. He's on his way back."

Maynard held the outer door open for them. "What happens next, Inspector?"

"I can't tell you that, exactly, Mr Maynard," Caine replied. "I shall be handing the case over to our drugs division. You'll no doubt be hearing from them." She stopped, buttoning her coat. "In the meantime, our officers will continue their search of the premises. I daresay what happens will depend on what they find."

Maynard followed the two police officers back across the quadrangle. "The effect on the school will be catastrophic. The press will be all over us for months."

"Oh, I doubt that, Mr Maynard." Said Caine. "It's a nine-day wonder for them. You, however, are going to have to live with the consequences for some time to come."

He sighed and took off his glasses to rub his eyes. "I suppose you're right. What we *are* going to do though is

216

find out who's responsible and expel them. Perhaps, then, things will get better."

"You think one of the pupils is responsible?"

"I should be very surprised if any of the staff were involved." He was shivering a little as the wind gusted across the quad. "I have some ideas about the senior pupils, though."

"Which you will, of course, pass on to us." They walked in silence for a long moment. The emergency vehicles had left and the extremities of the buildings were dark where the illumination from the tall Victorian lamp standards, placed at regular intervals around the square, did not reach. "You realise, of course, that this is a police matter," Caine went on. "Anything you know, any suspicions you have, are of interest to us, Mr Maynard. Do you want to say anything now?"

He shook his head. "No. I have no proof, Detective Inspector, just a few suspicions." He paused, looking out across the quadrangle to the tall buildings on the other side. "I take it you will be making that call on our neighbour, Mr

Beckett? You will be passing his door on the way back to town."

Caine frowned. Nothing had been further from her mind than the need to make the call on the antiques dealer. Maynard had touched on the subject earlier, when they had seen Beckett's house from the upstairs window and had thought it an inappropriate topic for discussion. Then an inquiry into his alleged involvement in witchcraft had hardly seemed relevant to the tragic events of the evening. So, what had changed Maynard's mind?

"Do you think I should?"

Maynard shrugged as though the matter was of little consequence to him; his eyes, however, were telling a different story. "As I say, you are more or less on his doorstep."

Caine glanced at her watch. It was only just after nine o'clock, not an unsocial hour, and it was true that she and Wendy had to drive right past Beckett's house on the way back to the station.

Wendy waited until they were in the car before asking, "Have you decided whether we're calling on Beckett?" She switched on the ignition.

Caine thought for a moment. "We are in the area and I daresay it wouldn't do any harm. You said you'd heard rumours about these strange goings on, Wendy? What have you heard about Beckett?"

"I believe he's a bit eccentric, Ma'am. I've seen him about town and I've heard rumours. People talk. He's never been on the wrong side of the law so far as I know, but as a local businessman he has a high profile and people do talk about anyone who's in the least bit out of the ordinary." Wendy turned up the heating and directed the stream of warm air on to the windscreen, which, with their breath coalescing on its surface, had clouded over. "There's been talk now and then about him, you know, the odd bit of scandal but it's been legit and lawful, so we've not been involved." She let in the clutch and steered the car around the outside of the grass at the centre of the quadrangle, turning towards the archway leading to the school's exit.

"So, what exactly makes him weird?"

Ice was beginning to form on the asphalt of the driveway and Wendy steered the car carefully between the brick piers of the arch. "I suppose he's a character, bit of a **Black Sabbath merchant**, if you see what I mean. He often dresses all in black. He's olive skinned and he has dark, piercing eyes and he's very tall, he must be well over six feet. It makes for a peculiar combination. You could imagine him in a graveyard flitting between the tombstones in a black cloak couldn't you, so you can't really blame people for thinking he's some kind of a devil worshipper." She giggled, Caine thought a little nervously. "If you ask me he just does it for effect, all those black clothes and things. He probably thinks it helps sell antiques."

"How long has he lived in the area?"

"Most of his life I gather, but I wouldn't really know. He's much older than me. In his mid fifties I should imagine. According to Bernie Crouch he did a bit of travelling in his youth, India, Tibet, places like that."

"Interesting character," said Caine. "I suppose, as we are passing…" she mused, drumming her fingers on the plastic fascia. "Well, we may as well. Actually, it might be useful to get some insight on his neighbours."

"Neighbours? Oh – you mean this place, the school." PC Doyle swung the car out of the school's driveway and turned right, back towards town, dipping the headlights against the oncoming traffic.

The gate leading to Beckett's Antiques Emporium, as his establishment was described on the display board at the entrance to the long gravel drive, was open. They turned off the road, the car's headlights picking out the tall trees on either side, black and gaunt against the dark night sky and reflecting off the windows of the tall, two storey Georgian house. The lights were on in the downstairs rooms and as they came into the car parking area, within range of their automatic sensors, halogen floodlights snapped on. There was a red Ford Fiesta, parked beside the

221

steps leading up to the heavy front door. DC Doyle drew

her car up behind it and switched off the engine. There

were no curtains at the window beside which they had

parked and they could see through into the brightly lit,

spacious room. There were a few items of furniture,

covered with dustsheets, in the centre, beneath a cut glass

chandelier. A mobile decorator's scaffold stood to one side

of the fireplace.

"Looks like he has the workmen in," observed

Wendy.

"At least there's someone here," Caine unbuckled her

seatbelt and opened the passenger door. "Let's go see the

Wizard."

Marcus Beckett lived up to the verbal caricature

Wendy Doyle had drawn. He was tall; something over six

feet six inches Caine estimated and, although at leisure,

wore an expensive suit, black, unrelieved by any less

severe colours. Beneath his jacket he wore a polo necked

sweater, also black. His hair was dark and slicked carefully

down. His eyes were large and intelligent, his gaze

piercing. The flesh of his face was swarthy, olive, hinting at Middle Eastern or Mediterranean origins.

It had taken Beckett over two minutes to respond to their ring at the doorbell and then he had appeared in the doorway very suddenly, as though the door had vanished rather than swung back on its hinges. It brought with it a gust of hot air from inside the house. Now he filled the open doorway, looking down on the two police officers with an air of disdain, one hand holding the door, the other stroking his long chin.

"We're closed." His voice was deep and cultured, the eyes that looked down at them cold and unwelcoming. "We shall be open again on Monday morning at 10.30 am. I suggest you come back then."

The door was already half closed before Caine spoke. "Police. Sorry to disturb you, Mr Beckett." She held up her warrant card. "I'm Detective Chief Inspector Caine of the Fen Molesey CID, my colleague here is Detective Constable Doyle. We'd like a few words with you if we may."

Beckett held the door half open and looked down at them as though considering her request. "I can't say that it's convenient, Inspector, but I don't suppose any other time would be any more so."

He stood blocking the doorway. They could feel the heat from the hall curl around his body.

"Do you think we might come in, Mr Beckett?"

"I suppose so, if you must, though why on earth you should be calling on me on a peaceful Saturday evening I really cannot imagine." He opened the door fully and allowed them to walk past him into the spacious hallway. It was bright and airy, well lit by a glass chandelier suspended from the top of the stairwell. There was the smell of gloss paint in the air and the walls had been freshly decorated with regency style wallpaper. All the space, apart from a narrow corridor down the centre, was crowded with items of antique furniture, obviously stock moved from the two front rooms, which, Caine surmised, probably served as salerooms and were now being decorated. They waited while Beckett closed the heavy front door and then followed his black-attired figure through to one of the back rooms, passing the richly carved wooden staircase on the way.

The room into which he led them was small in comparison with the other rooms in the house, but still large by modern standards. It reminded Caine of cluttered Victorian parlours she had seen in museums. It was stuffed with old furniture, chairs and tables of polished wood, armchairs, a couple of whatnots, bevel edged mirrors and a glass fronted cabinet containing a variety of clocks and watches; the majority of the items were unmistakably antique, others, equally obviously, cheap reproductions. A marble bust of an obscure Roman Emperor stood on one of the tables, beside it a pair of gilt bronzes depicting flappers in typical poses, young ladies elegantly dressed in 1920s styles, fingers wrapped around long cigarette holders bearing long cigarettes. The walls were almost covered with paintings and lithographs of various shapes and sizes, some portraits of people in period costume, others of animals, horses, dogs, a huge African bull elephant, swans

225

on the gleaming waters of a lake; others depicted town and country, forests and woods, industrial buildings tall with red brick chimneys, architectural drawings, workers taking in the harvest. In the far corner, beneath the window, was a partner's desk, its leather top strewn with documents, books and papers. To one side of the desk, totally incongruous, a computer VDU stood on a modern, purpose-built computer table. Beside the other end of the desk was a breakfront mahogany bookcase, its shelves lined with leather bound volumes. A log fire burned in the Adam style fireplace set in the centre of the opposite wall, throwing off an intense heat that hit them as they walked into the room.

In front of the fire, draped across a cherry red chaise longue and reading a magazine, was a young woman. Her body was covered by a black silk dressing gown, out of the bottom of which stretched a pair of long and shapely legs. The folds across her breasts revealed the edges of a black negligee made of the same material. Her hair, worn medium long so that it brushed her shoulders as she turned her head towards them, was black; her eyes, set in an oval, well shaped face heavy with make-up, were deep brown and she squinted as though she was having trouble focussing. They widened as Beckett came into the room with the two police officers.

"No, don't get up, Kelly," said Beckett with a wave of his arm. "These people are from the police. Come to disturb our peace this Saturday evening." He turned to the two officers, "This is Kelly Beacham. Miss Beacham is a friend."

The young woman, who, Caine thought, was probably a lot more than a friend so far as Beckett was concerned, followed his suggestion and remained lying on the chaise. She pushed herself up on to her elbows to take a better look at them and let her magazine drop to the floor. "Oh, right," she frowned, almost as though she had not heard him or, at least, if she had was not in the least interested in what he had said. She seemed about to add something, but her mouth tightened into a fine line and she turned her face away from them, towards the fire.

"Do sit down," Beckett gestured vaguely in the direction of two chairs that stood on one side of the fire, he himself walking over to a drinks trolley and picking up a carafe of whisky from the Tantalus that stood upon it. He poured himself a generous measure. "Would you like a drink, Inspector, Constable?"

Caine sat on one of the chairs on offer and motioned for Wendy to sit beside her. "No, thank you," she answered for both of them. "We won't keep you very long, Mr Beckett."

"What was all that noise before?" asked Kelly as though she had suddenly woken up to their presence. "I heard a couple of squad cars going by an hour or so ago. Or was it an ambulance? Anyway, it was a siren of some sorts. Bloody loud it was too." She was still having difficulty focussing her eyes. Caine wondered if she should be wearing glasses. "Is that why you're here?"

"There was a disturbance up at the school earlier on, Miss," said Caine. "But that isn't why we're here." She turned to Beckett. "There have been reports recently of bonfires in the woods adjacent to your house, Mr Beckett."

There was a high-backed wooden chair, almost a throne thought Caine, on the other side of the fireplace and Beckett walked to it and sat down slowly. "You probably mean in my private woods adjacent to the house, Inspector. It's all my land, you know."

"Fine. But why the fires?"

"Why not? I have a gardener who occasionally thinks it a good idea to burn off some of the rubbish, Inspector. I'm sorry if the authorities have suddenly decided it's a fire hazard. We wouldn't want the great forests of Essex swept away by a great conflagration now would we? I shall see he takes even greater care in the future."

"It's not exactly the fire, Mr Beckett – well, it is in a way – it's the fact that he appears to be burning off your rubbish at midnight." She could not resist adding, "And probably on the nights of a full moon."

She thought she could detect a twinkle in his eye. "Why should he not, Inspector? I leave Bill to his own devices. He knows more about gardening than I'll ever know. If he wants to burn rubbish at midnight, then I say let him."

"But apparently he doesn't do it alone. I understand there are a number of people with him. And they dance naked around the fire."

Beckett smiled, showing a set of strong white teeth. "Ah! You're referring to my little parties, Inspector. Why didn't you say so?"

"Hardly parties," said DC Doyle. "A party isn't running around naked in the woods in the middle of the night, not in December. That's not *my* idea of fun."

She had crossed her legs and now Beckett leaned towards her, peering over his whisky glass and running his eyes slowly along them, from ankle to thigh. "Well, my dear," he leered, "I think you're missing a lot in life." She blushed uncomfortably and uncrossed her legs, smoothing her skirt down and giving him a look of withering disgust.

"Do you practise black magic, Mr Becket?" Caine asked sharply.

His eyes lingered for a moment on Doyle's legs before he turned his head towards Caine. "And if I do?" he asked, smiling at her again.

"Do you?"

"*If* I did, would it be illegal? Could you prosecute me and my friends for dancing naked around a fire in my own woods?"

Caine shook her head. "I don't suppose I could unless you and your friends were making an exhibition of yourselves in a lewd and unseemly manner likely to cause a breach of the peace."

He chuckled and sipped his whisky. "Pure malt. Delicious. Are you sure you won't try some?" She shook her head. "Of course, you are still on duty. But, to return to the subject in hand – I take it there has been a complaint from that great seat of learning situated beyond the borders of my property?"

"Upton Grange School, yes."

"And they – the Principals no doubt and the senior staff - are complaining that the poor, deprived lads and lasses who attend the school *may* – I say *may* – have been subject to lewd and unsuitable sights – viz., human bodies, both male and female, in a state of undress cavorting around an equally naked fire in the woods – *my* woods – late at night?" Caine nodded. "Then I suggest, Inspector that they do not look. We don't do it for their benefit you know."

"Then for whose benefit *do* you do it?"

Kelly Beacham giggled loudly. Caine thought she had fallen asleep, but obviously she had been following the conversation from her reclining position on the chaise longue. "What a stupid question. He does it for his own good. That is one hell of a dirty old man you're looking at, Inspector whatsits."

"Thank you, Kelly" said Beckett coldly, his hard eyes flickering from Caine to the young woman. "I think I can handle this conversation quite adequately by myself." They flicked back to rest on Caine's face. "I hardly think for whose benefit we do it is of any interest or importance to you, Inspector, unless of course you would like to join."

232

"Join what, Mr Beckett?"

He smiled, his teeth showing white against his olive skin. "Our little religious group." He sipped his whisky again, pausing to swirl the liquid on his tongue before swallowing it with obvious enjoyment. "Ah! I can see doubt on your face, Inspector and on yours, Constable, but there is just as much legitimacy in the old pagan religions as in the newer ones. And, much as our enemies in the established churches dislike the fact, we are free, in this country at least, to practice them." He held his hand up to stop Caine from interrupting. "Unless, of course, Inspector, we were to indulge in infanticide or the sacrifice of virgins which – perhaps unfortunately – we do not. Though I'm bound to say it *would* add a little spice to our proceedings."

Kelly giggled again. "And he'd like that, the dirty old bastard!" She returned Beckett's withering gaze unflinchingly. "And he would do it if he could find any virgins! Well, he wouldn't exactly *sacrifice* them, if you know what I mean." She turned away in a fit of giggling.

"So, the allegations that you're running a witches coven are true," said Caine.

Beckett nodded, taking another sip of his whisky and rolling it around his tongue. "Yes, but as I say, Inspector, it's all perfectly legal and above board."

"Legal it might be," said Caine, "but aren't you in the least bit worried your activities may be seen by the young people at the school?"

"You're appealing to my better nature, Inspector – I must warn you, I don't have one. So far as I am concerned the people in the school shouldn't be looking. It's hardly my fault if their headmaster has no idea of discipline." Beckett finished his whisky and placed the glass carefully on a small coffee table at his side. "The school's a mess, the kids do exactly as they please. If anyone has grounds for complaint, it's me – with the shenanigans they get up to they're a constant nuisance."

"You don't approve of the way the school is run, Mr Beckett?" asked DC Doyle, a hint of irritation in her voice,

"I would have thought a free-thinking attitude is exactly your style. You don't exactly conform, do you?"

"Being a free thinker doesn't mean living without discipline," said Beckett. He seemed to tire of the conversation and stood up. "Now, if that's all you have to discuss, Miss Beacham and I would like to get on with our evening."

"Interesting character," said Caine a few minutes later as they drove out on to the road.

"I suppose there is nothing we can do about these midnight orgies he's been having?"

Caine shook her head. "Not really. He's right that we have freedom of worship in this country, so long as that's all they're doing he's not breaking the law. It would be different if we had positive proof he was involved in outright debauchery in full view of the school kids, but so far that's not the case."

"I don't know why they do it anyway. They must be nuts to cavort about naked in the middle of December. I wouldn't fancy it myself." Wendy slowed the car at the

235

crossroads, flicking on the indicator to make a right turn towards Fen Molesey town centre. "That Beacham woman was stoned up to the eyeballs, of course. They say it helps to keep out the cold. Maybe we should have searched the premises for pot."

"Maybe, but we didn't have the resources to go through a place like that. With all that furniture and stuff there there's a million places you could hide dope," Caine yawned. "One thing's for sure though – Beckett was teasing us. He was very cock sure of himself. The chances are if he's into drugs he wouldn't keep them on the premises." She opened her handbag and took out her car keys as the car turned into the high street. "The man's a weirdo, but at least I've seen him, just as The Super ordered. Now we can forget Marcus Beckett and concentrate on more important matters, such as the great train murder."

CHAPTER EIGHT

"You should have telephoned, Derek," said Mark Dolby irritably. He was in his shirtsleeves and he shivered as he strode down the drive to meet the car. His daughter opened the passenger door as he approached. She had been crying. "Are you okay, darling? Here, Derek, what's been going on?"

Donna ran into his arms, the tears again streaming down her face. White faced; Lorna came to the front door. "What on earth's going on? Donna, darling, what's happened?"

Derek climbed wearily from the car and slammed the door. He came slowly around the front of the vehicle and pushed his way through the half-closed gate, his face grim in the yellow light of the street lamp. "It's Emma," he said. His voice was strained. "She's disappeared."

"What?" Dolby's head jerked up as though struck. He had heard the expression far too many times in the past. Hearing his friend say it chilled him to the bone. "What do you mean **she's *disappeared*?**"

"It's true, Daddy." Donna stepped back from him and wiped her tearstained face with the back of her hand. "She was with Sara and me at the dance and then when we were ready to go home, we couldn't find her."

"That's right," said Derek, shaking his head as though he was in the middle of a bad dream. He clutched at the gatepost for support. He had spent the last hour hunting for his missing daughter and the strain was showing on his face. "I've – *we've* been looking for her – I know I should have phoned, but the battery on my mobile was flat and then I just got caught up in the search. She's never done this before, gone off without telling anyone, I mean." He looked desperately at his watch. "And it's late. It's nearly a quarter to one. Mark, I hope you don't mind, but with you being in the force I thought you'd know what to do."

"The first thing is not to panic," said Dolby with more reassurance than he felt, "I wish you'd rung earlier, though – we've been worried about Donna. Sara's all right I take it?"

Derek nodded and walked slowly up the drive, his face working, showing his emotion. "Yes – she's at home with Pauline. I asked her to ring you and Lorna, but they're both in a bit of a state."

"That's okay, Derek, I'll ring them – just to say you've got here okay." Lorna joined Dolby and gently eased Donna away from him. "I'll check if Emma's come home under her own steam – you never know with kids do you? She might have got separated from the girls somehow and missed you when you came to collect them. Perhaps she got a lift home with somebody else."

"No," said Derek. "if she'd had a lift home she'd have been there by now. I'm just worried that if someone did give her a lift they might have stopped off somewhere and…you know we're only at the back of Pods Wood, they might have…" he broke off, almost in tears.

239

Lorna took Donna by the hand. "Come along inside out of the cold, darling. Daddy wants to speak to Uncle Derek."

"I need to speak to Donna, as well," said Dolby. "Come in Derek – I want to know exactly what's been going on."

He followed his wife and daughter into the house, guiding his friend before him. Lorna took Donna into the lounge and sat her down in one of the high-backed armchairs. "I'll get you a hot chocolate, darling, you look like you could do with something hot inside you." She turned to the two men who had come in after her. "Would you like coffee?" They nodded and she left the room to go to the kitchen.

"Sit down, Derek," said Dolby, indicating the settee. He himself paced up and down, gathering his thoughts. "Now, Donna, darling, tell me exactly what happened."

"I don't *know* what happened," the young girl sniffed and wiped away a tear with the handkerchief her mother had pressed into her hand. "All I know is, Emma wasn't

240

with Sara and me when it was time to go home. Uncle Derek said he'd come for us at half past eleven and he's always on time, so a few minutes beforehand Sara and I looked around for her so we could all go out together, but she wasn't there."

"Was the place crowded?"

Derek laughed ironically. "Crowded? You've got to be joking. You can't swing a cat in those places, let alone dance. And the noise! I don't know how the kids stand it."

"So, she could have been there couldn't she?" insisted Dolby, sounding a little more positive. "If it was that crowded you might not have seen her in the crowd."

"No – we'd thought of that," said Donna, a little indignant. "We thought we might get separated, there were so many people, so we arranged to meet each other just inside the entrance about five minutes before Uncle Derek was due to arrive. We've done it before, only this time Emma didn't show up."

"Okay. So, she wasn't there," said Dolby, deflated. He turned to Derek. "How old is she, Derek? Sorry, I've lost track!"

"She was sixteen a few weeks ago." He rubbed his eyes. "She has been a bit wild recently. You know, it's a phase they all go through."

"Does she have a boy friend?"

"No – at least, not that we know of. They're a bit secretive at that age."

Dolby looked across at Donna. She was more composed now and seemed about to say something. "Has she, Donna?"

"I think she *has* been seeing somebody. Sara says she's seen her with someone, an older boy. Practically a man really."

Derek frowned and leaned forward in his seat. "She didn't say anything. Pauline and me, we had no idea. The secretive little minx!"

"There you are, then," said Lorna entering with a tray of steaming mugs. "She's probably gone off with him,

242

whoever he is and forgotten what time it is." She placed the tray on the low coffee table. "I rang Pauline, Derek, Emma isn't home yet, but don't worry, I'm sure she'll turn up soon."

"I hope you're right, darling," said Dolby, looking doubtful.

"They usually do turn up, don't they," Lorna rejoined, making an effort at being cheerful. "You've said so yourself, Mark, I don't know how many times. As a rule, young missing persons don't go missing for long."

"Yes, yes, statistically. I shouldn't worry too much, Derek, as Lorna says, Emma'll probably be safely home by the time you get back."

"I just hope you're right," said Derek. He looked at his watch and stood up. "I'll be on my way, then." He said. "And thanks."

"You'll let us know?" Lorna walked with him to the door.

Dolby heaved himself up from his chair. He had drunk a little more than usual at dinner on the understanding that Lorna was driving home and the red wine was having its usual effect on him. "Yeah, Derek, keep in touch." He said wearily. "But like Lorna says, she'll probably be home when you get there."

CHAPTER NINE

Caine was in the shower when Dolby rang the following morning. She rang him back.

"Sorry, I had a bad night last night. I didn't really want to get up this morning." She told him about the schoolboy's death. "I know it's not down to me to find out who was responsible, but I just keep thinking about it. Whoever it is, I'd like to see them behind bars."

"I know the feeling." It was just after eleven o'clock and the news from Derek and Pauline Atterwood's household was not encouraging. "I had my own little upset last night. One of Donna's friends has disappeared. They went to a dance together and she didn't come home. Do you want me in at the station this morning, Jackie, only I thought I'd go round and see the parents? See what I can do."

Caine reached over and poured hot water into the coffee pot. "I hope it sounds worse than it is. Is the girl in the habit of going off by herself?"

"Emma? No, apparently not. That's why it's so worrying. When I heard about it late last night we thought she'd just gone off with a boyfriend and forgotten the time, but she hasn't come home yet and it's not looking too good. I just hope it's not going to be another job for us!"

"God no, I hope not!" The coffee was almost boiling and it burned a little as it went down. "That's the last thing we need. Don't worry about coming in this morning, Mark. As a matter of fact, I don't think I'm going to bother myself. I'm expecting Alison over later on and there's lots to do here."

"Any breakthroughs on the Winters case?"

"Nothing that I'd call a real breakthrough. I'll fill you in on the details tomorrow."

"What about our interview with Mrs Hartnell? Anything scheduled on that yet? How are you by the way, Jackie? That was quite a knock she gave you."

246

"Oh, I'm fine. No bruises so far as I can see. And no, we've heard nothing from the hospital. Maybe it's just as well. We'll chase it up in the morning."

"Okay, I suppose I'd better get on."

Dolby sounded despondent. Caine imagined his mind was already moving on to consider what he was going to say to his friends when he met them to discuss their missing daughter. This was always a bad time, when nobody knew just how serious a missing person case might turn out to be. She hoped there would be some good news when he went around to see them.

"I'll see you at the station in the morning then," said Caine. "Oh and keep us posted about the girl."

"Yeah, I will," he sighed heavily. "But I've got to admit I haven't got a good feeling about it."

"Maybe it's just you, Mark. You've had a pretty bad night by all accounts. We're all in danger of getting things out of proportion."

"Yeah, yeah, I know, don't tell me – most so-called *missing persons* turn up again within forty-eight hours, laughing and joking like it never happened. Let's just hope Emma's one of those."

Within seconds of Caine putting the telephone down it rang again. It was Sergeant Poole.

"You asked me to let you know if we found anything at the school," he said. "There was some stuff in the senior boys' rooms, Ma'am. Cannabis. Not exactly what we were looking for – as you know we were after ecstasy and meth."

"Well done anyway. Was it well hidden?"

"Oh yes, we came on it by sheer chance," said Poole. "It was stuck down the barrel of a telescope."

"Pardon? Run that past me again."

Poole laughed. "It's okay, you heard right, Ma'am. Believe it or not it was stuffed down the barrel of an astronomical telescope. Seems the two lads who occupy the room are into astronomy. The school actually teaches it. Anyway, they've got two or three telescopes – different sorts, I don't know the details, but it's expensive gear, their families must be very well heeled. As I say, though, it was sheer luck we found the stuff – the telescope was in its box, but one of our lads is a bit of an enthusiast and he fancied trying it out. He knew something was wrong as soon as he put his eye to the eyepiece; there was something blocking his view, so he unscrewed the barrel to see what was in the way and there it was. A little plastic bag of cannabis – not much, but enough to bring a charge. It was carefully sellotaped to the inside of the tube."

"But you didn't find any of the stronger stuff?" Caine asked, disappointed.

"No. We won't be able to charge the two lads on the Rebus case, I'm afraid – their names are Hill and Sullivan by the way – but at least it's a start."

"Fine. And thank you, Sergeant, for letting me know." Caine put the receiver back on its rest. She sighed, disappointed that the source of Nicholas Rebus's ecstasy remained undiscovered. But, as Sergeant Poole said, it was a start and it could be that Messrs Hill and Sullivan would point their collective fingers at the local drug dealers.

Caine's daughter, Alison, arrived just before lunch. The weather being cold but bright they ate in the conservatory at the back of the house. Newly built by the previous owners it was double glazed and centrally heated. With Jacqueline Caine's eager consent, they had left it well stocked with indoor plants – among them mother-in-law's tongues, tradescantias and philodendrons. A host of other plants, whose names were a complete mystery to the new occupant, wallowed in the wintry sunshine of the airy, west facing room, filling the air with a range of heady scents.

"Is the boy's death one of yours, mum?" asked Alison finishing the last of her pasta and reaching across the glass topped table for her diet coke. "I mean, is it down to you to investigate?"

"No, thank The Lord." Caine settled back in her chair and looked out through the double-glazed panes. The previous owners had been keen horticulturalists and the garden, now resting through the winter, was well laid out and stocked. "There's no real mystery to it. It was drugs related, so the drugs division can handle it – and welcome

250

to it." She had spent most of last night thinking about the boy's death, about what a complete and utter waste of a life it had been and she had burned with anger at the stupidity of it all. She had fallen asleep thinking that, although she hated many aspects of her job, she was lucky to be concerned with deaths which, in the ordinary course of events, were single incidents brought on by the normal vices of mankind – lust, greed, passion, common or garden anger. Rarely had the cases she had investigated during her long career been concerned with organised crime of the kind that had resulted in her husband's, Jonathan's, murder over twenty-five years before; somehow death by drugs was dirtier than the sort of crime she was used to. She was glad she could pass this one over to the drugs division. "Anyway, darling, I'd rather not talk about it." She looked down the garden again. The shortest day of the year was approaching and the sun, already low in the sky, was now partially obscured by storm clouds, which, as forecast, were moving rapidly in from the north. "Let's go for a walk by the river before the rain gets here. We'll clear the table later."

The garden was well over a hundred feet long and eighty wide. Its size was one of the few things that had made Caine hesitate about buying the house when she moved into the area earlier in the year. Would she be able to manage it? Not by herself certainly, but the estate agent assured her there was a local handyman/gardener looking after it, an individual who went by the name of 'old Jimmy Fernlow'. He had worked for the previous owners for years, tending the front and back gardens on two half days a week basis, under the watchful eye of Mrs Anderson. The results of his toils were very pleasing thought Caine as she and Alison made their way up the garden and they promised well for the warmer weather. Mrs Anderson had chosen to have mainly lawn, with narrow borders running down each side. On the right, there was a high wooden fence against which she - or old Jimmy - had planted a variety of plants, which in their stark winter garb, Caine did not recognise, but which she was sure would be in keeping with the garden's character; on the left, against the red brick wall of the neighbouring house's orchard, were climbers such as clematis and roses, fronted by tall shrubs - lavatera, lilac and azaleas and closer to the path, cornflowers, geraniums and foxgloves. At the back of the garden, in the lee of the fence and the lime trees that gave the house its name, was a small herb garden and vegetable patch.

Beyond the garden were the banks of Trickett's Brook, an obscure tributary of the Blackwater, reached by opening a gate set in the five-foot high perimeter fence. Caine and her daughter walked through on to the towpath, closing the gate carefully behind them, feeling the nip of the wind as they left the comparative shelter of the fenced off garden.

"The neighbours keep telling me I should fix a padlock," said Caine ruefully. "Apparently this gate's an open invitation to the burglaring fraternity." She smiled. "They haven't yet cottoned on that I'm a copper!"

"Well, you should anyway," her daughter told her. She looked across at the distant wood that broke the horizon towards Beacon Hill. "It'll help keep away all the nasty little ferrets and stoats that inhabit the wildwood."

Clouds were gathering in the north, threatening to bring premature darkness to the bleak December day and the grass at the side of the river was still wet from the frost the sun had barely melted away. They were glad of their thick coats and pulled their hoods up over their heads. Their sturdy boots crunched loudly in the hard mud as they set off along the towpath.

"The people at work can't wait to hear the inside story on the train crash murder – it's so gruesome!" Alison said, breathing out heavily and watching the clouds of water vapour drift slowly away on the air.

Caine snorted her disapproval. Her daughter liked to tease her about her job and the secrecy that had, of necessity, to surround her investigations. She gave her the stock answer. "They'll have to wait for the trial, the same as everybody else."

254

Alison went through their usual ritual and pretended to pout. "That's really mean. I am the investigating detective's daughter after all, and they do expect me to come back with the goods."

"There aren't any goods at the moment," retorted her mother, "You and Joe Public know almost as much about the murderer as I do."

They stood for a moment at the edge of the bank, under the branches of an old willow tree, each with her own private thoughts, looking down into the rippling water and catching a faint, indistinct flash of silver as a fish swam up towards the surface. Then they walked on, following the curve of the brook as it widened out before them, the slowly moving water quickening its pace as it moved ever closer to the river. As they rounded a bend the figure of a lone fisherman came into view. Dressed in khaki waterproofs he was crouched beside the water on a portable campstool beneath a large umbrella, the long black shaft of his fishing rod resting on a metal tripod and arcing out over the centre of the brook. An empty landing net lay on the grassy bank beside him. He seemed deep in thought, one hand resting lightly on the rod, the other supporting his bearded chin, and his eyes fixed on the float that bobbed on the swiftly moving water. There was something about him that seemed familiar to Caine and she examined him more closely as she and Alison approached. He turned towards them as he heard their boots crunching on the frost-hard grass and she recognised the deputy head of Upton Grange School. He looked back at her uncertainly.

"Good afternoon, Mr Maynard," she said. "Mr Wilson's back at the school helm then?"

His brow furrowed as he recognised her. "I suppose," he said gruffly "that's one way of saying 'what are you doing here when you should be at the school sorting out the mess'." He secured the shaft of the rod on the tripod and stood up. "The truth is, Detective Inspector, I was so blazing mad I think I'd have murdered our dear Headmaster if I hadn't come away when I did." He looked around him, zipping up his windcheater as a flurry of cold wind chased its way along the bank, bending the stems of the bulrushes that stood in the water on the opposite bank. "You know of course that two of our senior boys were found with drugs in their room?"

Caine nodded. "Yes, Sergeant Poole rang me this morning."

Maynard nodded, "Toby Wilson, the headmaster - has been bending over backwards to get them off the charges. I told him to expel the little brutes and let them take the consequences of their own actions."

"They'll take those anyway, won't they?"

He smiled ruefully. "Not necessarily. You know as well as I do, Inspector, that's not exactly how the system works. Besides, using undue influence to get them off doesn't exactly help them to become good citizens; at least I don't think so. And that's exactly what Wilson has been up to. He doesn't know where to look next for another pair of influential boots to lick."

"It wasn't ecstasy we found, though," said Caine, "So, we can't charge the two boys in connection with Rebus's death."

"I know and that's the point I've been trying to make. Hill and Sullivan – those are the two boys involved – will be charged with possession of drugs, not with drug pushing and it's going to be a fairly minor charge; as I understand it there wasn't much cannabis found. I told Wilson to let them face the music, especially as they're undoubtedly guilty – it might teach them a much-needed lesson." He turned towards Alison. "Aren't you going to introduce me to this delightful young lady, Inspector?"

Caine smiled. "Yes, I do apologise, Mr Maynard." She laid her hand on Alison's arm. "My daughter, Alison. Alison, Douglas Maynard. Mr Maynard is the Deputy Head of the Upton Grange School I was telling you about."

Alison took off her gloves and shook Maynard's hand. "I was sorry to hear about the boy, Mr Maynard. It must have been quite a shock."

He removed his wire-framed spectacles and rubbed his tired eyes. "Yes, you might say that…"

"But what about Rebus's death?" asked Caine, "Isn't anything happening on that?"

He nodded. "Oh yes. The school governors are conducting an inquiry and – until it's over – I'm on suspension."

"An inquiry? I would have thought *you'd* be a major player."

"I am," he replied brusquely. "You might say that I'm *the subject* of the inquiry, purely because I happened to be senior body at the time Rebus's death occurred." He laughed bitterly. "Their time would be better spent trying to find out where young Rebus got the stuff."

"Hill and Sullivan must be highly suspect," suggested Alison.

He laughed again, without humour. "Not according to Wilson. He says they're innocent victims, that the stuff was planted on them." The big man shook his head in despair. "He's so unbelievably naïve you wouldn't believe it. I just

259

can't convince him that Hill and Sullivan are a couple of spoilt overindulged brats; their parents give them anything they ask for, especially Duncan Hill's – do you know, apart from his BMW convertible, he's got his own speed boat moored down at Maldon? The lad doesn't know he's born. A shake up with the police is just what he needs to wake him up to the real world!" he smiled again. "Sorry, I'm going on a bit. I shouldn't let it get to me like this. Anyway, what brings you here? Do you live nearby?"

"Yes, just around the bend up there. Lime Tree Cottage."

"Yes, I know the property. Used to belong to the Andersons. Both their sons attended the school until a few years back. They live abroad now I believe." He put his glasses back over the bridge of his nose and turned away from them, squatting down to adjust the position of his fishing rod. "Sorry, but I've got some heavy thinking to do."

"You must be freezing out here, Mr Maynard," said Alison. "Surely you're not going to stay out here much longer. It's getting dark."

As if in answer Maynard pulled the draw strings of his waterproofs more tightly about him and sat down on his stool. "I enjoy the solitude," he said quietly. "A man – or a woman for that matter – must have time and solitude to think properly and I need to do a lot of thinking. Perhaps I'll see you around."

"Sounds like he's in a bit of a spot," said Alison. They were tracing their steps back towards the cottage, walking more quickly as the sun slipped below the horizon and the icy wind blew mountainous rain clouds across the sky towards them. "I feel sorry for him. He looks like a nice man, but he must be nuts to even think about staying out in this weather." She shivered.

"Anglers are like that," said Caine, "Anything to get away from it all. It strikes me, though, that our Mr Maynard has plenty to get away from at the moment." The first fat drops of rain splattered onto the hood of her waterproofs and she drew the drawstrings in more tightly. "Still, I hope he's not too pig headed and gets himself under shelter soon. That umbrella thing he's got didn't look too safe and it looks like it's going to be a pretty rough night."

By the time they got back to the house the rain was hammering down on the thatched roof and cascading over the gutters. Caine groped in her handbag for the door key; rain running down from her hood and into her open bag. Alison stood back so that her shadow did not obscure the lock on the door and peered up at the roof of the house.

"I hope the thatch holds out. It can't be as waterproof as tiles can it?"

Caine found the key and fitted it into the lock, pushing the door open with a sigh of relief. "Thank the lord!" She stumbled into the hall and grappled with zips and press-studs to undo her heavy anorak. "Sorry, darling, what were you saying?"

Alison pulled her parka over her head. "About the roof. I hope the thatch is rain proof."

"Of course, it is, dear. They've been using it for hundreds of years haven't they? They would hardly have gone on using it if it wasn't, especially in this country." She looked down at the pool of water that had run off their coats. "I'd better get the mop to this – be a dear and carry the coats through to the utility room. You can hang them up near the boiler."

Alison took the coats and gave them a final shake before carrying them along the narrow corridor to the back part of the house. When she came back Caine was mopping at the water with the mop she had fetched from the cloakroom. "Well, I hope you're right. You know what damage a leaky roof can do and I wouldn't like to have to redecorate the whole house."

Caine squeezed the mop down into the bucket. "Perish the thought! You are coming to help clear out the box room on Saturday though, aren't you? You know I couldn't do it without you."

263

"Course I am. I want that room, it's much nicer than the one you usually put me into. And you never know what we might find. Some of those boxes haven't been opened since we lived in that dreadful top floor flat in Walthamstow. I must've been all of six years old and I remember you chucking all that stuff into boxes and saying we'll chuck it out if we haven't used it by this time next year. Fat chance! You're a real hoarder, mum, it must be your birth sign."

"This time it's the dump for most of it, darling, I promise. In fact, I'll let you make the decisions on what to keep and what to throw away. I can't be fairer than that. Come on Friday evening and we can make a nice early start in the morning."

CHAPTER TEN

DS Mark Dolby came into Caine's office at just before a quarter to eight the following morning, carrying two cups of black coffee. She looked up from the report she was reading. He looked tired and drawn and the knot of his tie was askew. "'Morning, Mark. You don't look too good."

Dolby placed the coffee cups carefully on her desk and slumped down into one of the guest chairs. "'Morning, Jackie," he gestured vaguely towards the cups, "I thought you might like one."

"Thanks, I would at that. I assume there's no news about the girl."

"No. It's not looking too good. No one's heard anything from her since Saturday night. She's been gone for nearly thirty-six hours. Someone's going to have to make a decision soon."

"You mean about a search?" Caine unscrewed the top of her fountain pen and made a note on a checklist. "Yes, but the Super's not going to like it. It'll be the second one in three days and you know what manpower's been like, what with the virus and everything else."

Dolby shrugged. "Whether he likes it or not we've got to mount a search soon."

"He'll fight it, you know. He's been on at me already this morning about the waste of resources on the train crash area search. The man's a joke - how did we know we wouldn't find anything? How do we *ever* know if we're going to find anything? That's why it's called *a search*." She sighed. "Anyway, Mark, if I know Hansen he'll try to hold off for a bit longer yet. He doesn't like searches, even when we already have a murder victim – they're too labour intensive and they cost too much."

"I know, I know, but you just try convincing Emma's parents she hasn't been missing long enough to start looking for her in an organised way!" He rubbed his eyes again, picked up his coffee cup and gulped at the steaming liquid. "Anyway, with your approval I'm going to see him to ask if we can get something started."

"Of course, you can go see him, Mark, but don't assume he'll let *you* handle it." She laid down her pen and picked up the coffee cup. "You know the missing girl. You're a personal friend of her parents. In those circumstances it's not always a good thing to get too closely involved." She took a sip of coffee. "Besides, we need you on the Winters case."

"Okay, point made," he said irritably. "Look, I'm sorry, you're right, but I won't feel any happier until we've found young Emma. Derek and Pauline are going spare – you can imagine. And I'm getting quite a bit of flak from Lorna and the kids – Emma was the sister of Donna's best friend, for God's sake! – I mean, *is* the sister!" he sighed. "Anyway, where do we go from here on the train murder? When can we interview our star witness again?"

"I'm hoping we'll be able to see her some time today." Caine told him. "I was just going to call the hospital."

DC Wendy Doyle popped her head around the door and peered in. "Good morning, Ma'am, Sergeant Dolby, sorry to disturb you, but I thought you should know, we've got the dead woman's husband downstairs."

"Ah! Mr Winters, all the way down from Yorkshire," said Caine, pleased. Perhaps they would get a few answers from him. "You'd better show him up, Wendy."

"I don't think so, Ma'am. He's in a cell. He was arrested last night trying to break into Mrs Mears' house. One of the neighbours raised the alarm and the local boys booked him for breaking and entering. When they realised who he was they whisked him straight down here."

"Good!" Caine swallowed some more coffee and stood up. "Then we'd better see him in his own quarters hadn't we." She looked across at Dolby. "Do you want to sit in on this one, Mark, or would you prefer to go and confront Hansen about young Emma?"

Dolby dropped his empty plastic cup into the bin under Caine's desk and stood up, yawning. "I'll see the Super if you don't mind, Jackie. The sooner he gets to know the situation the better, it might take some hours for him to come round to my point of view."

"Right. You can join us in the interview room when you're ready." Caine turned to DC Doyle. "Let's hear what Mr Winters has to say for himself then, shall we, Wendy?"

Leonard Winters was a tall, thin man, his face almost skeletal. He was sitting at the interview table when Caine and DC Doyle entered the room and he looked up at them from eyes sunk deep into his clean-shaven skull. He wore four or five earrings in each of his ears and as he turned towards the two officers his black donkey jacket opened to reveal a tattered yellow sweater. Below his worn denim jeans he was wearing heavy workman's boots.

"Good morning, Detective Chief Inspector." His voice was smooth and educated and he smiled at Caine's reaction. "Didn't expect me to speak like this, did you? Not from the look of me, anyway. Quite a surprise isn't it! One glance at me and you'd expect my every sentence to be punctuated with a goodly helping of the F-word, wouldn't you? *Didn't you* I should say, because of course you

269

bloody well did. I saw it on your face." He laughed again. "You middle class prigs are all the same – I can read you all like Janet and John books."

Caine shot a questioning glance at DC Doyle who smiled back nervously and shrugged her shoulders as if to say 'don't look at me, I haven't spoken to him before either.'

Caine gestured for Doyle to sit at the table and sat down beside her, opposite Winters. She smiled at the man, shifting her chair beneath her while she composed herself. "We will be recording this interview, Mr Winters."

"Even if I object?"

"Even if you object, Mr Winters." She nodded to DC Doyle who leaned forward and switched on the wall-mounted tape recorder. Caine recited the required introduction to the interview and then continued. "First of all, Mr Winters, my condolences on the death of your wife."

"Yes, it was quite a shock. Can't say as I'm going to grieve too much though. Let's be honest about it, Inspector, there was no love lost between Marion and me. We married young you see. It was a bit of a university lust match if you see what I mean, though we thought it was the real thing at the time of course, most people do at that age, which only goes to prove that on the whole we're the greatest load of plonkers that ever lived!"

Caine, irritated by the man's flippancy, ignored the comment. "I understand, Mr Winters, that the officers who detained you on Mrs Mears' premises are seeking her confirmation as to whether or not you are to be charged. I'm not particularly interested in that aspect of the affair, to be honest, but what I do want to know is what you were doing in her house?"

"What? At the old bat's place?" Winters interlaced his fingers and flexed them against each other. The sinews crackled audibly. "I had to get some of my wife's things. It's as simple as that."

"What things?"

"Oh, this and that." He unlaced his fingers and yawned. "Sorry, I'm a bit knackered you understand, I didn't have too good a night. The cells up in Colchester nick were pretty naff, but yours are even worse."

Caine sighed. When she first clapped her eyes on Leonard Winters she had had the feeling they would have a hard time getting anything useful out of him. Evidently, he was one of those people on whom civility is wasted. "Do you know what I think, Mr Winters, I think you were there to find your wife's will and dispose of it. You were aware she had changed it recently and that you were no longer a beneficiary, weren't you." Winters looked away, up at the high window, which was being buffeted by quick bursts of rain. "And I think you were also aware that Mrs Mears had a number of valuables on the premises."

"No, I wasn't aware of any such thing," declared Winters, a little rattled. "I wasn't there to take any of the old girl's belongings. I was only after what was – *is* – legally mine. My wife's stuff. That's all. I wasn't after any will."

Which was probably just as well thought Caine, because there wasn't one. But she wasn't about to let him

272

know that. He could stew in his own juice so far as she was concerned. "I'll accept that for the time being, Mr Winters. Where were you on Friday afternoon?"

Winters grinned. "I've been expecting you to ask me that, Inspector." He leaned back in his chair and folded his arms across his chest. "I was in Harwich if you must know. Unloading my truck, well anyway, the truck I was driving."

"That's your job is it? Truck driver?"

Winters nodded. "RTE – Rotherham Truck Enterprises. I've been with them for about four years give or take. They'll confirm it and they'll also confirm where I was on Friday. It'll all be in my log."

"We shall certainly check it, Mr Winters." Caine thought back to her interview with Mrs Mears. "When did you last speak with your wife, Mr Winters?"

He screwed up his face, thinking. "A few weeks ago, Inspector."

"You sure about that?"

Winters waited a few moments before he nodded again. "Yes. I think so. And don't ask me what we talked

273

about because I haven't got a clue. The only thing I can say is that we usually ended up having a slanging match. That's why we split up in the first place."

Caine looked at her watch. "Thank you, Mr Winters, we'll be holding you at least until we hear from our colleagues in Colchester on whether Mrs Mears wants to press charges." She stood up, saying for the benefit of the recording machine "Interview ends at eight fifteen a.m."

DC Doyle leaned over and switched it off.

"Bit of a peculiar character, Ma'am," she said as they made their way back to Caine's office. "If he's a university graduate what's he doing driving a truck?" She pressed the button for the lift and stood back.

Caine shrugged. "Dropped out," she said. "You don't hear much of it nowadays, Wendy, but in my day – way back in the nineties and noughties – a lot of the intelligent ones were doing it."

"You're not that old, Ma'am! Anyway, I don't understand it. If you're intelligent you should be doing more than driving a truck up and down the country, you should be putting something back into society."

"Maybe Mr Winters thinks he is – come to think of it, he's probably right. If it wasn't for truck drivers we wouldn't have any goods in the shops." They stepped out of the lift and turned into the corridor. "Anyway, it's a matter of values and how you, as an individual, see them. Winters strikes me as being a deliberately bombastic individual who'd do anything to prove he's different from the common herd."

"Would that include murdering his wife?"

Caine shrugged. "I shouldn't think he'd want to go quite that far, but who knows?"

Mark Dolby was waiting in her office and looking very gloomy when she and DC Doyle returned. "I hope your interview was more fruitful than mine," he said, turning away from the window where he had been watching the incessant rain beat down on the pavement outside. "Hansen wouldn't budge. Said a girl of sixteen should be able to look after herself. So far as he's concerned we sit on our hands until there's good reason to believe there's been foul play."

"Much as I expected," said Caine. She sat down and beckoned DC Doyle into one of the guest chairs. "So, what do we conclude on our Mr Winters, Wendy?"

Wendy Doyle seated herself and crossed her legs comfortably. "Like you said, he's a bit of a bombastic character, but I can't really see him as a wife killer. I'll see if there's anything on line."

Caine made a note on her pad before continuing. "He was lying, of course, about when he last spoke to his wife. But I don't think there's much behind that except to try to keep us in the dark about how much he knows concerning her new will. It's just the sort of thing a difficult sod like him would do."

"How would he know his wife's movements on the day in question, though?" queried Dolby. "He spoke to her the day before, Mrs Mears told us that, but she – his wife - didn't know she'd be on that particular train at that particular time. So how was he supposed to know it?"

Caine nodded. "Well, somebody knew. Or else it was a totally random killing. That's possible, but it doesn't make much sense."

"Someone could have been following her," suggested Wendy Doyle. "That O'Hanlon man for instance. Maybe he made contact with Winters and they cooked it up between them."

Caine nodded thoughtfully. "Not impossible by any means, Wendy. By the way, how are you getting on with the hit and run cases? Anything break yet?"

Doyle shook her head. "No, Ma'am. I haven't had much time for it, but anyway the whole thing seems to have dried up. Still, at least we're not getting any new incidents."

Caine made a few more notes and then tore the sheet of paper from the pad and passed it over to the young DC. "Follow up on these points, please Wendy. I don't honestly think Winters had anything to do with his wife's death, but it's as well to cross the 'T's and dot the 'I's. Check his movements on Friday afternoon in particular. Oh - on the question of O'Hanlon - anything further from our friends in Yorkshire?"

Doyle shook her head. "No. I've asked them to trace his whereabouts, but it's early days yet."

"Let Mark and I know if anything comes in on that." Caine turned her attention to the notes she had made the day before. "Now, what about those CCTV records? Any news on them?"

Doyle shook her head again. "I've got a couple of the girls going through them, but they're pretty time consuming and – dare I say it? – sitting and staring at a TV screen with pictures of people walking up and down station platforms is dead boring. That train went through a lot of stations and it's surprising how many cameras they have at each one. Of course, some of them were out of order, facing the wrong way, or – believe it or not – just not switched on. Also, some of the video machines attached to the cameras had no SD cards in them. What a way to run a security system!"

"Yes, remind me to send in the station security officer to give them some advice," said Caine dryly.

Dolby smiled. "Still, I imagine matching up the faces of the people in the train with their TV pictures as they came and went is a pretty tall order."

"Especially when the idiots supposed to be running security on the railways don't turn their confounded machines on," Caine agreed irritably. "Or, on the odd occasion when they do – forget to reload the video machines with SD cards. It's impossible - but there we are - it may be all we've got." She shook her head in disappointment and moved on to the next item. "The man in the blue suit. It's remote I know, shooting at the moon, but just on the off chance I'd like someone to visit all the dry cleaners in the area to see if anyone's handed in a pair of muddy blue trousers for cleaning." She ticked the item off her list. "Apart from that and the remote possibility we might just get a bit of sense out of our only witness, Mrs Hartnell, I can't say we're making much progress in solving this one."

Dolby was standing at the window again, watching fascinated as the rain hit the pavement outside. It ran swiftly down to form long streams in the gutters. "What do we know about the other woman in the carriage?" he asked. "The one that was killed in the crash?"

"Nothing much," said Caine, turning over some papers on her desk to locate the passenger list compiled at the scene of the accident. She found it and ran her finger down to the section marked 'DECEASED'. "Her name was Hillary Martin. That's all we know." She looked up at him. "Frankly, I hardly think it's relevant. She was probably dead before Nurse Winters was attacked and as she's no longer with us she can't tell us what went on. So, what's your point, Mark?"

He shrugged and turned to face her. "The point is that there isn't a point. It's just something we've not thought about, that's all."

"I'll see what we can find out about her," said DC Doyle writing the name in her notebook. "You never know, it might just turn up something."

280

Caine reached for the telephone receiver. "Let's see if Mrs H. is in a fit state to talk to us, shall we?"

The news was better than she had expected. Mrs Hartnell was well on the way to a complete recovery from the injuries she had sustained in the train crash and was expected to be discharged from hospital later that day. There was, of course, her mental state to be considered, Staff Nurse Rierdon confided; that was still questionable, but she was making reasonable sense and had quietened down since her unfortunate outburst on Saturday morning. Subject to Dr Hamilton's confirmation they could come in and see her at their convenience.

"There's no time like the present," said Caine, "We'll be along in half an hour or so. And thanks." She replaced the receiver and turned to the other two officers. "No sense in hanging about on this, we've precious little else to go on. I only hope Mrs H. gives us something concrete at last."

They stood up to go.

"Be careful where you park, Mark," said Wendy Doyle with a mischievous grin.

"I don't need reminding about that, thank you," said Dolby ruefully. "Those beggars nearly made me late on Saturday and they charged me sixty quid for the privilege."

Dorothy Hartnell was sitting up in bed reading a magazine when Caine and Dolby entered the room. Her face had a little more colour. She continued to read, and it was not until Caine introduced herself and her colleague that she put the magazine down and peered closely at them.

"You were here before, weren't you?" She spoke slowly as though she was concentrating on each word. Her manner reminded Caine of a small child.

"Yes, Mrs Hartnell," said Caine. "Unfortunately, you were unwell at the time."

"I don't remember much about it." Her eyes flicked to one side and she frowned. "Not now, please," she said sharply, "Can't you see I'm busy?"

"I'm sorry," said Caine, confused, "but we thought you'd told the nurse now was a convenient time for you. If it's not, of course…"

"I wasn't talking to you," said Dorothy Hartnell, glancing again to the side and mouthing words that neither Caine nor Dolby could interpret. She looked at them again. "It's all right, I may as well talk to you now. You'll only keep coming back until I do."

Caine, rapidly losing hope that this interview would prove fruitful, sat on the chair close to the bed whilst Dolby carried the other one from beside the wall and set it down beside her.

"Thank you for seeing us, Mrs Hartnell," said Caine. "We'd like you to tell us, please, exactly what happened while you were on the train last Friday."

"It crashed," said Mrs Hartnell.

Caine nodded slowly. She wasn't quite sure if the woman was being deliberately obtuse, but obviously they would have to phrase their questions carefully if they were to get any useful responses. "Yes, I know, but who was in the carriage with you at the time? Do you know what happened to them?"

"I don't really remember. It's very confused." Dorothy Hartnell took off her spectacles and rubbed her eyes. "I think there was someone in the carriage with me," Her voice faded before she said, more stridently. "I don't remember. I don't really *want* to remember."

Caine groaned inwardly and wondered if, once again, she and Dolby were wasting their time. The whole case seemed to hinge on getting lucid answers from this woman, but she appeared incapable of addressing their questions sensibly. How much longer would it be before she gave them some helpful answers? The Detective Inspector glanced at her colleague in frustration.

He shrugged sympathetically, and then leaned towards the woman in the bed. "Perhaps it would help if you told us a little more about what you were doing that day, before the accident," he suggested.

She looked to her side once again and mouthed more meaningless words before turning back towards him. "I'd been shopping."

"Where?"

"In the big shops. I like to go up to the big stores now and then. They have things you can't get in Colchester."

"You mean Harrods, Harvey Nichols, Selfridges, places like that?" asked Caine.

"Yes. The West End."

They had found no evidence in the murder carriage that any of the passengers had been on a special shopping trip. "Did you buy anything?" asked Caine.

"No."

"Nothing at all?"

"No. I didn't see anything I wanted to buy. Besides, we don't have much money to spare. But it doesn't matter, I just like to look in the shop windows at the things."

"So, you were window shopping," suggested Dolby.

"And when you had done enough window shopping you

decided to come home again. Did you travel from Oxford Street to Liverpool Street by underground?"

Mrs Hartnell nodded. "I don't really like to travel on the tube. I get lost. But it's easier than on the buses. I get lost even more on those buses."

"Were you by yourself?" asked Caine. The sudden thought had crossed her mind that, perhaps, Dorothy Hartnell knew one or both of the other ladies in the carriage. Maybe she and Hillary Martin, the woman who had been killed in the crash, had known each other? It seemed unlikely that Dorothy would have known Marion Winters, the murder victim; and what they knew of Mrs Winters' movements during the day in question made it even more unlikely, but Caine was aware that curious coincidences do sometimes occur. And they sometimes led in curious directions.

Dorothy's answer was enigmatic. "We are never really by ourselves, any of us. There are always *others* with us."

"I don't believe that is what Detective Inspector Caine meant, Mrs Hartnell," said Dolby, trying hard to hide his irritation. "Of course, you're never alone when you're out shopping, there are always other people in the shops, if only the shop assistants. What she meant was, did you have a companion with you?"

"We all have many companions on our journey through life." There was a strange echo in Mrs Hartnell's voice. "Our loved ones, those who have gone before, are constantly with us."

Caine groaned inwardly again and glanced helplessly at Dolby. She remembered what Mrs Hartnell's husband had said to them about his wife's ability to 'see' people who were no longer alive. The Doctor, David Hamilton, had said the same thing, only he had been scathing in his rejection of the idea. If Dorothy Hartnell was a spiritualist who genuinely believed the dead were with her constantly, although on another, unearthly plane, she probably also believed that true justice must wait for the next world; on this basis could she ever be a reliable witness? Caine

287

doubted it, but at the moment Mrs Hartnell was all they had and she clung to the hope that, in spite of everything, the woman had actually witnessed something significant at the scene of the murder; something that could help in their investigations. For that reason alone, it was worth continuing what had, so far, been a farcical interview.

Caine sighed and asked. "Yes, I know what you mean, Mrs Hartnell. You're talking about those who have passed on, aren't you?"

"Yes. I'm pleased you understand. I think you may well have second sight, Detective Inspector."

"No, I don't believe so - I'm not so fortunate," said Caine, a little embarrassed, "but I have known those who do possess the power and I understand what you mean." Out of the corner of her eye she could see Dolby staring at her in disbelief. In truth she did not dismiss out of hand the concept of life after death; she had thought about it, as most people do at various stages of their lives, though she had never really made up her mind what she actually believed. But she seemed to be putting on a convincing

288

performance at the moment and if it brought results from Mrs Hartnell in the form of remembered details of the murder then that was all to the good.

Mrs Hartnell seemed to approve of Caine's comments. "That's nice. I believe there really is a way for you, my dear, you're not wholly oblivious to the true path, like so many others." She looked accusingly at Dolby. "But you, young man, you are to be pitied and you will one day regret your scepticism." She had put him down as a complete non-believer and now she turned back to address her remarks to Caine. "You are right, my dear, many of our most cherished and loved have passed on to higher planes. But those of us who are blessed with The Sight can still feel their presence; if, of course, they wish us to feel it."

Dolby almost lost the battle with his irritation. "We're not talking about those who have passed on to a higher plane, Mrs Hartnell, we're referring to those who are still here on this one, this rock-solid thing we call the earth," he stamped his foot for emphasis, "the *real* world with *real* people. What we want to know is, whether or not

289

you went shopping with a living, breathing companion on Friday last, and did you travel home on the train with them."

The woman on the bed seemed unperturbed by his outburst. "Even those who have passed on are still living, Detective Sergeant," she declared with an air of finality. "It is only the body that dies when we pass over, the spirit continues for ever."

Caine tried another, more straight forward tack. "That may be so, Mrs Hartnell, but the point is we need your help in trying to find out what happened on the train last Friday evening. So, please, try to remember who was in your train carriage before the train crashed. Can you do that for us - please?"

There was a pause before Dorothy Hartnell answered. "There were two other people in the carriage. Two women."

Good. It wasn't much, but it was a start, thought Caine a little more optimistically. Perhaps they were beginning to get somewhere at last. "That's very good, Mrs Hartnell. Do you remember anything about them?"

Again, there was a pause before she shook her head. "No, I can't remember much about it at all. I'm sorry."

"Try, Mrs Hartnell, please. Think back to when you were in the carriage with them, just before the crash. Think about when the train was in the tunnel – it was dark and then, after a minute or so, you came out into the light again. What did you see there in the carriage when you come out of the darkness?"

Dorothy Hartnell shifted her legs in the bed and pushed herself up against the pillows stacked behind her back before closing her eyes and resting her fingertips against her temples. "I'm trying very hard to visualise it, my dear – Ah! Yes, it's coming back to me now. I can see it all again. I'm in the carriage and there are two other women with me. One of them is wearing a nurse's uniform. She's tall, with dark hair, not very old. Thirty five, forty perhaps, and she's reading a magazine." Her voice had taken on a dreamy quality and she rocked slowly back and forth, bending at the hips, as though in rhythm with a moving train. "The other woman is older, much older…"

Hardly, Caine thought, Hillary Martin was, if anything, a few years Dorothy Hartnell's junior. It was strange how people attributed age to people they did not know, intriguing how, in almost all circumstances, they thought of themselves as younger.

She became aware of a sudden change in the tone of Mrs Hartnell's voice and stared in disbelief at her face, where a subtle and inexplicable metamorphosis was taking place. As Jacqueline Caine watched, fascinated, the woman's features softened, the flesh seeming to flow and transform; the eyes within their sockets expanded, changed colour from green to light blue, the lips became fuller, more heart-shaped, opening to reveal a set of almost perfect white teeth, the hair became darker and thicker. The skin on her hands loosened, the fingers, tips still resting against her temples, lengthened and the wrinkles on the gnarled joints smoothed out. Her voice, as she spoke, became one or two octaves higher.

"This is the way I would have been, but for her. She ruined it all, you see."

Dolby was staring at Mrs Hartnell, equally dumfounded.

Caine finally found her voice, but the words seemed totally inadequate, not up to the situation. "What do you mean, Mrs Hartnell, are you all right?"

The figure on the bed turned its head towards her, the mouth turning down and the youthful eyes blazing with hatred. "I would have been! I would have been! I would have been!" And then the face contorted and twisted as Mrs Hartnell's voice shrieked through from somewhere deep inside her, shrill and quavering. "I didn't mean it to happen, darling, but I couldn't stop her! Please forgive me!"

As though something had snapped within her, her head jerked. Her body heaved, the flesh quivering as a long sigh escaped her lips and she fell forward in a dead faint, her chin resting on her chest.

"I think I need a cup of coffee," said Caine a few minutes later. "Correction, I need several cups of coffee." She and Dolby were making their way down the long corridor towards the hospital admissions area. After they had pressed the emergency button Staff Nurse Rierdon had ushered them unceremoniously out of Mrs Hartnell's room, telling them that, if they knew what was good for them, they would not come back. Still bemused by their experience they had trooped back down the ward and out into the corridor towards the exit.

"You and me both," agreed Dolby. "Though something a bit stronger wouldn't go amiss."

"You're right," said Caine, "but they're not likely to have Scotch whisky in a hospital canteen, so coffee it'll have to be. I suppose strong and black would be too much to hope for."

They sat at a corner table, she running her fingers around the top of her empty coffee cup, he twisting the stem of a plastic spoon in his fingers until it snapped.

294

"What the hell went on in there?" he said finally, dropping the pieces of broken spoon into his empty coffee cup. "We both saw it, didn't we? The way she changed."

Caine shook her head, baffled. "You mean we *think* we saw it."

"I **know** I saw it," Dolby told her emphatically. "What did she do to us to make us believe it was real?"

"I don't know." For the third or fourth time Caine ran through the events in her mind. "But maybe it *was* real. I've read about things like this. She was obviously in some kind of a trance."

"Yes, but how did she manage to make her features change like that? It wasn't just the flesh, it seemed like the whole bone structure." Dolby squeezed his plastic cup angrily. "She tricked us, somehow the woman tricked us."

"I don't know. I don't think so."

"Of course, she did. I don't know how she did it, but she had us for a couple of lemons. It must have been some sort of music hall trick. All that – '*it's coming back to me now. I can visualise it*'. Closing her eyes and pretending to go off into a trance!"

"But why, Mark? What would she have to gain by pulling the wool over our eyes like that? We weren't accusing her of anything." She looked around the busy dining room. "God! I need another coffee, how about you?"

"Yes, thanks Jackie. Hot and as strong as they can make it."

"So, what could Mrs Hartnell possibly have to gain by doing what she did?" asked Caine again. She had managed to persuade the lady behind the counter to put an extra spoonful of coffee into the cups and now she returned and placed them carefully on the table. "Assuming, of course, it was some sort of a trick. She's not a suspect. She wasn't on the hook."

Dolby's grin was twisted. "I know, she was just helping us with our inquiries." He picked up his coffee cup. "Well, she certainly did something to us, Jackie, an illusion of some sort. And I don't like it. Why do that if she didn't have something to hide?"

"You're not suggesting it was she that garrotted Marion Winters are you, Mark?" Caine sipped the coffee carefully. At least this time it was dark and strong and almost dangerously hot. "Don't forget that Marion Winters was murdered *after* the train crash – by then Dorothy Hartnell was injured. I doubt she could have killed her while she was in that condition. And what about the murder weapon? We'd have found the garrotte on her somewhere and if she threw it away, we'd have still found it." She smiled grimly, "I suppose if nothing else it would have made all that searching worthwhile. And, last but not least, what was her motive?"

"I don't know. You may be right." Dolby broke open a sachet of sugar and shook the contents into his coffee. "But by the same token can you argue with the fact that we both saw her face change beyond recognition. She got younger, Jackie! As we watched!"

297

Caine nodded again. She smiled. "I know – the years fell off her – believe me, I wish I could learn how it's done!"

Dolby grinned and stirred his coffee, lifting the cup to his lips. "Yes, but seriously, how do you explain it?"

Caine sighed. "I don't. I can't." She drank again, thinking hard. "I've read about this sort of thing. She was obviously in a trance when it happened. There's a lot we don't know about, Mark."

"Yes, I know, but I just don't believe in all that malarkey!" said Dolby. He put his cup down emphatically. "And please don't try and tell me it was the work of her spirit friends." He looked across at her and began to twist the new plastic spoon she had brought back with his coffee. "You don't believe in all that stuff, do you? When we were in there with her it certainly seemed like it, but I thought you must have been humouring her. You were, weren't you?"

"Well, yes, I suppose I was," said Caine, frowning. But was she? She had thought about the possibility of an

298

afterlife, but not in depth. Maybe because she lived with death all the time. In her job it was all around her. Other people's deaths. You couldn't afford to think about it too much or the sheer horror of it would get to you and you wouldn't be able to do the job. You just had to develop a thick, protective skin. On the few occasions when she had given it more than a cursory thought, she felt a little intimidated. It was not something she wanted to think about too much and yet, she had always felt, instinctively felt, that there *was* something there, beyond death.

"Mark, I just don't know *what* I think," she said finally. "I'll grant you something went on in that room that we don't understand, but I don't know what it was. Hypnosis maybe. Perhaps the woman's a hypnotist. I just don't know. But I keep coming back to the same question – *why*? If she did it intentionally, *why* did she do it? If she was involved in Marion Winters' death and she didn't want us to know then why didn't she just pretend she'd forgotten everything or that she was unconscious when the killing was taking place? It doesn't make sense."

299

Dolby looked into the black liquid in his cup and nodded grimly. "No, it doesn't. The whole thing doesn't make sense." He lifted the cup to his lips and drained it. "So, where does all this leave us so far as finding Marion Winters' killer is concerned? Nowhere it seems to me."

"We'll have to pursue our other lines of inquiry," said Caine. Although the morning was scarcely halfway through she felt tired, hopelessly drained.

"You don't think we'll get any more out of Mrs Hartnell then?"

"Do you? After what that nurse said we certainly can't go back to her until she's out of hospital – they think we're ruining her chances of recovery. Even if we see her at home, we'll have to watch our step or we'll have the husband suing us for upsetting her mental equilibrium."

Dolby laughed dryly. "Mental equilibrium? I shouldn't think the woman's had any of that for years!"

"You may be right. Anyway, I think we'll have to give up on our dear Mrs Hartnell for the time being. She's going to be about as useful as an inflatable tart in a whorehouse!" Caine

300

grinned at his shocked look. "Oh. Come on, Mark – when are you going to get used to the idea that I spent my first three years in the force walking the beat in Soho? That's tame compared with some of the things I know about!" She stood up. "Anyway, we may as well forget miracle breakthroughs on this one. We're just going to have to plod our way through to the truth the hard way!"

CHAPTER ELEVEN

Dolby was on his way to the station when the call came through. Two days had passed since Emma's disappearance. There had been no news of her since late on Saturday when she had missed her rendezvous in the dance hall with Donna and Sara. Superintendent Hansen had stubbornly resisted an official search. On Monday afternoon, when it had become clear that Emma was not returning home, her parents, Pauline and Derek Atterwood, had expressed their fears to the local press. Thereafter, a single telephone call from the editor of The Fen Molesey Gazette had been sufficient to convince Hansen he had better set a search in motion or face a barrage of appalling publicity from the local press – even the nationals, it was hinted, might be tempted to join in if the girl stayed missing very much longer. A team had been hastily cobbled together– headed by DCI Fred Hopkins, called from his influenza sick-bed - and from seven o'clock until almost eleven that evening police officers had been knocking on doors around the area in which Emma had disappeared; appeals for information had gone out over the local radio stations. So far, the response had not been promising, but they had worked late into the night, following up even the most tenuous leads, fighting their weariness – and the bitterly cold night - with a grim determination founded entirely on the hope of finding the girl. By the early hours of the morning feelings of negativity were running high. Now, early Tuesday, every minute was filled with the knowledge that the next telephone call might carry dreadful news.

Dolby's hands were shaking as he acknowledged the radio call.

"Bernard Crouch, here, Mark. Bad news, I'm afraid. We've got a report that a young woman's body's been found in Upton Woods."

Dolby's blood ran cold. "Any ID?"

"No, Mark, sorry!"

"How old is 'young', Bernard?" Dolby tried to keep his voice steady.

"Sorry, Mark, we haven't got that information either. All I know for sure is that the victim's female and – okay, she's young, but I don't know how young. She was found about twenty minutes ago on the edge of Upton Woods. Someone was taking his dog for an early morning walk and found the body. I rang you as soon as I heard."

Dolby steeled himself for a few long minutes of uncertainty.

"Tommy Poole and his partner are on their way there in their squad car," Crouch told him, "I sent them as soon as the dog walker phoned in. Oh, and I've also dragged Fred Hopkins out of bed. He sounded pretty bad, but he'd said he'd be there."

"I know, Bernie, he was in a right mess last night. The Super should never have put him on the case," A car was coming towards him and Dolby dipped his headlights. "If he doesn't watch it he'll be down with pneumonia." He realised he was talking to keep his mind occupied.

"Conscientious sod isn't he. But what else could the Super do? The flu together with this bloody virus are turning into a right epidemic!" Crouch also was talking for the sake of it. He went quiet for a moment, his voice replaced by static. "I'll let you know if anything else comes in before you get there."

"Does DCI Caine know?"

"Not yet," Crouch replied through a crackle of static. Dolby turned into Inworth Lane where the road sloped down towards Upton Woods. The narrow lane was overhung on both sides by an avenue of tall chestnut trees. Now devoid of leaves their bulk nevertheless blocked out most of the dawn light from the sky and was evidently having a similar effect on the car's radio transmissions. "I thought you might like to get there and have a look before I trouble her," Crouch continued through the static.

"Thanks! Get on to her now for me will you, Bernie. I don't see why she shouldn't have the pleasure of knowing as early as possible." Dolby came to a sharp bend in the road and slowed his car almost to walking pace. He was at the lowest point of the narrow lane, where it dipped and swung sharply to the right. A layer of mist had suddenly wafted across the road from between the trees. He switched on his fog lamps. "Tell her I'll meet her at the scene."

He had been surprised at Jacqueline Caine's lack of enthusiasm when, on the previous day, he had told her he wanted to join DCI Hopkins' search team.

"We really need you for the Winters' investigation, Mark."

"Yes, I know that Jackie, but Emma's parents are my friends. Lorna and Pauline are old school mates. They see each other practically every day. It just doesn't seem right me not helping them find Pauline's daughter. I've known the kid her whole life."

"I know how it seems, Mark, but we have to be professional about this. You're a senior man. DCI Hopkins has his own back-up team. Hsearcxh mee might think we're interfering."

"That's rubbish!" had told her Dolby heatedly. "He should be grateful for my help. I know the girl and her family – I might be able to get information from them that no-one else can!" Dolby was surprised at Caine's objection to his suggestion. He was making it with the very best of intentions – with the possible exception of the parents no one wanted to find the missing girl more than he and it seemed out of character for Jacqueline Caine to be unsympathetic to the idea that he should lend his expertise to the effort. But maybe she was more concerned about their lack of progress in the train murder case than she showed? Hansen had come on rather heavily about her getting a quick solution; she must be worried over their lack of progress and his constant reminders that no woman could walk the streets safely whilst the killer remained free.

She had relented a little. "Okay, you're right. But Mark I really do need you on this bloody train murder." She had paused reflectively. "OK, Mark - let's just go through what we've got on Winters – Lord knows there isn't much – and then you can offer yourself as a volunteer in the Emma search. I might join you – it could do us both good to get away from it for a few hours, help clear our heads. How does that sound?"

"Fine." He understood where she was coming from, but his acceptance had been grudging. They seemed to be getting nowhere fast with the train murder and he wanted to get away from it, to involve himself in the search for Emma; *now*, this very minute, not after yet another go through all the seemingly useless paper they had accumulated on the Winters' murder, all of it leading nowhere. Finally, he had sat down in one of the office guest chairs and crossed his legs, forcing himself to be patient. "So, where do we go from here with the Hartnell woman?"

"Nowhere for the time being," said Caine. "I've a feeling we'll have to go back to her in the end – she's the only positive link we've got – but let's give her a couple more days to get over the trauma of the train crash. I don't want a repeat of last time. Perhaps we'll have better luck with her when she's at home."

"Yes, maybe she'll tell her husband and we can get it out of him." He sighed. "It's just typical that our one and only witness turns out to be a complete fruitcake!"

"Oh, I wouldn't call her that," said Caine, "Whatever she is, she's not mad. And don't forget what happened this morning – it was weird, but there must have been something behind it. I can't think what though." She turned back to her file and flicked through the pages of another report. "You're right about her being our only lead, though, there's nothing here of interest from any of the other passengers. No one saw anything, it seems, they were all too busy looking after themselves when the train came off the rails."

DC Wendy Doyle knocked on the door, interrupting their discussion. "I've just had a call from Ted Bottomly." Caine looked at her quizzically. "You know, the cheeky sod from North Yorkshire who was trying to get off with me. Actually, he sounds very nice. He has a really sexy voice."

"I don't think we need to know that Wendy, but since you mention it what did he have to say with this really sexy voice?"

"Sorry, Ma'am," she blushed. "He's been over to that place in Rotherham where Mr Winters' works – you know, he's a truck driver with them – and they've confirmed Winters was in Harwich last Friday afternoon. He had a consignment for the docks."

"So that puts him out of the picture," said Dolby. "Our options are getting narrower all the time."

"Not necessarily," Wendy sat down and consulted her notebook. "Apparently the guy at the transport company talked a lot. Winters got to Harwich at just after twelve noon and Ted – DC Bottomly – said the man in the office made some remark about him having time to swim the North Sea before he got his truck back. They had to unload it first and then reload it with stuff to go back up north and, on top of that, he had to have a number of rest hours."

"You mean he had time to drive down here, kill his wife and get back to Harwich again?" asked Caine.

310

"Apparently it takes them hours to do the turnaround, so it's not impossible," said Wendy. "But he'd have needed another vehicle wouldn't he, to get down here? His truck was being unloaded so he couldn't use that."

"Just like I said," said Dolby," that puts Lenny Winters out of the picture. Where would he get another vehicle? Besides, how would he know where to find his wife? He would have assumed she'd be at Mrs Mears' house, not travelling in a train. And even if he spoke to Marion Winters the night before she couldn't have told him where she'd be. The train journey only happened because Mrs Mears had a stroke on Friday morning and that came totally out of the blue!"

"I agree. There's no way Winters could have known where his wife would be," said Caine. "So, it does look as though we can forget him as a likely suspect, unless of course he was in cahoots with O'Hanlon and he did the dirty deed. Any news on him?"

"Nothing," said Wendy. "They can't trace him, so he could have been anywhere on Friday afternoon. One thing's for sure, though, there's no sign of him or Mr Winters on the videos." She took a couple of photographs from her file and passed them across the desk to Caine. "DC Bottomly emailed these down to us. This first one's O'Hanlon – as you can see he's got the most enormous beer belly, so we'd have spotted him on the recordings a mile off. The other one's Winters."

Caine studied the photographs for a moment before passing them back. "They look like Laurel and Hardy," she observed, "You're right, they'd certainly stand out on a video, especially as a duo."

"So, it's unlikely they're in a conspiracy," commented Dolby, taking a quick glance at the photographs. "I take it there's nothing else of any interest on the CCTV recordings?"

"Zilch," agreed Doyle. "We've been through all of them a couple of times."

"Thanks for your efforts with the CCTV records Wendy." Caine ticked a couple of items off her check list and screwed the top back onto her fountain pen. "How many stations were there where the security videos had no film in them or weren't working?"

"There were a lot of duds, I'm afraid, Ma'am," Wendy told her, looking bleak. "Four stations, with nine cameras that weren't working. It would be just our luck if the killer actually got on the train at one of those. If he beat it immediately after the train crash there'd be no record of him ever having been on the train." She stood up. "What shall I do with the SD cards? Send them back?"

"No. Lock 'em up until we've cracked the case," Caine told her. "You never know, we might need them again!"

"So, where do we go from here?" asked Dolby. "It seems to me we're no further along the road to finding the killer than we were on Friday evening."

Caine closed her file and stood up, walking towards the window. The lights were coming on in the street outside and it was starting to rain again. "Yes, I know, it's depressing," she said. "And you're right, Mark, we don't seem to have come very far. If only we could get something out of that Hartnell woman."

"Doesn't she remember anything at all?" asked DC Doyle. She had not been with them when they had interviewed Mrs Hartnell earlier in the day and they had not mentioned the trance incident. "Perhaps we could try hypnosis. It's sometimes good for memory loss."

Caine smiled grimly. "I don't think so, Wendy. Her psychological state's in enough of a mess as it is. We can't risk making it worse!" She turned back to Mark Dolby. "Okay, Mark, go and see if you can find Fred Hopkins and offer him your assistance. See what he says. I might join you later, but for the time being I think I'll head for the canteen. At the moment nothing seems more desirable to me than a nice cup of tea and, maybe a buttered scone."

Dolby had spent the rest of the evening and half the night out in the bitter cold helping to supervise the search for Emma Atterwood. He hadn't had much rest the night before either, what with the discussions he'd had with the Atterwoods and helping them with their inquiries with

Emma's friends and relatives. Now he realised he had not been thinking straight when Sergeant Crouch told him where the young woman's body had been found. There were two entrances to Upton Woods and Crouch had not told him which of them to go to. He cursed the delay and, pulling into the side of the road beneath the overhanging branches of one of the huge chestnut trees, called through to the station again.

"Mark Dolby again, Bernie. Which end of the woods am I looking for?"

"Upton Road." Crouch told him. "There's a parking area a few hundred yards up on the left. It's a favourite spot for ramblers. You come off the road and then there's a path that runs into a bit of a meadow before the woods start. Apparently, the body's up there, near the trees, a few feet off the pathway."

"Yes, I know the place you mean. It's near the school."

"Yes. You go past Beckett's Antiques place first, then the meadow and woods. The turn off's just before you reach the school."

Dolby made the mental adjustment and followed Inworth Lane until he came out onto the Upton-Fen Molesey road. He turned left away from the town, entering the heavy early morning traffic. The mist that hung over the surrounding countryside drifted across the road in thick damp patches hindering his progress. The sun, low in the eastern sky and trying to break through the thick grey clouds, had so far made little impression on the white frost that clung to the metalled surface and the wheels of his car slid dangerously on the many sharp bends of the B road that was barely wide enough to carry two-way traffic. It was a few minutes past eight when he passed Beckett's Antiques Emporium, a big square Georgian house set well back from the road. A large gold on green notice, placed strategically beside one of the two brick piers standing on either side of the entrance to the imposing drive invited passers-by – especially those interested in genuine antiques

316

and objet d'art – to call in and browse, without obligation. He travelled on for a few hundred yards more, looking out for the left turn that would take him into the woods.

A few seconds later he saw the flashing blue lights of a police car and pulled off the road, bumping over the wet grass into a wide clearing. In spite of the advancing dawn light the headlights of his car were still on and their beam picked out the tall trees at the edge of the woods and swept across the silhouettes of the two police officers beneath them. They had been huddled together as the light passed over them and now they turned and started to make their way towards him. He brought his vehicle to a halt and switched off the ignition, throwing his door open and stepping out into the frigid air. The cold caught at him and he pulled the zipper of his anorak up to his neck and turned up the collar before gesticulating to the two officers and making his way towards them.

"Morning, Mark." Sergeant Tom Poole greeted him with a wave of his hand. "Not a very good one though, I'm afraid."

Dolby's stomach seemed to turn a somersault inside him and his step faltered. The moment he had been dreading since late on Saturday evening had come. "It is Emma then!" He started to run forward, towards the body that lay huddled at the side of the path a few yards beyond Poole and his companion.

Poole caught the look on Dolby's face and realised the impression his words had conveyed. He glanced quickly at his companion; a young officer Dolby did not recognise. Obviously, a raw recruit and not yet used to examining corpses at close quarters, his face was pale and drawn; he was biting his lip and blinking as though to hold off his tears. He turned away as Dolby ran by.

"No, Mark, it's not Emma." Poole called to him. "At least, I'm almost certain it isn't. This woman's too old. She must be twenty-five, maybe thirty. It's hard to tell. But she's not sixteen and she doesn't fit Emma Atterwood's description."

Dolby stopped his headlong rush and hesitated, torn between the temptation to rage at the Sergeant for his

318

insensitivity and the need to satisfy himself, once and for all, that the body lying beside the path, just a few feet away from him, was not Emma's. He saw the injured look on Poole's face and drew a deep breath of cold early morning air into his lungs before turning back towards the body. "Okay. Let's take a closer look."

Poole stood beside him as he knelt down beside the still form of the dead woman. As Poole had guessed she must have been about twenty-five years old, perhaps a year or two older. She was dark haired, well built and tall, possibly five feet six or seven. She lay on her back; her long coat open to reveal a white blouse stretched tight across her bosom, beneath that a long navy skirt. Her eyes were wide open as though, when she died, she had been staring up at the sky. The tip of her tongue protruded between the generous flesh of her lips. Her neck was slightly twisted and, in the increasing light of dawn Dolby could just make out the rope that still encompassed her throat. It was blue and white, the different coloured strands entwined together, biting hard into the white flesh, the ends

319

trailing down into the mud. There was no knot. The killer

had merely thrown it over her head, probably from behind

and pulled the ends tightly across each other, releasing

them when his work was done. Dolby's eyes moved back

to her blouse, the front of which was askew and, he now

saw, torn; one of the buttons was missing, small traces of

thread hung loose where it had been; the others were

misaligned with their respective holes. Her dark, almost

black hair was long, dishevelled where the night wind had

swept it curling across the surface of her face. A sheen of

moisture – frost, perhaps – clung to her skin. Her

stockinged legs, which were long and shapely, were close

together, her high-heeled shoes encrusted with mud, but

still firmly on her feet.

"No, it's not Emma Atterwood," said Dolby. He was

ashamed to feel the relief that was sweeping over him.

Why should this young woman's death –evidently violent –

be any less of a tragedy than that of the missing girl? Her

loved ones would still grieve her loss, still grasp at fond

memories of her when she was a baby taking her first

320

faltering steps into childhood, a teenager making the mistakes of the young on entering the world of adults, a young woman, living, loving, making her way in life. He felt suddenly sad and very helpless. "I don't know who she is." His voice grated from the dryness in his throat.

"It's odd," said Poole. "I've got the funny feeling I've seen her before, but I can't place her." His colleague, the younger officer had returned to his side and was looking down at the body, concern creasing his brow. "What do you think, Bennet? You're closer to her age, have you ever seen her before?"

PC Bennett shook his head. "She was a good looker, Sergeant, and her face is sort of familiar, but I can't say I can place her."

Dolby stood up, his eyes still on the woman's face. "Now you mention it there is something vaguely familiar about her face," he murmured. "We'll know soon enough." He took a few steps back. "No handbag." He looked across at the other two officers. "Apparently she was spotted by an early dog walker. I daresay this path is used a lot by dog

321

owners, so we'd better get the place taped off as quickly as possible, before any more come along. Tom, ring through to Bernie Crouch and organise a few more bods to help stake out the area. I daresay he's alerted the SOCO team but remind him just in case."

When Caine arrived about twenty minutes later the photographer had done his work and departed and the scene of crime team was busy within the small copse. Dr Williams had arrived a few minutes before her and, with Dolby beside him, was crouched over the body as she crunched over the frozen ground towards them. He turned his head towards her as she approached.

"G'Morning, Jacqueline, another strangulation, I'm afraid." He ran his gloved hands gently under the dead woman's chin, lifting it slightly to reveal the rope around her neck. "But I doubt it's the same man as the train murder. Different rope for a start, this is a nylon twine, used for marine purposes. You see a lot of it on the boats down in Malden marina." He turned his attention to the dead woman's hands, lifting each of them in turn, holding

322

onto the right one and peering at it intently for a few seconds. "We could be in luck here; she may just have scratched her attacker – I think there's a few particles of skin under the nails. I'll know better when I can scrape it out and have a DNA test carried out."

Dolby stood up. "The Doc was just about to tell me how long she's been dead." He turned to Williams. "What do you think, Peter?"

"Hard to say when it's this cold. We've had a pretty cold December so far and it was well below zero during the night." He stood up and looked at his watch. "I can't pinpoint time of death for you at the moment, but I should be able to make an educated guess when I get the body back to the lab."

Caine stared down at the dead woman. She frowned. "It was recent, though, wasn't it? Not more than two or three days."

"I was thinking more along the lines of yesterday evening," said Williams. He pulled off his rubber gloves and threw them into his bag before bending down and closing the clasp. "What?"

"No, no you're absolutely right," said Caine. She crouched down beside the body and studied the dead woman's face for a few seconds. "I know for a fact she was alive on Saturday evening, because I saw her. Her name is Kelly Beacham – Marcus Beckett's girlfriend." She had started to push herself up into a standing position when something bright caught her eye. One of the drawer strings of her anorak had caught a thread from the sleeve of the dead woman, pulling it aside to reveal an expensive wristwatch. Caine peered at it more closely before reaching forward and pushing the dead woman's sleeve a couple of inches further up her arm. "I think this confirms it." The glass face of the watch was cracked and the second hand was motionless. "Her watch stopped at…" She moved her head closer, "…ten-0-three. She must have knocked it in the struggle and cracked the glass."

Dolby came nearer and peered down at the broken watch. "Maybe she hit it against something while she was being strangled." He straightened up. "It could be a real stroke of luck."

Caine nodded. "Yes, I'd say it fixes the time of death pretty accurately."

CHAPTER TWELVE

"With respect, sir, there's nothing to indicate the two cases are connected," said Caine.

Superintendent Edward Hansen glowered at her from behind his desk. He had had a late night at a Rotary 'do' the previous evening – something to do with a senior member becoming a grandfather for the fourth time and celebrating accordingly - and he had not been terribly happy when that idiot Crouch rang him at home early - very early - to inform him that he had yet another murder on his manor. His head was still throbbing from the effects of mixing his drinks and he needed another cup of hot, strong coffee; but his Secretary, Deirdre, had taken it into her head to go off to the Ladies and he hadn't a clue how to make one for himself. He grimaced. "The fact that the cases are probably unconnected is hardly relevant, is it Chief Inspector?" He leaned back in his swivel chair his sheer mass putting a huge strain on the pneumatic pistons governing its ability to rise and fall and twist and turn.

"The fact is that at the moment you are practically the only senior officer I've got who's able to stand up without falling over sideways."

"I know, sir, it is a bit unfortunate about DCI Hopkins." He had collapsed that morning at the scene of the latest murder. "He should never have come out this morning – he was obviously much too ill."

"Yes, the hospital says it's pneumonia now. The man's an idiot! Fancy going out on the job in that state – and in this weather!" Hansen seemed conveniently to have forgotten that it was he who had called Hopkins from his sickbed in the first place, not realising that Jacqueline Caine and Mark Dolby were already at the scene. "That's my whole point isn't it, Chief Inspector? The man's not fit and able enough to conduct this new investigation."

Caine sighed. "But with all due respect, sir, Mark Dolby and I only went out to the scene because Sergeant Crouch asked us to. My team and I are busy with the train crash murder. And you've been insisting that that **has** to be cleared up, on the double."

"I know that don't I?" Hansen replied irritably running his hand over his forehead as if to sweep away his headache. "It was me put you in charge of the case!"

"So, I don't see how I can manage this latest murder as well, sir – not if you want me to get any results on the train murder. It's baffling enough as it is. We all seem to be running around in circles."

Hansen gazed across at her through his tired grey eyes. He suddenly sneezed violently and scrabbled in his trouser pocket for a handkerchief. Maybe he was about to go down with the virus or whatever Hopkins and most of his other officers had, if so, he didn't really give a damn. He felt in need of a few days' bed rest, although he would have preferred an afternoon on the golf course. "Don't make things even more difficult for me, Jacqueline."

"I'm just making the point, sir that as there seems to be nothing in common between this Upton Woods murder and the train murder I'm going to have to run two totally separate investigations side by side. Our manpower's stretched to its limits as it is so I don't see how I can hope to devote sufficient time to either of the two cases."

Hansen blew into his handkerchief and sighed wearily. "Excuse me." He shook his head. "I take the point, Jacqueline. I'm just asking you to get some sort of a result."

Caine shrugged helplessly. "Some sort of a result? There *is* only one acceptable result and that is to get the right man, or men." Hansen looked about to burst. "Okay, I'll do my best, sir, you know that. But it'll take time – and to be perfectly frank we've been getting practically nowhere with the train murder. As I say, we're just going round and round in circles." She looked across at him with what she hoped was an appealing expression. "I'm worried, sir, there's a killer running about out there and we're not getting any closer to catching the bastard!"

"Don't I know it, Detective Inspector!" Hansen replied gruffly, "And now you can make that *two* killers who are running around free on *my* particular patch of

England. Yes, I've read your report on the train murder –
very little progress there if I may say so – a particularly
unpleasant affair. And please bear in mind that the press
are getting increasingly impatient with us." He sneezed
again, this time not quite so heavily.

"They would be, wouldn't they? All they're
interested in is quick results. So far as they're concerned it
doesn't matter whom we arrest so long as we arrest
somebody!"

"Well, they certainly want somebody's blood – and
soon." He heard Deirdre returning to her office next door
and punched his intercom. "And you can tell DS Dolby
that unless we get some results on the Atterwood girl I'm
going to call that search off. We haven't got the resources –
half the men, and that of course includes the women - are
down with this confounded virus thing."

Caine had stood up ready to leave, now she sat down
again determined to fight Dolby's corner. "That's hardly
fair, sir!"

"It's not a question of what's fair and what isn't fair, Jacqueline, you know that. We can't afford to have dozens of officers traipsing up and down the freezing cold countryside looking for a girl who's most probably just run off for a few days of postponed lust with her boyfriend. She's sixteen years old for God's sake, not six!" He held up his hand, perhaps realising he had gone a little too far. "Okay, I suppose that's a pretty harsh view and the parents wouldn't understand – neither would I if she was my daughter, I suppose, thank God I had two sons! – **But the point is** we've no reason to believe she's come to any harm and, until we do, my force has greater priorities that need attending to." He suddenly remembered the intercom was on and barked into it "Get me a large black coffee, please Deirdre, with plenty of sugar – oh! And one of those cinnamon doughnuts!" He looked up at Caine again. "Thanks, that'll be all, Detective Inspector – and let me have some results soon if you would."

"On both cases?"

"Of course, on both cases!"

331

"Oh well, I suppose we've done it before," said Dolby a few minutes later. He sat opposite Caine in her office looking through the photographs of the girl they had found dead in the woods a few hours earlier. "They managed to get these to us double quick, I must say."

"That's the beauty of digital cameras."

"Yes, brilliant," Dolby studied one of the images for a few seconds before passing it to her across the desk. "Anyway, it's not the first time we've had to double up – or even triple up - on our workload, is it? I can remember, two or three years ago, working on two cases of murder, an arson case and a charity fund fraud all at the same time. The fraud case took weeks to clear up, we were working our grey cells to the bone I can tell you - and then, wouldn't you know it, the perp got off with a few hundred hours community service; the arson case took months before we made an arrest - it got so bad I thought I was going to be fired – pun intended!" He massaged his forehead, pressing his fingers around his eye ridges. "It ain't easy working multiple cases, I don't need to tell you that, Jackie! But let's not forget we haven't found Emma yet. We can't just give up on her."

"No – we can't, Mark. But I can tell you Hansen isn't going to let the search go on for much longer." She sighed. What could she say? She knew his concern had sharpened since the new murder victim had been found. Had Emma also fallen foul of the killer? "We've all been there," agreed Caine, "And we all know working on so many cases isn't to be recommended. It's not going to be easy, but on reflection it's not so bad as all that. At least we can concentrate on this new case while we're deciding which line to pursue on the other one. And the search we're having to do up at Upton Woods now means our men can look out for Emma while they're at it."

He grimaced. "I suppose that's true – not that we want them to find anything." He stood up and paced the floor, forcing himself to think more clearly. "Right. So, how are we going to split the two cases?"

"We won't initially," said Caine. "I was thinking about it on the way back from The Super's Office. Unless someone has a brilliant lead on the train murder or an unexpected break turns up, for the next couple of days we'll all concentrate on the new case."

"Well, it'll give us time to reflect. Maybe by then we'll have something more positive on O'Hanlon's whereabouts," suggested Dolby. "It would be useful to eliminate him from our inquiries. And we can see our friend Mrs Hartnell again on Thursday or Friday." He laughed. "Perhaps we should just ask her who killed the woman – well, both of them, actually - she reckons she's in touch with the other side."

"If only it was that easy," said Caine, smiling, "But maybe it's just as well she can't - we'd both be out of a job! Anyway, at least by Thursday she'd have been home for a few days. She may even be a little more sensible." Caine had given a lot of thought to the strange events that had occurred during their last interview with Mrs Hartnell, but she had drawn no conclusions. It had been a deeply puzzling and disturbing experience that did not fit in with her accepted views of normality and she hoped it would

334

not be repeated. She had swept the unpleasant implications of the incident under a mental carpet. "In the meantime, we've got a bit of a lead on the Upton Woods murder. At least we know who she is!" Caine scanned the top photograph again. It depicted the dead woman lying face up on the muddy ground.

"Didn't stint on her clothes, did she."

"How do you mean?"

Caine smiled. Unsurprisingly Dolby was unfamiliar with the differences between expensive and inexpensive women's clothes. "I recognise the label on that blouse. It's a *Santu*, the sort of stuff well-off young girls wear – must have set her back at least two hundred pounds. And the skirt looks like a *Valentino* – four hundred quid of anyone's money."

"Phew – not mine!" Dolby was suddenly glad his wife and daughters were more reasonable in their demands for up-to-date styles, although Donna was beginning to show an unhealthy interest in designer labels. "Any idea what she did for a living? Or do you think her sugar daddy provided the gear?"

"Could be. You can never tell these days where the money comes from." She peered more closely at the picture, noting the tear in the dead woman's blouse, the misalignment of the buttons as though she had re-dressed in a panic. "Looks like there could have been a sexual assault. It definitely doesn't look like the same MO as the train case."

"Doc Williams told me to wait for the autopsy so far as a sexual motive is concerned, but he's quite certain the ropes used to strangle the two victims were different." Dolby leaned across the desk and ran his fingernail across a part of the close-up photograph of the dead girl, tracing out the clearly visible rope about her neck. "This rope is multiple strands. It's much thicker and heavier duty than the one apparently used in the train murder. We'll have more details when forensics have finished their examination, but if we're comparing the two murders on the basis of what was used to kill them then there is no real comparison."

"That's not to say they're not the same killer, though," said Caine. "It seems to me perfectly reasonable he could have used different rope." She dropped the photograph on to the top of the pile and leaned back in her swivel chair. "But then there really are no similarities in the MO are there? I think we have to assume there's no connection."

"Yes, there's hardly any areas of similarity," agreed Dolby. "The murder scenes are quite different; the second victim isn't a nurse – she's not even dressed in a nurse's uniform; the weapons used have nothing in common, except for the fact they're both rope or string. I suppose we should be glad we haven't got a serial killer on the loose." He leaned back in his chair and crossed his legs. "Do we know anything about the girl, apart from the fact that she was Beckett's girl friend?"

"No. It was sheer coincidence Wendy and I bumped into her at his place on Saturday evening. Otherwise, we wouldn't have had a clue who she was. At least knowing her identity is a bit of a start."

"And there was no handbag at the scene," Dolby reminded her, "Which is strange."

"It may be in the vicinity, of course, the SOCO team's still checking the area, but it is unusual for a woman to go anywhere without her handbag, so the inference is the killer took it."

"Possibly, although it doesn't look like your typical assault and robbery, does it. Anyway, as we know her name Wendy should be able to trace her address quite easily. I wonder if her parents live in the area."

"If they don't we'll have to get our friend Beckett to carry out the identification," said Caine, "although both Wendy and I are more or less certain it is Kelly Beacham, we'd better make absolutely certain." She looked at her watch. It was just after 9.30 am. "I think we'll go and speak to Beckett now. Hopefully, he hasn't got wind of what's been going on and it's always useful to be able to see a person's face when you break the news."

In the cold light of day Caine was better able to appreciate the size of Beckett's house. It was genuine Regency period, built along the lines of a minor stately home in the mid eighteen hundreds and probably housed seven or eight bedrooms. It stood in grounds extending to ten or more acres, parts of which bordered on the public woods where Kelly Beecham's body had been found. In front of the house was a large area of gardens, part of which had been turned into a car park able to accommodate a dozen or more cars, essential to the success of Beckett's antiques business. A low fence separated his area of woodland from the public woods and those within the grounds of Upton Grange School; it was likely, thought Caine as Dolby guided the car up the long drive towards the house, that all the land in the immediate vicinity had once been owned by the Squire who had built Beckett's house and that it had been sold off in parcels over the generations. Now it stood tall and imposing, a good example of a minor Palladian style Manor House.

It was just after ten o'clock when they drew up beside a white delivery van in the parking area at the front of the house. The van driver, dressed in a black donkey jacket and oil-stained jeans, called something over his shoulder as he came down the steps towards them. Caine could not make out the words, they may have been foreign, but she glimpsed Beckett in the hallway scowling back at the man, as he slammed shut the rear doors of his van and hurried around it to climb into the driving seat. Beckett, obviously not seeing the two police officers, turned on his heel and made his way down the corridor towards the back of the house.

"Dutch," said Dolby nodding at the man and indicating the name and address printed on the side of the van. "I've heard tell Beckett deals a lot with the continent."

There was a note on the front door of the house apologising for the inconvenience caused to customers of Beckett's Antiques Emporium by the decorating work but assuring them it was open for business. They climbed the steps and walked through into the hall where, amongst the

340

clutter of antiques moved out of the showrooms whilst they were being decorated, an elderly lady, dressed in a dark blue business suit, was doing something mysterious with a porcelain vase. She looked up as they approached and gave them a businesslike smile through a set of slightly buckteeth.

"Good morning, sir, madam, are you here for anything specific or are you just *browsing*?" She made the latter alternative sound anything but respectable and Caine got the impression that she, evidently a sales employee of the Beckett Antiques Emporium, did not look kindly on mere browsers. It seemed she would take to them much more readily if they exhibited a passion for a particular sort of antique, the more expensive the better.

"No, we're not here on business, not antiques business anyway," Caine showed the woman her warrant card and introduced herself and DS Dolby. The woman looked slightly alarmed and almost dropped the vase, depositing it, with shaking hands, onto a small piecrust topped table. "We'd like a word with Mr Beckett, please."

341

"I'll get him for you," She turned and scurried along the corridor towards the room in which Beckett had conducted his conversation with Caine and DC Doyle a few days before.

Dolby picked up the vase and turned it slowly in his hands. "Not exactly my taste, but not bad I suppose, if you like that sort of thing. Do you reckon any of this stuff is genuine antique?"

Caine ran her finger along the top of the piecrust table, noting the marquetry. "Some of it must be or the man wouldn't still be in business."

Dolby wandered across to a tall glass cabinet displaying a range of clocks and watches, peering through the glass at one of the labels. "Crikey! Eighteen thousand pounds - he certainly knows how to charge."

Beckett's assistant appeared at his elbow again and shook her head reprovingly. "Not at all, Sergeant. That is a genuine Thomas Tompian, made around 1786 and it's certainly worth that much or more. You couldn't find a finer example."

"Is that so?" said Dolby, impressed in spite of himself. "It is pretty magnificent I must say. What about that little watch on the shelf above? That I do like."

"And well you should, Sergeant," she said, "that's also seventeenth century. Abraham Breguet made it just before he left Switzerland to work for Louis XV in Paris. There's no price on it because it's practically priceless."

Dolby shrugged. "Oh well, maybe Mr Beckett could repair the Seiko I've got at home, that's about as posh as I get, I'm afraid."

"Don't think he couldn't, Sergeant," the woman replied reprovingly, "Although he prefers quality Mr Beckett really is a very good clock and watch repairer. He has restored quite a number of good pieces in his time." She turned to Caine. "He will see you now, Inspector, if you'd like to come this way."

As she finished speaking the door to one of the front rooms opened and a young man came into the hall. The white overalls covering his stocky, well-built body were splashed with various coloured paints and a few wisps of copper red hair showed at the edges of the baseball cap that was pulled tightly down over his head. He was carrying a litre can of paint in one hand and a brush in the other and he did not seem to notice the two police officers as he walked, head down, across to the room on the other side of the hall.

Caine was about to make a comment to her companion when Beckett's voice boomed down the hall towards them. "Good morning, Inspector - what can I do for you now?" He approached them, hand outstretched, black clothes standing out starkly against the brightness of the newly decorated walls. "Haven't reconsidered, have you?" He caught the puzzled look on Caine's face and went on, "Joining my little coven, my dear!" He laughed heartily at his own joke.

Caine ignored the remark and took the outstretched hand. His grip was firm. "Good morning, Mr Beckett. This is Detective Sergeant Dolby. We're not here about the matter we discussed the other evening. I'm afraid it's much more serious."

"Ah! Then I hope you're here to explain the very tiresome police activities that have been going on all morning over in the woods, not two hundred yards from my front door! I hope so and I also hope that all those flat-footed coppers are there for a good reason – they're enough to scare away even my most law-abiding customers!"

"I can assure you they're there for a very good reason, Mr Beckett," said Caine. "A young woman's body has been found in the woods." She was watching his face closely. He showed no surprise, no emotion whatsoever.

As Caine was speaking Beckett's female sales assistant came out of the end room. She slowed as she heard Caine's words.

"How dreadful!" Beckett said quickly His eyes still showed no emotion. "But it's not the first time that has happened – unfortunately, woods and forests in general are known as the play haunts of villains and cut throats." He stroked his chin thoughtfully. "That certainly explains why there's so many coppers to the square foot over there, but what has all this got to do with me?"

"We believe the young lady concerned was known to you, Mr Beckett," said Caine, still watching his face carefully. "She was here in the house with you when I called in on Saturday evening. You introduced her as Miss Kelly Beacham."

This time Beckett reacted, his jaw dropped and his eyes narrowed. The elderly lady, now well within earshot, gasped and, her face blanched. She found her way to a chair and sat down heavily.

"Are you quite sure it's Miss Beacham?" asked Beckett after a few seconds.

"Oh yes, quite sure. There will have to be a formal identification, of course, but it seems pretty certain."

"And she was murdered?

"There's no doubt about that."

"When did it happen?" Beckett still showed no sign of emotion.

"We're not absolutely sure," replied Dolby. "We'll have a better idea when the post-mortem has been completed." He took out his notebook and opened it, flicking through the pages to find the next unused page. "Perhaps you wouldn't mind telling us when you last saw her?"

Beckett looked across at his elderly sales assistant, who had recovered her composure and was now following the conversation avidly, her eyes alert. "Perhaps you'd better come into my den, Inspector, Detective Sergeant." He turned in the direction of the back of the big house, beckoning them to follow. He looked over his shoulder at the woman. "Perhaps you wouldn't mind keeping an eye on things Felicity, while I'm helping the police with their inquiries!"

They followed the tall man down the hall, twisting and turning between the packed ranks of furniture. Beckett nodded towards a crowded coat stand.

"You can hang your coats there if you like," he said. "I always keep the place fairly warm, for the benefit of my customers.

Caine took off her topcoat and hung it beside a rather tattered old sweater, carefully avoiding the strands of dark blue wool that had snagged from it and now hung down in tight little clusters. Dolby hung his beside hers. In the back-room Beckett went straight to the drinks trolley and selected a decanter of whisky from the Tantalus. "I don't suppose you'd like to join me, Inspector, Detective Sergeant?"

"Thank you, but no," said Caine. "It's much too early in the morning for us." She noticed his hand was steady as he poured the amber liquid from the heavy cut glass decanter into a matching whisky tumbler. He motioned towards two armchairs and she sat in one of them, smoothing her skirt down over her knees. "Perhaps you wouldn't mind answering DC Dolby's question, sir?"

"Not at all," said Beckett. "I hope you don't think I'm acting suspiciously, Inspector. The truth is I am more than a little shocked by your news."

"That's not surprising, sir," said Dolby. "So, when did you last see Miss Beacham?"

"Last night. She was here, with me, until, I suppose, about nine thirty. The last I saw of her was when she drove

348

off in her car. She seemed perfectly all right at the time."
He took a sip of his whisky. "There's very little else I can
tell you."

"Did she say where she was going?"

He shrugged. "I assumed she was going home. She
certainly didn't say she was going anywhere else. Excuse
me."

The melodious beeping of a mobile telephone ringing
somewhere in the furniture cluttered room broke into
Beckett's speech and for the first time since Caine and
Dolby met him he appeared flustered. His eyes shot in the
direction of the sound and he got up from his chair,
annoyance showing on his face. "I told that young fool not
to leave his mobile around!" He went quickly towards the
door, his eyes searching amongst the various artefacts
before bending down and picking up the offending
instrument. He looked closely at the keypad before
pressing one of the keys. The ringing stopped and he put
the telephone to his ear. "Sorry, wrong number!" He
barked abruptly, touching another key and slipping the

phone into his pocket. He walked back towards his seat, calmer now. "I beg your pardon, Inspector, Sergeant, you know what these workmen are like, you have them in to do a couple of rooms and they wander all over the place poking their large inquisitive noses into what really doesn't concern them. And, of course, they leave their belongings strewn all over the place." He sat down again and reached for his whisky glass. "Where were we?"

"You were just telling us you thought Miss Beacham was on her way home when she left you, Mr Beckett. And that would be at about nine thirty?" Pen poised Dolby was looking into his open notebook.

"Yes, but that's all I can tell you. She went off and I haven't seen her since."

"And she appeared normal when she left?"

"Quite normal, Inspector. She had a little trouble starting the car as I recall, had to turn the ignition key three or four times, but in the end it fired up and she went off much as usual."

"You knew her well?" asked Dolby.

350

"Oh, I won't deny we were having a little bit of a fling together," said Beckett, unabashed by the admission. "Why not? She wasn't married and neither am I – there was a bit of a gap age-wise I suppose, and some people probably thought I was a bit of a sugar daddy to her, but I've never cared much about gossip."

"How long had you known each other?" There was, thought Caine, something about Beckett that many women would have found attractive. He was a big man made to seem larger by his sombre attire. Today he wore a black suit, the slightest hint of a crimson stripe showing in its fabric, a navy shirt buttoned down at the collar and a tie of slightly lighter blue. The effect was sombre, even sinister and she suspected this was intentional. Some members of her sex would find this creepiness intriguing, even attractive. She was not one of them.

Beckett was studying her through his dark eyes. "She was a member of my little group, of course, joined about eighteen months ago. A very enthusiastic member as a matter of fact. She'll be a great loss." His smile was

351

twisted and unnatural. He took another sip of whisky. "I don't suppose I could interest you in replacing her?"

"If you are suggesting I become a member of your witches' coven, then no thank you!" said Caine with a small shudder she hoped Dolby would not see.

At her rebuttal he had looked up from his notebook, but his gaze was directed towards Beckett. "Do you really practice witchcraft here in Fen Molesey, Mr Beckett? Do you really believe in all that stuff?"

Beckett regarded him mockingly. "I suppose you're going to tell me it's nothing but superstitious nonsense, Sergeant. I can assure you it's not. The history of the Satanist movement goes back a very long way, far beyond the time of Christ." He laughed. "One day people will learn the truth!"

"But it's all a lot of hocus pocus!" Dolby insisted.

"And Christianity isn't? Don't make me laugh, please!"

Caine could see the interview deteriorating into a slanging match and intervened quickly. "This is all very

352

interesting, gentlemen, but returning to the matter in hand and to last night, Mr Beckett, can you tell us exactly what your movements were during the evening?"

Beckett shot an amused look across at Dolby. "As I said, I was here with Kelly until about nine thirty. After she left, I went out to do a little business."

"Where?"

"Notley Seward, you probably know it, Inspector, lovely little village not far from here. I had a netsuke I'd found for a customer, lovely little ivory piece."

"Your customer's name?"

"Shelbourne, Jonathan Shelbourne. He lives in the Old Rectory. He deals a lot in Japanese goods."

"And he can confirm you were there, with him, between what times?"

"About 9.45 and 10.15. The business didn't take long. He'd seen the little fellow before – the netsuke that is, made in Japan in the eighteenth century – and he'd rung earlier in the day to say he'd take it, so I said I'd take it over. Which I did, Inspector."

"And Mr Shelbourne will confirm that?"

"Oh yes, he'll remember, it was only last night and he gave me three thousand pounds for the piece. Cash. He'll remember it alright – he's probably re-sold it for five or six thousand!"

"And you came straight back here afterwards? You saw nobody else?" asked Caine.

"Oh yes, straight back. I had a bit of work to do, on the computer. I went up to bed at just after twelve o'clock."

"You say you went to see Mr Shelbourne at just after half past nine, Mr Beckett," said Dolby dubiously, "isn't that a little late for a business call?"

"For a normal business, perhaps, but I don't suppose anyone would call the antiques business *normal*, Sergeant; it's a very incestuous industry, everyone knows everybody else and it's a case of all friends together, if not friends then brothers and sisters in the trade." He laughed. "No, I don't think you'd say a ten o'clock call between dealers would be out of the ordinary. And, to answer your other question, 'no' I saw nobody else, apart from Shelbourne,

354

and nobody saw me, there *is* no one to see me here in the house. I live alone, Inspector." He smiled his unnatural smile.

"Do you know of anyone who might have wished Miss Beacham harm?"

The big man shook his head. "No, I don't, Inspector. May I ask, if she was raped?"

Caine was a little surprised at the callousness of the question. "At this time we really couldn't say, sir; we have to wait for the results of the autopsy. Do you have Miss Beacham's address by any chance? My assistant at the station's probably located it by now, but if you have it it may be useful."

"Yes, I can give it to you, Inspector, if you wish. She had a flat in Luckett's Grove, in Upton – Eccles that is - I think the block is called Luckett Towers, but I need to look up the number. She shared with another young lady, I believe." Beckett swallowed down the rest of his whisky and went across to his desk. It was piled high with papers and he scrabbled around moving some of them for a moment before picking up a small black leather directory. He flicked quickly through the pages. "Yes, here it is. Number 7 Luckett Towers, although there's hardly anything towering about the place; as I recall the rooms are anything but spacious and the one time I went there I had to duck my head to get through the doorways." He closed the directory and dropped it back onto the table. "Is there anything else I can do for you, Inspector, Sergeant?"

"Yes, do you know where we can locate her parents?"

"They live in Brentwood, I know that much, but that's all. I never actually met them. There was no reason why I should – I wasn't going to marry the girl was I?" He smiled his non-smile again. "Perish the thought! Maybe the girl she lived with – what was her name? – Michelle - would be able to help you."

"Thanks – oh, one other thing – can you give us a description of Miss Beacham's car?"

"Yes. A Ford Fiesta. Red. About three years old. I don't remember the number plate details, I'm afraid," said Beckett. "I take it it was near the body?"

"As it happens it wasn't," Caine told him. She stood up. "One other thing, Mr Beckett, where did Miss Beacham work?"

"At the Fen Molesey branch of the Anglia bank. On the High Street." Dolby nodded silently; that was why the woman's face had been so familiar; he banked there and had probably seen her behind the counter. "I'm not that sure what she did there, banks and money on the whole don't interest me." He eased himself up out of the armchair and led the way to the door of the room. "If I can be of any further assistance, Inspector, Sergeant, don't hesitate to give me a call." He opened the door and ushered them out into the hallway.

"I wouldn't trust that man as far as I could throw him," said Dolby as they got into the car afterwards. "And considering the size of him that's not far." He turned the key in the ignition.

"I can't say I exactly took to him myself," said Caine. "I felt as though he was hiding something."

"I'll get someone to check his alibi as soon as we get back to the station. Better still…" he pulled his mobile phone from his pocket, "I'll get Wendy to do the honours now." He dialled and spoke into the phone for a few moments before leaving it on standby and slipping it back into his pocket. "Where to now, Chief?" He reached down to switch on the car's heating system.

"The place they found Kelly Beacham's body. I'd like to walk over the ground a bit, get to grips with the layout."

"The SOCO boys'll still be there I should think. They've got a very large area to search."

Caine loosened the top two buttons of her coat as she felt the blast of warm air from the heater. "Didn't think much of Beckett, did you?"

"Don't tell me you liked him, Jacky! What a ponce with his black suit and his almost black shirt! Do you think he dies his hair?" Dolby steered the car out onto the B road towards Upton Eccles.

"If he does it's very well done. There was just a hint of grey, even red on his sideburns, but you'd hardly notice."

He changed gear. "And what about all this occult stuff? Is he really into all that?"

Caine shrugged. "Apparently. I'm totally ignorant of the subject myself, except it seems our good citizens can do exactly as they like so far as religious practices are concerned. Belonging to a coven and worshipping Satan isn't illegal per se and frankly I'm only interested in that particular aspect of Mr Beckett if it's relevant to the murder."

Dolby nodded thoughtfully. "What with dear old Mrs Hartnell we seem to be getting more than our fair share of weirdoes in these cases."

Kelly Beacham's body had been found not far from a pathway near the entrance to the public woods, which were no more than a hundred and fifty yards along the road from Beckett's house. Dolby slowed the car to make the left turn into the parking area, the limits of which were marked off by police barrier tape. There were three other Fen Molesey Constabulary cars parked to one side and he pulled over to join them, waving his hand at the uniformed constable who stood on duty at the edge of the meadow that lay beyond the parking area. Beyond him, amongst the trees, they caught an occasional glimpse of some of the officers busily combing the area for clues, the yellow and blue of their Day-Glo jackets bright against the dark background of branches and tree trunks.

The sun had been well up for over two hours and Caine felt its weak, wintry warmth as she climbed out of the car and set her feet – sensibly and comfortably housed in wedge heeled boots - down on the muddy surface. It had been churned up by the tyres of the many vehicles coming and going during the course of the morning and the gravel

360

laid down as a poor attempt to improve the surface and make the area into a more serviceable car park had had little effect other than to cause the recent rain to gather in inch deep puddles. She tried to avoid them as she and Dolby made their way towards the pathway.

"Have we got a statement from the man who found the body?"

Dolby nodded. "Yes. I saw him earlier on while I was waiting for you to arrive. It seems he was out walking his dog when he spotted her. This is a favourite haunt for dog walkers. The woods aren't vast, but they make a pleasant walk for anybody who doesn't want to overdo the rambling bit." He looked around him at the tall beech trees, set some way back, denuded of foliage and standing gaunt against the bright winter sky. They joined the path that crossed over the meadow. "People come here in the summer for picnics and things, though it beats me why. There's no view. Lorna and I like to have a view when we go for a picnic."

They came abreast of the policeman standing guard over the entrance to the marked off area and nodded to him.

"Morning, Simpson," said Dolby. "Had any visitors?"

PC Simpson stamped his feet against the cold and walked across to them, blowing on his hands. "Morning, Inspector, Sarge, nothing much, just a couple of people wanting to walk their dogs. They weren't too happy when I told them we're off bounds here, at least until our men have finished searching the area." He frowned; a seasoned beat man, in his early thirties, and shook his head sadly. "Of course, as soon as they realised what was going on they took it very reasonably and sloped off to find somewhere else to walk their pooches – either that or they rushed off home to be the first with the gruesome news." He paused. "Oh, by the way, Ma'am, DS Whitlow – he's in charge of the search here – he asked me to tell you they've found the woman's car."

"Where?"

"A few hundred yards up the road, Ma'am, not far from the school entrance. Looks like it was abandoned. The SOCO team are on their way."

"Thanks, we'll take a look at it later."

Simpson looked at Dolby. "Excuse me asking, Sergeant, but is there any news on the missing girl? Emma Atterwood? Only we were told to look out for any signs of her here, you know, while we were searching…"

Dolby frowned and shook his head. "Nothing. There's been no sign of her – of course this little lot hasn't made anybody feel any better about it."

"Who did you say was in charge of the search?" asked Caine.

"DS Whitlow, ma'am."

"Okay, sorry – I don't think I've heard the name before."

"He's been loaned from Chelmsford, I believe, ma'am," Simpson explained. "He and the lads are out there amongst the trees, mostly over in that direction." Simpson waved his arm vaguely towards the trees. "They're working their way through the woods on either side of the track."

They followed the track across the meadow stepping in the muddy ridges kicked up by a host of boots and horses' hooves until they reached the marked off area in which Kelly Beacham's body had been found. Apart from the fact that the body had been removed it looked much the same as it had when they had been there earlier, a bleak grassy knoll at the edge of the earthen pathway that, a few feet further on, snaked away into the woods. Caine squatted on her haunches and ran her eyes over the small area of grass that had been flattened by Kelly Beacham's body.

"He didn't try to hide her, did he Mark?"

Dolby squatted down beside her. "No." He continued her line of thought. "And there was no struggle either – apart from the small areas that our guys have flattened down with their size twelve boots and where they laid the stretcher while they loaded the body onto it of course, there's no sign of the ground being disturbed."

"So, she was probably not actually murdered here – she was killed somewhere else and her body was carried here afterwards. Whoever left it here was fully prepared for it to be discovered."

"That doesn't make sense though, does it," said Dolby. "Why carry her all the way here if you're not going to bother to cover her up? She might as well have been left where she was killed."

"Yes, curious." Caine stood up. "It may not have been intentional though, leaving her here in full view. Perhaps the killer panicked – someone may have been coming, or he thought he heard someone coming so he just dropped her body here and ran off." She walked slowly up the path towards the trees. "She was hardly off the path at all, it was obvious that anybody walking along here would see her, especially a dog walker – the little critters have a habit of fishing bodies out of the ground and they couldn't have missed this one." She looked around the marked off area. "With the way all this mud's been churned up there's no chance we'll get any decent footprints. I wonder if they've found anything more interesting further away."

Dolby followed her as she moved slowly along the path and into the woods. Now, on either side of them, they could see the other police officers moving steadily between the trees, peering down at the ground, their eyes searching the undergrowth.

"There's Paul Whitlow," said Dolby, pointing through the trees at the figure of a stocky man bent almost double as he peered at the ground before him. "He used to be with F M before he transferred to Chelmsford. Bit of an awkward customer as I recall, always gives you the impression he's got a giant chip on his shoulder, but he's basically an honest cop." They moved towards the figure amongst the trees. "'Morning, Paul," he called, "found anything we can use yet?" They made their way across to him.

The Sergeant straightened up at Dolby's voice and rubbed the small of his back. He was short for a policeman, probably less than five feet seven inches, but heavily built, a man who looked as though he could look after himself in a fight. There was a livid scar running down the left side of his face. He scowled and shook his head dolefully. "No, anyway, it's my guess the killer didn't come this way at all. He was probably disturbed and beat it straight back to his car."

"Maybe," said Caine. "DCI Jacqueline Caine." They shook hands. "I understand the woman's car was abandoned on the road a few hundred yards up."

Whitlow nodded. "Dunno if abandoned is the right word. Found by an AA patrolman would be more accurate. Red Ford Fiesta. Ran out of petrol. Now, if you don't mind – it's bloody cold out here and I would like to get on with this search."

Caine worked her way around a blackberry bush and kicked away the fronds of a long bramble that was trying to attach itself to her leather boots. Her eye was caught by wispy strands of dark blue amongst the white of the slowly melting hoar frost still clinging to the thin branches and she stopped to reach out towards the top section of the bush. "What's this?"

Whitlow came quickly across. "Oh, that's nothing. I've seen two or three similar bits on the bushes hereabouts. They're just bits of material snagged off people's clothes while they were berry picking. You get a lot of berry pickers in this neck of the woods."

"Not at this time of the year, though," retorted Dolby. "You're talking August and September, Paul, not December!"

"Precisely my point," said Whitlow. "Those bits must be months old. They're not worth worrying about."

"But we don't know that for certain, do we Sergeant?" Caine pointed out icily. "For all we know one or two of them might have snagged off somebody's clothes much more recently – last night for instance - and until we know one way or the other we should treat them as potentially interesting." She looked Whitlow straight in the eye and he looked away. "I think you'd better gather them up and put them into evidence bags, Sergeant, don't you - and tell your team to do the same."

"But I tell you it's a waste of time, Ma'am!" said Whitlow. "I've seen this stuff before. People wear jumpers and the wool or whatever fibres they are get snagged on the bushes. Happens all the time in the berry picking season and you can tell the stuff here's months old – the weather's been at it, you can see that for yourself."

"Me? I wouldn't know the difference between last night's snagged wool and stuff that was left here six months ago," said Caine, keeping her voice quiet. "And I don't think you would either, Sergeant, much as you think you would. So, why don't you just humour me and put the stuff in your little paper bags for analysis by the forensic experts, there's a good chap."

Whitlow was about to reply when one of the other searchers, about thirty yards away and closer to the fence that separated the public woods from those belonging to Upton Grange School, shouted across to him. "I think I've got the handbag, Sarge."

Made of fine black leather and displaying the logo of an expensive designer brand on its side, it lay against a thick clump of brambles about fifteen feet in from the track through the woods.

"That's hers all right," said the policeman who had found it. He stood a few feet away from the bag, looking down at it intently. "I know that logo, it's a **Santu**, same as the blouse she was wearing."

"How come you know about blouses and handbags then, Dickie?" asked Whitlow as the three other officers came towards him. "Dickie Bird, ma'am," he said, by way of introduction. "You may have seen him around. Seems he's an expert on ladies' clothes." He sniggered. "You may want to ask his advice sometime, Ma'am!"

PC Bird blushed. "Don't be like that, Sarge. I know cos my missus is always on about that stuff. Not that she can afford it, mind, not on her wages, but she's said that's what she'd like if she could afford it." He leaned forward to take a closer look. "It's bloody good leather, actually."

Dolby moved up beside him and pulled on his gloves.

370

"Don't move it, yet, Mark," said Caine. "By the way, that's good observation on your part, PC Bird – Dickie – not many men would've known that particular logo. Well done." She leaned forward to study the handbag and then turned and looked around her. They were in a small clearing and there were small saplings and bramble bushes - some of them well over six feet high - all around them. "Notice anything about the position of the bag, Sergeant Whitlow?"

The short, stocky man shook his head. "It's been chucked away and this is where it landed," he said. "What else is there to say?"

Dolby and Bird looked around them, turning slowly on the balls of their feet.

"I see what you mean, Ma'am," said Dolby. "We can't see the path from here and the bag's up against this piece of bush, facing away from the path." He walked towards the wire fence that marked the woods they were in from those belonging to the school. It was only a few yards away. "The bush is pretty big –well over six feet high – so it's extremely unlikely it could have been thrown from the path, unless whoever threw it chucked it really high, in which case it probably wouldn't have lodged up against the bush like this," he turned back towards the handbag, "it's caught in the brambles a good eight to ten inches from the ground – but if it had been thrown from the path it probably would have bounced off the bush and come to rest on the ground."

The others nodded, Whitlow without enthusiasm.

"That means it was probably chucked over the fence from the school side," said Bird.

"Precisely," said Caine. "I think we'll probably have to try a few experiments ourselves, just to see whether the theory holds water, but the chances are you're right. Whoever threw the bag away was probably on the other side of the fence, on school property."

"We don't know for sure though, do we," said Whitlow, frowning. "And we won't really know even if we experiment and the bag lands in the same place every time we chuck it over the fence. I can't see the point."

372

"The point is," said Dolby, with an exasperated glance at Caine, "that if we can establish that it was probably thrown over the fence from the school side then whoever threw it must have been on that side, in the school grounds. It narrows things down a bit."

"Yes, well, I suppose it might," admitted the Sergeant grudgingly, "but maybe before we start all this experimentation you're so keen on we should make sure that *is* the woman's bag and not something just left here by some other bint having it off in the woods with her boyfriend."

"What? In this weather, Sarge?" said Bird. "You've got to be joking."

Dolby picked up the bag and unzipped the centre section, slipping his gloved hand inside and removing a black leather credit card holder. He flipped it open and read the details on the first card. "Yes, it's Kelly Beacham's, not that there was much doubt." He dropped the credit card holder back into the bag and removed a leather purse fat with bank notes. "Look at this little lot. I think we can rule

373

out robbery as the motive." He unzipped the other compartments and peered quickly into them. "Nothing much else of any interest."

"What? No mobile 'phone?" said Whitlow dryly. "I thought they were compulsory for anyone under the age of thirty. It's like they were born with the ruddy things – like bloody appendages!"

CHAPTER THIRTEEN

The red Ford Fiesta had been pulled off the road on to the grass verge beside the busy B road and now it was flanked front and back by two police cars, their blue lights flashing. Dolby pulled in behind them and set the hazard lights before carefully checking the road behind and opening his door. Caine stepped out onto the dew-wet grass on the passenger side and walked towards the Fiesta. Its doors were open and two police officers were kneeling down beside them, the top halves of their bodies out of view inside the car. A third officer stood by the bonnet watching. He nodded his recognition and walked slowly towards them.

"You almost missed us, Ma'am, DS Dolby. The truck should be along at any moment now to take it back to the station for a good going over by forensics."

As he spoke one of the other officers pulled his head from underneath the steering column of the little car and straightened up. Caine recognised Sergeant Edward Briggs from the fingerprint division. He nodded and came over.

"Good morning, Eddie. Anything significant?"

He shook his head. "It's hard to say, Ma'am. Plenty of the girl's prints, of course – at least I imagine they're hers, I just need to double check on that." His quick, intelligent eyes twinkled behind the thick lenses of his spectacles. "And there's a couple of dabs on the outside door handle. I don't think they match the girl's though."

"You think someone pulled her car door open?" asked Caine.

"Could be," replied Briggs. "I'll be able to do a better guessing job when we get the car under cover."

"Any signs of violence?"

"No. Nothing obvious. We'll be able to tell for certain after we've got it back to the station and given it a thorough going over."

Caine walked slowly to the rear of the car, her eyes searching the grass verge and the edge of the road. "Did somebody check for tyre marks? Other vehicle's tyre marks?"

Briggs nodded. "Oh yes, we've got that covered. A second car did pull up behind her." He pointed to a line of tyre marks on the muddy verge. "The photo boys have taken a couple of dozen shots of them, and Marty back there – the guy with his head under the Fiesta's passenger seat - has a plaster cast that would do well in the Tate Modern. If we can find the car we'll match the tyres okay, no sweat. Oh, and there were some other tyre marks as well – they'll almost certainly be from the AA man's vehicle. We'll have to double check that to eliminate them."

Caine nodded thoughtfully. "Good. What do you think, Mark?"

"There's a definite pattern emerging. Kelly leaves her lover's house and sets out for home, but she's forgotten to fill up her petrol tank – Beckett said she had trouble starting – and she only gets a few hundred yards before she

377

runs out of fuel. She stops here and is just wondering what to do when a nice friendly passer-by passes by. She thinks he's a knight of the road come to rescue her in her hour of need and he offers her a lift to the nearest garage to pick up some petrol. She goes with him and instead of a knight he turns out to be a sexual deviant. He rapes her, kills her and dumps her body. How does that sound?"

"Gruesome," said Caine, "but probably close to the truth, although we don't yet know if Kelly Beacham *was* actually raped." A huge truck rumbled by on the road and she rebuttoned her coat against the resulting slipstream. "I know I should know this; I was there only a couple of days ago, but how far away from here is the school entrance?"

"Upton Grange? No more than a hundred yards I'd say," said Dolby, "if that. The entrance to the drive is just around the next bend."

Caine nodded thoughtfully. "Right. We need to get somebody up there right away to see if anyone saw anything suspicious last night. People hanging around, that sort of thing. Catch them while it's still fresh in their

378

minds. But I was also thinking that a few words with Kelly Beacham's flatmate – the one Beckett mentioned – could be useful. They lived up at Upton Eccles, but she's probably at work and that probably means going back into town."

"Well, there's no point in both of us going up to the school," said Dolby. "How about if I go see them while you hitch a lift back into town with Eddie here? Okay by you, Eddie?"

"No problem so far as I'm concerned. Do you think there's a connection with the school then?"

"Possibly," said Caine, "We already have the distinct probability that Kelly's handbag was thrown into the woods from the school side, which implies the killer went into the school grounds afterwards."

"Why should he do that?"

"Because he lives there," suggested Dolby. "Although dumping it there was hardly calculated to throw us off the scent, was it? Which, I must admit, worries me a bit."

Briggs groaned. "Don't tell me I'm going to have to fingerprint the whole ruddy school. Three hundred rich, over privileged brats plus a horde of schoolteachers – we'll have dozens of top lawyers from London all over us for weeks claiming harassment and police brutality against minors!"

"They're not **all** rich," said Dolby. "Some of the kids get there on scholarships."

"Don't blind me with statistics, Mark. They may not all be gold plated plutocrats, but they're stuck-up little snobs none the less. We'll be up to our noses in red tape."

"There's no need to panic, Eddie," Caine assured the fingerprint specialist, "it won't come to that. There are various categories of brat we can ignore, at least for the time being – some of them would be unlikely to have attacked Kelly Beacham – the girls for starters. But we may eventually have to check on all the male staff and senior boys. We'll just have to see what our inquiries throw up in the next day or so, that's all."

"Well, I'm going to need help anyway I should think," Briggs said gloomily. "You know what the staffing situation's like at Fen Molesey at the moment, what with this ruddy virus epidemic. I'll be lucky to get a dinner lady from the station canteen. I'll be on it for weeks!" he glanced towards his car. "Well, if you're fit Ma'am, I'm just about done here for the time being - I'll pick up where I left off when the car gets back to the station."

Michelle Cooke was Assistant Person Friday for Wyngarde Serviced Offices, situated in Wyngarde Place, a recently refurbished office block at the rear of the Sainsburys store's car park off Fen Molesey High Street. DC Wendy Doyle had first traced Ms Cooke's identity via a telephone call to the department of the local council looking after the electoral register; and then her whereabouts by means of a radioed message to a police squad car, which happened to be in the Upton Eccles area. The officers in the car stopped off at the block of flats formerly occupied by the murdered Kelly Beacham and made inquiries of the neighbours as to the location of her flatmate, Michelle Cooke. They had been unusually lucky in finding a well-informed neighbour who not only knew the two young women by sight and sound, but also was on extremely good terms with them. She, Mrs Lebus, an elderly widow, after a gruelling search through her memory, had directed the officers to Wyngarde Serviced Offices, through whose glass and aluminium entrance doors Detective Chief Inspector Jacqueline Caine was to pass less than two hours later.

Inside was a lobby leading off, on the right, to a flight of stairs and on the left to a glass entrance door leading to the main offices. On the wall beside the door was a large board showing the names of the businesses for which Wyngarde provided office services. Caine paused to study it, having found in the past that inspiration sometimes came from the most unlikely quarters. There were more than a dozen names listed alphabetically from "A" for Access Accountancy through "H" for T.Hickman Garden Services to "Y" for Young's The Electricians, but no "Z". Providing

382

serviced offices for small businesses was, she decided, a prosperous sector in which to be. She pushed open the door marked "Wyngarde" and walked through into the reception area.

She was greeted by a middle-aged woman with dyed hair and short legs, the upper reaches of which were thrust into open view by the abruptness of her skirt and the tallness of the stool upon which her buttocks were firmly placed. She was sitting behind a low beech wooden counter, a telephone switchboard on her left side and a computer console on her right. She smiled widely at Caine's approach across the polished wooden floor, cracking the layers of makeup encrusting her face and bidding her visitor a hearty welcome.

"Hello. I'm Vanessa. What can we do for you, dear? Do you have an appointment? We don't see representatives without an appointment. Mr Diggs is very hot on appointments, dearie, so you can't get in to see him without one, I'm afraid. He's a very busy man, is our Mr Diggs, he's got Serviced offices in Chelmsford too you know *and*

Colchester *and* Ipswich and he's negotiating at this very moment – I put the call through to him only a couple of minutes ago – for a whole new operation in Cambridge…"

Caine flashed her warrant card and uttered the words usually calculated to silence the orally verbose, "Police. DCI Caine, Fen Molesey CID."

Vanessa was unflustered. She plunged on, not even changing verbal gear. "Oh, if you'd said so before I would have known, wouldn't I? It's no good springing a surprise like that on a girl, is it? If I had known then I could have asked Mr D. if he could see you without an appointment, as a special favour like, but now he's on the telephone on this very important call and I really can't disturb him. More than my job's worth that'd be, to disturb him, I mean…"

"I don't want to see your Mr Diggs, thank you, however important he might be," said Caine, in a desperate attempt to stem the flow. "I believe you have a young lady by the name of Michelle Cooke working here?"

"Oh, you want 'Chelle do you? Why didn't you say so? If you'd like to wait over there on one of them chairs,

I'll call her for you." She indicated one of the two black imitation leather armchairs placed strategically between the glass and aluminium doors and the freshwater dispenser and turned to shout along the narrow corridor behind her. "'Chelle, there's a Police Lady to see you!"

Michelle Cooke emerged from the corridor a few minutes later, the leather of her shoes clattering loudly on the hard wooden floor. A small woman with short dark hair, wide framed spectacles and a worried frown she looked older than her twenty-three years. She wore a white satin blouse and a long black skirt with a short split up the side.

Caine rose to meet her. "Miss Cooke? I'm DCI Jacqueline Caine, Fen Molesey CID. I wonder if I might have a few words with you?" She looked across at the elderly Vanessa, "In private?"

Michelle Cooke, flustered and more than likely a little scared, nodded, looked around her and finally beckoned for Caine to follow her. "Yes, we can use my room." Caine wondered momentarily why she did not refer to it as her 'office' and then realised, as they emerged into a large chamber at the end of the corridor, that it was indeed a 'room' rather than an 'office'. Measuring about twenty feet by fifteen it was chock full of filing cabinets, tall shelving units stacked with unopened boxes of paper, a coffee and tea machine, a single desk with a computer on top, a series of printers, a photocopying machine, a small table housing a postal franking machine and a coat stand burdened down with at least a dozen coats, hats and umbrellas. Miss Cooke went behind her desk and sat down indicating a straight-backed chair to one side of her. "Please sit down, Inspector." She indicated the tea and coffee-making machine. "Can I get you something to drink?"

Caine was about to shake her head and then remembered she hadn't had a drink since breakfast, which had been some hours before. "Yes please, coffee, no milk or sugar."

"Good, I'll have one as well, I think." It was also a good idea in that a coffee might help to calm Michelle's nerves.

Her hands were shaking as she made the coffee and brought the two polystyrene cups back to the desk. "Excuse the plastic cups, Inspector, only we don't have proper china except for Mr Diggs' special guests and, of course, if any of our clients have special people to see them then they ask me to get out the proper stuff for them."

Caine took one of the cups from her. "What do you do here, Miss Cooke?"

"What, me myself, or do you mean Wyngarde's Serviced Offices?" She went on without waiting for an answer. "Well, Wyngarde's hires out office space to small firms on a short-term basis, you know, like three months at a time, even a month in some cases, it's useful for small firms who can't afford to pay much up front, like for instance when they're just starting up. Then me and Vanessa, we provide them with secretarial services, typing and word processing, sending e-mails, booking hotels and travel tickets for them, that sort of thing." She stopped to sip her coffee and then asked, "What do you want with me, Inspector? Is there something wrong at home?"

Caine wasn't sure whether Michelle was referring to the flat in Luckett's Grove, Upton Eccles which she had shared with the unfortunate Kelly Beacham or to what she probably regarded as her proper home, that of her parents or family-home someplace else, and so she did not answer the question directly. "I believe you rent a flat in Luckett's Towers, Luckett's Grove, Miss Cooke?" Michelle nodded. "And your flatmate is a Miss Kelly Beacham?"

"Has something happened to Kelly?" Her eyes clouded over and she blinked back tears, removing her glasses to wipe her eyes.

"I'm afraid so. Her body was found in Upton Woods this morning. She's been murdered. I'm extremely sorry to have to bring you this news." There was no easy way to say it. There never was. Getting it out quickly, in simple unambiguous terms, with no possibility of a misunderstanding was usually the best course.

They had left the door to Michelle's office room open when they came in and now the older woman, Vanessa, appeared in the doorway, whether innocently, to charge with coffee or tea the ceramic mug she was carrying, or because she was curious to know why a Police Inspector had turned up and asked for her colleague, Caine did not know or care. She was useful now, when the inevitable flow of tears came flooding down the cheeks of the younger woman and was immediately at her side with a box of tissues procured from out of nowhere.

Caine waited, drinking her coffee, while the young woman, comforted by the older, composed herself. "I hope you don't mind, Michelle, but if you are able I would like to ask you a few questions. It is important that we find out as much about Kelly as we possibly can." She took out her notebook and pen and sat waiting patiently. Michelle Cooke was probably the person who knew most about the murdered woman's personal life. It was important not to hurry things.

Michelle nodded, using a tissue to wipe away a tear. Vanessa, having completed her ministrations, had deposited herself on the edge of the younger woman's desk, crossing her legs beneath her short skirt. She watched the proceedings eagerly, listening, and Caine had no doubt she would join in with the subsequent dialogue; not a bad thing if, as Caine strongly suspected, she was privy to much of the goings-on of Miss Cooke's private life.

"Have you known Kelly Beacham for long?"

Michelle nodded, sipped her coffee and began to speak, slowly at first, but then with increasing rapidity as though she wanted to get the interview over as quickly as possible so she could go away somewhere to cry in private. "Over a year. I'd just got this job here and I was looking for a place to live locally. I'd been with my parents up till then, up in Ipswich and I was looking for a job and I applied to Mr Diggs through the Ipswich office and was travelling down by train every day and then Vanessa here she said she'd put me up for a few weeks to make it easier for me and then she invited me to go along with her to a

390

party and I met Kelly and got talking to her, her flatmate was leaving so I said where was it and could I take over the room…and that's how I got to know her…"

Unbidden Vanessa took up the story. "Oh yes, Kelly and me go back a long way one way or another. She was your real party girl she was, couldn't keep her down you couldn't, she was a real laugh, life and soul of any party. I suppose that's why old Marcus – he's her lover as at the moment - took up with her, he likes them uninhibited and full of life and of course Kelly's a real looker – sorry! – I should say she *was* a real looker." She stopped momentarily to draw breath.

Caine slipped into the gap. "You said 'Marcus' – that wouldn't be Marcus Beckett would it? The antiques dealer with a place out on the Upton road?"

"Yes, it would – do you know him?"

"We have met." Caine smiled to herself. Her hunch about Vanessa being a useful source of information on the murdered woman's background was paying off. Curious, though, how all events during the past few days seemed to centre on the area of the Upton Grange School and the exotic Mr Beckett. "He took up with Kelly did he?" She asked, feigning surprise.

"Oh yes," said Vanessa emphatically, "well, she was the sort of girl he'd always be looking out for, wasn't she, someone intelligent – she was that you had to give it to her – she was a girl who kept her mind and her legs wide open, if you get my meaning…" Her words trailed away as though she suddenly realised she might be saying more than she should. She was, after all, talking to a Police Inspector and how much of his private life with young Kelly would Marcus Beckett want her to divulge to the Police?

"She was a member of his coven, of course," said Caine, egging her on.

"You know about that do you?" Vanessa looked relieved. Thinking perhaps that she may not, after all, have let slip anything not already known to the police. "Well, yes, she was I think, not that I know much about that sort of thing, you know, it was just something she let slip once in a while, talking about what they – the members – got up to at their sort of 'meetings' or whatever you'd like to call them."

Michelle Cooke broke into the conversation again. "It was disgusting the things that went on…and bad – I mean sort of *evil.* I think they were worshipping the *devil* – can you believe that sort of thing goes on nowadays? I wouldn't have. I only went once, to this gathering Mr Beckett was holding down at Maldon, he's got a big boat moored there. It was in the summer. I went with Kelly, of course, she asked me if I'd like to and I said I would because I didn't know what went on, and we had a row about it afterwards, but I wouldn't go again…no way! I couldn't stand that man Beckett - he's…weird! Really weird!"

"Kelly went to his 'parties' though, she went regularly?" asked Caine her eyes on Michelle but watching Vanessa who was at the edge of her vision. The older woman was looking distinctly uncomfortable at the line of questioning. Michelle nodded. "These activities that were going on at Beckett's 'parties' – were they of a sexual nature?"

Michelle nodded again. "Kelly said she didn't care." Her voice lowered and she blushed and looked down at her desk, picked up a paper clip and began to twist it between her fingers. "I don't want to speak ill of her, not after…after what's happened to her, but I think Kelly was over-sexed. She couldn't get enough of it if you ask me, the kinkier the better. She used to tell me about it, what went on…" she paused, looked up appealingly, "I don't have to tell you what she said do I? I don't think I can…it wasn't nice what went on at his so called 'parties'."

"No, you needn't tell me, Michelle. I daresay if I need to know the details I can get them from somebody else." Caine looked meaningfully across at Vanessa who scowled and turned her head away. "We already know that Kelly was having an affair with Beckett, he admitted it quite openly, but perhaps you could help us fill in some of the other details on her life. I believe she worked for Anglian Bank?"

"Yes," said Michelle eagerly, "at the branch on the High Street." She seemed pleased that the subject of Marcus Beckett's activities had been dropped for the time being. "She was a Junior Manager there I think, in charge of some special accounts she told me. It was quite a big job, but she was very clever."

"Well paid I suppose?"

"Yes, I think so. She didn't talk much about her job, but she always had plenty of money."

"He was generous with her too, Marcus Beckett was," volunteered Vanessa. "I saw him give her some money once, a great fat wad of notes. Twenties and fifties. They thought no-one knew, it was on the sly like, but I saw it alright."

The telephone on Michelle Cooke's desk rang. "Sorry, I'll keep it short," said Vanessa with a nod of apology to Caine. She picked up the receiver, "Hello, Wyngarde Serviced Offices…Hello Mr Hickman…"

Caine tried to ignore the interruption. "Did Kelly ever tell you why Marcus Beckett was giving her money, Michelle?"

Michelle shook her head. "No. We never discussed it," she replied thoughtfully. Then she nodded slowly as though the whole matter suddenly had become clear to her. "I see it now, though," she giggled nervously. "I suppose I'm a bit naïve. Beckett was her sugar daddy. He paid her for doing what they did together." She blushed. "That's how she could afford all those designer clothes. Her wardrobe's full of them. She was always out buying clothes. She'd pass some of them on to me when she got fed up with them."

Vanessa finished her conversation and put the telephone down. "Sorry about that, Inspector, business call you know, we do have to keep the business running no matter what. Would you mind if I just pass this message on to Michelle?" Caine sighed and waved her on. "Sorry. Michelle that was Mr Hickman again. You know how he's been going on about his young mate Trevor not turning up for work since Monday, well he's decided he's going to give him the push, so he asks would you put a new advert in the paper for an apprentice gardener to replace him."

"I'm not surprised," said Michelle with an apologetic smile at Caine. "That Trevor was useless as far as I could see."

"You're right there," said Vanessa. "He was a right one he was. All he was interested in was the girls – tried to get a couple of goes at you as I recall, 'Chelle." She giggled like a young schoolgirl. "Even tried flirting with me a couple of times, but I soon told him where to get off. Can't trust a guy like that, anyway, they never settle, they're always off *somewhere*."

Caine sighed again. "When you're quite ready to continue with the questions, Ladies?" The two women smiled their apologies. "Thank you. Now, Michelle, when did you last see Kelly?"

"Yesterday evening after work," she twisted the paper clip savagely between her fingers. "She used to run me home in her car in the evenings, most evenings, when

397

she wasn't going straight out from work. We'd come in to town in the mornings together as well."

"Did she go out again yesterday after you got home?"

"Oh yes, we got back at just after six and she had a shower and went out. I think she was going to see *him*."

Caine made a note in her book. "Were you concerned when she didn't come back?"

"No. She often stayed with him overnight. To be truthful I didn't really want to know too much about what she did with him. I liked her, I liked Kelly, but I couldn't see what she saw in Marcus Beckett – what with the way he dresses, all in black like some creature from a horror film - he wasn't even in her age group - and if we talked about him it usually developed into a row, so we avoided the subject." Michelle paused and frowned. "I wasn't concerned she didn't come home last night, but…"

"Yes…?"

"I don't know. I just thought I saw her car at the side of the Upton road this morning, from the bus and I

398

wondered how it got there and should I tell someone, but then I thought maybe it wasn't her car, but somebody else's. I didn't have time to check the registration number." She paused again. "You said they found her in Upton Woods – it *was* her car wasn't it!"

Caine nodded. "Yes, it was. Apparently, she ran out of petrol on her way home from Beckett's house. I'm sorry." She finished her coffee and put the empty cup down on the desk. "And you didn't see her again after she left to go out?"

Michelle shook her head. "No, but when I saw her car this morning it reminded me about the phone call."

"What phone call?"

"There was a phone call at the flat last night at about a quarter to ten. The phone rang, but when I answered there was no one there, just someone playing loud, pop music. I didn't like it, it was too noisy, not at all my kind of music."

"Nothing else, just loud music?"

She seemed uncertain. "I couldn't hear anything clearly, but I think there were faint voices, sort of a long

399

way away. I thought it was a wrong number so I hung up and forgot all about it."

"Until you saw the car this morning. What did you think then – why did it remind you of the phone call?"

"We've got one of those phones at the flat that tell you who's ringing. I didn't really notice at the time, when the call came in, but when I thought about it this morning I thought it was Kelly's mobile number."

"You know her mobile number?"

The girl shrugged. "Sort of. I've got it written down, just in case. It starts with 079…I think; it's miles long like all of them. Anyway, I thought I recognised it."

"And your phone doesn't show the name of the person ringing you?"

"No – only the number. It's a bit old fashioned."

"But you think Kelly tried to ring you at quarter to ten last night?"

"About that time, but as I say because she didn't say anything and all there was was this horrible music I thought it was a wrong number and I hung up. Oh no!" She groaned suddenly and wrung her hands together, "You don't think she was being attacked when she rang me do you? To call for help?" She began to weep again. Vanessa put her arm around her comfortingly and pushed a tissue into her hand. "Poor Kelly! She was being raped and murdered and I just ignored her call for help!"

"You weren't to know," said Caine. "It wasn't your fault."

With a visible effort Michelle pulled herself together and smiled weakly. "Is there anything else I can tell you, Inspector?"

"The music you heard over the telephone, do you know what it was?"

She shook her head. "No. It was pop of some sort, but I'm not very keen on the latest stuff. It's just thump thump thump isn't it? I prefer proper music."

"Quite right" said Vanessa who had remained silent for some time now, listening intently, no doubt looking forward to relaying the conversation word for word to anyone who cared to listen to her. "They don't know how to write decent songs anymore. Give me Abba or George Michael any time over this latest lot!"

"But you might recognise it, Michelle, if you heard it again?"

The young woman shrugged. "I might. Do you have any idea who might have been playing that music then?"

It was Caine's turn to shrug. "It could have been anybody, I'm afraid." She sighed and yawned. "Excuse me, it's been a hard few days." She stood up. "Is there anything else about Kelly Beacham that you think might be helpful? We know she was having an affair with Beckett, but did she have any other friends?"

"When I first knew her she did have another boy friend," said Michelle, "What was his name? Simon I think it was, I did meet him briefly – he was very nice, quite dishy."

"What happened to him? I suppose Kelly broke it off when Beckett started to take an interest in her?"

"Oh no - Simon died a couple of weeks after I moved in with Kelly. It was very tragic. She was really upset."

402

"Tragic? How did he die then?"

"He took an overdose," said Vanessa, interjecting quickly. "Committed suicide, silly young buggar."

"No, it wasn't that sort of overdose," said Michelle hotly. "Not medicines or anything like that. The inquest decided he died from a drugs overdose - heroin I think they said. It wasn't pure or something and he took much more than he should have. Funny thing was, he wasn't an addict. He used to smoke a bit of coke, but nobody knew why he took that filthy stuff. It was all in the newspapers, Inspector, maybe you remember it."

Caine shook her head. "Sorry, I wasn't working in Fen Molesey at the time. Did Kelly have any other friends? What did she do in her spare time, apart of course from her occult dabblings?"

"She was a member of a choir," said Michelle. "And she went to rehearsals once a week, on a Thursday, most weeks. I know she was a bit of a raver at parties and things and she didn't care what she got up to, but she was quite keen on classical music and singing and things like that.

403

Poetry too. She used to sit and read poetry books some evenings when she didn't go out. I think she wrote some as well, you know, she was a complicated person and really clever."

"You say she belonged to a choir? Do you know the name?"

Michelle shook her head. "No. I don't know the actual name, but it was something to do with the Upton Grange School."

Caine leaned forward, her interest quickening. Here it was again, that connection with the school. "What on earth did Kelly have to do with Upton Grange School?"

"She was an Old Girl," said Vanessa. "She went there as a day pupil. Won a scholarship there she did. She might have been a bit mad and peculiar and stuff, and not at all fussy whose bed she put her body into, but she *was* bright. She got a good education at Upton in those days and from there she went on to University." She sighed. "Now it's all been wasted, of course, but you could see it coming if you knew where to look."

404

Caine wondered where the woman got her information but decided not to press the matter. "And she had friends at this choir? Old school friends?"

"I suppose so," said Michelle. "She didn't talk about it much. She played the music and practiced her parts quite a lot in the flat and sometimes in the car – she had a good voice, actually - but she didn't talk very much about the people in the choir. I don't think she had any special friends there."

"There is someone who would have liked to have been," said Vanessa with a leer. "That guy that runs the choir, Deputy Head of the School he is, and he teaches music, what's his name? Mainwaring or something. He was all over her, at least he would have liked to have been."

"You mean Maynard." Michelle corrected her.

Caine looked up from her note taking. "Really? Douglas Maynard? He doesn't look the type."

"Believe me they're all the type, Inspector," Vanessa assured her. "There's no man alive doesn't want to get into a good-looking girl's bed!" She laughed. "I know, you're wondering how I know all this about Mr Maynard, Inspector. Well, I'm not making it up that's for sure. Michelle and me, we've been to a couple of the Choir's concerts – not really my style, of course, but my hubby Arthur rather fancies himself with the classical stuff. He wanted to go so I went along for the ride. Anyway, during the interval when we were having a cuppa in the canteen place next door – I think they call it the refractory or something – we was having a bit of a mingle with the people from the choir, you know, like you do at those sorts of things and it was quite obvious Maynard fancied a bit from young Kelly. Fair drooling at the mouth over her he was."

"Maynard was flirting with Kelly Beacham?"

"Well, I didn't actually hear what they were saying, not in so many words I didn't, but a nod's as good as a wink as they say. You can back me up on that, can't you 'Chelle."

The younger woman shook her head. "No, Vanessa. That wasn't the way I saw it at all. He was just being nice to her. He's known Kelly for years – he was a master there when she went to the school you know – I think he was just trying to persuade her to stay away from that old creep Beckett. Leastways, that's what Kelly told me afterwards."

Vanessa laughed dryly. "It's time you grew up, dear," she said, her voice distinctly frosty, "you could see Maynard would have been all over her if he'd had half the chance!"

"You still surprise me," said Caine thoughtfully. "I always thought I was a pretty good judge of character and I've met Mr Maynard. He didn't seem that type to me."

"Well, I can only speak as I find," said Vanessa huffily.

"Will you want to go through Kelly's things? You know, at the flat?" Michelle asked, with an obvious effort to change the subject.

"Yes, I plan to send one of my officers over there as soon it's convenient, if that's okay by you. I think it might be very helpful."

"Whenever you like. I don't have anything to hide," said Michelle. "Kelly had the bigger of the two bedrooms; it's to the left off the hall as you go in. She kept all her private stuff in there. You'll need a key I suppose."

"We've got one," said Caine. "There was one in Kelly's handbag, on her key ring."

"Oh! What if the killer saw it?" said Michelle, alarmed. "What if the killer gets into the flat?"

"If he did he only *saw* it, Michelle," said Vanessa with a look of disdain. "He couldn't have had a copy made of it could he, girl? Not by looking at it - so how do you suppose he's going to get into your flat?"

The young woman blushed with confusion. "Sorry, you're right, I just thought, well, he killed Kelly and we don't know why, he might…you know."

"What? Come back and do you in as well, darling? Get real! If you ask me, you see too many blooming TV Detective movies!"

"There's not much chance of the killer having a key," said Caine tactfully, "but in case you're worried, Miss Cooke, you should get the lock changed." She stood up. "Well, if there's nothing else you can tell me, I'll be on my way." She walked towards the door of the room, manoeuvring around the photocopying machine and the heavily burdened hat stand. "If anything else occurs to either of you I can be reached at Fen Molesey Police station."

CHAPTER FOURTEEN

"So how did you get on at the school, Mark?" asked Caine as he came into her office later that afternoon. He was carrying a file and he dropped it onto her desk before sitting down wearily. "You don't look too pleased – and I hope you're not expecting me to read through that pile of paper. What is it, anyway?"

"Believe it or not it's the personal files of everyone at Upton Grange School!"

"You're joking!"

"No. Scouts' honour. Maynard insisted. I mentioned that we thought someone on the school premises had chucked the handbag into the woods and that we might need to make inquiries into some of the people at the school. He took serious umbrage at that, said I was being presumptuous, that we have it in for them because of that drug find on the school's premises."

"What's happened about that, by the way? Have they brought the two boys in – what were their names? Hill and Sullivan?"

"Yeah, but they let them go. From what I can gather Toby Wilson, the Headmaster, seems to have leaned on a few people – nothing non-kosher, apparently, but it was a first offence etcetera etcetera, so they let them out."

"Not 'off' I hope," said Caine.

"Not completely, they'll be up before the beaks again in a week or so. Anyway, Maynard takes the view that virtually **anybody** could have walked up the drive and lobbed Kelly Beacham's bag over the fence; and if we *really seriously* think the killer is one of the staff at the school, or a pupil – heaven forfend! – He was as dramatic as that! - Then we're welcome to go through this little lot. He said he had instructions from the Head to bend over backwards to help us. Said it might help repair the PR

411

damage they've been suffering after the drugs episode at the weekend. As you know, the papers have been slaughtering them. Anyway, I still don't know if he was having me on or not."

"I doubt it." Caine opened the ring binder and flicked through some of the pages. "I suppose the files on the teachers and some of the seniors might prove of some use if we get to the stage of *suspecting* any of them specifically, but I don't think we want to go through all the rest, do you?" She peered more closely at one of the pages. "Passport size photos too with every CV, very organised." She closed the file and pushed it back across the desk to Dolby. "We'll get Wendy and her team to have a look through them if need be. But what about your talk to the other people at the school? How did that go?"

"Not so bad. It could have been a lot worse. But did you realise half the kids have gone?"

"Gone where?"

"Home for Christmas. Most of the boarders." He nodded towards the calendar that hung behind her on the office wall. "It's end of term day today, believe it or not. When I arrived most of the loving mothers and quite a few of the fond fathers were there driving their delightful progeny home for the Xmas holidays. Of course, some of the senior kids drive their own cars and I met some of them going out as I came in, driving like bats out of hell they were. Looked like they couldn't get away from the place fast enough."

"That's modern school kids for you," Caine said dryly, "They don't realise how well off they are." She leaned back in her chair. "So - half of our possible eyewitnesses to the dirty deed in the wildwood are no longer there!"

"Precisely. I did what I could with the rest though. After a bit Maynard sort of resigned himself to the fact that the school might be involved – by the way, the murdered woman – he referred to her as 'girl', force of habit, I suppose – he knew her, apparently she was an Old Girl." Caine nodded. "Ah! You knew that! Anyway, Maynard organised a snap assembly in the big hall – impressive place, actually, all wood panelling and that kind of stately

home stuff – and I stood up and spouted at the remaining

kids and staff, told them what the score is and asked

anyone who thought they might have seen anything

interesting or useful last night to come forward and speak

to us."

"Any response?"

"Zilch so far I'm afraid."

Caine nodded thoughtfully. "How many kids are

there still at the school then?"

"A few of the boarders – about twenty of them so far

as I can gather," Dolby told her. "Those that have to wait a

day or so before they have somewhere to actually go home

to – a lot of the parents are abroad, of course – and the day

kids – they're all off from tomorrow. Plus, the staff are still

there. They hang about 'til the end of the week,

apparently, to mop up the necessary paperwork and do a bit

of preparation for next term. Mind you a good many of

them actually live on the premises or in the immediate

area, so there'll only be a few who'll be really difficult to get hold of after the end of the week."

"Hmm. Not good though is it, our killer may be one of those who've buggered off! And Maynard? How come he's no longer suspended from duty?"

Dolby smiled. "He is actually quite a decent sort of chap when you get to know him. He's obviously been under a lot of strain recently. Anyway, he told me the school governors had had second thoughts about his suspension – apparently, it happened when they suddenly realised they were actually paying him to sit by the riverside and fish. I had the opportunity of asking around other members of staff and it seems the school inquiry into the drug incident is still ongoing, but they seem to have reached the conclusion that Maynard wasn't to blame. Apparently, their thinking at the moment is that Toby Walters, the head, is the more culpable on account of the fact he had a perfectly good anti-drugs policy – drawn up by Maynard incidentally – but he didn't want it implemented in case it gave the school a bad name, if you can believe such rot."

"Good. What about statements from the staff?"

"You mean alibis for last night?" Dolby folded his arms across his chest. "I've got a couple of people working on it. It's a bit like looking for a needle in a haystack, though. All in all, there must be nearly thirty members of staff to be accounted for, plus the senior boys, half of whom are no longer there. Mind you, from the size of some of the younger kids I'd say we might have to extend the list of suspects right down as far as the twelve-year-olds. I couldn't believe how grown up some of them look! By the way, how did you get on with Kelly's flatmate?"

Caine summarised her interview with Michelle Cooke. "I don't really think I discovered anything of significance."

"What about Maynard though? Interesting that he may have fancied young Kelly."

"Oh, I don't believe that for a minute. Truth be known that woman Vanessa was probably jealous – could be she fancied him herself."

"Yes, but there is a link there, between him and Kelly Beacham. And he *does* live at the School – *and* the handbag *was* chucked over the school fence."

"Bit obvious though isn't it? Oh, I don't say it's not worth following up, but there must have been a lot of the school people linked to her through the choir. I just doubt that Douglas Maynard had a sinister involvement with her. He just doesn't strike me as the type."

"What type do you have to be to fancy a woman and end up killing her when she doesn't come over?" asked Dolby sceptically.

"Trust me, I'm a woman, we have something called intuition," said Caine. "Which may sound like an unprofessional way of putting it, so let's just say in my opinion Maynard had nothing to do with Kelly Beacham's death. Investigate him if you like, Mark, but I'm sure you'll come to the same conclusion."

"I will." He yawned. "Have you seen Wendy Doyle since you've been back?"

"No. Should I have done?"

"No. It's just that she rang me a few minutes before you got back. Seems there's another dog-walker wants to tell us what he saw in the Upton Woods, or environs thereof, yesterday evening. Wendy said she'd have taken it, but she'd just managed to establish the address of Kelly Beacham's parents and she wanted to follow it up before the press got to them."

"She's going over there to see them personally?"

"Yes. I didn't order her to; she just said she'd take it on. I don't envy her the task, I must say, but she doesn't complain – she just gets on with it.

"Right, we could do with a few more like her. Anyway, we may not need the parents' help for a formal identification, Beckett seemed in no doubt that it was her - but it'll be just as well to get the point cleared. They might even *want* to see her – you never can tell how the next of kin'll take it." She stood up and went to the window. The

418

sky was overcast, but it had stopped raining. "So, what's this about a new witness?"

"Another dog-walker. Wendy left the details with me. Guy by the name of Holmes, lives in Menzies Gardens. Apparently, his house and land backs on to Beckett's antiques emporium. He claims to have seen something interesting while he was out walking his dog yesterday evening."

Caine smiled. "You don't think he could be the famous Sherlock Holmes do you, walking the Hound of the Baskervilles?" She stood up. "Yeah, I know it's not funny, Mark, but it's about all I can manage in the way of humour at the moment. Besides, it's not raining for once, and I feel like going out again. Let's get over to this Menzies place shall we and see what Sherlock has to offer in the way of inspiration."

Menzies Gardens was a small development of ten very large, five and six bed roomed houses situated to the south of Marcus Beckett's estate. Built of red brick in the

neo-Georgian style in the nineteen seventies the houses lay

well back from Inworth Lane, a turning off the B road to

Upton Eccles and the road along which Dolby had

travelled that morning on his way to view the body of

Kelly Beacham. The gardens were wide and long, most of

them with large parking areas overhung by gaunt, mature

trees, their branches white with hoar frost in the chill of the

approaching evening.

Number Seven was three quarters of the way down

the cul de sac, a big house green with creepers climbing up

the sidewalls and with heavy lace curtains at the windows.

Dolby turned into the drive and parked. They left the car,

buttoning up their coats against the stiffening wind and

walked up the drive towards the front door. They were

about to press the bell when a large dog appeared around

the side of house and ran towards them, barking furiously.

It stopped a few yards away bearing its teeth and growling

half-heartedly as though it was just going through the

motions and had no intention of attacking these trespassers

to its property. Behind it sauntered a tall, elderly man dressed in old, heavy tweeds and smoking a grimy meerschaum pipe. Caine looked at Dolby and smiled, but neither of them said anything. The elderly gentleman stopped and surveyed them from a distance.

"Down, boy, down Mags!" He came closer, up behind the hound and laid a steadying hand on its shoulder. "You'd be the Police I take it." He said, presumably to Caine and Dolby and not the dog. He looked down the drive. "Unmarked car, I suppose that means you're CID?"

"Yes sir," They walked towards him, Caine reaching into her handbag for her warrant card, which she held up in front of him. "Fen Molesey CID, sir." She introduced herself and Dolby. "I understand you contacted the station this morning, about the woman found dead in the woods."

"Correct," said the old gentleman, as though she had won a major prize. His handshake was firm. "Name of Holmes, Krishna Holmes, on account of being born in India and having parents with a very vague sense of humour. Thought their kid was going to grow up to be a

421

god – god*like* perhaps, what do you think?" He struck a pose in front, displaying his prominent aquiline nose in silhouette. "Not so bad, eh? But not exactly godlike – not the genuine thing I'm afraid. Disappointing for the mater and pater. Died disappointed I daresay. Still, only human and feeling more that way day by day, the more ancient I become. Can't stop the march of years, though, eh?" The dog, whose name, Caine assumed, was 'Mags', had stopped barking and Holmes caught hold of its collar and swung it round the way it had come. "Side door I think is indicated. Haven't got my front door key and was just seeing the dog was okay in the garden when you chaps arrived."

They followed Holmes around the side of the house, passing through the garage and then into the large countryside style kitchen. Mags ran through the door and into some other part of the house while a handsome old lady rose to greet them. Tall and thin she was dressed in a long tweed skirt and a warm woollen jumper decorated with gambolling lambs. "You'll be the police, won't you,"

422

she said. Her voice was high and sweet, like that of a little girl. "Would you like a cup of tea, it looks very cold outside."

"Is," confirmed Holmes. He introduced them. "Detective Inspector – forgotten your name – and Detective Sergeant – haven't got a clue, I'm afraid, head like a sieve these days, that's why I write everything down – anyway, you'd better give me your business cards before you go just in case I think of anything else to do with this case." He turned back towards his wife. "This is my wife, Frances."

Mrs Holmes started to do things with a kettle over by the sink while her husband indicated they should take a seat at the large refectory table in the centre of the room. He sat down opposite them and lit his pipe, puffing away for a few seconds before taking a notebook from his pocket and flicking through the pages. "Tea'll be ready in a minute or two," he said, "Meanwhile here's what I sketched last evening."

"What kind of tea would you like?" asked Mrs Holmes taking a large china teapot down from a shelf beside the work surface. "Lap San Sou Chong, Earl Gray, Assam or just tea tea?" Her voice rose. "And Krishna, will you please not smoke that filthy pipe in here."

Holmes ignored her and puffed energetically at the meerschaum, releasing a cloud of sweet-smelling blue smoke into the air.

"Just tea tea," said Dolby.

Caine nodded. "Make that two tea teas for us, thank you Mrs Holmes."

"What exactly did you see yesterday evening, Mr Holmes, that you think might be of interest to us?" asked Dolby.

Holmes placed his pipe on the table and then turned the notebook towards them so they could see the page more easily. In the centre was a line drawing of a motorcar. It was expertly drawn, with every detail shown including even the slight scuffs at the edges of its bumpers. Holmes smiled and, in his enthusiasm, put down his pipe to turn the pages. "Used to be a graphic artist, commercial products, toothpaste tubes, ladies' legs in sheer silk stockings, boobs in brassieres and beer in bottles and barrels, you name it I used to draw it. And of course, motor cars." He said. "But always preferred natural things." He flicked through some of the other pages which were devoted to drawings of wildflowers, trees and small hedgerow creatures, with an occasional bird thrown in. They were all very well executed.

"These are brilliant," said Dolby, "but it was the car you wanted to show us, wasn't it? Would you mind telling us why?"

The old man looked a little disappointed that the police sergeant had called his attention away from his other drawings. "Oh. Right. Correct. Yes." He turned the pages of the book back to the drawing of the car. "Ford Puma. Dark blue. Six months old I should think. Parked on the edge of Upton Woods last night at 7.30 pm when I walked by with Mags. Still there at 9.30. Nobody in it. Driver came back and drove off at 9.37pm. Thought it was a bit suspicious being parked there empty – wondered what the driver was doing – where he'd gone, you know, so made a note just in case. Just as well in the circumstances. This morning woman found dead in woods. Not three hundred yards from where car parked. Put two and two together, arrived at four and rang you lot. Helpful or not?"

Caine studied the drawing for a few seconds. "It could be very useful indeed, Mr Holmes. This is the actual number plate of the car? Good. We'll make a note of it." She reached for her bag and then saw that Dolby was taking a photograph of the drawing with his phone. "But where exactly was it parked and how can you be so sure about the times it left? Surely you weren't watching it all the time?"

Mrs Holmes brought the teapot over on a tray together with a collection of fine china cups and saucers and a large barrel of biscuits. She sat down next to her husband, deftly picking up his pipe and depositing it carefully on the work surface behind her. She lifted the teapot to pour. "Milk?" She did not wait for an answer but

426

poured the milk and then stirred it into the brew before handing cups to Caine and Dolby. "It's nice to see the local police actually putting women officers in senior positions. I always think women are so much more responsible than men, don't you dear?"

"Thank you, Mrs Holmes," Caine replied, taking the cup and saucer from her. "Yes, we can hold our own against the men if we're given half a chance."

"Show you in a minute," said Krishna Holmes in answer to her question about the timing. "Bit suspicious, what? Empty car for two hours or more and then away like a bat out of hell at half nine. Makes you think he was up to something."

"He? You actually saw the driver of the car?"

Holmes looked pleased with himself. "Oh yes, tall, burly chap. Dark clothing almost like he didn't want to be seen. Saw him coming through the trees back to the car, get in, drive off."

"But it must have been pitch black in the woods at that time of night," protested Dolby beginning to wonder if they were wasting their time. "I don't see how you could have seen anything at all let alone a man in dark clothes. Is there a street lamp there or something?"

The older man shook his head, enjoying himself.

"So where exactly *was* the car parked?" asked Caine. She drank the tea quickly, eager to get on. "Perhaps you'd like to show us."

"Finish up, finish up, Sergeant," said Holmes waving his thin arms at Dolby. He stood up and made for the door. "Come along then and you'll see."

Holmes strode out of the room into the central hallway of the house. Caine and Dolby followed him up the stairs onto the top landing and then through into a room at the back of the house. It was cold in there and Caine saw that the window was wide-open letting in the chill winter air. In front of the window, mounted on a metal tripod, were a pair of night vision binoculars, beside them an empty chair and on the floor beside it a large book opened at a page illustrated with photographs of birds. Holmes sat down and put his eyes to the binoculars swinging them around for a few seconds and twirling the focussing knobs.

"There," he said, finally bringing the binoculars to rest, "No cars there tonight, but that's where it was." He touched the fine adjustment on the binoculars. "You could still see the tyre marks on the ground this morning in spite of all the rain we'd had – the place is partially sheltered by trees." He stood up. "See for yourself."

Caine sat down and looked through the binoculars. They were focussed on a corner of the woods behind the house and she could see the asphalt of the lane running beyond. She thought she could just pick out the faint line of marks made by a car's tyres, although the rain that had fallen last evening and during the day had almost washed them away.

"Where exactly are we looking?" she asked Holmes, taking her eyes from the binoculars and looking through the window. She could see over his back garden to the darkly silhouetted trees.

He pointed. "Over there. Building on right is Beckett's antiques place. Behind that his garden, on the edge, where the road curves – that's Inworth Lane – Upton Woods. Beckett's got a narrow back drive that runs into it. Puma car parked on the edge, just off road, under the trees. Couldn't have seen it in summer, too much foliage. Last night, no problem. Not with these." He patted the binoculars affectionately. "And, I admit, a little bit of help from the moon."

Caine stood up and made way for Dolby. He sat down and put his eyes to the eyepieces, twirling the focussing knobs.

"Amazing how much you can see with these things at night," said Holmes. "Designed for it, of course. Got a badger set down there you know. Often watch, though main interest is birds." He picked up the book that was lying on the floor beside the chair. "Seen quite a few of these beauties – oh yes! – and there's a barn owl nesting somewhere hereabouts. See him hunting regularly."

Dolby stood up. "So, you saw the car through these binoculars?"

"Correct. Parked right there. That was later in the evening, of course. First saw it half seven, out walking Mags. Was still there two hours later when I came up here. Thought, 'this is damned strange.' So, kept an eye on it, ran off that quick sketch and lo and behold! Just after nine thirty this joker in dark clothes turns up. Carrying binoculars. Gets in. Drives away. Ask myself – 'what's he been doing in the woods?' No answer then, but this morning heard news bulletin – woman dead in Upton Woods, probably murdered, so I rang your lot."

"You say this person was carrying binoculars? Night sights like these?"

"Couldn't say. Didn't get that good a look at them. But damned suspicious, what? Reckon he was our man?"

"It's hard to say," said Caine. She walked to the door. "Thank you for getting in touch with us, Mr Holmes. This may be a useful lead and we will follow it up. If you think of anything else that may be relevant please do give us a call."

Back in the car Caine took out her mobile telephone and rang through to the station. "I need ID on a car – Ford Puma, dark blue – registration…" She read out the detail from Dolby's phone. "Right, thanks, ring me back." She reached for her seatbelt. "Bit of a weirdo that fellow Holmes."

"This case is full of them," agreed Dolby, strapping in. "Still, what he gave us might be interesting. Do you want to drive around to take a look at the place where the Mondeo was parked?"

"Yes, while we're in the area. I'm a bit puzzled as to why it was parked for two hours with nobody in it, but the driver – whoever it was – had binoculars with him so he was obviously looking at something. But what? At night in the middle of the woods in the depths of winter – the mind boggles."

"Could have been a peeping tom, I suppose," said Dolby.

They drove out of the cul de sac and turned right into Inworth Lane following the edge of the Menzies housing estate and passing the back of Marcus Beckett's land until they reached the curve in the road where the mystery Mondeo had parked the night before. Dolby drew the car up at the side of the road a few yards short of the narrow drive leading up to the rear of Beckett's estate and switched on the hazard lights. They left the car and walked up the road towards the trees.

Dolby pointed at the ground, which was soft and muddy underfoot. "You can still see the tyre marks." A little further on the impressions were much deeper. "Do you suppose we should get some casts of these, just in case?"

"Might be as well, I suppose." Her mobile rang. "This'll be the station with that ID." She put the telephone to her ear and listened to the caller for a few seconds. "That doesn't make sense" She responded, obviously puzzled. "Are you quite sure? Right. Okay. Thanks." She switched off and slipped the phone back into her pocket. "It gets weirder," she said.

"What?"

"That car – the Ford Puma – it's registered to the Met."

CHAPTER FIFTEEN

"What's a Met car doing on our patch?" asked Dolby.

"You don't suppose it was an official visit do you, Jackie?"

Caine shrugged. "Search me. Maybe an off-duty officer took it into his head to do some bird watching."

"Not impossible, I suppose, but it doesn't seem very likely in the middle of a freezing night in mid December," replied an unconvinced Dolby. "But do you think whoever it was could have been mixed up in Kelly's murder."

"Well, if it was a copper in the car it's slightly less possible he might have topped her than if he was an ordinary citizen," said Caine, "but you do get bent coppers, unfortunately and we can't rule it out. Besides, if he actually was here snooping about in the woods, he might have seen something, so we ought to try to trace him."

"Which means going through The Super," said Dolby. "He's not going to like it, a Met car on his patch without his say-so."

"Assuming it **was** without his knowledge," said Caine turning back towards the car. "He doesn't always tell us what's going on in our manor, you know." She rubbed her hands together. "Come on, it's getting pretty raw out here, it'll be dark soon and I could do with something a little stronger than a cup of tea tea. Let's get back to my office, I've got a fresh bottle of whisky whisky in my filing cabinet and I think this cold definitely merits the definition 'medicinal purposes'."

The public counter behind which Sergeant Bernard Crouch was working was barely visible in the press of bodies lined up in front of him. Four uniformed officers were grappling to keep a group of young teenage boys and girls in line, trying to ignore their shouted insults. The girls, three of them, wore their hair short and in multicoloured shades ranging from crimson to purple, their skirts – in spite of the weather - up almost above their waists, their tops almost below their bosoms, their legs black stockinged, coaxed into narrow, nine-inch-high wedge-heeled boots. The boys, four of them, wore their hair not at all, preferring smoothly shaved scalps; their legs were partially covered by torn worn blue jeans, their feet by heavy Doc Marten boots and their torsos by tee shirts and studded leather jackets.

One of the girls kicked out at the female officer holding her, catching her just below the knee.

"Stop that!" Yelled Crouch, who had long since lost his cool. "Get back in line!"

"She asked for it!" retorted the girl, speaking through the metal ring that protruded from her lower lip. "She was touching me up, the filthy dyke!"

Caine and Dolby walked into the melee as they made their way back into Fen Molesey police station after their visit to Menzies Gardens.

Crouch shouted above the hubbub to attract their attention. "DCI Caine, DS Dolby, Thank Gawd you two are back. Got a bloke waiting for you, Manager of the

437

Anglian Bank in the High Street. Wouldn't say what it was about, only that it's urgent. Hope you're not overdrawn!"

"Where is he?" asked Caine, ignoring the last remark and deftly avoiding a kick thrown in her direction by one of the girls. "Watch it young lady or I'll tie a rope through that nose ring and string you up by it."

"Room 6," Crouch yelled as the two detectives pushed through the swing door into the corridor. "It was empty and he seemed harmless enough to let into the inner sanctums." He turned his attention back to the invading forces. "Shut up you little buggars or I'll throw you all in the cells..."

"Nice bunch of kids," said Dolby as they walked through the swing doors and into the corridor beyond. "What do you suppose the Anglian Manager wants?"

"Must be connected with the Beacham murder," said Caine as they paused outside the door to room number 6. "She worked there and it's too much like coincidence for him to turn up for any other reason." She paused, her hand on the door handle. "Mind you, we haven't released the name of the murder victim, so I wonder how he knows?"

The man sitting at the table in the small interview room sipping tea, without enthusiasm, from a plastic cup rose as the door opened and extended his hand towards Caine as she and Dolby entered. He was small and dapper, conservatively dressed in an immaculate navy suit with just a hint of pink stripe, highly polished black shoes, and a military style tie knotted up to the collar of a pristine white shirt. His thinning hair was brushed carefully back from his forehead, but there were one or two stray strands encroaching his ears, curling over the metal rims of his spectacles.

"Good evening, I'm Frederick Carter, Manager of the Fen Molesey branch of the Anglian Bank, but I expect the officer on the desk told you that."

"Yes," said Caine. She introduced herself and Dolby and they sat down on the opposite side of the table. "What can we do for you Mr Carter?"

He resumed his seat. "I felt I should come in and see you as soon as we became aware of the – er…" he hesitated, "…the situation. Normally we would first have carried out a very full investigation, but in the circumstances, well, it's best you know as soon as possible."

"What circumstances, Mr Carter?" asked Caine.

"Why, the death of the poor woman, Kelly Beacham," he replied, confused. "I understand she was found in Upton Woods this morning and that she'd been murdered. Are you telling me that is not the case?"

"No. You're information is quite accurate," said Dolby. "News travels fast, even when it's not supposed to. We haven't yet released the identity of the murder victim, Mr Carter, so may we ask how you came by this information?"

"I had no idea the news hadn't been released," said an embarrassed Carter, "but I can assure you the information was come by quite innocently, Inspector, Sergeant. When Miss Beacham didn't turn up for work this morning one of

440

my staff rang her home number. She didn't get any reply, so she tried her mobile, again without any luck – it seems we had the wrong number in our records; then someone suggested we try her flatmate, a Miss Cooke, I believe – Miss Beacham had her work number programmed into her extension. It was Miss Cooke, I believe, who informed us that Kelly, Miss Beacham – had been murdered."

Caine nodded. "She shouldn't have said anything yet, not until the next of kin had been told, but I must admit I didn't think to ask her not to." She noticed Carter had finished his tea. "Would you like another cup?" He refused, without managing to condemn the brew too much and she considered having one herself; she was still a little cold from her trip out to Upton Woods and was missing the whisky she had promised herself and Dolby on their return to her office. "You mentioned 'a situation', Mr Carter, what exactly did you mean by that?"

He hesitated, said finally, "We've had the internal auditors in recently, Inspector and – well, to cut a very long story short – they are a little concerned with one of the accounts Miss Beacham has been handling. There is a suspicion, well, more than a suspicion, I suppose, that one of the bank's clients has been laundering money and that Miss Beacham was aware of the situation. However, most regrettably, she had not passed her suspicions on, either to her superiors, to myself, or to the National Criminal Intelligence Service."

"And you thought this might be relevant to Miss Beacham's death?"

Carter nodded. "Naturally. Particularly as it's fairly common knowledge that she has been having an affair with the client concerned; normally that wouldn't arouse our suspicions, we're a reasonably open-minded organisation and if one of our employees happens to be unmarried and wants to conduct a romance with an equally unmarried client, then we say good luck to them, but in this case…"

"You suspect collusion," offered Dolby. "And probably quite rightly too, sir. It does seem too much like coincidence."

"The client is, of course, a Mr Marcus Beckett," suggested Caine.

"Well, yes," said Carter, surprised, coughing to hide his embarrassment. "Naturally, our clients' affairs are normally kept strictly confidential, but in the circumstances, I felt we should advise you."

"Thank you, Mr Carter," said Caine. "We're very grateful to you for your prompt action and I'll see the information concerning your client is passed on to the appropriate department." She indicated the file he had placed on the desk. "I take it those papers are relevant to the case."

Carter nodded, picked up the file and handed it across to her. "I had copies of the documents specially made. It's all fairly straightforward provided you can follow a set of accounts, but naturally my staff will be available to assist should your people require it." He stood up and turned towards the door. "Naturally, the information will have to be passed on to the NCIS. I trust you won't hesitate to contact my staff or me if we can be of any further assistance, Inspector, Sergeant. Thank you for your time."

Caine and Dolby followed Carter out of the interview room and made their way up to her office where she opened the bottle of Glenmorangie and poured two small measures.

"Unusual that," said Dolby, sitting in one of the guest chairs and sipping at the whisky. "You don't often get bank managers who are that helpful. In fact, you don't often get bank managers full stop. We're lucky to have a branch these days let alone a manager in it."

Before answering Caine rolled the whisky around inside her mouth, anticipating the warmth passing through into her system. "Too right! They're closing branches left right and centre, expecting everyone to go on-line. But I suspect that Mr Carter was worried at the implications of Kelly Beacham – one of their trusted employees - being murdered by person or persons unknown." She paused thoughtfully." Anyway, it seems to me that if Beckett's been laundering money it's pretty certain he's tied up with

444

the drugs trade and that can get pretty nasty. Poor Carter must be wondering who's next for the strangler."

"Yes, so am I, as a matter of fact," agreed Dolby. "This could put a whole new complexion on the situation. In the first place it puts Beckett firmly in the frame as her murderer, wouldn't you say?"

"Could be, Mark, except for one thing. At the time Kelly was killed he was with his client, Jonathan Shelbourne, that fellow who lives out in Notley Seward. He confirmed Beckett's alibi."

Dolby nodded reluctantly. "Yes, and by all accounts he's a pretty reliable witness." He sighed, "all the same it's a nice theory."

"Which doesn't add up to a row of beans," said Caine. "Like you, I wish it did, I don't like that guy Beckett any more than you do, but we have to face facts, Mark. Kelly Beacham died at just after ten pm and at that moment Beckett was cosily ensconced in The Old Rectory at Notley Seward selling a Japanese thingy to a Mr Jonathan Shelbourne, dealer in antiques." She finished her

445

whisky, put her glass down on her desk and reached over for the file that Carter had left with her. She opened it and flicked through the pages. "I suppose the NCIS bods will be able to understand all this, but it leaves me cold." She put the file down and picked up the one on the train murder. "I suppose the implication that Beckett's been laundering money may give us a bit of a lead on Kelly's murder, which is more than we have on this other case. Mark, this has not been our week, has it?"

"Not so far," Dolby stood up and walked across to the window. It was dark outside and he watched the people on the street scurrying by in the light of the yellow lamps. "If it's not Beckett – and as you say unless he can be in two places at once, it can't be – who else is it?"

"Someone at the school? It seems pretty certain Kelly's handbag was chucked over the school fence into the woods."

"Maynard?"

"I don't think so, but nothing's impossible. It could have been any number of other people from the school,

446

though. We're definitely going to have to follow that up. It might help when we've had the full path. and forensic reports."

Dolby came back to the desk and sat down again. "Maybe it was one of Beckett's friends."

"How do you mean?"

"Well, if he's up to his ears in the drugs game he'd know plenty of people willing to rub Kelly out, to protect their own interests. Maybe she knew too much."

"And I suppose she could have been blackmailing him," agreed Caine. "As you say, he might have hired an assassin to carry out the job." She reached for the telephone, "Which reminds me, I need to have a word with our bossman, Hansen, to see if he knows anything about that mysterious Puma driver from the Met, who just happened to be hanging around in the woods on the night of the murder." She picked up Carter's file again. "And he can tell me what he wants done with this bank file on Beckett. No doubt he'll want us to go carefully on that.

You know the syndrome, mustn't upset a man like Beckett, he's something or other in the local pecking order."

"Yes, I guess we need a bit more on him before we can move," agreed Dolby. He looked at his watch. "Maybe I'll trot over to Kelly Beacham's flat and have a look though her things. I don't know exactly what I'm looking for, but it's just possible she may have taken documents from the bank, something that might incriminate him." He stood up. "I suppose her flat mate might be home and could let me in, but it might be as well for me to take the set of keys we found in Kelly's handbag."

There were three keys on the ring. "I think Michelle Cooke told me the Chubb and the gold Yale are Kelly's door keys." She looked closely at the other one. "She didn't mention a third, so maybe that's an office key."

"Yeah, or maybe it's the key to her lover's heart," commented Dolby dryly, "Always assuming he's got one." He took the keys from her. "It doesn't really matter so long as one or other of them fits the lock." He moved towards the door. "There's no knowing what I'm going to find there, Jackie, so I'll see you here in the morning."

"Right. Don't call me unless you find anything earth shattering. I've promised myself a long soak in a hot bath tonight. I may even wash my hair. Oh, and by the way," she stopped him at the door, "you'd better ring Michelle Cook and let you know you'll be at her flat – if she walks in on you she'll have a fit!"

CHAPTER SIXTEEN

"I reckon it points straight to Beckett," said Dolby. They were having breakfast in the canteen the following morning. The Detective Sergeant sliced through one of his sausages before continuing. "She had well over five thousand quid in cash stashed away down the bottom of her undies drawer. It *must* have come from him; she wouldn't get her hands on that sort of money, otherwise, not in cash anyway. In her sort of job she'd have it in her bank account. It almost certainly comes from the proceeds of drug running." He sighed. "Yes - Unless I'm much mistaken we'll find Beckett's caught up in that scam as well – he probably uses a bit of cannabis to get his satanic orgies going, oil the wheels so to speak." He opened his mouth to receive the sausage and chewed on it with appreciation. "They don't do a bad breakfast here, do they

450

Jackie? Does you good, especially on a freezing cold December morning."

Jacqueline Caine heaped scrambled egg over her toast before nodding her agreement. She chewed thoughtfully and took a sip of tea. "You're probably right about the drugs, Mark, that ties in with the money laundering, but we've still got to get some real proof that Beckett killed Kelly. Don't forget his cast-iron alibi."

"The Shelbourne man? Yeah!" Dolby said gloomily. "I suppose even Beckett couldn't be in two places at once, unless of course he's a real occult wizard." He paused to sip his tea. "Which wouldn't surprise me. I've been making a few inquiries into his background. He's led a pretty weird life. Spent years out East. India, Tibet, places like that. Got himself involved with a load of spooky cults, apparently and did a few unusual jobs. Would you believe that at one time the man was a circus performer?"

Caine smiled, trying to imagine the tall, swarthy antiques dealer performing in the big top. "Doing what?"

"A snake charmer – and I kid you not." Dolby laughed. "Ran one of those little side shows. And then he did a stint as ringmaster. Unbelievable, isn't it?" The Detective Sergeant chewed for a moment and then swallowed. "Oh, and he did one of those escape acts, you know, being trussed up in a sack and chucked into a locked box with chains around it, then dropped in a tank of water. Had to work his way out before he drowned – Houdini-style. That sort of thing."

"Hmm! Interesting man. I can see why he could take in a young girl like Kelly Beacham. And there were some incriminating papers in her flat?"

"Yes, hidden away, but not very cleverly. I've been through them and it's pretty obvious why the Bank's auditors became interested in Beckett's account. There were large amounts of cash going in that he hasn't even attempted to justify. Young Kelly must have been onto him pretty quickly at the beginning, probably blackmailed him to keep her mouth shut. Once they had the arrangement going he probably thought he didn't have to bother any more. He expected her to look after the banking details."

Caine finished her meal and pushed the plate away. "She was obviously blackmailing him and equally obviously he decided he might as well make the most of it. She was an attractive girl and he evidently has a very active libido, that is if the rumours about orgiastic witch ceremonies are to be believed. Frankly, I don't know whether to believe them or not." She dabbed at her lips with her paper napkin. "And it certainly gives him a motive to kill her when he got tired of her. So far as he was concerned she was dangerous. The only thing is – apart from the Shelbourne alibi - and that's going to be pretty difficult to break – why did he make such an amateurish job of it?"

"How do you mean?"

"He's an intelligent man. Surely if he did intend getting rid of her he'd have done it much more professionally and in such a way he wouldn't be incriminated. As it is the body was left right on his doorstep."

Dolby popped the last piece of fried egg into his mouth and chewed on it for a few moments. "I see what you mean. You're right. If he'd got one of his cronies to do her in, he'd have organised it so it happened a long way from his patch, not right next door." He pushed his plate away. "So, we really *can't* pin it on him and he's our number one suspect. I think we'd better start looking elsewhere!"

Caine pushed her chair back and stood up. "Yes. It looks like the usual routine plod. Let's start by going through the statements from the people up at the school. Maybe someone saw something."

Dolby nodded. "I've just got a few bits and pieces to go through on my desk and then I'll join you."

When he walked into Caine's office half an hour later she was sitting at her desk peering down at an A4 sized sheet of lined white paper. She held it up with gloved hands and waved it at him. "Here's somebody else who doesn't like our local Grand Wizard, Marcus Beckett, Esquire."

She dropped the paper back on her desk. Dolby came closer and looked down at it. Large black printed type had been cut from a newspaper or magazine and stuck to its surface.

"*For Kelly's killer look no further than Marcus Beckett. Watch the broken hands*." Dolby read out loud. "Bit corny isn't it? Straight out of a Victorian melodrama. When did it arrive?"

"It was in the morning's post," said Caine. She leaned back in her chair and took off her glasses to rub her eyes. "I'm not sure what to make of it."

"I'm not surprised," Dolby sat down on the other side of her desk and crossed his ankles. "Whose hands are supposed to be broken?" he laughed dryly. "Just when we were writing Beckett out of the plot. Of course, it could be purely malicious."

"Yes, I imagine a man like him must have accumulated a lot of enemies in his time." She picked up the sheet of paper again. "Obviously whoever sent it wishes to remain anonymous, but I wonder if the boys and girls in the forensic lab'll be able to get anything from it."

"You mean by way of identifying who sent it?" Dolby stretched across the table and was about to pick up the used white envelope before he realised he was not wearing gloves. "I'd better not touch it, but is this the envelope it came in?"

"Yes. The post mark's local so that's something of a clue." Caine picked up the envelope and turned it over. "They've written the address by hand, which indicates we're dealing with an amateur, but that doesn't get us very far. How many people in Fen Molesey are past masters of the poison pen letter?"

"Do you think we should take it seriously, Jackie? I mean, it might just be somebody venting their spleen against Beckett."

"It probably is and it's also probably a total waste of time, but we're going to have to follow it up, just in case. We'll send it down to the lab and see if they come up with anything." She took a paper bag from her desk drawer and dropped the letter and envelope into it. "Anyway, you're just in time to meet our visitor from the Met."

"The Met? Don't tell me Hansen's managed to nail Puma man."

"Yes, he surprised me as well." She looked down at the notepad on her desk. "DS Bill Hayland, Drugs Division, Metropolitan Police. Seems he was on a surveillance job on Tuesday night, the night of Kelly's murder. Believe it or not he was watching our dear old friend Beckett." She removed her spectacles again and polished the lenses with a small chamois leather she had taken from her handbag. "Hansen told me he practically had to blow his top before the Met people would agree to co-operate with us, but he got there in the end. Hayland should be here in the next few minutes. By the way, any news yet on young Emma Atterwood?"

Dolby shook his head glumly. "No, her parents have heard nothing. And Hansen's called off the search

"Umm. That's bad, Mark, but I suppose, until we have something more definite to go on…"

"You mean another body?" Dolby said gruffly. "Can you imagine how her parents feel?"

"No, I don't suppose I can, Mark, but Hansen's right in a way. Our resources are already stretched to breaking point trying to piece together clues on the two murders we *have* got; we can't really spare the manpower to go on looking for her."

Dolby stood up and went to the window. "When are we planning to see Mrs Hartnell again?"

"I haven't got anything organised on that, Mark. To be honest, what with all this with Beckett and Kelly Beacham it almost slipped my mind. And, to be even more honest, I've been avoiding the thought of another encounter with that woman."

"You mean the trance business?" said Dolby. "I still find it difficult to get my head around it and I don't want any more of the same either, thank you very much."

"I don't know that we can avoid it for much longer," said Caine wistfully. "She may be the only hope we'll ever have of finding Marion Winters' killer. Maybe we should pay her a visit this afternoon."

"If we must," said Dolby reluctantly. "I'll give her husband a ring. Hopefully she'll be a bit more with it by now." He sat down again. "I suppose there's nothing new on the train murder. No new avenues of inquiry have occurred to you?"

She shook her head. "No. I've been thinking about it a lot. Of course, the press are still breathing down Hansen's neck and he has a go at me every time I see him, but you can't make bricks without clay and we can't get any further without some sort of a breakthrough." She spread her hands helplessly. "So, unless we can get Madame Hartnell to come across with something useful, we are – to put it bluntly – up that famous creek without a paddle."

Her telephone rang and she picked up the receiver. "Ah," she said, "We'll be right down." She replaced the receiver. "It seems our friend DS Hayland has arrived.

Let's go see if Puma man has anything useful to add to the other jig saw puzzle."

Detective Sergeant William Hayland was tall and thickset and probably in his mid forties. He wore thick, high-necked navy jumper and faded corduroy trousers of a similar colour. He had thrown his blue windcheater carelessly onto a chair by the door of the interview room and sat beside it, his legs outstretched, on the only other guest chair. On the desk were the remains of a plastic wrapped sandwich and a folded newspaper. He stopped chewing, swallowed and rose lazily as Caine and Dolby entered the little room, extending a large hand towards them.

"Bill Hayland. I understand you might have some information for me. About this geezer Beckett." There was a cockney burr to his voice.

"Funny, because I thought you were here to fill us in," Caine replied after they had got the introductions over. "I tell you what, we'll show you ours if you'll show us yours!"

Hayland puckered his leathery face into a grin. "Sounds okay to me, Inspector. Who's going first?"

"How about you, Sergeant?" suggested Dolby, moving the other man's windcheater off the chair and on to the desk. He sat down. "It's our patch, technically you're our guest."

"Right," Hayland leaned over, picked up the sandwich wrapper, and lobbed it expertly across the room, where it bounced off the wall and dropped squarely into the wastepaper bin. "Harlem Globe Trotters eat your hearts out! Okay, so what exactly do you want to know?"

"What you were doing in the Upton Woods on Tuesday night."

"I was observing a guy by the name of Marcus Beckett" replied the burly policeman. "Purports to be an Antiques Dealer, but we've got other ideas as to where he gets his dosh. Oh – and by the way – this is strictly between you and me – we don't want any leakages, know what I mean!"

"I'm not sure we do," replied Caine frostily. "We keep a tight ship here in FM."

"Funny that," said Hayland. He leaned over and took the folded newspaper from the desk, flipping it open to the second page. "Young woman – attacked and murdered in woods – blah blah blah," he read." – the police have stated that her watch was smashed during the attack and fixes the time of death at just after 10.00pm blah blah blah." He tossed the paper across for Caine to read for herself. "That's not the sort of detailed info we let out where I come from, so I reckon there must have been a leak."

Caine quickly skimmed through the report and handed the newspaper to Dolby. "OK, I take your point. That is pretty serious and there'll be an inquiry as to how that particular piece of information got out. But that doesn't answer our question as to what exactly you're doing conducting inquiries in our neck of the woods."

"Well, we've suspected for some time there was someone in these parts handling drugs distribution for a widespread dealer network. Thought it might be Beckett,

462

had our eyes on the bastard for quite some time as a matter of fact. Anyway, we had a pretty strong lead originating in the smoke – London that is – and we followed one of their couriers, to see where he'd lead us – a guy named Foote, 'Footy' to his mates. I was the last leg of the tail, if you'll excuse the pun and I took over from the bloke before me about five miles outside Fen Molesey and followed Footy all the way to Beckett's place. He went in the back entrance and I parked a bit round the bend, left the car there and hiked through the woods to where I could see what was going on." Hayland pulled the notepad on the desk towards him and tore a small section from the top sheet, folding it a number of times until it was small enough to go into his mouth. He used it as a toothpick, sliding it between his large, uneven teeth, punctuating his words. "I had a good view – up a tree as a matter of fact. I could see right into Beckett's house and I had a pair of Zeiss night viewers – very powerful." He smiled. "Beckett doesn't seem to have invested anything in opaque drapes, probably thinks he's not overlooked – big mistake - I could

see everything that went down. And I mean *everything*."
He winked lasciviously at Dolby. "Quite interesting it was
too."

"So, what *did* you see?" asked Caine a little irritably.
Why couldn't the man just tell them without prevarication?

"Footy handed the stuff over to Beckett, they had a
bit of a barney over something, don't ask me what, but
Footy got a bit upset. I think Beckett threatened him or
something, there was a lot of voices raised, but finally the
little feller left, not looking all that happy, I must say. He
went just as the young woman arrived. He had a few words
with her, but she gave him the cold shoulder."

"What young woman?"

"Search me. She just turned up. Dark, tall, slim, good
looker, nice figure, dressed in a navy skirt and white blouse
beneath a classy outdoor coat." Hayland smiled lecherously
at Dolby again and winked. "Much younger than Beckett,
but she was his piece of skirt, that was quite obvious. They
went inside together and up to one of the bedrooms. I could
see them quite clearly – no curtains!"

"What time would that have been?" asked Caine.

Hayland leaned over to his windcheater and removed a much smaller notebook from one of the zip-up pockets. He opened it and flicked through the pages. "I got there just after 7.15 pm, so this must have been round about 7.30, give or take."

"A neighbour tells us your car was parked on that spot at the back of Beckett's place from about 7.30 until just after 9.30."

Hayland nodded. "They might have seen the car there between those times of course, but I wasn't in it."

"But you've just told us the courier, Footy or whatever his name is, left at about half past seven, Sergeant," said Caine. "And the woman arrived at about the same time. Why didn't you leave then?"

"For all I knew the girl was there to collect that little package the courier brought with him. She may have been there as the next part of the distribution chain. So, I waited to see whether she took it with her."

"And did she?" asked Dolby.

Hayland smiled. "No. When Footy gave it to Beckett he put it on a little table in full view of the window. He didn't move it. Not the whole time I was there. And I had a pretty good view. It was still there when the woman left."

"And you stayed there watching the house, the whole time Beckett was in there with the woman?" asked Dolby. "Incidentally, she was almost certainly Kelly Beacham - she was found dead in the woods yesterday morning – murdered."

"Ah!" Hayland nodded. "The woman in the paper - that explains your interest in Beckett! Bit busy in Fen Molesey at the moment, aren't you? What with that train murder last Friday."

"We'll manage," said Caine. "You watched Beckett's house until when?"

"Until the girl left."

"And what were they doing all that time?" Caine realised as she asked the question how inappropriate it was. She inwardly cursed herself.

There was the slightest hint of embarrassment on the Met officer's face as he glanced across at Dolby. "Please!" He said wryly, "Can't I leave that to your imagination?" He frowned. "Don't think I enjoyed it, Inspector, stuck up a tree in the middle of the countryside with the temperature below zero and the wind whipping round me arse. It was brass monkeys out there I can tell you. It wasn't exactly my favourite assignment."

"And you waited there, watching, until you saw Miss Beacham leave?" asked Dolby.

"Yes. I told you. She went at just after half past nine and she didn't take the package with her. It was still on the table and it hadn't been moved. Anyway, I watched her go – quite a mover she was, very tasty, nice pair of legs – well, I couldn't see them then, of course, not under her long coat, but I'd seen them before when she was…you know – with Beckett. Anyway, she got into her car and drove off down the main drive from the house. I unfroze my arse and beat it back to London, arriving home some time after eleven o'clock – I stopped off for a warming drink and a bite to eat on the way." He leaned forward

aggressively, "Does that satisfy you, Inspector?"

"And Foote, the courier, he'd definitely gone by

then?"

Hayland shrugged. "So far as I know, but he drove

out the front entrance, didn't he. I didn't follow him so I

wouldn't know whether he hung around or not, would I?"

"But you could recognise him again?"

"Oh yes. No problem. He's got a record as long as

your arm and we've got mug shots from all angles. Here,

you're not thinking he might have done the girl in are

you?"

"The thought had occurred to me," said Caine. "He

could have lain in wait for her as she drove out."

"Why?"

Caine shrugged. "Any number of reasons. Lust. Or

maybe he also thought she was part of Beckett's

distribution service and would have the pot on her when

she left. Perhaps he thought he'd pinch the stuff back,

make a few quid for himself. There's no honour amongst thieves you know."

It was Hayland's turn to shrug. "Not impossible I suppose, I wouldn't put it past the little skunk. He's a right pox on society, not unknown for beating up on women. But, if that's what happened he must have been a very disappointed bunny, cos the stuff didn't leave Beckett's place. Now, what've you got for me?"

"About Beckett? Not much," said Caine. "You probably know everything worth knowing already. There's a suspicion he's involved in occult practices and he's rumoured to run a local witches coven."

Hayland grimaced. "We know all about that, thanks, he's been under surveillance one way or another for months. I'm looking for something we *don't* know."

"And there's a fair chance he's been money laundering."

Hayland yawned. "We know that too, Inspector, had our suspicions for weeks. You got any real proof though? That'd be something to make this morning worthwhile."

"We've got a few files from his bank," volunteered Dolby. "The manager seemed to think the evidence is all there."

"Good. We can move in on the buggar then. I'll just get the final okay from my people."

"Hang on a moment," said Caine. "We've got a murder case here. Beckett's girl friend has been murdered and this investigation of yours is likely to muddy the waters."

"Sorry, Inspector," said Hayland, "but I think my lot are ready to move – we've been dying to get our hands on this load of rats. We're going to turn his place over as soon as we can get in there." He stood up. "We've probably got enough to make some charges stick, but maybe we'll find a bit more, really nail down the coffin lid. Of course, if he was involved with the woman's murder, then that's all to the good. One way or another we'll have the scumbag on toast."

Caine sighed. "I don't like it. I'd sooner spend a bit more time investigating the murder. We haven't got a clear enough picture yet."

Hayland moved towards the door. "Listen, if we don't move now Beckett might do a runner. We've got enough to hold him on, so let's do it, before he gets out of the country."

Caine sighed. "Well, I'm relying on you to have enough to hold him on, Sergeant."

"Precisely why I want to bust his place as soon as we can. I think we've got enough already, but a bit more won't do any harm, will it Inspector?"

She looked at her watch. "Okay, but you'll have to clear this with the local Drugs Division – they'll want to send someone along."

"No problem," said Hayland easily.

"We'll also have to get a warrant, we can't just burst in on him. A statement from you would be helpful, Sergeant. Together with the suspicions we've got we should be able to persuade one of our local beaks to come across." She stood up. "Shall we aim to visit Beckett at about four this afternoon?" She came around the desk towards the door. "Thanks for your co-operation, Sergeant, it's much appreciated." She stopped. "Oh, and it would be very helpful if you could let us have full details on this man Foote, the drugs courier you were talking about."

"No problem there, Inspector, it'll be a pleasure. And you can have your statement as soon as you like. Point me in the direction of a desktop and I'll knock one out for you. After that, a visit to one of your locals would be appreciated, unless of course you want me to help you get that warrant."

"No thanks, I think we can manage that much for ourselves, Sergeant," said Dolby. He opened the door. "Our Desk Sergeant, Bernie Crouch'll get the local sorted out for you. If you ask him nicely he may even trot down there with you – quite partial to a liquid lunch is our Bernie."

They passed DS Hayland into the capable hands of Sergeant Crouch and walked back to the lift. "We might be able to get this Beckett character on some sort of drugs charge and money laundering, but I'm not sure that session added much to our knowledge of who murdered Kelly Beacham," said Dolby. "Do you think it might have been the drug courier?"

"Nothing's impossible. It's worth checking out. Anything's worth checking out." The lift doors opened and they stepped inside. "I wonder if we could tie Beckett's alibi, Jonathan Shelbourne, to this drugs scam?"

"You mean the drugs might have been Beckett's real reason for going over to see Shelbourne on the night of the murder?" Dolby nodded thoughtfully and rubbed his hands together. "Interesting possibility. Now that would be progress – it would blow Beckett's alibi to Kingdom Come."

They stepped out into the corridor and made their way towards Caine's office. "Yes, Beckett might not have been at Shelbourne's place at the time Kelly was killed. The sooner we get to have a look around Beckett's house the better. Let's get cracking on that warrant."

"What about our visit to the Hartnell woman?"

She pushed open the door to her office. "Yes, we shouldn't put that off any longer, Mark." She stood for a moment thinking before continuing across the room to her desk. "Look, you take care of the warrant. I'll get Wendy to come to the Hartnell's with me."

CHAPTER SEVENTEEN

DC Wendy Doyle manoeuvred the car into a space outside the small, terraced house halfway along Bridge Drive, between an old, but well cared for Ford Puma and a neglected looking blue Corsa. She set the handbrake and switched off the ignition.

"Here we are, boss, number 16. Wouldn't think it belonged to a builder and decorator would you?"

"Cobbler's syndrome," said Caine. Doyle looked puzzled, "The cobbler's too busy making other people's shoes to make them for his own family," she explained, opening the car door. "Anyway, let's hope Mrs H. is in a more receptive mood than last time."

Number 16 was probably the most run-down house in Bridge Drive. The paint around the window frames was cracked and pitted, the pebble dash mildewed and the glass in the top section of the front door cracked. The small

475

metal gate at the entrance to the front path squeaked loudly as Caine pushed it open and she trod carefully on the cracked paving leading up to the porch. She pressed the doorbell and then, hearing nothing, banged the handle of the letterbox against the frame two or three times, creating a noisy clatter. There was still no response and she bent to lift the flap of the letterbox and look through into the hall. A light was on in the back of the house. A dank, musty smell of dampness reached her nostrils.

Dorothy Hartnell, when she came to the door a few minutes later, looked tired, but she seemed a little stronger than she had in hospital. Her head was still partly bandaged, but her cheeks were a healthier colour. She toyed nervously with the belt of her long winceyette housecoat. A flicker of anxiety ran through her tired eyes as she recognised the Detective Inspector.

"Oh! It's you. More questions I suppose." Her body language showed her hostility and nervousness. She sighed and let go of the door wearily. "You'd better come in, I suppose." She stepped to one side to let the two officers pass.

"I hope you're feeling a little better, Mrs Hartnell," said Caine, her nostrils wrinkling at the dankness of the tiny hall.

"I still have headaches from the injuries and my arm is stiff, not to mention my ribs- they were very badly bruised. My husband thinks I should sue the railway company, but I don't know…is it worth it? This…" She pointed to her body and her voice rose sharply, "…is just an earthly shell and when I'm gone it'll be empty and useless, a crumbling piece of dust and clay. Ashes to ashes…"

They stopped momentarily in the narrow, dingy hall, beside a small telephone table. The telephone was a collector's piece thought Caine, one of the old, square, black ones with a circular dial. Beside it were a large notepad and a plastic penholder holding a biro at the end of a coiled plastic cable stuck to the wallpaper.

"Don't take any notice of our crumbly walls, Inspector," said Mrs Hartnell, a note of bitterness in her voice, "my husband's always telling me he's much too busy doing other people's houses to bother with his own."

"Couldn't you get your son to do it, Mrs Hartnell?" asked Caine, relieved that she was looking so much better physically, but still concerned there had been little change in her mental condition. Still, perhaps this time their interview would yield some useful results. For that reason alone it was important they convince the woman they were on her side and win her confidence. "I hear he does a good decorating job."

"Oh no, it's not a job for my Reginald," Mrs Hartnell replied. "As it is Henry should not work him the way he does, but I can't get neither of them to see sense. Reginald even says he enjoys it, the silly boy!" she indicated a door to their right." You'd better go through."

They went into the small front room. It was crowded with large pieces of furniture including two armchairs in which Mrs Hartnell indicated they should sit, and a double settee, all of which were covered in a heavily flowered upholstery. Heavy curtains, also flowered, hung at the tall sash windows and there were bookshelves around the walls lined with old leather-bound books and an occasional brightly coloured paper back. A tea pot and a solitary cup and saucer stood on the small table between the two armchairs a few feet away from the coal effect gas fire which added the only note of cheer to the drab little room.

"I hope we haven't interrupted your tea," said Caine.

"No, I've finished. I was just communing with a few of my friends," said Mrs Hartnell, without attempting to explain where her 'friends' had gone. There was no sign of a telephone extension in the room. "They left when they saw you arrive." She peered around the room before seating herself on the sofa. "We're alone now, at least I think so."

Wendy Doyle gave Caine a puzzled look.

"We're sorry to disturb you again," said Caine. "We hope you'll understand, Mrs Hartnell, that we do need to ask you about what went on in the train carriage last Friday, when the young woman was murdered. The nurse."

The other woman's eyes, until now placid, flashed angrily and her voice rose again. "Stop this! I told you in the hospital that I couldn't help you! I don't remember anything!"

"You remembered being in the train carriage," said Caine, feeling her confidence for a fruitful interview slipping quickly away. "*And* you remembered there were two other women in there with you. Did anyone else come into the carriage?"

"I've told you before, I *don't remember*," shrilled Mrs Hartnell. She suddenly put her hands to her forehead and rocked the top half of her body backwards and forwards. "I had a headache before you came and you're making it worse with your questions, questions, questions!" She dropped her hands and started to fidget with the belt of her housecoat. Her eyes were staring past them at the wall.

"I'm sorry," Caine chewed on her lip for a moment, her eyes on the other woman. She did not know why, but she had the feeling Mrs Hartnell was playing with her, holding something back. She tried to keep a note of sympathy in her questioning, but her voice hardened. "I'm sorry, but do try to remember, Mrs Hartnell, please, it could be vitally important. The killer, whoever he was, could strike again at any time. Every woman in the Fen Molesey area could be at risk. We've got to find him!"

"I tell you I don't remember," the other woman sighed. Her voice dropped again. "All right, I'll try." She closed her eyes and furrowed her brow in concentration. Caine shot a worried look across at her colleague, who was watching the events with a fascinated frown. She hoped the woman was not going into one of her trances. "No. No." Mrs Hartnell's voice was unchanged. She shook her head and opened her eyes again. "I must have fainted when the train crashed, that's why I don't remember anything." She paused. "Except... I'm *sure* nobody came into our carriage after the crash."

481

"What about before – just before, maybe?"

She shook her head emphatically. "No. I'm sure **nobody came into the carriage**."

"But what about what you said to the Paramedic at the scene of the accident?" asked Caine. "You mentioned a man didn't you?"

Mrs Hartnell made a vague gesture. "Did I? I don't remember. It's all a complete blank."

"Yes, you said 'leave him alone' – who did you mean by '**him**', Mrs Hartnell?"

"I don't know. I keep telling you I don't remember any more."

They sat silently for a few moments before Caine sighed and stood up. "There's nothing else then?"

The woman shook her bandaged head. "No - there's nothing else, Inspector. Now, will you please leave me alone? I'm very tired."

It was a quarter to six in the evening when DCI Caine and DS Dolby knocked on the door of Marcus Beckett's house. They were accompanied by four other officers, among them DC Wendy Doyle, DS Bill Hayland of the Metropolitan police and two men from the Fen Molesey drugs squad. The antiques store had closed a few minutes earlier and Beckett was alone when he opened the door. He seemed unconcerned when Caine showed him the warrant and told him they were there to search the premises.

"And what, pray, are you searching for?" he asked, with exaggerated politeness.

"Drugs," Hayland told him before Caine could say anything.

Beckett eyed the Met officer up and down sceptically. "I don't think I've had the pleasure of meeting you before. Who are you?"

"Detective Sergeant Hayland, Metropolitan Police."

A flash of concern crossed the big man's face, but he recovered his composure immediately. "Ah! The Met! We are coming up in the world. Why don't I feel honoured?" He turned to Caine. "Search by all means, Detective Inspector, although I can't think why you hope to find drugs here. I have absolutely nothing to hide," His eyes, behind the veil of casual amusement, were cold. "Just make sure nobody breaks anything will you? I have a lot of valuable antiques in this building and I don't want any of your jackbooted bobbies knocking anything over or stepping on anything priceless."

"I can assure you we'll float about the place like butterflies," said Caine, leading the way into the hall. "You heard the gentleman, boys and girls, treat the place as if it was your own."

Beckett smiled contemptuously. "Search away then, Inspector." He turned away from the door and started down the hall. "And good luck – this is a very big house, you know. Pity the decorators have been in, I've had to move a lot of the furniture around and even I don't know where anything is. So – happy hunting, but you'll never find what you're looking for."

As he spoke a small van approached up the drive and came to a stop in front of the steps leading up to the front door. "Ah! That'll be the sniffer dog and his trainer," said

484

Caine. She noted with some satisfaction the slight flicker of alarm that flashed across Beckett's features. "If there's anything here the dog'll find it, don't you worry about that. Not allergic to dogs are you sir? Only you look a little concerned."

"Not at all, Inspector. Now, if you don't mind, there's no point me wasting my time watching you and your merry henchmen at play, so if you'll excuse me, I shall go and do some real work of my own."

"I hope you won't mind if PC Scott here accompanies you, Mr Beckett." Caine nodded to one of the uniformed officers. "I'd like him to keep an eye on things."

Beckett's lip curled. "Then the first thing he'll see me do is telephone my solicitor."

Scott, a slight smile on his lips, followed the tall man along the hall and into his office.

"Nice move, Inspector," said Bill Hayland with a grin. "You could see the buggar was rattled. At least he won't be able to move the stash with young Scottie watching him. Where do you want us to start?" He walked over and opened the door beneath the stair well. "How about if me and Wendy here take a butcher's down in the cellar?" He flicked the light switch. "Oh, what a pity, looks like the light bulb's gone," he turned to Doyle and grinned lasciviously, "Don't you worry, darling, you and me ain't scared of the dark are we? You just cuddle up close and I'll see you all right!"

"Wendy stays with me," said Caine sharply. Puma man had irritated her since the first moment she had clapped eyes on him. "And if you don't stop harassing her you're out of here and there'll be a report to your Super tomorrow morning. Have you got that?" Hayland nodded, tight lipped. "Now you're the one on the Drugs Squad, so I assume you're something of an expert. You tell us where you think we should start looking – and let's have a sensible suggestion shall we?"

"Ask the dog," suggested Dolby. "He's the *real* expert!"

The advice from the dog handler, PC Dundridge, was "You look and we'll sniff" and with that suggestion the

486

officers began a slow search of the big house. Their task was made more difficult by the large number of articles on view and the fact that many of the items of furniture, moved while the front rooms were being decorated, still occupied the hallway. Dundridge, a thin wiry officer sporting a moustache that seemed totally out of keeping with his bald head, took the dog, a two-year-old black Labrador named Durante (for his formidable olfactory powers) up the stairs to begin the search, advising the human officers to "just turn a few things over down here and, if you find anything suspicious, give Durante here a shout. He responds very well to wolf whistles and bitches."

Caine watched the others disperse into the big house and began a slow search of the furniture in the hall. There were plenty of places you could hide a stash of drugs. Antique vases from various periods, small wooden writing desks no doubt fitted with secret drawers by the skilled joiners who had made them so many years before; porcelain pots of various shapes and sizes, marble busts which – for all Caine knew – might be hollow; snuff boxes, jewel caskets and any number of other elaborate kinds of box. Beckett could have hidden the stuff in any of them. If he had then Durante would find it, the sniffer dogs rarely failed. Unless of course it was not here. Beckett might have managed to get the stuff out of the house before they arrived. According to the man she had posted to watch the house that morning, he had not left the premises all day, but he had had plenty of customers calling in to view his range of antiques; one of them could easily have been an accomplice. Come to think of it, the antiques showroom was the ideal front for drugs distribution. Hide the stash in any number of items and have a regular customer – the next link in the distribution network – come in, buy it and take it away. It couldn't have been easier. Perhaps this search *was* going to be a waste of time.

Hayland had left the door to the cellar open and Caine wandered over to it and peered down the steps, feeling the cold that, in defiance of the rules of physics, seemed to emanate upwards, from out of the darkness. Experimentally, she flicked the light switch up and down.

Mondeo man had been telling the truth, the light was not working. On impulse she pulled her torch out of her overcoat pocket and turned it on, directing the beam down the steps, expecting to see dust and cobwebs, perhaps rows of wine racks covered with the grime of decades. If they ventured anywhere cleaning ladies most certainly did not descend into cellars. But to her surprise the light reflected back from a gleaming marble floor, tessellated in many different colours, marking out the edges of some ornate central design. Fascinated, she moved slowly down the stairs, playing the light of her torch over a series of tall pillars, faced with marble, which, she now realised, held up the ceiling of the cellar. It had been excavated downwards to make it much deeper than a conventional cellar and must have been at least nine feet high. In the centre of the tessellated floor was a five-pointed star, a pentagram, fashioned from black and white marble, beyond this a stone slab about seven feet long raised on a plinth. Around the room at measured distances, a number of shadowy alcoves were marked by unlit torcheres. Caine turned her attention back to the raised slab, playing the beam of her torch over it. A few feet above the slab, set high on the wall, was the carved stone face of a man, grotesque, distorted, twisted lips set in a cruel line, eyes glaring in the reflected light, red tipped horns issuing from the forehead. Here was the devil in Beckett's satanic temple – the rumours were true then; the man *was* some sort of a satanic wizard. She shivered and stood hesitating on the bottom step for a few seconds considering whether to search the place. A dank smell reminiscent of a mixture of mildew and incense reached her nostrils and the skin on her arms tightened into goose bumps. The air was much colder down here than up in the house and there was a draught coming from somewhere. The tiny hairs on the back of her neck rose and she shivered again before turning to climb the stairs up to the hallway. She would leave the search of this place to Durante and his handler.

As she turned on the stair, she was startled by a noise from the steps above her. She looked up. Somebody, a man, was standing at the top of the stairs, peering down at her, his body a black silhouette. His face was in shadow, but the light streaming down from the hallway bathed the top of his head, suffusing the unruly mop of his hair with a blaze of flickering, red-tipped flame. Startled, she dropped her torch. It hit the marble floor with a crash and the light went out. Her heart beating faster than she cared to admit she cursed and reached down in the darkness to pick up the torch, feeling blindly around for a few seconds before her fingers closed on its hard plastic case. She flicked the switch back and forth a few times, but it did not respond. Her heart pounding in spite of herself she turned again and climbed the steps.

The figure had gone from the top of the stairs, but as she came through the cellar door and out into the brightly lit hall she was startled to find Reginald Hartnell standing just a few feet off, staring at her, his lips slack and his mouth working, sucking something. His eyes were wide, anxious. As she sought to regain her composure he swallowed whatever was in his mouth and then stuffed his baseball cap back onto his head, covering the bright red of his hair. Then he turned and made his way quickly along the hall towards the front door, out into the night.

"What was he up to?" The voice was Dolby's. "Jackie - You look like you've seen a ghost! Are you okay?"

She nodded and laughed weakly. "Yeah, fine. I was down in the cellar having a look around and he came to the top of the stairs. It's quite spooky down there and I have to admit he gave me a hell of a fright. It wasn't his fault though, so not to worry."

Dolby leaned through the cellar door to sweep the beam of his torch down the steps into the dark cavern beyond. "I see what you mean by spooky. This must be Beckett's devil worshipping temple or whatever you call it. Pity we can't bring him in for running a place like this. I suppose there's nothing down there we can hold him on?"

Caine shrugged. "I didn't stop to find out. We'll let the dog have a sniff around. Has anyone found anything yet?"

Dolby shook his head. "Nothing incriminating. There are just too many places to look. Anyway, I don't think there's anything here, Beckett's much too clever to leave any evidence."

"Well, we know he's been involved in money laundering and that ties him in with Kelly Beacham."

"Yes, but we've got no evidence he killed her, have we?"

CHAPTER EIGHTEEN

"We can't hold him, Jackie, not on the drugs nor on the money laundering charges. We haven't got enough evidence and his solicitor's been screaming blue murder most of the night." Dolby stood by the window of Caine's office and looked at the rain sweeping across the street. It seemed just as gloomy inside. "I wish that idiot Hayland hadn't been so keen to get in there!"

Caine yawned. She could not believe this was happening. They had found only the barest evidence of cannabis at Beckett's place last night– a few tiny traces of dust were all the sniffer dog could come up with – so they had brought Beckett in for questioning on suspicion of money laundering. "He underestimated Beckett. How long will it take for the NCIS to put a laundering case together?"

Dolby shrugged. "Could be weeks. They've an enormous pile of paper to go through. And we've also drawn a blank on his alibi – he *was* with that fellow Jonathan Shelbourne. The man's a pillar of his local community and one of the neighbours saw Beckett getting out of his car to go into Shelbourne's house. The time tallies exactly with what Beckett claims."

"I suppose this neighbour couldn't have been mistaken?" asked Caine, realising she was clutching at straws.

Dolby shook his head. "I really don't think so. There's a lamppost near where Beckett parked and the neighbour recognised him. Said he's seen him before - lots of times - at the antiques shop and around town. After all, you couldn't mistake Beckett could you – he's a one off."

"And it looks like he's getting off," said Caine, with a poor attempt at humour. She pulled the Kelly Beacham file across the desk towards her and flicked idly through it.

"We'd better let him go I suppose, or we'll be all over the tabloids. I can see it now – Desperate Cops arrest wrong man on drugs charges."

DC Wendy Doyle put her head around the door. "Sorry to trouble you, ma'am, Sergeant Dolby," she said apologetically, "but there's a lady downstairs says she wants to see the officer in charge of the Beacham case. She gave me this." She was holding a brown envelope in her gloved hands. "I think you'll need to put plastic gloves on –It's an SD memory card and there may be prints on it." She placed it on Caine's desk. "I don't know what's on the card, but the lady seems to think it's important. I think you'd better see her – and soon, she says she's in a hurry and she keeps looking at her watch."

Intrigued, Caine donned her plastic gloves and removed the memory card from the envelope. "What do I do with it?" she asked, "You know I'm not much good with all this tech stuff."

"Here, Ma'am – let me," Wendy took the card from her and inserted it into the SD slot on the side of Caine's computer, pressing the appropriate keys on the keyboard and clicking the mouse when prompted. After a few seconds a picture jumped on to the screen.

"Him again! Why do you suppose he keeps cropping up?" It was a rhetorical question; Caine did not wait for an answer. "Phew! This is X certificate stuff, Wendy, I hope you didn't look at it too closely!"

"I haven't look at it at all," replied the young police officer.

Caine clicked through three more photographs. "God! They're a bit graphic!"

"I wonder if they knew they were being photographed!" commented Dolby.

"You mean did they know they were starring in '*Sex with Satan in an Essex Village*' – unexpurgated? I doubt it," replied Caine. "Beckett's a bit of an exhibitionist, but these look like the work of some high-tech peeping Tom, not a professional sex snapper."

"When were they taken?"

Doyle clicked the mouse a number of times, bringing up the property details of the particular photograph they had been looking at.

"06.12. - 6th December." Dolby glanced quickly at the calendar. "That was Friday. Three nights before Kelly Beacham was murdered." He turned to Caine. "If it had been the same night I would have wondered if our Puma Man, Hayland of the Met, was involved. He said he watched Kelly and Beckett together that evening. Now we know the sort of thing he was watching, the dirty beggar!"

"No – he wasn't there. He didn't start his surveillance until after he'd followed Foote, the drugs courier, to Beckett's place."

"But why would *anyone* take photos like this?" asked Wendy. "They're really over the top. They're seriously disgusting!"

"People take photographs like this for all sorts of reasons, as you well know, young lady," said Caine, standing up. "But it's no use us speculating. Maybe the woman who brought them in will be able to supply some of the answers."

Marjorie Weston looked as though she had just left her horse at the town-drinking trough while she came in to purchase a packet of crisps. In her mid to late fifties, she was tall and broad, dark haired and sun tanned and wore a dark brown hacking jacket above khaki jodhpurs and black leather riding boots. She turned her weather-beaten face away from the window (she had been watching the rain) as Caine, Dolby and Doyle entered the small interview room.

Caine introduced Dolby and herself. "You've already met DC Doyle, Mrs Weston." She placed the envelope containing the SD card on the table between them. "Perhaps you'd like to tell us how you came by this computer card."

Mrs Weston looked at her watch before she said anything. "I really am in a hurry – I have a riding lesson to give in less than half an hour – so I'll tell you as quickly as I can. I run the Inworth Riding Stables, Inspector, near Upton Eccles. We're just off Inworth Lane, you probably

499

know it. Well, to cut a long story very short, Gemma, one of my girls, found that disgusting piece of technology on the floor while she was mucking out the stables this morning. Fortunately, she didn't realise what was on it."

"You mean it was on the floor in your stables?"

"Yes, but don't ask me how it got there. I thought nothing of it until I put it into my desktop computer in the stable's office – to see whether it needed to be handed back to its owners, you understand, but I couldn't believe what was on it. Then, of course, I recognised the people involved and, in view of that poor girl's murder I naturally thought I should bring it to you in case it has any bearing on the – er – case."

"Well, thank you, you did the right thing," replied Caine. "It may or may not be relevant, but thanks anyway."

"How do you think it got onto your stable floor" asked Dolby?"

"I really don't know! I can only surmise it came in with some mud caught on one of the horses' hooves. It was certainly covered in mud when Gemma, our stable hand, came across it."

"More to the point, Mrs Weston, do you know who took these pictures? Not one of your pupils I presume?"

"That really is not funny, Inspector, to suggest that any of my young ladies would indulge in…" she waved her hand towards the incriminating envelope, "…such disgusting pornography!"

"So, you don't know anything else about them?"

"Nothing, but I recognised that man – that Beckett person," she blushed, "his face - you can see his face in one of the – er – poses – and that young tart of his showing off everything she's got. Anyway, as I said, I realised it may be of interest to you in view of the fact that – well, she's been murdered, hasn't she? And the body was found near one of the bridle paths we use nearly every day. I thought there might be some connection."

"So, you think it was picked up from the mud on the path on one of your horses' hooves and carried back to your stables," said Dolby. "It makes sense."

501

"I'm glad it makes sense to you." Mrs Weston rose from her chair. "I'm just pleased to get rid of the disgusting thing. Now, if I may, I'd like to be away to that lesson." She hovered for a second and reached into her brown leather handbag. "My card in case you need to contact me, Inspector and, of course, if you like to ride, you'll know where to find me." She turned towards DC Doyle, "And you, young lady, should you ever need riding lessons I can promise you an excellent deal. I'm sure that with your figure I'd soon have you up in the saddle. I hope I've been of some assistance."

Wendy Doyle made a face at the receding figure as she went through the open door and out into the corridor. "Silly moo! I've been riding since I was four years old!" She turned back to Caine. "Well, now we know where the SD card came from the question is - is it going to be of any use to us?"

Caine thought for a moment. "Maybe. The thing is, what was it doing on the bridle path, possibly near Kelly's body? Assuming, of course, that Mrs Weston's surmise is correct, and it did come into her stable premises on a horse's hooves." She tapped her fingers on the tabletop and went on thoughtfully. "Suppose, just suppose, somebody had been watching Beckett and Kelly Beacham performing in his bedroom – some Peeping Tom – and suppose he'd taken these photographs – there may even be a video on the card, we haven't seen it all - and suppose he was the one who picked Kelly up that night when she ran out of petrol and he tried to force himself on her – to take advantage of her – after all, he's been lusting after her for ages and seeing her in bed with Beckett really turned him on…"

"And" said Dolby, following through Caine's line of thought. "She won't come across, doesn't fancy him, so they have a fight. They struggle with each other in the car and one way or another he kills her. But while they're fighting each other, somehow or other, the SD card falls out of the car door or window; and it gets covered in mud and sticks to the horse's hooves when one of the riders makes her way along the path sometime later."

"So, who took the photographs?" asked Jacqueline Caine. "If Mrs Weston's surmise is correct – and it seems pretty plausible to me – then find the smutty photographer and we've almost certainly found Kelly's killer."

"And there's a fat chance of finding any fingerprints or DNA on the card," Dolby interjected, "Not after all the mud's been washed off."

Caine inserted the SD card into her computer console again. "Mark, get on to Tony Ash in Photography and ask him if he can get us blow-ups of these. It might be useful to see them in more detail – no cracks please!"

"Perish the thought," said Dolby lifting the telephone receiver and dialling. "What if he says he's too busy?"

"Tell him what's on the pictures – I guarantee he'll have them in the computer system before you can say 'randy policeman'!" She clicked her computer mouse, brought up the pictures on the card again and peered closer to the screen. "I thought so, but I wasn't sure..."

Dolby was speaking on the telephone and looked over inquiringly.

"What?" asked DC Doyle.

Caine beckoned her around the desk and pointed to the screen. "Look - Whoever took these pictures was **higher up** than Beckett and Kelly. They were at an angle, looking down."

"Up a big tree in Beckett's garden, maybe?" suggested Doyle. "Those funny wispy things at the edge of the picture could be branches."

Dolby finished his telephone conversation and replaced the telephone receiver. "Tony says to send the card over and he'll blow them up right away. He seemed quite keen, can't think why." He grinned and leaned across to look at the pictures. "Are there any tall trees on that side of the house?"

"I can't say I remember," admitted Caine. She clicked the pictures off the screen and released the SD card from its slot and then stood up. "There's only one way to find out." She turned to Doyle and handed the card to her. "Get it over to Tony Ashe pronto, Wendy and tell him I'd like the blow-ups by this evening, if that's possible. I've

got a feeling this is going to lead us somewhere at last."

It was raining again as Dolby drove out of the police

station car park and turned along the High Street towards

the Upton road. The pavements were busy with shoppers,

hurrying along, their umbrellas bobbing up and down,

swerving to avoid each other, adding colour to the drab,

wet scene. The traffic was heavy and they rolled slowly

past the row of High Street shops that Caine's daughter,

Alison, referred to as skull-numbing; M&S, Next, Tesco

Metro, Boots the Chemists, Boots the optician, Superdrug,

and umpteen mobile phone outlets, all the names that,

across the country, were draining individuality out of

Britain's towns and cities. The only name with local

associations was Hengert's, the department store and even

that, it was rumoured, was under offer from a well-known

chain. Dolby stopped at the traffic lights alongside

Jefferson's DIY and switched on the car's blower system

to clear a patch of condensation from the inside of the

windscreen.

"Nice to see Mr Hartnell's busy," he said, glancing out of his side window and gesturing towards a van parked in the service road at the side of a group of shops. Caine looked across and watched the retreating back of Reginald Hartnell as he carried tins of paint, 5 litres in each hand, around the back of the van and up the exterior stairway to the flats above. A shouted expletive from the pavement on her side of the car drew her attention away from him and she watched sympathetically as a young mother struggled up the last few steps of the subway with a heavily laden pushchair, swearing profusely at the other pedestrians as they jostled to get by in the teeming rain.

"She would have found it easier to come up the slope," opined Dolby.

Caine nodded, deep in thought. Seeing Hartnell's van had reminded her of his wife. Had she really seen nothing of the killer on the train? She had been quite definite, but Caine had come away from their last meeting with the nagging feeling that she was holding something back.

It was still raining steadily when they arrived at Beckett's house a few minutes later. He was back from his night at the station and they saw him as they drew up beside the entrance door of his Antiques Emporium, standing at the window of the furniture show room, tall and composed, one hand in his trouser pocket the other resting on the shelf of a Victorian whatnot. He smiled at them through the window and raised his hand in mock salute.

"He's a pretty cool customer, no doubt about that," said Caine stepping out of the car and pulling her coat more tightly about her. "He's totally cock-sure of himself. You wouldn't think he'd spent half the night watching us search his house and then the other half in a police cell would you? I wonder if he's really that pleased to see us."

Dolby grimaced. "I doubt it, but at least we're not after *him*, for the time being anyway." He locked the car doors and slipped the keys into his coat pocket. "Are we going around the back first?" She nodded and he walked around to the boot and lifted the lid. "I'll grab an umbrella."

Dolby unfurled a large golfing umbrella and held it over them as they walked around the side of the house towards the back. They nodded at Beckett as they passed. He, still seemingly unconcerned, nodded back and then walked away from the widow, around various items of furniture to the door of the room.

There was a wide patio at the rear of the house, stretching down to the lawn that ran for over a hundred feet before breaking into an herbaceous border and, finally, a low wicket fence. Beyond the fence was the part of Upton Woods that was attached to the property. The trees – mostly birch, with a smattering of spruce - were fairly tall, being above or level with the roof of the house, but the upper branches seemed insubstantial.

"There's no way a fully grown man could climb up any of those without the branches giving way," opined Dolby. "The nearest one that could have been a possible is that sycamore," he pointed, "but it looks like the top branches have been pruned. Quite recently I'd say. It's not really high enough either." He squinted against the rain.

"And that tall building beyond must be the school dormitory quarters."

Caine nodded thoughtfully. "Yes, that tree surgeon Hickman who came in to say he'd seen a suspicious character walking across the fields near the scene of the train crash; he mentioned cutting down a sycamore in the school grounds. Last Friday as it happens. He was on his way from the school when he saw his suspicious character."

Dolby remembered mention of it in Hickman's statement. "They couldn't have been up *that* tree then." He turned to look back at Beckett's house. "Perhaps we should nip up to the bedroom, the one he and Kelly were performing in, and take a squint out of the window. Wherever the bloke taking the photographs was we must be able to see it from there."

Caine was still gazing in the direction of the school. "I don't think that'll be necessary, Mark. In fact, I think we'll do it the other way round. Let's get back to the car."

CHAPTER NINETEEN

"Your officers have already searched those rooms," said Douglas Maynard. It was a few minutes later and they were in his office where they had interrupted his toils at a large wallboard on which was inscribed a complicated timetable. He sat down at his desk and nodded wearily to the two guest chairs. "You may as well sit down while you're here." He leaned forward and dropped his marker pen onto the desk. "So, what makes you think you'll find anything else up there?"

"It's nothing to do with drugs, sir," said Dolby. "We're investigating the murder of Kelly Beacham, the young lady found dead in the woods."

Maynard nodded and took off his glasses. He wiped the lenses with his handkerchief and replaced them on his nose before replying. "Oh yes, poor young Kelly. She was an ex-pupil of the school, you know."

"You knew her?"

"Oh yes, Inspector. She was an independent lass who went through some wild phases, but I was hoping to see her settle down." He shook his head wearily. "It's dreadful, isn't it? To see these young lives snuffed out prematurely like this." He smiled weakly. "You know she belonged to the Upton Choir – she'll be sadly missed."

"You're in charge of the choir I believe," said Caine, thinking back to what Kelly Beacham's flat mate had told her. He nodded. "You saw her often there?"

"Usually once a week. She had a nice clear voice." He stood up. "Anyway, those rooms. I doubt there's anything up on the fourth-floor boarding rooms that are relevant to her murder. I've already told you I don't think anyone at the school had anything to do with it."

"We think you may be wrong," said Caine.

"Have you got new evidence then? *Clear* evidence I mean that points in that direction?"

Caine hoped Maynard would not insist on them obtaining a warrant. It would take time and she doubted they had sufficient evidence at this stage to wheedle one out of a local magistrate. But it was important they look at the rooms on the fourth floor of the school in order to get that evidence. Catch 22. "We have very strong suspicions, Mr Maynard." She smiled and changed tack. "Astronomy is one of the school's subjects I believe?"

Maynard nodded, not quite sure why she had changed the subject. "Er – yes – we do include astronomy as a science option for the older pupils. Some of them are interested. It is a fascinating subject, but you're referring of course to the drugs that were found stuck to the inside of that telescope. I thought this had nothing to do with drugs."

"I can assure you it hasn't. But the telescopes - one or two of your pupils have them?"

He nodded again, now even more uncertain where the conversation was heading. "Yes. Duncan Hill and Lee Sullivan have some rather good instruments, but you already know that." His eyes narrowed. "If it's nothing to do with drugs I can't see why you're so interested - they actually do use them for star gazing, nothing more than that

I can assure you and I fail to see what it has to do with the murder of that poor girl."

Caine smiled. "They may use them for their astronomy, but we think they might also put them to other, quite different, uses. At least, someone up there on the fourth floor does."

Maynard looked puzzled again. "What 'other use'?"

"I take it that as they were allowed bail on the drugs charges they've gone home for the Christmas holidays," said Caine, adroitly side-stepping the question. Maynard nodded. "One of them has a car I believe."

"Yes. Hill has a convertible. He and Sullivan left the school for the holidays yesterday; I believe they went together in Hill's car. They live quite close to each other – Hill's in Great Yarmouth and Sullivan is from somewhere up in North Lincolnshire. I think Hill drops him off at a station somewhere along the line. Anyway, they're not here."

"So, it won't do any harm if we trot up to have a look at their room, will it."

514

Maynard rubbed the back of his neck wearily. "Okay, you win, Inspector, but I shall insist on knowing what this is all about. For the life of me I cannot understand how either Hill or Sullivan can be connected with the murder of Kelly Beacham. They're a little wild, I admit and they obviously got themselves drawn into this drug thing, but they *are* just schoolboys." He stood up. "I'll get the keys to the rooms and we'll go up, but I shall want a full explanation."

The telescope had been packed away in its box and laid on top of the small wardrobe in the boys' room. Maynard did not demur when Caine asked him to bring it down and assemble it.

"It looks pretty powerful," said Dolby as Maynard took the long sleek barrel out of its casing. "More than enough to do the job, I'd say." He helped steady the tripod as the deputy headmaster secured the two parts together with the large metal retaining screw. "And look, there's a place here to secure a digital camera. Taking those photographs would be a doddle."

515

Maynard looked up from his task. "What photographs?" He stepped back and experimentally pivoted the barrel of the telescope on its fitting.

"Let's call them studies in human biology," said Caine. She and Dolby carried the telescope closer to the window. "We think they may have been taken using this." She peered down into the finder and twiddled the focussing knob, at the same time swivelling the barrel of the telescope left and right. "Ah! Yes – that's about it." She gave the furled knob a quick, final turn. "Perfect. Spot on. Take a look at that, Mark."

Dolby took her place at the finder. "This has got to be it."

"Got to be what?" asked Maynard impatiently. "Will you please tell me what the deuce you're talking about? What has this telescope to do with the murder of Kelly Beacham?"

Dolby straightened up. "We'll tell you in a minute, sir, but first of all would you like to take a look?"

Maynard bent over the telescope, looked through the eyepiece and then turned the focussing adjuster a couple of times. "What am I supposed to be looking at?"

"Your neighbour, Beckett's, bedroom," said Caine. "We have every reason to believe that your two nice young senior pupils have been watching him cavort in bed with his lover – and for good measure they've been taking photographs of the proceedings."

Maynard lifted his head and stared at her. His chin dropped. "They've been *what*?"

"They're peeping Toms," said Dolby brusquely. "They've been taking dirty pictures of their subjects *and*…" he paused, glanced across at Caine.

"*And* what?"

"*And* we believe they're implicated in the murder of Kelly Beacham." Caine told him.

"That's ridiculous," said Maynard, angrily. "I know those two boys, they are a little libertarian and – okay, they occasionally go out on a limb and they're obviously implicated in this cannabis business– but they're **not** capable of **murder**! I don't believe that!"

"With all due respect, what you believe or don't believe is not that important, sir," Dolby told him brusquely. He looked around the room. "Shall we search the room now, Ma'am?"

Caine nodded. "While we're here, though I shouldn't think we'll find anything incriminating. They probably got rid of anything suspicious when Kelly's body was found."

"You're wrong about those two, I'm sure you're wrong," said Maynard, taking off his spectacles and wiping the lenses nervously with his handkerchief. He shook his head. "Look – I think I'd better let the head know what's going on here – will you excuse me? You can stay and get on with whatever it is you have to do." He backed towards the door. "If you could come and see me before you leave the school premises, I'd appreciate it."

"Oh yes, we'll need the boys' home addresses," said Caine. "Oh, and by the way, what day does the council collect the school's refuse?"

518

Maynard looked at her as though she was out of her mind. "Tuesday."

Later that afternoon Duncan Hill's car was transported from his home just outside Great Yarmouth. It arrived at the forensic laboratories a few hours before the schoolboy, his father and the family's solicitor, accompanied by DS Dolby and a uniformed officer, drove up in front of Fen Molesey Central Police Station. They were ushered through the reception area and into number one interview room at just after nine thirty that evening. A few minutes later Caine's car arrived from Pinchbeck, just outside Spalding, carrying Lee Sullivan and his parents; their solicitor, it was understood, would meet them in the station as soon as he could disengage himself from a private function. DS Dolby met them in the reception area.

"I've got the other boy in room two," he told Caine. "It wasn't an easy journey down I can tell you."

"Nor mine," said Caine. She turned to Sergeant Wallace at the desk. "Put these people in Interview Room

519

2, Bill, and get some food organised for them, anything they want within reason. After that, rouse Wendy Doyle for me, if she's still around, I need to speak to her." She turned back to Dolby. "A quick word, Mark." He followed her into the small office behind the front desk. "Did Hill say anything?"

Mark shook his head. "No, as soon as his father realised I was there on serious business he called in his solicitor. Difficult beggar, he told the boy to remain silent. The only thing I managed to get out of young Duncan was that he hadn't a clue who Kelly Beacham was; first he said he'd never heard of her, then he said he'd never met her."

Caine sat on the edge of the desk. "Same with my lad, only they couldn't get hold of their lawyer, so it was the parents told the boy to clam up. They knew that much; they didn't need a solicitor."

"Where do we go from here then?

The door opened and DC Wendy Doyle came in carrying a manila folder and a box file. "You wanted me, Ma'am?"

"Yes, though I must admit I'm surprised you're still here. Any news from Forensics on the boy's car?"

"No, Ma'am, nothing yet," Wendy replied. "I've been busy going through those statements and I've been looking through Kelly Beacham's personal stuff," she indicated the box file." You know, just in case we missed anything the first time. I sort of forgot what time it was.

"What about the waste bins at the school?"

Doyle grimaced and sat wearily down on one of the guest chairs. "That was a bloody awful job, Ma'am one of the few times I've wondered why I was so eager to get into the CID! Anyway, your hunch the refuse collection would be re-scheduled for the run up to Christmas was spot on. The council's running nearly two days late, we managed to find some prints." Caine smiled, pleased. "They'd been ripped into pieces, of course, but I matched up a couple without too much trouble. They were pretty raunchy I can tell you! I've passed them over to the lab for matching up with the digital images we found on the SD

Card; but there's no doubt in my mind that they came from there."

Caine picked up the box file and rested it on her knees. "Have the boys admitted anything?"

"Fat chance," said Dolby, moving a pile of papers from a chair and sitting down. He yawned and looked up at the wall clock. It was very nearly nine forty-five. "Hill told me he doesn't even know the woman, never met her. He's a cocky little beggar. A right spoiled little sod if ever I saw one."

"What was it Graham Maynard said about him?" asked Caine thoughtfully. Tired, she rubbed her eyes. "Oh yes, over-indulged, that's the way he put it. And he's not far wrong either, the kid has his own state-of- the- art convertible and, by all accounts, a speed boat down at Maldon Marina."

"And he said he'd never met Kelly Beacham?" asked Wendy Doyle, "That's interesting, or at least it might be." She opened the box file and took out a large envelope, leaning forward to shake the contents on to the desktop. A pile of loose photographs fell out and she rummaged among them. "Here it is." She passed one of them over to Caine. "I haven't seen Hill or Sullivan, so I'm not sure if it *is* them, but that's definitely Kelly. They're on a boat down at Maldon, you can recognise the quay behind them, there's that little Chandlers' shop in the background."

Caine studied the photograph for a moment and then nodded and passed it across to Dolby. "Yeah, that's them. Cosy together aren't they, the three of them."

Dolby studied the photograph for a moment and then dropped it back on the desk. "Those lads have been lying through their teeth, which comes as no surprise, of course, the little gits. If they didn't know Kelly *very well indeed* then I'm a Dutchman. They're all over her and she's loving it, look where they've got their hands."

Doyle picked up the photograph again. "They're not wearing much, so it must have been taken in the summer." She turned over some more photos, searching. "There's another one of her somewhere, with Marcus Beckett. He has a boat down there as well, I think. Here it is." She pulled another one from the pile and passed it over to Caine. "One of the boys is with them, but I'm not sure which is which."

"It's Duncan Hill," Caine confirmed. "Well spotted, Wendy. At least this gives us the opening we need. Just let them go on pretending they didn't know Kelly Beacham! And *this* snap definitely links them to Beckett, so we can have a go at them on the drugs angle, too."

"Do you intend confronting them with that tonight?" asked Dolby, standing up. "It's getting pretty late. I know they're both legally over age, but they're still at school and we don't want to give their lawyers any excuses for claiming harassment."

Caine held back a yawn. "I know what you mean. It's been a long day, but I think we'll see them now and give them something to think about overnight." She leaned over the desk and tapped the photograph depicting the two boys with the murdered woman. "They can't argue with this and if our hunches are correct and the forensic boys and girls

524

deliver on the car, we should be home and dry by tomorrow morning."

Duncan Hill, tall and self assured beyond his years, his long fair hair neatly combed, showed his teeth in a smile, but his eyes remained cold and appraising. He had clean-cut features, a firm jaw and a straight aquiline nose. His skin was dark, retaining a hint of tan from the long days spent on the playing fields and at the wheel of his speedboat, moored down at Maldon marina, and there was a long scratch, still slightly raw, running down his cheek. He looked casually at the photograph and then threw it back across the table as though it was of no consequence. "That's me and Lee Sullivan, yes, I can hardly deny that can I? And the woman, I sort of remember her, vaguely. We meet lots of women down at the Marina in the summer, it's a famous flocking place for the birds. Obviously, we met her then, when the photo was taken, but apart from that I'm afraid my mind is a complete blank, Inspector. I've told you before I don't *know* the woman so I can't think why you keep on going on about her!" He peered across the desk to look at the photograph again. "Been murdered has she, poor cow?" He crossed his Armani jeaned legs and smiled across at Caine and Dolby. Beside him his solicitor, a tall thin man by the name of Herman Porter, wriggled uncomfortably.

"Okay, Mr Hill," said Caine. "How about this gentleman then? Do you know him?" She showed him the photograph of himself, Kelly Beacham and Marcus Beckett.

Hill smiled lazily and yawned widely to show his boredom. "You're really not a very inspired detective are you, Inspector? Everyone in Fen Molesey knows him – Mr Beckett is town weirdo, so it's me and the weirdo and his bird standing together on a boat down in the harbour. What does that prove?"

"It proves you know the woman was Beckett's girl friend," said Dolby with some satisfaction, although it didn't really prove much at all. Still, the cocky little sod was bound to trip himself up sooner or later. At least he had had the good grace to turn a little pale when the photographs were produced. Now he was nervously fingering the scratch on his cheek. Interesting, that scratch. Doc Williams had said the murdered woman had traces of skin under her fingernails – would they match up? Dolby smiled to himself and wondered how the lad would react when they told him they also had the explicit photographs of Beckett and Kelly. "Are you sure you wouldn't like to change what you said earlier?"

Duncan Hill shook his head. "I'm not saying anything else."

"Sleep on it," advised Caine, standing up. She directed her next words to Porter who looked as though this was the last place he wanted to be at nearly eleven o'clock on a Thursday evening. "Perhaps you'd like to advise your client that it's time he started to tell us the truth, Mr Porter. We do have a lot more interesting things coming along tomorrow morning by the way. Have a good night."

"I hope you're right, Jackie, about the interesting things for tomorrow morning," said Dolby in her office a few minutes later. "But what if forensic ***don't*** come up

with the corroborating evidence?"

CHAPTER TWENTY

Dolby sounded relieved as he answered Caine's question. Like her, he was obviously tired through lack of sleep. He had had a late night and now an obviously early morning. "No, it's not Emma, Jackie – she still hasn't shown up. It's worse in a way - it's another nurse."

Caine's heart sank. She kept the cordless telephone pressed to her ear as she made her way back into the bathroom, her other hand clutching the towel around her naked body. "Where did you say they found her?"

"Down one of the pedestrian underpasses in the High Street."

"Any ID?"

"Don't know yet. All Bill Wallace would say was it's a nurse – *another* nurse. Apparently, she's in full uniform. Looks like it happened when she was making her way

529

home from the hospital last night. I'm on my way over there now."

"Okay. I'll see you there." Caine pressed the 'off' button on the receiver and placed it on top of the low-level cistern before shaking off the towel and stepping back into the shower. Another nurse. If there were other similarities with the train crash murder they probably had a serial killer on their hands and whoever it was must have some sort of fixation on nurses. She squeezed shampoo from the plastic bottle and massaged it vigorously into her hair and scalp. At least that was some sort of lead, she reflected, however tenuous – all they had to do now was find someone who had a penchant for murdering nurses. And maybe now they would have to think about police protection for Mrs Hartnell; she was still their only witness to the train crash killing and, in spite of her protestations that she could remember nothing about the murder Caine still nurtured the hope that something would come back to her. They had to protect the woman. She sighed and then smiled to herself. Dolby's joke about Mrs H. making use of her contacts on '*the other side*' to find out who was responsible for the killings wasn't really so ridiculous. It would have saved them a lot of time and trouble. Pity things didn't work that way.

It was a quarter to eight when Caine arrived at the scene. The High Street was only a few minutes walk from Fen Molesey Central and she drove in and parked her car in the police station car park before walking across, snug in her Barbour raincoat and preferring to ignore the slight drizzle than suffer the inconvenience of carrying an umbrella. The sky was still dark, but the High Street shopping area was well lit and she found the underpass easily enough. A uniformed officer stood at the top of the steps, the approach to which had already been taped off, and although she did not recognise him, he obviously knew her.

He nodded sombrely as she came up to him. "Morning, Ma'am. DS Dolby and the doctor are down at the bottom of the steps. Take care on the way down, they can be a bit slippery in this drizzle and it's dark, only one

of the lights down there is working."

She nodded her thanks and lifted the tape to duck

beneath it, making her way down the steps towards the two

men huddled at the bottom. One of them looked up at her

approach and she recognised Mark Dolby in the dim light

of the lone sodium lamp located on the wall at the entrance

to the foot tunnel. It was dark and forbidding; there were, it

seemed, no lights at all working in the area where the body

had been found. Dolby's collar and tie were askew;

evidence of his hurried scramble to get dressed when news

of this latest killing had reached him. Beside him Peter

Williams, the Police Surgeon, was intently studying the

figure on the ground. The woman lay on her back, her eyes

closed, her face and clothes sodden from the rain that had

fallen steadily throughout the night. She had short blonde

hair and a fine boned face filmed with moisture from the

rain; she could not have been much more than twenty years

old. Her arms were bent up towards her chest, the fingers

of her hands bunched into fists; her legs, beneath the light blue skirt, were curled up in the foetal position.

"It's the same MO," said Williams wearily, looking up and nodding to Caine as she approached. "Morning, Jackie – not a good one, I'm afraid. Same style as the train crash murderer. A string garrotte." He pushed his trilby hat slightly up over his forehead so that he could scratch his head thoughtfully. "The bastard's at it again – it looks like he's targeting nurses." He sighed and stood up. "I'll be able to tell you more when we get her in for the autopsy, but for the moment that's about it." He pulled off his rubber gloves, stuffing them into his pocket. "Don't expect anything from me until this evening, though, I've got a pretty tight schedule as it is, administering medical skills to the living."

"Any ID?"

Dolby nodded. "She had her ID tag from the hospital on her. Janine Foster. Student nurse at Fen Molesey General. She looks about 20 years old. Her purse was in her pocket, so it doesn't look like robbery." He turned to Williams. "What about timing, Doc? When did it happen?"

Williams shrugged. "Dunno, Mark. As you know, it's difficult when the weather's like this. Body cools off very rapidly. If you were to press me, I'd say some time late last night. Elevenish maybe. I honestly don't know. If she was on her way home from the hospital or whatever you'd do better finding out what time she was seen leaving her shift. Add ten or fifteen minutes to walk here and that'll be more or less when she died."

"Thanks," said Caine gloomily. "We'll do that. Funny, though, that nobody found her before this morning."

"Not really," replied the doctor. "Not many people come down here when it gets really dark. They're scared this very thing'll happen to them – and they can't rely on the local coppers to protect them anymore."

"Fair comment," said Dolby ruefully. "The other thing is that the dossers use these places to bed down. Someone might have seen her lying here and assumed she

534

was homeless and dossing down for the night. It's a sad reflection on our society."

"Yes, well, you find me a government that knows the solution to that particular problem," said Caine, looking down at the body. She turned again to the doctor. "Any sign of rape?"

Williams shook his head and then shrugged. "Not so far as I can tell at the moment, won't know the answer to that until I've examined her properly. But her clothing doesn't seem to have been disturbed." He buttoned his heavy overcoat, turned down the brim of his trilby hat and picked up his case, turning towards the steps. "I'll be in touch. Happy hunting."

Caine watched him go and then looked slowly around the dingy area. It was all shadows and dirty grey concrete decorated with graffiti and, in the slowly falling rain, it depressed her even more. This was not the sort of place a lithe and vital young woman should meet her death. She suddenly felt the need to get away from the place and turned towards Dolby. "Anything else we need to do here,

535

Mark? We have unfinished business back at the station, with Masters Sullivan and Hill." She laughed dryly. "This is all we needed isn't it though, another dead nurse and a likely serial killer. Thank heavens the Kelly Beacham case is looking a bit more positive. Perhaps we can clear that up and get back to tracking down the train killer."

Dolby nodded his agreement. "Yes, there's nothing else we can do here for the time being. I've had a quick look round and the SOCO team are on their way over. We can get back here later, if necessary, when they've finished."

"No news on Emma Atterwood, then?" Caine asked Dolby a few minutes later as they crossed from the High Street to turn into the car park of the police station. They had plodded along together silently until then, each with their own thoughts.

"No. Not a word. Pauline and Derek are out of their minds. They think the worst."

"Naturally, as a parent I'd be inclined to think the same." They waited as a vehicle turned across their path and into the police station car park and then they set off towards the front entrance door. "What do *you* think?"

Dolby hesitated. "To tell you the truth, Jackie, I don't know what to think anymore. The more I've probed Derek and Pauline and the more inquiries we've made at her school the more obvious it is that Emma was – *is* – a bit of a tearaway. She's headstrong, with a mind of her own."

"So?"

"So, there's a fair chance she's not lying dead somewhere. On the other hand…" His voice trailed off as he pushed the door and held it open for Caine.

When they got to her office the forensic report on Duncan Hill's car was lying on her desk. She picked it up and skimmed through it, noting the relevant points. "It's only a preliminary report, Mark, but I think we've got enough here to continue our questioning."

He was standing by the window watching the traffic build up in the street outside, the people alighting from the buses at the stops and bustling by on their way to work. The scene, yellow lit as the luminescence of the streetlamps faded slowly against the light of the rising sun, was almost surreal. He thought of a Lowry painting.

"You still think it's the boys? Only I can't help wishing we could find something to incriminate that man Beckett."

"Don't let him become an obsession, Mark. He didn't kill Kelly Beacham. He was somewhere else at the time. We'll get him on the other charges though. All in good time." She dropped the report on to her desk. "Everything points to the two schoolboys. You've only got to look at the evidence forensic have picked up from the boy's car." She looked at her watch. "It's all here, in the report, Mark, read it while I organise some coffees – then we'll go and talk to them." She stood up. "Oh – and I think, initially, we'll concentrate on young Lee Sullivan – he shows more signs of cracking than his friend Duncan."

The pale-faced boy nodded respectfully, as Caine and Dolby sat down at the table opposite him and his solicitor, a short podgy man in a brown suit and white shirt that stretched and bulged at his midriff. He announced himself as Gerald Jacobson and handed Caine his card, which he took from a voluminous briefcase reclining on the floor beside him.

"Please bear in mind my client's tender age, Inspector." His voice was slightly squeaky. "I shall be paying particular attention to the tone of your questions. And I have already noted your reluctance to allow Mr Sullivan's parents to be present."

"Oh, I don't think you need worry yourself about that, Mr Jacobson," Caine replied pleasantly, wondering what sort of law practice the man ran. She doubted he had dealt much with serious crime. Lee Sullivan might be still at school, but he had the physique of a fully developed, mature man, being well over six feet tall and big framed. Caine estimated his weight at something over fifteen stone, a man not to be ignored in a rugby scrum. He was wearing jeans, a blue sweatshirt with the BOSS logo emblazoned across it and Doc Marten boots. His eyes were quick, intelligent and distinctly worried. He was vulnerable, in spite of his physical size and his reluctance to be questioned in the presence of his parents (to avoid their embarrassment or their condemnation?) "It wasn't my doing, Mr Jacobson. I think Lee made his preferences quite clear."

They had been through the necessary recording preliminaries, so now Caine opened her file and took out the photographs of Beckett and Kelly Beacham, developed by the police photographer, together with the torn ones found in the Upton Grange School garbage bags. She placed them, re-assembled and encased in transparent plastic envelopes, face down on the tabletop. "I'm going to show you some photographs, Lee, and I want you to tell me if you've seen them before and whether you and your friend Duncan Hill took them." She turned one of them over, watching the boy's face.

He looked at them and a flicker of fear flashed across his brown eyes. His face, already pale, drained completely of colour.

The lawyer, Jacobson, gasped. "I must protest, Inspector," he spluttered. "This is sheer filth!"

Caine ignored his outburst. "Well, Lee - do you know the people in these pictures?"

The boy hesitated. He was close to tears. He nodded slowly. "Yes. It's Mr Beckett, who runs the antiques business near the school. And the girl – the woman – that's Kelly Beacham, but we didn't kill her, Miss, honestly!"

Caine turned over a couple of the torn prints. "We found these, in the garbage bin at your school, Lee. They have *your* fingerprints on them, *and Duncan's*. So, you have seen them before, haven't you?"

Lee Sullivan nodded, his face pale.

"Did *you* take these photographs, Lee, using a digital camera and your telescope, the one that's in your dormitory up at the school?"

He nodded again, licking his lips nervously with the tip of his tongue. "Yes, me and Duncan, we sort of saw Mr Beckett and Kelly in his house one night, while we were playing with the telescope. We hadn't intended to – I mean, we weren't being peeping Toms or anything like that..."

Dolby laughed humourlessly. "Oh, come off it, lad! You don't take photographs like that without intending to!"

The boy sniffed back his tears. "That was *his* idea, sir, Duncan's, he had a thing going for Kelly – we'd met her down in Maldon in the summer you see, on the boats – he has a speedboat down there in the Marina and Mr Beckett also has one – a proper boat his is, much bigger than Duncan's..." His voice trailed off and he blinked back the wetness from his eyes. "But we didn't kill her, we really didn't."

Caine opened her file and replaced the photographs. "We'll come to that in due course, Lee." She took out the forensic report. "Now, we know that Kelly Beacham's car ran out of petrol on the Upton Road, near the woods, at some time after half past nine on Monday evening. We also know that on that night Duncan's car was parked near hers – there were tyre prints in the mud a few hundred yards from where her body was found." She paused. "What exactly happened on that night, Lee? Were you with Duncan when you picked Kelly up?"

Lee took a sip of water from the glass on the table. "Yes, Miss, we – er - me and Duncan – we finished our prep work for the evening at just after half past nine and he suggested we go out for a spin in the car, we often do that – we listen to the music –his car's got a really great sound system and we can play it really loud without anyone complaining – and then we maybe stop off for a drink somewhere…" he frowned as he realised what he had said and then hastened on, "…at a coffee bar usually, but that evening just as we were driving down the Upton road towards town, well, we noticed this car at the side of the road." He stopped, sipped at the water. "As soon as we realised it was Kelly, Duncan stopped to ask if there was anything we could do to help. She said she'd run out of petrol and he suggested we take her to a garage to pick some up and she came in the car – it's a two door, so I climbed in the back and she got in beside him – and then, well, Duncan went a bit funny."

"How do you mean, funny?" asked Dolby sharply.

"It wasn't me, sir, it was him. He didn't drive to the garage as he said he would, he just drove down the Upton Road and then pulled off into the woods. He started to come on to Kelly, you know…"

"Did you have the prints with you, the photos?"

He nodded. "Yeah. Duncan kept the SD card in the car – less chance of someone finding it; and even if they did – well, they wouldn't know what was on it. Would they? Not without a laptop. He said we had to keep them safe – the card and the prints we'd printed out that is - know where they were at all times, in case somebody else found out about them. He didn't mention them to Kelly though, not at first, not until she…you know…"

"Until she what..?"

The young man blushed. "Duncan said to her, you know, how about if me and him, well…" he hesitated. "He sort of asked if we could …you know – 'bonk' her."

Jacobson had been following this monologue with a constant frown on his face. "What do you mean 'bonk'

544

her?" he asked darkly. "Do you mean have – er…" he glanced across at Caine hesitantly, "have– *sex* - intercourse with her?"

Lee Sullivan gulped and then nodded.

"And what happened then?" asked Caine. She glanced pointedly at Jacobson. "Don't be shy, Lee, we all know about this sort of thing."

"She just laughed at him, Miss. Called him a stupid kid or something – and said that anyway she wasn't that sort of a girl. So, Duncan got really angry with her."

"What did he do?"

"He showed her the photos – the ones with her and Beckett having it off and doing things together. He said she *was* that sort of girl and the photos proved it! Well, she looked at them and called us a couple of names. Then she took out her mobile and tried to call someone on it, I suppose 'cos she wanted to frighten us off or something – I don't know who she rang because Duncan stopped her and then she started screaming to be let out of the car, but all he did was to paw at her body and - and…" he paused again to gather his wits. "You know, he put his hand under her coat and pulled at her blouse and things and tried to kiss her. She hit him, scratched him across the face and then she managed to open the door and get out of the car... the last we saw of her she was running away into the woods." He paused. "That's the last Duncan and I saw of her, I swear."

"What time was this, Lee?" asked Caine.

He shrugged. "About ten, I suppose, or maybe a bit before. I don't really know. She ran away from us, Miss. Don't you believe me?"

Caine ignored the question. "What did you do then?"

"Duncan just drove off and we drove around for a bit before going back to the school. We didn't talk much about what had happened – I didn't want to raise the subject and get Duncan worked up about it, he can be pretty mean when he's in a bad mood. But then on the way back to school he kept going on about the photographs and how Kelly was bound to tell on us, so we had to get rid of them. We knew the school rubbish gets collected on a Tuesday morning, so we tore them up – the photos - and put them in one of the big rubbish bins, making sure they went to the bottom." He paused, looking puzzled. "How did you find them, Miss?"

"The Council didn't empty the bins on Tuesday this week, Lee," said Caine. "Christmas rota or something, they do a re-shuffle of their collection schedules. Otherwise, we'd have missed them." She turned back to her file. "And you're quite sure you never saw Kelly Beacham again?"

The boy nodded.

"She ran away from Duncan's car and into the woods?"

He nodded again. "Yes. Don't you believe me, Miss?"

"Sorry, Lee," said Dolby softly, "but we're having a little bit of a problem there. Kelly was in the front seat of the car you say."

"Yes, sir, it's two door – I got in the back when we picked her up. She went in the front passenger seat."

"And not in the back? That's funny," Dolby kept his voice low and calm, "Peculiar I mean, because we've found traces of her face powder and a few of her hairs on the back seat, plus one or two other things that were obviously hers. And you say that neither Duncan Hill nor you had sex with her?"

The boy was holding back his tears. "No. I told you," he retorted desperately. "She wouldn't let us."

"Peculiar again, Lee, because a pair of her panties were found stuffed into the back seat squab. Curious that, isn't it! Why would she take her panties off in the back of your friend's car?" Lee Sullivan's face was ashen. "But it gets worse, Lee, much worse. You see, Kelly was strangled with a piece of rope – two ply marine rope to be precise, blue and white, the sort of stuff people use when mucking about in boats. Fibres from that rope – the *same* one, not just one like it – were found in Duncan's car. So, are you still sure Kelly Beacham ran away from you that night, into the woods?"

The boy shouted his reply. "She did, I tell you. She ran away! We didn't kill her!"

Nearly four hours later Caine sat at her desk and bit into a cheese sandwich. Dolby, opposite her, chewed at a piece of lettuce protruding from the edges of his turkey salad baguette and then sipped at his coffee.

"They did it all right," he said. "They won't admit it, but it's all there isn't it." He took a big bite of the baguette and chewed industriously.

She nodded. Duncan Hill's statement had agreed with Lee Sullivan's in almost every detail except that the roles of the two boys had been reversed. In Duncan's version Lee had been driving, it was Lee who lusted after Kelly Beacham and it was Lee who had had the fight with her, Duncan sustaining his scratched cheek only when he intervened between them. But according to both boys' version of events, repeated over and over again during the course of the morning, Kelly had fought with them, escaped from their car and then ran away into the woods. They had not seen her again.

"Do you think we'll get them to admit to the rest of it?" asked Dolby.

549

"That they killed her? Who's to say? Four hours this morning didn't wear either of them down and I don't know how much longer we can go on questioning them. If we overdo it their lawyers will be all over us." She sipped her coffee thoughtfully. "At the end of the day how far we go depends on the CPS, I suppose, but personally I think we've got enough to charge them. How do you feel about it, Mark?"

He thought for a few moments. "Yes, I'd go along with that. We've drawn a blank on all the other possibilities – Beckett couldn't have done it because of the timing, his friendly drugs courier is almost certainly out of the picture, there's only the most tenuous link with him, so we come back to the two boys. They've admitted Kelly was in their car with them, there was Kelly's stuff in there that shouldn't have been and they obviously tried to have sex with her; I don't know and they're not telling."

Caine agreed. "Yes, Mark, we can't ignore the forensic evidence – Duncan Hill's car's full of it."

550

Dolby nodded. "They're both lying through their teeth about killing her – up to that point they're probably telling the truth, more or less, except they're trying to muddy the water by blaming the actual assault on each other. They've set it up between them; they've had plenty of time."

"Yes, it looks like it. Now it's Lee's word against Duncan's and vice versa, although I'm more inclined to believe Duncan was the instigator. He's a pretty cold fish I must say and he's probably threatened Lee if he doesn't go along with the deception." She paused thoughtfully. "There's just one thing that bothers me – if they were intending to rape her how come she was strangled with a piece of rope? It doesn't quite add up."

"How about if she put up a fight and they killed her by accident," suggested Dolby, "and then they used the rope to throw us off the scent; make us think she was killed by the same maniac that did for Marion Winters?"

He was interrupted by a loud knock on the door, which opened to admit a large head covered with bushy grey hair. The face beneath it, beaming and bearded, was that of Bob Hawthorne, the Fen Molesey force's chief forensic officer.

"Hope I'm not interrupting anything," he bowled into the room waving a file of papers triumphantly in the air and guided his six-foot frame to a guest chair. He slumped into it and leaned forward, still waving the file. "I've found her!"

"Hallo, Bob," said Caine, putting down the remains of her sandwich and dabbing at her lips with a paper handkerchief. "*Who* exactly have you found?" She asked ungrammatically.

"The poison pen letterer," said Hawthorne, equally ungrammatically. "If that's what you want to call her. It's as good a name as any, except for her real one of course and as it happens, I'm pretty sure I know that too. Mind you, I nearly never got round to it what with all the other stuff you've been throwing my way – how did it go by the way, the young woman in the woods? Have you charged anyone yet?"

"We were just discussing it," said Dolby. "It looks pretty positive."

"Got to be the car owner - no doubts in my mind. The fibres are definitely from the same bit of rope and those panties in the back of the car were definitely hers, no arguments. So far as I'm concerned that case is all wrapped up bar the trial." He opened the file and leaned forward. "Now, the reason I'm here – that poison pen letter," he pulled the letter from the file. It was enclosed in an envelope. "Very interesting. Melodramatic, but interesting. At first it looked like there was nothing on it to give us even the remotest clue," he looked across at them, his eyebrow cocked. "But never underestimate the ingenuity of us scientific folk. Ever heard of Fibre memory? No – don't lose any sleep over it, you're not alone, most people haven't. I have, of course. All it means, in this particular context, is the impression that gets left in the sheets of paper *under* the one you're writing on."

"You mean when you write something on the top sheet of the pad and it comes through very faintly on the one beneath?"

"Got it in one. Only on this particular sheet of paper there didn't seem to be anything – but it looked like the paper came from a pad, so I thought 'give it a try' with cross light photography – I won't go into that, far too complicated. Let's just say it worked. There **was** *something* on the paper, written on the sheet above the one bearing the poison pen message and impressed onto it from the above sheet." He paused, smiling.

"*What*?" asked Caine impatiently. Didn't the man know she had another two murders on her very busy hands?

"A number." He read from the file. "01968214546, to be precise. It turns out to be a phone number."

"Come on Bob," said Caine. "Is that number supposed to mean anything to us?"

"I'll put you out of your misery," said Hawthorne with a grin. "I didn't know it either, but I've got some pretty intelligent people in my team and one of them came up with the answer almost immediately." He paused again.

"Well? Get on with it, Bob!"

"I hesitate because you're going to have trouble believing this," said Hawthorne, obviously enjoying himself at their expense. "It's the emergency number..." he almost paused again but caught the dangerous glint in Caine's eye and went on, still smiling. "The phone number they gave out after last week's rail crash, for relatives and interested parties to ring for information."

"But this is nothing to do with the rail crash," Dolby declared. "The letter was going on about Kelly Beacham being murdered by Marcus Beckett. What's that got to do with the train crash? I don't get it."

"You will," said Hawthorne. "As much as I've got it so far, anyway and it doesn't make much sense to me."

"Is that all then?" said Caine, unable to follow his reasoning, if it was reasoning. "All you've got is a phone number, is that it, Bob? So why are grinning like some moronic chimpanzee?"

"Am I? Sorry." The forensic expert composed his features. "But that's not all. There were some other impressions on the paper, not just the number."

"Oh, come on, Bob, spit it out. We've got two other murders on our hands. We really can't afford the time for these schoolboy guessing games."

"Okay, okay. The impression of the postmark came through from the envelope. But there was something else, actually on the paper of the printed letters the poison pen writer used to spell out her message." He held up the sheet of paper and pointed. "It says '*For Kelly's killer look no further than Marcus Beckett. Watch the broken hand*." The perpetrator used words and letters cut from a magazine; some of them complete words and phrases. The piece '*look no further*' for instance was actually cut out as a complete section, together with the white paper around it, including the border of the magazine's page – those words were printed on the bottom line of a page of the magazine. That meant there was extra unprinted paper for any impression to show up on - and it did – the magazine must have been delivered through the post and whoever sent it used a franking machine with their logo on the printing plate." He smiled again.

"Are you trying to tell us the magazine's franking logo was actually impressed on the printed paper inside the envelope?" asked Dolby, unsure if he was following Hawthorne's explanation.

"Not all of it, just a section and it was extremely faint, but it was enough. We put it through our tests and we came up with this," he passed over a sheet of paper on which was written '*hic Her*' "That's one I made earlier."

"But what does 'hic her' mean?" asked Dolby, puzzled. "It sounds like Latin!"

"Let me put you out of your misery," said Hawthorne, "We made a computer search of the UK magazine directory, inputting '*hic Her*' and – lo and behold – it coughed up the words '*Psychic Herald*'. So, now we had two parts of the jigsaw. Firstly, the sender of the letter used a sheet of paper with the emergency number from the rail crash impressed on it and, secondly, he or she stuck *printed words on it, taken from the Psychic Herald.*"

"Dorothy Hartnell!" Caine exclaimed. "She was involved in the train crash and her husband would have written the emergency number down when he heard the news of the train crash over the radio. *And* she's a spiritualist - I'll bet she's on the Psychic Herald's mailing list!"

"I am impressed. That was very quick, Inspector," said Hawthorne, a little deflated that she had deprived him of the chance of prolonging his explanation. "You *do* have an advantage over us, of course - *we* didn't know she was mixed up with the spook world. We had to phone the Psychic Herald to see who was on their mailing list and then cross check it against the local people who rang the emergency number. But we got there. We also got the name 'Hartnell'."

"Well done anyway, Bob," said Caine, beaming, "that was an excellent piece of detective work. You haven't managed to work out what '***Watch the broken hand***' means have you? It's had us stumped."

Hawthorne shook his head. "It might be new world stuff, I suppose. They're very fond of riddles, aren't they? And they have affected ways of putting things, like with new wave poetry. Why make something understandable when, with very little effort, you can make it totally incomprehensible?"

"Thanks, that's a great help, Bob." Caine absentmindedly picked up the last portion of her sandwich and popped it into her mouth. "But wait a minute, what am I so pleased about? It doesn't matter who wrote the poison pen letter - we've already got Kelly Beacham's killers. But, on the other hand - what the heck has Dorothy Hartnell to do with Marcus Beckett?"

CHAPTER TWENTY- ONE

Caine and Dolby were on their way out of the station an hour or so later when they met Graham Maynard coming in. He was moving quickly up the steps and they almost ran into him as they stepped through the doorway. He was breathing heavily as though he had parked his car at a distance and ran all the way to the police station. He lurched unsteadily as the door opened before him.

"Oh, hello, Mr Maynard," said Dolby catching him by the arm to steady him. "You're in a bit of a hurry, aren't you? Anything wrong?"

"Yes, there is as a matter of fact," said Maynard angrily. "I hear you're charging those two boys with murder. Is that true?"

"Yes," said Caine. "We charged them about half an hour ago."

Maynard's shoulders slumped. "You've made a mistake. Those kids aren't murderers."

"We think they are, sir," said Dolby. "But I don't think we want to discuss it here, do you, on the steps of the station entrance. If you've got anything to add to our investigations perhaps you'd like to come and see us later."

"I'd like to talk about it *now*, Sergeant, if you don't mind," said the other man. He was still angry. He took off his spectacles nervously and started to polish them on his handkerchief, calming down a little. "I'm sure you've made a big mistake."

Caine looked at her watch. It was just after five o'clock. They were anxious to get to the bottom of the Hartnell-Beckett puzzle, but they had plenty of time to interview the Hartnells. "We were on our way out to an important meeting, Mr Maynard, but we'll give you five minutes." She turned and led the way back into the station.

"I just think you're wrong about them," said Maynard a couple of minutes later. They had gone through to the small office behind the reception area. "It's out of character

561

– at least for young Sullivan, he gets led on, you know, by Duncan Hill. I suppose I can believe they were into the sex thing, the photographs – that's sort of natural at their age - but I really can't believe they'd *murder* anyone. They've never done anything violent before."

"On the contrary – Duncan Hill was expelled from his previous school for breaking another pupil's nose," said Caine, "I don't suppose his previous school told you *that* when you checked his references, not in so many words, anyway. And he and Lee have been up in front of our desk sergeant on a number of occasions for causing a public nuisance. We also have reason to believe that, courtesy of one M. Beckett, Esquire, they're been mixed up in the drug pushing that's been going on at your school. They're not squeaky clean and sanitized, you know, either of them."

Dolby took up the cudgels before Maynard could reply. "And that's ignoring the fact that the two of them were actually under suspicion for drug offences at the time of the murder. Really, Mr Maynard, the mind boggles – what sort of excuse can you dig up to get out of *that*?"

Maynard floundered. "I didn't know about the broken nose," he admitted, depressed. "And I'm not denying they're implicated in this drugs thing, but look - they're just teenage boys, young adults, having trouble adapting to life, just like any other teenagers." He sighed. "Look, if you are going to charge them both please bear in mind that Sullivan is the weaker of the two characters. He's heavily under Hill's influence."

"We'll bear that in mind," said Caine. "But at the moment they seem to be equally culpable."

"I still don't believe they're killers."

"Sorry, but the evidence says they are," Dolby told him. "Look, sir, they've admitted assaulting Kelly Beacham on the night of her murder, there's no question of that *and* our forensic evidence says they went on to kill her. For some reason they won't admit to that, but they did it all right." He stood up. "Do you know what I think, Mr Maynard? I think you're only really interested in protecting the name of your school – after all, there won't be many parents lining up to send their kids to a school famous for its murderers will there?"

"I think that'll be enough," said Caine, also standing up. "Unless you have some sort of concrete evidence that will persuade us otherwise, Mr Maynard, we do intend to press charges against Hill and Sullivan." She moved towards the door and opened it. "Now, I don't think there's anything more to be said on the matter, do you?"

Caine and Dolby made their way out of the police station car park and turned left to walk through to the High Street, pulling their coats more tightly about them as the wind, racing up from the river, caught them in a prolonged blast.

"It's not getting any brighter," complained Dolby, looking up at the grey, cloud laden sky. "And we're not getting any closer to finding Marion Winters' killer. I honestly don't see the point of following up on that poison pen letter, even if it did come from Mrs Hartnell. We've already got Kelly Beacham's killers."

"I still want to know what the connection is between Hartnell and Beckett," said Caine. "So far as I'm concerned it's a coincidence too far!"

"So do I," Dolby assured her. "I'm not saying it hasn't got me intrigued, Jackie, especially when we know Marcus Beckett *didn't* kill Kelly. It's just that the Hartnell woman's a complete nutter – malicious letters are probably her thing - so I'm just wondering if we'd do better to follow our other leads than bothering with that letter."

They turned into the High Street. The wind dropped slightly and they lengthened their stride. "What other leads?" inquired Caine with an ironic laugh. "I know we thought we had plenty, but they've all fallen by the wayside, haven't they?"

"I still think it's possible there may have been some sort of conspiracy between Marion Winters' husband and that O'Hanlon guy," said Dolby. "If only we could lay our hands on him we might get somewhere."

Caine shook her head. "No, I think that one's fizzled out too, Mark." They manoeuvred around a young woman

565

pushing a double width pushchair out of Boots. "Look, we may as well follow through on the poison pen letter, if only to satisfy ourselves that it leads nowhere. And don't forget, Mrs H is still our one and only witness."

"If you can call her that," said Dolby, "I suppose we could charge her with wasting police time."

"We could at that, Mark," Caine nodded thoughtfully. "If she's been holding out on us, as I suspect she has, maybe that could give us a bit of leverage."

"Well, I just hope we're not wasting our time, Jackie. Wouldn't it be better to ask Mrs Hartnell about it straight out than go to her old man?"

"We'll have a shot at him first," said Caine. "It'll be useful to get his version, plus the possibility we might actually get a sensible reaction from him. She's been pretty useless so far – and I still think the letter's so much fantasy. I'm just interested to know why Mrs H. actually sent the thing."

"To do Beckett a bit of harm, I suppose," suggested Dolby.

"Precisely, that's pretty obvious. But the question is *why*? What do you suppose she has against the man?"

They passed Tesco Metro, picking their way through the bustling shoppers. At the end of the High Street the entrance to the pedestrian subway was closed off with incident tape and they glanced over the railings at the still continuing police activity in the underpass and then walked around the side of Jefferson's DIY store to the back of the shops. They passed Henry Hartnell's parked van and climbed the concrete staircase leading to the flats above. A lurid estate agent's sign announcing the premises were 'to let' was attached to the side of the building, next to the front door, and they pushed it open and walked into the dingy interior. The place smelt of paint and old boiled cabbage and there were traces of dampness in the air. They could hear the sounds of a radio playing pop music in the back room and they headed in that direction.

Henry Hartnell, paintbrush in hand, met them at the door. His blue dungarees were spattered with many tints of paint, as was his blue baseball cap. He looked tired. "Oh, it's you," he said without enthusiasm. "I don't know what's been going on down there in the subway, but it's nothing to do with us."

"We haven't come about that, sir," Dolby told him. "We're still investigating the rail crash murder."

"Oh yes, I daresay, Dotty says you came to see her again on Wednesday. Quite upset she was. Why can't you leave us alone?"

"Life isn't that simple, Mr Hartnell," replied Dolby. "We have a murder investigation on our hands – two murders now – and we need to ask you some questions."

The smaller man backed into the room. Behind him his son Reginald paused in his work of wallpaper hanging. He was halfway up a stepladder, the string of his plumb bob swinging wildly on its cord as he turned to look at them. His eyes were vacant, but he nodded to them, his jaw limp, before turning back to his task, winding up the string with meticulous care to take the metal weight into his big hands.

"I don't know anything about your murders," said Hartnell, "neither does my wife; we've got nothing to hide." He walked to the windowsill and turned the radio's volume down. "What did you want to ask me?"

"Do you know Marcus Beckett, Mr Hartnell?" asked Caine.

"Yes, of course I do. Reginald and me have done some work for him. I don't like him, but I know him."

"Why don't you like him?"

Hartnell's gaze was evasive. "He's not a man you like easily, is he? At least I don't think so."

"There must be a reason, Mr Hartnell. There's always a reason," said Dolby. "Is it the same reason your wife doesn't like him?"

"You know about that?" Hartnell could not hide his surprise.

"About what?" asked Caine.

Hartnell frowned and laid his paint tipped brush carefully down on the windowsill next to the radio. "Er - about him and Dotty. It was a long time ago – I thought I

569

was the only one she ever told, but of course you've got

records and things you can look up."

"What exactly are you talking about, Mr Hartnell?"

asked Dolby "*What* was a long time ago?"

He looked from one to the other, his eyes furtive. "I

thought you said you knew – but if you don't then I can't

tell you! It's not the sort of thing a respectable woman likes

talked about. It's very personal."

"Your wife knows Marcus Beckett, doesn't she," said

Caine, changing tack. There was a note of accusation in her

voice. "She knows him very well, doesn't she?"

Hartnell shook his head. "No, she doesn't. She used

to, but not now she doesn't."

"How do you mean she used to? Come on, Mr

Hartnell, don't make us read the riot act to you – this is a

murder inquiry. We need to know."

"She wouldn't want you to."

Dolby pressed him. "What are we talking about here,

Mr Hartnell? What is it your wife wouldn't want us to

know? We'll find out sooner or later, so you may as well tell us and stay out of trouble."

Hartnell's face crumpled with dismay as he fought with his dilemma. "She'll not like me telling you this, but..."

"But what?"

He turned and looked at his son who had now moved over to the pasting table to stir a bucket of wallpaper paste with a long stick. He worked at it energetically, whistling through his teeth, ignoring his father and the two visitors.

Hartnell held his hand up to his mouth and whispered. "Outside. I'll tell you outside."

He led them out to the hall and along the corridor to the front door. "I didn't want to tell you in there in case Reggie heard, only you see, he's not mine."

"What do you mean he isn't yours?" asked Dolby.

The other man blushed. The revelation was taking a lot out of him. "Sssch! Not so loud! He might hear, he may not be very bright, but he's got good ears. He's not really my son. He's illegitimate. My wife had Reginald before we were married. He isn't mine. He's – er – **his**."

"You don't mean your wife and Marcus Beckett…?" Said Caine. "You **do** mean that. They were lovers."

"I don't know if you'd call them lovers, exactly," said Hartnell, blushing with embarrassment. "She was young then and I don't need to tell you what that Beckett is like with women. I reckon he gets them under some evil, diabolical spell. Anyway, he treated my Dotty very badly, that Marcus Beckett. She's never forgotten it."

"You've worked for him recently though, haven't you," said Dolby. "How come if you and your wife hate him so much?"

"Oh, we've done the occasional decorating job for him, I don't deny that, but that's been for money." Hartnell replied defiantly. "He's got pots of cash and I've charged him over the top for the privilege I can tell you. I didn't do it because I enjoyed it, no way. A man in my station in life can't afford to turn down a cash job when it comes his way. Anyway, there was another reason."

"What was that?"

"Beckett wanted to get closer to Reggie – he said he was his son and he wanted to get to know him. Dorothy didn't like that, but I thought there was no harm in it. I thought it was time the buggar took some responsibility for Reggie - after all, he ran off as soon as the kid was born. Dotty never saw a penny out of him for years – it's time he paid something back for the way he treated her. If it hadn't been for me coming along when I did it would have been very hard for her to manage, I can tell you! What's going to happen now?" He asked anxiously, "Reginald mustn't find out he's not my kid, Dorothy and me made that clear to Beckett before we agreed he could see him. It would really upset the boy if he found out now. He thinks I'm his dad."

"He won't find out from us," Caine assured him. "One other thing, Mr Hartnell, do you know why your wife should send us a letter accusing Marcus Beckett of murdering Kelly Beacham?"

The little man shook his head. "Who? Oh, that'd be the young woman found dead in the woods near his place the other morning. Did she do that, my Dorothy? She doesn't like him, of course, but…well, sorry, I don't know nothing about it." He yawned and rubbed his eyes with the back of a paint-stained hand. "Excuse me, I've not been sleeping very well lately, nor has Dorothy, not since that train crash, she's been very upset since then she has, nightmares and all sorts she's had, tears and tantrums and tempers, and walking in her sleep, all sorts. I'm very worried for her. But then of course she has the sight, you see, she's not like other people." He shook his head again. "Been sending you letters has she, about murderings has she? That don't sound good at all."

"So, you can't help us?"

"No, I don't know anything about any letters, Inspector. I don't like you to keep troubling her, but it seems to me the only one who'd know about *them* is Dorothy herself."

"Oh! How did you know it was me?" Dorothy Hartnell sat in her chair in her tiny front room and stared at them. "It was silly, I knew I should have typed the envelope."

"It wasn't the envelope that led us to you," said Caine. "It was that magazine you took the printed letters from. Why did you do it, Mrs Hartnell? Why did you send that letter?"

She sighed and rubbed the bandage at the side of her head. "So, you would know the real truth about who *really* murdered Kelly Beacham."

"We *know* who murdered her, Mrs Hartnell," said Dolby. "You weren't telling the truth in that letter. It's my belief you knew Beckett was having an affair with Miss Beacham and you hate him so much you wanted him to take the blame for her death. Isn't *that* the truth?"

"Absolutely not, Sergeant." She turned to Caine. "You have empathy, Inspector, tell him what I said in that letter is true. It's all true."

"It's not," Caine protested. "No way is it true. What makes you think *I* think it is?"

The other woman smiled mysteriously. "Because you can *feel* it. You're not blind like he is," she indicated Dolby. "You must be able to *hear* her, telling you. Telling you from beyond the grave."

Caine sighed wearily. The whole thing was getting out of hand. They could not have chosen a worse key witness if they had tried. "I don't know what you're talking about, Mrs Hartnell."

Mrs Hartnell smiled again. Her eyes seemed to roll across their sockets and focus on the wall behind Caine. "You *know*, Inspector, don't pretend, you *must* be able to feel her presence, she's standing right behind you. She's tall and brunette and very good looking, wearing a blue coat and a navy skirt. If you turn around now you'll be able to see her. You will I'm sure you will."

Caine felt a wave of coldness sweep over her and, in spite of herself she turned to look behind her. There was nothing there but faded wallpaper and bookcases lined with old leather-bound books. She turned back to face the other woman. "I can't see anyone, Mrs Hartnell. Please, let's be sensible about this. Whom are you talking about?"

"Kelly, of course. Kelly Beacham. She's telling you right now who was responsible for her death – and it wasn't those two young men!"

Dolby had been following the conversation with a look of absolute disbelief on his face. "Oh, *please*, Mrs Hartnell, don't you think this has gone on long enough? You may have had a bit of concussion from the train accident, but you're not seriously trying to tell us you've been in contact with a dead woman."

She regarded him with narrowed eyes and stuck out her bottom lip. "People like you understand *nothing*!"

"I understand this much," said Dolby, equally stubborn, "you're wasting our time, Mrs Hartnell. This is a murder investigation and if you're not very careful you'll be on charges of obstructing the police in the pursuit of their inquiries. *Now*, what was the *real* reason for sending that letter to the Inspector?"

Mrs Hartnell sighed and shook her head disdainfully. "I've told you the reason. If you're too blind to see, then that's your affair."

"If you can talk to dead people, Mrs Hartnell," said Dolby, leaning almost menacingly towards her, "then how come you say you can't remember what happened when Marion Winters was murdered? All you have to do is call her up – I'll bet she'd tell you *exactly* what happened. Then you could pass the information on to us and that would be an end of it. We wouldn't have to keep coming around to question you!"

Dorothy Hartnell looked across at Caine. The Detective Inspector hoped it was not an appeal for help – she could hardly admonish Dolby for expressing much of what she herself was thinking.

"That's not the way it works," Mrs Hartnell said. "It's not like telephoning a person. People from the other side have to *want* to communicate with you – if they *don't* then you get *nothing*."

Dolby laughed derisively. "I suppose you get the woman from BT telling you they're unobtainable. That's *very* convenient."

Caine made an attempt to bring the interview back on to a sensible track. "You don't deny sending the letter though, do you, Mrs Hartnell?"

"No, I sent it. I had to help the poor girl. I couldn't turn her away when she came to me. She'll never rest easy until that man pays for his crimes."

"Then perhaps you could tell us what you mean by *'watch the broken hand'*?"

The other woman looked puzzled. "I sent it, but I don't know what was in it, Inspector. Kelly decided that. I was in a trance state when she did it. My only waking involvement was to put it in the post."

"Now I've heard everything," muttered Dolby. "You admit you sent it, but you don't know what was in it! Pull the other one, please, Mrs Hartnell!"

Her eyes narrowed and the look she threw across at him was vicious. "I am a medium, Sergeant," she said, speaking the words very slowly. "A person from the other side can make use of my physical body. When that happens, I very often have no idea what they are doing. Kelly composed that letter without my intervention."

"You mean the ghost of Kelly Beacham took charge of your body, cut words and phrases out of a magazine, stuck them to a sheet of paper and then *you* posted it?" said Dolby contemptuously. "You must think we were born yesterday, Mrs Hartnell, you really must! I've never heard such a load of codswallop in my life, and I've been about!"

Her voice was even, emphatic. "*I posted* it, that's *all*. It was there in the envelope when I came out of the trance, so I knew she intended it should be posted."

Caine stood up. "I think that's enough, Mrs Hartnell. It's a pity you haven't seen fit to co-operate and I have to tell you we shall be seriously considering charging you for wasting our time. Perhaps you'd like to give the matter some serious thought. If you decide to co-operate you know where to reach us but failing that we'll be in touch with you early next week to tell you whether we intend to charge you with wasting police time." She moved towards the door.

Dolby stood up and joined her. "Think about it, Mrs Hartnell. The way things stand you'll be up before the magistrates by this time next week."

CHAPTER TWENTY-TWO

"Forget it, Jackie, the woman's an absolute nutter," said Dolby savagely as they got into the car outside the Hartnell's small, terraced house. "She's riding rings around us. Even if we could get a lucid statement from her, it wouldn't be worth the paper it's written on. The defence would tear her evidence to shreds." He switched on the ignition, put the car into gear and shot out into the centre of the road, narrowly missing a passing cyclist and hooting at him as though Mrs Hartnell's inability to act as a reliable witness was entirely his fault. "She's just a vindictive woman who wants to get back at her ex-lover who dropped a kid on her twenty odd years ago, nothing more, nothing less." He braked at the T-junction and waited to turn right. "I still think we should have asked her about Reginald and her connections with Beckett."

"No, it was right to leave it for the time being. The woman's unstable enough as it is, talking about her guilty secret would only have made it worse," Caine, reached up for the buckle of her seat belt. "But you're right, of course, in every other respect, she'd make an unreliable witness and she's probably just got it in for Beckett, not that I blame her." She laughed dryly. "You know, I just think it's too much of a coincidence that *she* should be writing poison pen letters about *him* - especially when they're so closely connected to the two murders, possibly three."

"But that's all it is, Jackie, it's a coincidence. We *know* Beckett had nothing to do with Kelly's murder – he couldn't have been in two places at once - so Mrs H. is just floating a red herring, a dead one at that. Dead and stinking. If we had any sense we really would prosecute the woman for wasting our time."

"But who would have thought she and Beckett would-be long-lost lovers? I'd like to hear his side of the story. It might explain why they've both turned out to be such weirdoes."

But there was more to it than that, Caine thought, watching the black silhouette of the trees as they flashed by in the car's headlights. She could understand the woman being a little bitter about the man who had abandoned her and the child he had sired. It happened every day, but this had been more than twenty years ago. Did Dorothy Hartnell **really** hate Beckett that much after all this time? Surely the wounds should have healed by now. Or was there something else behind it? Something she, Caine, didn't know about? But even if there was, how could it possibly be connected to the train crash murder? That was their priority now, wasn't it? But useless as she was, Dorothy Hartnell was their only lead. They **had** to stick with her.

Beckett's shop was closed by the time they reached it, but the lights were on in the house and they pulled up in the almost empty car park. Felicity, Beckett's elderly assistant, came to the door when they rang and let them into the now tidy hall. She called to her employer that she must go, or she would miss her bus back to town, and that he had some late customers.

"I don't suppose he'd want to see you if he knew it was you," she explained. "The police aren't exactly at the top of Mr Beckett's popularity list at the moment." She went to the clothes rack and took down a heavy overcoat. "He shouldn't be a moment." She struggled into the coat, acknowledging Dolby's helping hand with a grateful smile and then went down the hall again to call out. "I'm off now, Mr Beckett. I'll leave these latecomers to you."

He came towards them out of the back room just as Felicity closed the front door behind her.

"Oh! It's you. What do you want? Haven't you given up trying to frame me?"

"I can assure you, sir, that was never our intention," Dolby said, stiffly. "We're here on a quite different matter. Would you mind answering a few more questions?"

The big man gave his twisted smile. "Still hoping I'll let slip something important?"

Caine came to the point. "Mr Beckett, do you know a Mrs Dorothy Hartnell."

The man nodded, without hesitation. "Yes. Her husband Henry and son Reginald have a decorating business – they've just finished working here as a matter of fact. What about her?"

"Is it true that you are Reginald's father?"

He gazed at them for a number of seconds before answering. "Did she tell you that?"

"Her husband told us. Is it true?"

He nodded. "Yes, it is. We had a *thing* together. It wasn't an affair – neither of us was married – that makes it a non-affair, doesn't it? Anyway, it was a long time ago and Reginald was one of the results. I didn't stand by Dorothy when she had the child and we didn't marry. I had no intention of marrying the woman."

"That comes as no surprise, sir," said Dolby. "You don't seem to be the marrying kind."

"An impudent comment, Sergeant, if not an altogether inaccurate one. But as it happens it wasn't my choice."

"How do you mean?"

"Simply that after Reginald was born little Miss Moffett – yes that really *was* Dorothy's maiden name! – Moffett - I think the expression is that she 'took against' me."

"Why?" asked Caine.

Beckett was standing by the hallstand and ran his hand lightly over the rich mahogany wood. He seemed to have decided to be friendly towards them, though his manner was slightly superior as if he thought he was in full control of the situation. "Oh, she had this notion that I was the embodiment of all evil. It's a long story." He nodded towards the open door of one of the showrooms. "Perhaps you'd like to take the weight off your feet. I know I would and there are some chairs in there. I want to sell them eventually, of course, but there's no reason why, in the meantime, we shouldn't avail ourselves of the comfort they have to offer."

He led the way through from the hall. The showroom was once again packed with items of antique furniture, the wood shining, the metal gleaming. There was a group of six Lloyd loom chairs set to one side, near the fireplace and he directed the two police officers towards them.

"Where was I?" he sat down, facing them, yawning widely. "Excuse me, but it's been a hard day. Plenty of activity in the shop I'm glad to say, lots of filthy lucre coming the way of Uncle Marcus."

"You said that Mrs Hartnell – Dorothy Moffett as she then was - took against you," said Caine, bringing him back to their earlier topic. "You were going to tell us why she did that, Mr Beckett."

"Oh yes. She thought I was the incarnation of the devil himself; you see. she had her spiritualism – oh yes, even in those days she fancied she could conjure up the dead; it was hell driving past a cemetery with her, I can tell you, you couldn't stop her gossiping with the inhabitants!"

He laughed loudly. "I'm exaggerating, of course, but she was really into what you might call the 'white' side of death and eternity. I, on the other hand, was more taken with the 'black' side, as you know it's the occult that interests me. She calls it devil worship."

"So, you disagreed and decided to split up?" Dolby suggested.

"Oh, it wasn't quite as simple as that!" Beckett frowned. "You'll have noticed, of course, that our son – Reginald – has 'problems', 'mentally challenged' is the present jargon I believe. Dorothy blamed me for his condition and for the other child's death – said it had happened because I consorted with the devil," he said the last few words mockingly. "That it was *Divine Retribution* – that her God was paying me back, nonsense like that."

Caine leaned towards him. "You said there was *another child's death*, Mr Beckett. What other child?"

Beckett shook his head in apology and looked more human than she had ever seen him. "Sorry. You didn't know, of course, why should you? Reginald was meant to be a twin. There was another baby in the womb with him, Reggie's sister. She was fully developed, but something happened to her and she died at the moment of birth, as she came out of the womb, or very shortly thereafter. Nobody's *quite* sure what happened, possibly she strangled on her umbilical cord. Dorothy blamed the midwife, but I told her that was unreasonable."

"I'm sorry," said Caine. "It must have been very hard for you and Dorothy."

Beckett smiled and gave a little shrug. "Oh, it wasn't easy. Dorothy insisted on giving the dead child a name – she called it – *her* – Stephanie – and we went through all the trauma of having a proper funeral and then mourning her. She – Dorothy – went clean out of her mind. Of course, I got the blame for everything, because I happened to be interested in the occult – devil worship she called it - and she was convinced that's what caused the problem. Divine retribution. She had tantrums and fits of depression and she actually physically attacked me a few times, believe it or not." He paused reflectively. "Well, it wasn't going to get any better, so when I couldn't stand it anymore, I upped and went on my travels." He yawned again. "It was a bad time, but in a way she did me a favour, got me out of a rut." He looked around him appreciatively, "as the result of which I haven't done too badly."

"And she hates you for leaving her?" asked Dolby.

"For that and what happened to the two kids? I suppose so, but to be absolutely sure you'd have to ask her. Anyway, what's all this about?"

Caine stood up. "You've just filled in a few holes for us, that's all. Thank you, Mr Beckett. We'll see ourselves out."

Doctor Williams was in Caine's office waiting for them when they arrived back at the station, drinking a cup of coffee and studying the pages of Lancet. He didn't get up as she came in, merely nodded towards a file on her desk.

"Sorry, Peter, we weren't expecting you," Caine took off her coat and hung it on the rack. "You're early."

Dolby hung up his coat and nodded towards the doctor. "Does this mean you've got the PM early for us, for once?"

"Yes, but I don't know why I bothered," Williams grunted, "You're never grateful. Here was I working like a Trojan on your behalf and not so much as the smell of a drop of Scotch, let alone a taste." He held out his cup. "You can drop it in there, thank you, Jackie."

"What a waste!" Caine poured a measure of Glenmorangie into his cup and sat down behind her desk. "Janine Foster," she read from the front of the file. "Poor kid. Have we got a positive ID on her yet?"

Williams nodded. "Wendy took care of it. The parents and a younger sister turned up while I was there. If there's one thing that would persuade me to give up this game it's being there when the parents view the body. Yuk!" He took a long gulp of the whisky-laced coffee. "That's better! This machine coffee needs something to liven it up."

Caine was reading the notes on the dead girl and turned over the page. "Same MO as the train murder, no doubt about that. Do you think it was the same weapon?"

Williams nodded. "Forensics will confirm it definitely by comparing the string fibres that have been left on the skin, but it's identical as far as I can see. It seems the killer must be carrying this garrotte string around with him." He paused to take another sip of the hot liquid. "And we've got the same funny mark on the skin of the victim's back, some sort of bruising caused by pressure, I think, a great deal of pressure. It was fading quickly, but I could just about make it out. Wouldn't have seen it though if I hadn't been looking for it. You'll see it on the close-up photographs. I can't think what might have caused it, though, it's a peculiar shape, bullet like and yet not a bullet - strange."

Caine finished reading and passed the file across to Dolby. "Thanks, Peter, we appreciate it. I hate having to do business with you, but you never let us down." She looked at her watch. "I'm glad you were early – I was hoping to get off at a reasonable time tonight, I've got Alison coming over this weekend to help me go through the box room – she keeps telling me I've got a lot of junk up there I ought to get rid of - so I need to nip into the supermarket for some bits and pieces of food. She's got an appetite like a team of horses, that girl! Then I have to pick her up at the station at eight o'clock."

Williams finished his coffee and stood up, throwing the plastic cup into the wastepaper bin. "I'll be off now then, Mary asked me to pick something up from the shops, as it happens, but I can't remember what. I'll have to give her a ring." He lifted his coat from the rack and stuck his hat on the top of his head. "Let me know if you've got any queries on anything." He picked up his briefcase and opened the door. "Have a nice weekend."

"Fat chance!" Dolby finished reading the file and passed it back to Caine. "Not much of any consequence in there. I was hoping we'd have some sort of lead."

Caine shook her head. "It's pretty lean in that respect. All we know is the killer pounced on her just as she came

594

out of the tunnel – which must have been completely dark by all accounts – it gets lighter there, just when you get to the steps leading up into the South side of the High Street."

"But why didn't he do it when she was in the dark? Why wait until she got out into the light?"

Caine shook her head. "Search me, Mark, I'm only the detective in charge." The telephone rang and she picked up the receiver. "Caine...Oh yes, sir, I'll be right down." She groaned and replaced the receiver. "I was expecting that. I am summoned to give an account of myself to The Boss of Bosses. He's heard about the Foster murder and he wants to know how things are going – evidently he hasn't realised there's a link with the train murder and that we've probably got a serial killer on our hands." She stood up and smoothed her skirt. "It should be fun telling him."

When she came into his office Superintendent Hansen was standing by the window looking out at the rain. "It never rains, but it pours," he said turning towards her. "I hear you haven't been doing much to stop it,

Detective Chief Inspector. You can sit down, by the way, you look a little tired."

She sat. "I wouldn't say I've been doing nothing, sir, we have managed to put together a couple of charges on the Beacham murder."

He turned towards her and scowled. "Yes, well done on that score at least." He sighed. "The trouble seems to be, Jacqueline, that as soon as you clear up one murder another one pops up in its place. It's like that Greek thing isn't it? Where whatisname's trying to kill off the skeletons and every time he kills one another one jumps up to take its place. Whatsitcalled?"

"I don't know sir, but it's hardly a good analogy. We're hardly overrun with skeletons or even dead bodies."

"No, I suppose not," he grunted. "The point is though that we have had three murders this week – four if you count that poor kid who died of a drugs overdose or whatever it was, up at Upton Grange School. Anyway, what's the latest on today's victim? It's another nurse I hear."

"Yes, sir and I'm afraid it's probably the same MO as the train crash killer."

He groaned and sat down heavily in his swivel chair causing it to lurch backwards on its castors, towards the window. "And I suppose there are still no clues as to the killer's identity? What about that woman who was in the same train carriage when it all happened? Can't she give us any help?"

Caine shook her head. "She claims she can't remember a thing. Concussion or whatever. And apart from that she's a bit weird. DS Dolby thinks she's a nutter and I'm not sure he's wrong. She's been sending us anonymous letters claming she knows who killed Kelly Beacham."

"Was she right?"

"No sir, she claimed it was that man, Marcus Beckett."

"Ah yes, the Wizard of Upton. Wouldn't put it past him, but of course you've already got the killers, so she's barking up the wrong avenue of trees there, isn't she? But what made her say it was Beckett in the first place?"

597

Caine shrugged. "Oh, she reckons she has an informant, but don't bother to ask who it is, the whole sad mess was trumped up by her for the simple reason that she wanted revenge on Beckett. Apparently, they were lovers way back in the Noughties and when she had his love child he walked out on her. She's never forgiven him."

"Really?" Hansen rubbed his chin thoughtfully. "The Noughties you say – it could be that Daphne, my wife, brought the poor little sod into the world – used to be midwife for the Fen Molesey area did Daphne, around about that time as it happens. I'll mention it to her. What was the woman's name?"

"Dorothy Hartnell, maiden name - believe it or note - 'Moffett' – Miss Moffett – no spiders or puns intended. She was unmarried at the time. Anyway, we've got nothing out of Mrs Hartnell, and the worrying thing is, we really have no other clues at all. All the other avenues we've explored on the Winters' case have led us nowhere. At the moment, we're totally stumped."

When Jacqueline Caine finally emerged from Hansen's office she carried with her very firm instructions to solve the two murders forthwith, without any more backsliding.

CHAPTER TWENTY- THREE

Alison had claimed the room as her own as soon as she realised how much better it was than the one she was using for her occasional weekend visits. That room was at the other end of the corridor and it was small and poky by comparison with this one, which was big and airy. Even with the clutter of cartons and boxes and other paraphernalia her mother had dumped into it when she moved in it was a much nicer room. The light streamed in through the large west-facing window overlooking the back garden and if you stood on tip toes you could see across Tricket's brook and over Tricket's Woods to Beacon Hill, nearly three miles away and the highest point in the area. The Andersons, previous occupants of the cottage, had not used the room –when they moved in they had used it as a storage room and so it had stayed over the nine years they had been there. Their children were abroad and there was just the two of them, so they had no need of it. Alison's mother fell into the trap of following their lead and so it had remained a box room. Until now. The décor, of course, left much to be desired, but that problem would be addressed just as soon as the room was clear of junk.

"We'll clean the place up as we go along." Her mother entered carrying a handful of dusters and the vacuum cleaner. She was wearing a pair of old overalls and had tied a silk scarf about her head. "There's going to be a lot of dust when we get going," she explained defensively as her daughter looked at her askance. "It's to keep my hair clean."

Alison, dressed in old jeans and a GAP sweatshirt that had seen better days, patted her baseball cap down onto her head and swished her ponytail. She wasn't exactly the doyen of fashion, but she thought she was dressed the more appropriately of the two. She ran her knife through the binding of the nearest box and ripped it open. "What are you keeping these for, mum? Surely you don't need them anymore."

Caine dropped the dusters on the floor in the corner and left the vacuum cleaner beside them. "What *these* are you referring to, dear?"

"*These* these," said Alison holding up a couple of copies of National Geographic magazine. "They're dated 2003 and the box is full of them."

"I meant to read them," protested her mother, "I just haven't got around to it."

"You know you never will, not with your job. Besides, they're beginning to smell a bit musty. I reckon you should chuck 'em. If you really really want to read them someday, when you're old and grey and I'm visiting you in your old people's home, you could probably get them on CDs or DVDs."

"Thanks very much, Alison, for saying you'll visit me, but I shall never go into a home. I shall die detecting, magnifying glass in hand."

Alison slid the box of magazines across the floor towards the door. "This lot'll be the 'chucking away' pile. I shall expect to see it much bigger than the 'keeping in the loft' pile." She turned her attention to the next box. "Seen anything of that dishy fishy guy? I wonder if he got pneumonia from being out in the rain?"

"You mean Mr Maynard, Deputy Head of Upton Grange School for Murderous Little Toffs? Yes and no. I mean 'yes' I have seen him and 'no' he didn't get pneumonia. We had a bit of a falling out actually. He seems to think Mark and I have made a complete cock-up of solving the Beacham murder."

"Oh, really, what's he complaining about then?" Alison opened the top of the cardboard box and took out a small book. "Looks like there's books in here – I suppose we'll have to go through them all, but by the look of the ones on the top they'd go down pretty well in a charity shop." She pushed the box over to the chucking away pile.

"He reckons the two boys didn't do it. You know, Hill and Sullivan, the two schoolboys. Maynard reckons

603

they're not capable of killing anybody. I don't know so much; they seem quite capable to me! Built like oxen, both of them. Their photos were in all the newspapers yesterday."

"Sure, I read the story. I always do when it's to do with Fen Molesey. You're the star mystery attraction in our office, so we guys always keep up with developments. I won my bet."

"What bet? You're not gambling, I hope, young lady, you know I've always discouraged it." Caine opened one of the cartons. "Good lord, I'd forgotten I ever had that hat. What on earth did I wear it for?" She lifted it from the box and unwrapped it from the bag in which had been stored. It was big, round and blue, with a red feather.

"Maybe you played the lead in "*Annie Get your Gun*", Alison suggested. She delved into another box. "Here's some old packets of wallpaper paste and some ancient rolls of wallpaper." She unravelled a foot or so of the paper. "I remember that we had it in the Walthamstow flat. Mum, you do keep the weirdest things. Oh, and look –

a complete set of decorating tools." She took them out of the box and laid them on the floor at her side. "A couple of scrapers in quite good condition, a pasting brush that's gone a bit bald, one of those stringy things with a weight on to make sure the wallpaper goes up straight, a pair of old and rusty scissors marked 'stainless steel' and 'made in China', a Stanley knife without a blade and one of those funny triangular scraper things for getting paint out of the corners of window frames. A motley lot I must say, but probably still useful so I won't throw it all away just yet."

Caine had put the hat on and was trying to see her reflection in the window glass, to no avail. She slipped it back into the plastic bag and threw it across the room to the chucking away pile. "I'm sure I'll never use it. Anyway, what bet was it you were talking about?"

"We've got this new guy, an Aussie, name of Bruce believe it or not and he bets on anything. Never mind about 'if it moves put your money on it', Bruce says 'if it *exists* you've got to bet on it'. So, he set this book up on how long it'd be before you and Mark Dolby solved this latest murder and I – having a great deal of faith in the infallibility of my mother, the great detective - said you'd have the case done and dusted before the weekend. So, I won thirty-five quid. I'll buy you dinner tonight if you like."

"You're on. I know this really expensive place out at Layer Marney. Your thirty-five pounds'll just about pay for the starters, but they're so big that's all we'll need." She went on to the next box. "I suppose we'd better get on, I'd forgotten how much junk I brought with me. It must have cost a lot of money to have it brought here."

"You should have chucked it **before** you moved! I told you at the time, but you never got around to it. That's what comes of being married to your job."

"I'm not married to my job. I found time to bring you up, didn't I?"

"Yeah, but you used to work exceptionally long hours. I missed you, mum. I still miss you, things haven't changed that much, you know, you work so hard I still hardly ever see you."

"Don't put it all down to me, young lady, you chose to work in London and get a place there."

"I suppose." Alison nodded reluctantly, "but that's where it's all at in the advertising industry. You can't really work anywhere else, can you?" She absentmindedly pushed the decorating tools about on the floor. "We'll keep most of these bits." She turned her attention to the next box. "But don't you get fed up with all those long hours?"

Caine nodded and cut the tape on another carton. "I suppose I should have labelled these on the outside, but as I recall it I was rushing about like a blue-bummed fly at the time. Good Lord, old shoes, I thought I'd chucked those away ages ago. Look, these were my favourites." They were brown leather, heavily scuffed and down at heel and sole. She threw them across the room to join the other chuckaways. "Even the best wear out sometime, I suppose, but to answer your question, yes, I do get fed up, especially at times like these when Mark and I and the team seem to be bashing our heads against a brick wall. Nothing seems to be going right with this train crash case."

607

"No leads at all?"

"The leads are there all right, but the bloody hounds seem to have escaped from the ends of them." She brightened. "I sometimes think *we're* the dogs, going round and round in circles, chasing our own tails."

It was just before seven o'clock on Sunday evening that Caine got back from dropping Alison at the station. She went straight into the kitchen to put the kettle on and then, while it was heating, settled down at the table to read the 'Weekly Review' from the Sunday newspaper. It was then she saw the big ball of sticky tac. It was stuck to the wall tiles above the marble topped working surface, next to the microwave oven. She remembered Alison had found the large unopened packet in one of the boxes on Saturday afternoon and asked why her mother was not using the stuff; apparently, it was unbelievably useful for attaching things to walls and such places without damaging the surfaces. Caine had forgotten she had the stuff, could not even remember when she bought it, or why. Alison took it out of its packet to demonstrate how flexible and useful it was and then sat cross-legged on the floor in her future bedroom playing with it like a child, as if it was plasticine, rolling it, twisting it, stretching it and pressing things into it to see what sort of impression they made. She must have stuck it to the kitchen wall before she left that evening, perhaps as a not-so-subtle reminder to her mother to make better use of the stuff in future.

Caine reached over to take the ball of plastic from the wall. It was untidy there, a blot on the neat ceramic tiles that ran along the wall behind the shining marble worktop. She had her reading glasses on; otherwise, the deep lines impressed into the plasticine-like material might not have caught her attention. Alison must have pressed something into it before she tired of the game and stuck the stuff to the wall. The shape of the impression reminded Caine of something, something she had seen quite recently, and she bent closer to peer at it intently. A thrill of recognition ran through her body and she turned and ran quickly through to the hall for her briefcase. She had brought home the files on the Winters and Foster murders, just in case she had time to look at them over the weekend; she had not, but now she was glad she had them and she carried them back to the kitchen. There was a particular photograph she remembered in the Winters file and now she found it and examined a detail on it, very closely, comparing it with the impression on the sticky tac.

With rising excitement, she reached for the telephone and dialled Alison's mobile number; she would still be on the train. She identified herself to her daughter, speaking quickly. "Alison, that sticky tac you were playing about with – you know, the stuff you found in one of the boxes…"

"Yeah. The stuff that's good for sticking things to walls?"

"Yes, darling, that stuff. You left it on the kitchen wall. There's an impression on it – you must have pressed something hard into it to make an impression. What did you use?"

Alison answered her question and before she put down the telephone receiver Caine felt certain she knew who had murdered Marion Winters and Janine Foster.

She rang Dolby.

He listened quietly. "You're quite sure the mark's the same as the ones on the victims?" He asked, yawning. He had been taking the rare opportunity of relaxing in front of the television and her call had woken him up.

"Certain Mark. I'd bet my reputation on it. But it's not just that, a lot of other things fit in too."

"Then what are we waiting for?"

"We're not, Mark. We'll bring him in now. We can't afford to wait until we're absolutely sure, we don't want another victim on our hands. Can you get away?"

The gears of Dolby's brain were now fully engaged. "But hang on a second, Jackie," he protested, "are we *really* certain it was him? He wasn't even on the train!"

"I'm not so sure about that, Mark. Remember, we thought all along that the killer walked away afterwards. First thing in the morning we'll ask the fingerprint people

611

if they can match the prints on that child's book we found in the train carriage."

Dolby grunted his agreement. "The book – yes, it would explain the book!"

"And we'll get Wendy to organise another search through the CCTV recordings – it would be useful if we could prove he **was** actually on the train - now we know who we're looking for we may find something." She paused, assembling her thoughts. "I'll give Wendy a ring now I think –it might be advisable to have an extra pair of hands." She sighed. "You know, Mark, I think we've got the killer, in fact I'm certain of it, but I can't say it gives me a great deal of pleasure."

"I know what you mean, but we can't allow sentiment to get in the way. The fact is he's dangerous."

"And I'm still not sure of the motive – I have some ideas, but I'm not sure."

All the lights were on in the dilapidated house in Bridge Drive when they drove up twenty-five minutes later. Dolby pulled his car past Henry Hartnell's van and into the kerb a few yards further down the road. Wendy Doyle got out of the car in front of them and came to the window to peer in.

"Evening, Sergeant, Ma'am," she nodded across at Caine. "Are we going straight in?"

The other two officers climbed from the car and joined her on the pavement.

"Yes. We may as well get it over with," Caine led the way along the pavement and pushed open the metal gate to number 16. It squeaked loudly and someone in the neighbouring house twitched their curtains and peered out, immediately losing interest and dropping them again when they saw it was only the Hartnells receiving visitors.

"The door's open," said Dolby. "That's a bit strange on a night like this."

"Maybe they're expecting us," ventured Wendy. She shivered and pulled her heavy coat closer about her.

Caine reached out to press the doorbell and then remembered her last visit, when it had not worked, so

613

clattered the letterbox. The sharp metallic sound carried loudly into the house. There was no reply.

Dolby pushed the door inwards, calling loudly. "Police. Is there anybody at home?"

A faint sound came from the back of the house.

"Weird," said Doyle. "Sounds like someone groaning.

"I don't like the look of this," said Caine. "We'd better go in and find out what's going on."

She walked quickly up the hall towards the back of the house. Behind her, Dolby opened the door to the small front room and peered in. "Nobody there."

As they came closer to the back of the house the sound Doyle had interpreted as groaning became louder. Caine turned the handle of the door at the end and pushed it slowly open. Beyond was a small kitchen that seemed to have been caught in a time warp. There was a butler sink in the corner, filled with dirty crockery and fed by taps that came straight out of the wall. On the opposite side of the room stood a heavy cast iron range, on which were gathered a number of dirty saucepans, each a different colour. Heaped logs burned in the grate. A heavy oak wood table, its surface scattered with brightly coloured playing cards stood in the centre of the room. On the floor beside the table, his head turned towards the police officers, lay Henry Hartnell. His eyes were open and he was staring at the ceiling, groaning loudly and pawing wildly, with both hands, at his throat. A heavy bruise darkened the upper part of his forehead.

"You're too late!" he said, his voice hoarse. "I tried to stop them, but you're too late!"

Dolby knelt down beside him and caught hold of his hands, easing them away from his throat. There were two thin red lines cut deep into his flesh, running side-by-side, right around his neck. "Looks like they tried to do for him, Jackie." He released the man's hands and felt for the pulse at his throat. "The rhythm's a bit erratic, but he'll live. We'd better call an ambulance."

Doyle took her mobile from one of her inner pockets and passed on the message.

Caine pushed a chair out of the way and knelt down on Hartnell's other side, opposite Dolby. "Who did this to you Mr Hartnell?"

He groaned again and his breath caught in his throat, as he tried to answer her.

She tried again. "Where are your wife and son, Mr Hartnell?"

Hartnell's eyes moved to find hers and he made an effort to breathe normally, managing to wheeze out an answer, the words coming in monosyllables, making them difficult to follow. "They've - gone to - get her. I tried to - stop them - but they – would-n't – lis-ten. Then they – lost it - got violent and – and – *this*! – I think they thought I was dead!" He paused, then wheezed out "They've gone to get her…"

"Gone to get who, Mr Hartnell? You must tell us."

He exhaled for a long moment and caught his breath again. "The nurse…!"

Caine shot a worried look at Dolby. "Which nurse, Mr Hartnell? It's important!"

616

The man shook his head and then closed his eyes. Concerned, Dolby felt for his pulse again.

"I think I know," said Wendy Doyle suddenly. She reached towards a group of playing cards that lay strewn across the tabletop. "These are tarot cards aren't they? They're something to do with black magic." She picked one of them from the top of the pile and handed it to Caine. "This one represents death and someone's written a name on it."

Caine took it from her. She shivered, although it was warm in the room. The tarot card was about the size of a normal playing card and bore the sombre tinted image of a skeleton wielding a blood-tinged scythe; all around the skeletal figure the hands of the dead reached upwards from the grave. The borders of the card bore the number thirteen in Roman numerals. Across the top section someone had written, in a long, sloping hand, the name "*Mary Bayliss*". Caine looked inquiringly at Doyle, waiting for her to continue.

"She's a nurse – actually a midwife - at Fen Molesey General Hospital," explained Doyle. "She's the one we keep coming across in the hit-and-run cases!"

They were too late to save Mary Bayliss. They found her lying on the floor of her bedroom, the now familiar twin marks of the plumb bob string channelled deep into her neck. Dorothy and Reginald Hartnell were picked up just twenty minutes later, making their way home in Dorothy's blue Vauxhall Corsa. They allowed themselves to be arrested without a struggle, Reginald quietly solemn, bemused by the proceedings, his mother overwhelmed by what she described as 'the sweetness of revenge.'

Superintendent Edward Hansen smiled at Caine and Dolby from the other side of his desk and, in his enthusiasm, dunked his biscuit in his tea. "You've got them to confess, Jacqueline, Mark, that's splendid, it really is, and I really don't see your problem."

"The problem is that both of them claim they carried out the murders *alone*," explained Caine. "And we don't think either of them is fit to plead."

Hansen looked from one officer to the other. "That's bunkum! Do you believe the woman sat outside in the car last night while her son did all the dirty work?"

"I don't know what to believe, sir. *He* says exactly that. *She* says the exact opposite."

"What? That *she* did it and not him?" said Hansen. "It seems to me they're both implicated – call it conspiracy to murder if you like. We've got evidence, haven't we?"

"Yes, sir, we've got evidence," said Caine ruefully. "We've managed to find a piece of CCTV tape that proves he was on the train – It's a particularly bad shot, from a rotten angle and the picture's blurred, but we've managed to enhance it enough to get a positive ID." She passed a still photograph, taken from the videotape, across to the Superintendent. "If we hadn't known who we were looking for we'd have missed it, but he's there all right, next to his mother, on the platform boarding the train. We also know

619

he *wasn't* on the train after it crashed. He evidently ran away. And we've got his fingerprints on a children's book found on the train afterwards, plus a packet of sweets he'd been eating. They all prove he was on the train. We've also matched certain fibres found on the victims' skin – on all three victims, the woman on the train, the girl in the subway *and* the murdered midwife –to those from the plumb bob that Reginald Hartnell carried and used for his work."

"What on earth is a plumb bob?"

"It's a tool used for hanging wallpaper, sir," explained Dolby. "It's a piece of string with a weight on one end. You dangle the weight near the wall and it helps to ensure the paper goes up straight."

Hansen still looked puzzled. "But how could it be used as a murder weapon?"

"Quite easily," Dolby told him. "We believe the string was doubled up into two strands and then thrown over the victim's head, exactly like a garrotte. The ends were then pulled tighter and tighter about their necks until

620

the pressure killed them. Fortunately for us the metal weight fell behind the back of the victim's neck and as the killer pressed the victim down it made a very deep impression in the skin leaving quite a distinctively shaped bruise that was easily spotted during the post-mortems."

Hansen nodded his understanding and dunked another biscuit, just managing to get the soggy end into his mouth before it broke off. "So, what's the problem? You've got all the evidence you need."

"Yes sir," said Caine patiently. "The problem is his mother says *she* did it – we think she's protecting him – and the bad news is we can't prove she's lying. It could have been her and not him. On the other hand, it could have been him and not her."

"But what about the motive?"

Caine frowned. "It's a little complicated, sir."

"So, it's complicated. I'm not an idiot, am I? I am presumably capable of understanding it, complicated as it might be." He swallowed another piece of biscuit.

"Yes, sir, of course you are, sir." Caine sipped at her coffee. "Well, the way we see it when Reginald was born, he was one of twins. His sister, unfortunately, died at birth and his mother, Dorothy, was extremely disturbed by the event. She became chronically depressed and developed an obsessive hatred for the midwife – Mary Bayllis as it turns out, the last victim – and for midwives and nurses in general – so much so that all through his life the boy, Reginald, was taught to hate members of their profession. She brought him up largely on her own – the father, Marcus Beckett, walked out on her. They weren't married."

"Oh yes, Beckett, you mentioned him the other day." Hansen nodded. "Funny how he keeps cropping up like a bad penny. By the way, I checked with my wife. Thank God, she wasn't the midwife that handled that particular stillbirth. Anyway, presumably there was a lot of trouble between this Hartnell woman and Beckett?"

"Yes sir, there was obviously some animosity between them, but he – Beckett – soon faded from the picture. He went travelling."

"So, you think it was this hatred of nurses that made Reginald Hartnell – or his mother – murder the nurses, garrotte them with this plumb bob thingy you've been talking about, that he carried because he was an interior decorator? There's nothing complicated about that, Inspector! I understand it perfectly."

"But what we haven't said so far, sir," said Dolby, "is that Dorothy Hartnell is a spiritualist. She seems to believe that the spirit of her dead daughter haunts her son –and even maybe her herself. She believes that her still-born daughter – she calls her Stephanie - was seeking to avenge her early death."

Hansen's eyes narrowed. He rubbed his chin thoughtfully. "Bunkum, unless of course, you believe in suchlike hocus pocus."

"It doesn't really matter what I believe, sir, the fact is that it's not the sort of defence her lawyers can use in court, is it?"

Hansen nodded his agreement. He took a long swig of his coffee. "No, but they could argue some mental disorder and that whoever did it would have been in some sort of a trance at the time they carried out the murders."

"We've taken advice on that, sir," said Caine, "from a psychiatrist, Dr Rees, from the local hospital. It seems this nurse obsession – which is quite plausible apparently - could have lain dormant for years; there was an underlying animosity towards them, but it was kept well below the surface until quite recently."

She paused and Dolby broke in. "Dorothy Hartnell, for some twisted reason, tried to harm the children for whom Mary Bayliss had acted as Midwife. There were a number of hit and run incidents with those kids and we now know that Dorothy's car – a blue Corsa – was involved."

Caine nodded. "But what triggered off the murders, we think, was the rail accident."

"How do you mean the rail accident could have triggered it off? The pain, the shock? What?"

"Bear with me, sir, if you would, it is a bit difficult to grasp. Mrs Hartnell herself says the spirit of her daughter, Stephanie, **took possession** of her at the moment the train came out of the darkness and into the light. Dr Rees takes a slightly different attitude – he thinks the emergence of the train from the tunnel, the passage from the darkness into the light, combined with the trauma and pain caused by the train accident were enough to send her – or her son, maybe both! – Over the edge. He likens it to birth itself – the passage from the dark of the womb to the light of the living world – a replication, if you like, of the conditions under which her infant daughter died."

"And that set her off, did it, in his opinion?" Hansen frowned. "I'd say it was a load of bunkum myself, but I suppose it might make a weird sort of sense to a psychiatrist. And this could apply to both the woman *and* her son?"

"Yes, sir, apparently." Caine told him, "They both suffered the loss of the infant and the boy's experience would have been fed and nurtured by the hatred his mother felt for the woman she convinced herself could have prevented it - the midwife."

"There's an analogy also in the method of the murders," Dolby pointed out. "The infant, Stephanie, apparently from strangulation by her umbilical cord. The rope or string used in the murders seems to reflect the manner of her death."

They drank their coffee while Hansen turned over the pages of the files in front of him. "This young nurse, Janine Foster, the second victim, she was killed on her way home, in one of the pedestrian subways near the High Street?"

"Yes, sir, it's more or less the same scenario," confirmed Dolby. "The underpass was totally dark that night – all the lights had been smashed by vandals – and the killer struck at the moment the girl passed out of the darkness and into the light."

"Weird!" said Hansen. "And that was at nearly eleven at night? How come the boy's mother claims she did it? Wasn't she still convalescing from the injuries caused by the train crash? Isn't that a flaw in her confession?"

"No sir," said Dolby. "She was physically quite capable of doing it, her injuries from the crash were largely superficial."

"But the son, Reginald, was working on a job only a few yards up the road. He was there, on the scene, obviously *he* did it."

"That may be so," said Caine, "but it could also have been his mother. Reginald was working very late that night, to finish the job. His father had left him to it – they seem to have put a lot of trust in that young man, bearing in mind his learning difficulties – and his mother claims to have gone out to fetch him home. The husband says she was acting strangely at the time, having bad dreams, walking in her sleep, all the signs of a disturbed mind. Anyway, she says she went out to find her son, they met the girl and she murdered her using Reginald's plumb bob."

Hansen finished his coffee and put his cup down. "So, they both *could* have done it."

"Yes, sir," Caine agreed, "and according to the psychiatrist it's probable that neither of them is fit to plead."

Hansen passed the files back to Caine. "Well, Inspector, I think this is one the CPS is going to have to sort out, don't you?" He stood up. "In the meantime, we've at least got the murderer or murderers behind bars."

CHAPTER TWENTY- FOUR

.

Sergeant Bernard Crouch looked up as Dolby walked past the front desk. "Well done, Mark, I hear you and DCI Caine have nailed the Great Train Murderers."

Dolby nodded. "Yes. But it's going to be a difficult case to try."

"Oh? Yes, I suppose it is a bit weird, it being a mother and son like that," said Crouch. "Anyway, Mark, I'm glad you've emerged from the Super's at last, I've been looking for you, or DCI Caine. There's a young lady says she needs to talk to you."

Dolby grimaced. "Do you know what it's about, Bernie? Only there's a call I need to make. Derek Atterwood left me a message asking me to ring him back. It may be news on Emma."

"Ask her yourself, she's over there," said Crouch indicating a young woman seated in the corner of the room.

Dolby followed his gaze. The woman – she was hardly more than a girl - looked up from the magazine she was reading and pushed a lock of dark hair out of her eyes. Slim and wearing a short skirt with a split up the side, showing her legs to advantage, she stood up nervously as he came towards her.

"Hi! Are you one of the officers investigating Kelly Beacham's murder? Only, I spoke to a lady detective last time." She blushed, held out her hand. "Sorry, you don't know me, of course. I'm Michelle Clarke, Kelly's flatmate. At least I was until…you know…"

"Oh yes, of course," Dolby shook her hand. "I'm Detective Sergeant Dolby. It must have been my colleague you saw, DCI Jacqueline Caine. What can I do for you, Miss Clarke?" The young woman looked around nervously. "I'll tell you what, we'll go through to the Sergeant's office, behind the desk. We won't be disturbed there and you can tell me what's on your mind."

"It's just that I heard that music again," she told him as she sat down in the tiny office. "Ms Caine, the Inspector, seemed to be interested in it when we spoke, so I thought I should tell you, just in case it's significant."

Dolby sat down behind the desk and took out his notebook. "I assume you're referring to the music you heard when you answered the telephone on the night of Kelly's murder? I have read your statement of course, Miss Cooke, but perhaps you'd like to fill me in on the background."

Her nervousness showed as she toyed with the metal clasp of her handbag. "Yes, that's right. I told the Inspector that when I answered the telephone all I heard was this thumpy music. It was awful. I think Kelly was trying to ring me on her mobile, at least I think it was her mobile number that came up on the telephone readout. Anyway, I heard that music again this morning."

"Really? Are you sure it was the same music?"

"Oh yes, I've got quite a good ear for music. I play the piano you see, not that we have one at the flat, of course, but I played a lot before I left home. Anyway, I was going along the High Street this morning and I went past

Our Price – you know, the CD shop – and they were playing it. So, I went in and asked one of the assistants for the name of the record." She opened her handbag and took out a tiny notebook, flicking through the pages to find the right one. "It's by a group named '*Penny And The Dreadfuls*' and it's called '*Night of the Bloody Corpses*' – I think it's dreadful." She shivered. "I don't suppose you've heard of it."

"As a matter of fact, I have, Miss Cooke," said Dolby. "There was a CD of that name in the car belonging to the people who, we believe, killed Kelly Beacham."

She stood up. "I hope I've not wasted your time then, Sergeant, only I know you've already found out who killed her."

"Not at all, Miss Cooke. Information is always useful. What you've told me helps to confirm Kelly was probably in that particular car when she tried to contact you." He stood up. "Is there anything else you want to tell me?"

She shook her head. "No, thank you, Sergeant. I have to go now, I'm on my lunch hour and I have to get back to the office. My boss, Mr Diggs, well, he's not very good if you're late back. I'll find my own way out." She turned and opened the door. "If I think of anything else, of course, I'll be in touch."

Dolby had written the names of the pop group and the CD in his notebook and now he sat down again and stared at them for a few moments. The fact the young woman had bothered to come in to tell him she had discovered these new details reflected on her good character and sense of public duty, but the information was not all that important. They had already established that Kelly had been in Hill's car on the night of the murder; he and Sullivan had admitted it. Should he bother to tell Jackie Caine right now or leave it until he saw her this afternoon? He had taken his mobile phone from his pocket in readiness, but now he slipped it back again and made for the door, stopping dead a few feet away from Crouch's desk.

"The mobile phone," he murmured to himself as the thought struck him. "She *must* have had it with her because she definitely telephoned Michelle Cooke. The music confirms it. So where is it?"

Crouch looked up from the notes he was making. "Sorry, Mark? Did you say something, mate?"

Dolby nodded. "Yes, I did, but don't worry about it." This needed thinking about. He made for the outer door. There was time for a quick sandwich at The Royal Arms and there was nothing like a swift pint of draught Guinness to lubricate the little grey cells. And while he was there, he could return Derek Atterwood's call.

There was someone with DCI Caine half an hour or so later, when Dolby, humming a not very melodious tune, knocked and then pushed open the door to her office.

She looked up and nodded for him to enter. "Hello, Mark. You know PC Bird," she indicated the officer seated opposite her. "You've arrived at just the right time, Dickie was telling me something that might prove interesting."

Bird nodded towards Dolby. "Good afternoon, Mark." He turned back towards Caine. "The thing is,

Ma'am, I wasn't quite sure how much DC Whitlow would have told you. I don't even know if what the AA man said struck him as being strange. To tell you the truth I didn't think it was strange myself, not until I got to thinking about it afterwards, anyway. Since then, well, it's been sort of nagging at me."

Dolby sat down. "What exactly are we talking about here?"

"Dickie Bird was with DS Whitlow when they bumped into the AA man who found Kelly Beacham's car by the roadside. Go on, Dickie."

"It's just that when the AA man hailed us down – we were on our way to the scene of crime to set up the area search – he said he'd come to Miss Beacham's car *as arranged* – she wasn't there, of course, but he used those words, *as arranged*. I don't think neither Paul Whitlow nor me thought about it at the time, we had other things on our minds, so we didn't follow it through. I hope I'm not speaking out of turn, Ma'am, Sergeant," he smiled nervously and shot a glance from one to the other. "But you know what Paul's like – well, maybe you don't - he's good at his job, he usually gets things done, but he's a bit abrupt with people. Anyway, he made some sarcastic comment to the AA bloke, so the man just jumped into his van and drove off."

"You didn't connect the abandoned car with the body?"

"Well, yes, we did, but the AA guy was complaining about being kept waiting for hours beside a locked car– I don't know how long he was there, but he carried on like it was *our* fault – so Paul Whitlow told him to put a sock in it, we had more important things to worry about and the other guy just said he'd leave us to it then and took off."

"And you didn't report it?" asked Dolby.

Bird blushed nervously. "Well, no, Sergeant – er – we didn't think it was important."

"I hardly think it was for you *or* DS Whitlow to judge whether it was important or not," Caine commented. "But to get back to what you were saying, what do *you* think the man meant by '*as arranged*'?"

636

"I assume he meant someone had telephoned the AA and asked for an engineer to come out to the car," said Bird. "But, that's quite normal, so as I say I didn't even think about it at the time. It wasn't until afterwards it occurred to me how sort of 'out of order' that remark was. Surely, the murdered woman must have made the call when she broke down the evening before."

"I see what you mean," said Dolby. "So why did the breakdown engineer turn up in the morning rather than the night before?"

"Where are the registration details of Kelly's car?" asked Caine. She opened one of the files on her desk and flicked through the pages. "Here they are. Anyone know the AA's breakdown number?"

Dolby pulled his wallet from his pocket and read it off from his AA Membership card. Caine dialled the number and then put the telephone receiver into conference mode.

The supervisor at the AA call office responded immediately. "Yes, I've got those details on the screen now, Inspector. What is it you want to know?"

"Was there a breakdown call-out request for that car on the night of Monday December 10th?"

"Yes, Inspector. In fact, there were two."

"*Two*? Are you quite sure? This could be important."

"Yes, Ma'am. The first one was at 9.44 pm and the second shortly afterwards at 10.14."

When the call ended Caine and Dolby sat quietly trying to digest the information they had been given. PC Bird looked puzzled.

"Something very strange is going on here," Dolby said finally. "I'm not sure what the hell we do next."

"Sorry," said Bird, "but – er – I'm lost. I've not been wasting your time, have I?"

"Not at all. In fact, I'm extremely glad you came to see us, Dickie," said Caine. "It may be that your timely intervention has saved us from committing a gross miscarriage of justice."

Bird looked pleased with himself, but still puzzled. "Why? What did all that on the telephone just now mean?"

"It's early days yet and I'm still trying to get my head around it," Caine told him, "But it seems that Kelly Beacham made a telephone call to the AA *ten minutes after she died*."

"Sorry, it doesn't make sense to me, Ma'am," Bird, confessed. "How could she make a phone call *after* she was dead? Someone's got something wrong somewhere!" He looked at his watch. "Excuse me, Ma'am, but I'm on duty in ten minutes. Is there anything else I can tell you?"

"No, I don't think so. We'll be in touch if anything comes up." Bird got up to leave. "Oh, and thanks again, Dickie. You did the right thing coming to see us."

"Bright young man," said Dolby as Bird closed the door behind him. "But what the hell was Whitlow thinking of not taking a statement from the AA patrolman? Bird says they realised there was a connection between the car and Kelly's body! It's just routine."

"Yes, you're right, and I'll see our friend Whitlow hears about it. But it's pointless speculating about that now." Caine stood up and turned to look out of the window. It was raining again. "Obviously Kelly Beacham could not have made that phone call if she'd been murdered at 10.03 as we thought – so our timing must be totally out." She turned back to her desk and sat down again, reaching for the Beacham file. "I'm just thinking, Mark. The *only* reason we assumed Kelly died at 10.03 was because her watch stopped at that time. We took the easy option, like a couple of amateur sleuths from a cheap detective novel!"

Dolby nodded. "You're right, Jackie, it *was* crass stupidity. Doc Williams couldn't be specific about the time of death, so we jumped to the conclusion that the watch was smashed when the killer strangled her."

Caine banged her fist angrily down on the desk. "We are *idiots*, Mark, absolute idiots!" She sat fuming inwardly for a few seconds. "But, think about it, don't you think her watch being broken at that particular time was *very*

640

convenient?" She stopped, her brow creasing with thought. "I wonder…is that possible? Excuse me, I'm just going to ring Bob Hawthorne in forensic." She picked up the telephone receiver and dialled. "Bob? Jackie Caine – the watch that Kelly Beacham was wearing – have you still got it? Good…I want to know *why* it wasn't working…Yes, I know the glass is smashed – I want to know *why*. What smashed it?" she paused listening. "You can subject it to any fancy tests you like, Bob, but we need to know *fast*, like this afternoon! Thanks." She replaced the receiver. "He's being his usual pedantic self, worse than a lawyer! He kept saying he can examine the watch for damage, but he can't necessarily say who or what *caused* the damage or when it happened. He'll get back to us later."

"Right. There was something else I had to tell you, Jackie," Dolby told her apologetically. "I almost forgot. Kelly's flatmate called in at lunchtime. Apparently, she's heard that music again – the stuff she heard when Kelly rang her on the night of the murder – and she thought she should tell us the name of the music. That's not important, but it occurred to me afterwards that we haven't found Kelly's mobile phone. She obviously had it when she was with the boys – she rang Michelle Cooke on it – so what happened to it afterwards? And where is it now?"

Bob Hawthorne placed the watch, in its protective bag, on Caine's desk. "Versace designer and *very* expensive. Whoever smashed it couldn't have cared much about destroying nice things."

"You mean it was deliberately smashed?" asked Dolby.

"Yes, I'm pretty sure it was deliberate," said Hawthorne. "Look at the glass on the watch face" he took a magnifying glass from his pocket and held it over the watch, "The glass was smashed, but my guess is that the watch just kept on going. The second hand was probably still sweeping, so whoever did it decided to take the glass off and hit the face with something that had a small, hard tip, to concentrate the force of the blow; possibly they used a jeweller's screwdriver. If you look closely you can see a

642

tiny dent halfway along the second hand, but – and this is crucial - it's in a spot where the glass face above it is undamaged. Obviously, the glass wasn't in the way when the hand was damaged. The glass must have been taken off. *That* couldn't have been accidental."

Caine borrowed his magnifying glass and peered at the watch face. She could just make out tiny indentations on the hands. "Yes, and they've done the same with the hour and minute hands haven't they?"

Hawthorne nodded. "Yes, I daresay they wanted to make a good job of it, so they whacked the other hands as well."

"But can you *prove* this damage wasn't caused accidentally?" asked Dolby.

Hawthorne shrugged. "I doubt that an accidental blow would have caused that sort of damage and, as we've seen, the glass face couldn't have been there at the time. Besides, it's…" he paused, "how shall I put it? *It's all too precise.* For a single, accidental blow to have caused this sort of damage it would have required impact with some object that had ***three very small points*** and – more unlikely still - each of those three points would have had to have impacted through the glass and with one of the three hands. It's just much too precise." He shook his head decisively. "No, Jackie, it's well nigh impossible it could have happened accidentally. But, of course, the battery's the clincher."

"What about the battery?"

"It was fitted in upside down."

"Upside down?" queried Dolby. "But it would never have worked like that."

"No, it wouldn't, but then I don't think it was ***deliberately*** put in upside down. For my money what happened was, whoever did the other damage didn't mean to touch the battery at all. His problem was that it fell out of its housing," the forensic officer pointed to the watchcase. "When you want to get to the hands or remove the crystal from the front you ***have*** to take the back metal casing off first. Do that and the mechanism – the body of the watch – drops straight off into your hands. What probably happened was that the battery compartment was a little loose and the battery actually fell out. In his haste to get the whole thing together again and back on the girl's wrist, the killer botched the job and put it in ***upside down***. That one simple little error, plus the damage to the hands and glass, puts accidental damage totally out of court. It ***was*** definitely tampered with. The question is – ***why***?"

"That's simple," said Caine with quiet satisfaction. "To make us think Kelly died at 10.03 pm instead of some time later."

CHAPTER TWENTY-FIVE

"I hope you've got it right this time," said Hansen in his office the following morning. "You don't know how embarrassing this is. That leak to the press about the broken watch was bad enough, now they'll be all over us accusing us of botching the investigation."

"We made a mistake, sir," said Caine. "I'm sorry. Admittedly it's embarrassing, but we haven't botched the *entire* operation – at least now we'll be arresting the actual killer."

"Yes, but we've held those two lads for – how long is it? – Three days – for something they didn't do. I suppose they'll be after compensation."

"They weren't exactly blameless, sir," Dolby reminded him. "They admitted assaulting the woman and we can still hold them for involvement in drug trafficking – we know Beckett's up to his neck in the racket and I'd bet

646

a month's salary the two boys helped him get the filthy stuff into the school. So, they're directly implicated in the death of the lad who jumped off the roof." He shrugged. "In any case, if Hill and Sullivan hadn't tried to rape the girl none of this would have happened."

"I don't know about that, though," Caine cautioned. "Beckett would have killed her at some time or other - so, what they did was to furnish him with the perfect opportunity not only to kill her, but to frame them."

"You're sure it *was* him?" said Hansen darkly, "Why? What reason would he have to kill her?"

"She knew too much," said Caine. "She knew he was money laundering for a couple of drug barons – we've had the full story e-mailed through to us from the Met. Drugs Division. She knew what was going on and she was taking money off him in return for keeping her mouth shut. Blackmail, in other words. I suspect he meant to get rid of her all along, but he thought he'd make use of her in the meantime, to work off his sexual excesses if you like. Anyway, when the incident with the boys happened the other night he couldn't let the opportunity slip by. He reckoned he could do away with Kelly and put the blame on Hill and Sullivan. It was the perfect set-up, or so he thought."

Hansen nodded. "So, what exactly *did* happen on Monday evening?"

"Well, we don't know for absolutely certain, sir," said Caine. "But I think we can make some very educated guesses. After Kelly Beacham escaped from the two boys she was probably a little shaken – she'd had a bit of a shock. She knew Sullivan and Hill and when she got into the car with them she didn't expect them to turn on her and demand sex. She could, of course, have gone along with them and given them what they wanted, but it turns out she decided to fight them off, and when she finally got out of the car the natural place for her to go was to Beckett's. He was her lover after all and his place was only a few hundred yards away; it was through the forest, at night and in the winter, but after what she'd had to put up with it looked like the easy option. When she got there, of course,

648

Beckett was out, but she had a key – it was the other one we found on her key ring – so she let herself in."

"Beckett, of course, was out making his delivery to Jonathon Shelbourne," explained Dolby. "So, Kelly made herself at home. She rang the AA again – she didn't want them going to her car that night, she'd probably had enough of being out in the freezing weather, so she reckoned she'd spend the night at Beckett's. It probably wasn't the first time. She arranged for an AA breakdown man to meet her at her car the following morning, with the petrol. That was a lucky break for us sir, because without it Constable Bird wouldn't have run into the AA man and we wouldn't have realised she made the two calls."

Superintendent Hansen had heard that part of the story and he nodded his agreement. "Have to keep an eye on that young man, Bird, he obviously uses his brain."

"Quite," said Caine, picking up the story. "The other lucky break, of course, was that Kelly used Beckett's house telephone to ring the AA the second time; she didn't use her mobile, we know that because BT confirms the call was made from Beckett's number at 10.14 that evening and the AA have the recording of Kelly's conversation with their operator. So, we *know* beyond a shadow of a doubt that Kelly went back to Beckett's place that night and consequently that she was alive the last time Hill and Sullivan saw her. We were hopelessly out of order there, I'm afraid." She sighed. "Anyway, when Beckett got back from his delivery and found Kelly there, in his house, he listened to her explanation as to why she came back and reckoned he was on to a good thing. Maybe he'd wanted to get rid of her for some time and suddenly saw his opportunity. He strangled her and then set out to implicate the two boys."

"They gave it to him on a plate," Dolby commented. "She'd been in their car that same evening, leaving traces of her hair, scent, face powder, all the things that the forensic lads are so good at finding; but for good measure Beckett planted her knickers and the rope he'd used to kill her, in the back of Duncan Hill's car. He knew the vehicle – she told him - and he knew where it would be parked, –

he was only a few hundred yards from the school car park, through the woods. His experience as an escapologist made it easy for him to break into the car; an expert can do it in a matter of seconds."

"Before he did that, of course, he tried to establish an alibi for himself," continued Caine. "He knew he'd be prime suspect. He's into watches and clocks, remember – he has a whole display of period instruments in his showroom and his shop assistant told us he carried out some of the repairs and restorations himself. Anyway, he thought that if he stopped Kelly's watch we would assume Kelly was murdered at precisely the time the watch showed when it was broken; he was very nearly right, I almost made the biggest blunder of my career!"

"And, ironically, if it hadn't been for that poison pen letter we probably wouldn't have looked more closely at the watch and seen that it had been tampered with rather than merely damaged in her struggle with the two boys" added Dolby. "That set us on the right path."

"Let's get this straight," said Hansen. "What you're saying is that Beckett *made* the watch stop at 10.03 – when he was actually at Shelbourne's, who could alibi him – so we would think that Kelly Beacham had been killed at 10.03 whereas, in reality, he didn't murder her until much later?"

"Precisely. He wasn't to know she'd rung the AA at 10.14 from his house telephone, *after* she was supposed to be dead!" Caine continued the narrative. "He first dumped Kelly Beacham's body in the woods, taking great care to ensure it would be discovered fairly quickly – he didn't want the evidence he was going to leave in the boys' car to grow too cold – and then he went through the woods, over the fence and into the school grounds, found their car and planted the rope in the boot and the pair of panties she'd been wearing in the back seat squab. The boys used some of the same type of rope themselves, so they would think nothing of it if they saw it in the boot; and the panties were well hidden down the back of the seat squab where *they* wouldn't find it, but *we* would. He also threw her handbag over the school fence and into the woods, ready for us to find."

"And we also know what happened to Kelly Beacham's mobile phone," said Dolby, "Beckett answered a mobile call while we were interviewing him on the morning after she was murdered. It didn't register with us at the time, but he had to scramble around a bit to find it and when he did he said it belonged to the decorator – Reginald Hartnell as it happened – but of course it must have been Kelly's. She had it with her when she came back to Beckett's house."

Caine nodded her agreement. "The call that Beckett answered was from Kelly Beacham's employers – we've checked with them. Beckett told them they had the wrong number."

"It seems conclusive," said Hansen. "You'd better go and bring him in. Don't want the bird flying the coop do we?" The two officers stood up. "Oh, by the way, Sergeant, good news about the Atterwood girl. I knew she'd turn up."

"Yes, sir," said Dolby. "Safe and sound I understand."

"Knew she would," said Hansen smugly. "Happens every day nowadays."

"There's news on Emma Atterwood, then, Mark?" said Caine as she closed the door to the Superintendent's office. "You didn't tell me."

"Sorry, Jackie, in the heat of what's been going on with Beckett I clean forgot to mention it."

"Well? I take it she's back home, safe and sound."

"Yep. Turns out she wasn't such a model of good behaviour after all. It seems she ran off with the tree man's assistant – you know, that bloke Hickman, it was his sidekick, Trevor - they did a few jobs on the Atterwood's garden some months ago and Emma must have taken up with him then. Real ladies' man from what I can gather. Anyway, she got herself pregnant – or I should say *he* got her pregnant. She didn't dare tell her parents, so she ran off to London with him."

"So, what brought her back?"

Dolby smiled grimly. "Turns out she hadn't actually told the boyfriend she was in the club. When she did he slung her out and took up with another girl. So poor Emma suddenly found herself all alone in the smoke with a baby on the way and no visible means of support. Luckily she decided that perhaps Derek and Pauline were the least of the many evils and she came home."

"Poor kid," said Caine. "I suppose the parents are well pleased?"

"Well, they realise that having a surprise grandchild is better than losing a daughter, if that's what you mean!" He opened the door that led out on to the car park. "Shall we go and pick up our old friend Marcus?"

It was well after eight o'clock that evening before Caine arrived home. They had had a long session in the interview room with Beckett and his solicitor. The antiques dealer had remained silent, admitting nothing but his name and address and she and Dolby, tired of his stonewalling, had finally decided to give up for the day. She had snatched a quick meal in the canteen and then set off for home.

The weather had suddenly taken a turn for the better and, although there was some low cloud, it was relatively warm for the middle of December. She helped herself to a whisky and then sat in the lounge for a few minutes in front of the television before deciding there was nothing worth watching on terrestrial and nothing but detective mysteries on Prime and Netflix, so she had switched off. Whisky glass in hand she wandered over to the French windows and looked out at the garden. The moon was high in the sky, riding through banks of fine clouds, and in its silvery light she could see the dark shape of Trickett's Wood a mile or so away. She felt pleased with the way things had gone during the last few days, but there was a slight sense of dissatisfaction. True, the three major cases on her patch were solved, but she and Dolby had got it badly wrong with the boys, Hill and Sullivan. They weren't squeaky clean (a more thorough search of their quarters, carried out since they had been arrested, had yielded traces of cannabis and amphetamines and she was sure more questioning would link them to Beckett's drugs activities), but neither were they murderers.

Even more damaging to her sensibilities, though, was the act of locking up a young man who was mentally challenged, even if he had been responsible for three murders; it may have been necessary, but it went against the grain. Was that the root of her mental malaise? Or was it that she really could not make up her mind whether Reginald Hartnell was guilty of those crimes? Was it possible that he was innocent and that his mother, poor sad woman, really was the responsible party? There was something strange about that woman – was she really a medium in touch with the spirits of the dead? Caine laughed out loud in the empty room. The whole concept was absurd – and yet…Jacqueline Caine shivered involuntarily and tossed the rest of the glass of whisky down her throat.

She put on her topcoat, slipped a torch into her pocket and walked out into the garden, along the path and out of the back gate onto the towpath of the river. There was a slight wind rustling the leaves of the trees, but beneath that she could hear the chuckle of the water as it sped on its way towards the Blackwater. She took out her torch and shone it down into the rushing stream, delighted to see the small dark shapes of tiddlers rushing towards the surface, attracted by the unaccustomed light.

The moonlight was stronger now; it was light enough to see without the torch, so she switched it off and pushed it back into her pocket before setting off along the towpath. She didn't know quite why she was walking here, alone by the river, but there was a feeling of anticipation as she approached the bend and then of satisfaction as she saw, against the distant light of the hurricane lamp, the huddled shape of the lone fisherman.

THE END

Printed in Great Britain
by Amazon

72787106R10373